"Williams populates her historical fiction with people nearly broken by their experiences."

— Foreword Reviews INDIES Finalist (Soul of a Crow)

* Gold Medalist - 2015

— Independent Publishers Awards (Heart of a Dove)

"Perfect for romantic mystery lovers ... a sweet, clever quickstep with characters who feel like longtime friends." *— Foreword Reviews (Wild Flower)*

"Set just after the U.S. Civil War, this passionate opening volume of a projected series successfully melds historical narrative, women's issues, and breathless romance with horsewomanship, trailside deer-gutting, and alluring smidgeons of Celtic ESP."

— Publishers Weekly (Heart of a Dove)

"There is a lot I liked about this book. It didn't pull punches, it feels period, it was filled with memorable characters and at times lovely descriptions and language. Even though there is a sequel coming, this book feels complete."

— Dear Author (Heart of a Dove)

"With a sweet romance, good natured camaraderie, and a very real element of danger, this book is hard to put down."

— San Francisco Book Review (Heart of a Dove)

Also By Abbie Williams

 The Shore Leave Cafe Series

Summer at the Shore Leave Cafe

Second Chances

A Notion of Love

Winter at the White Oaks Lodge

Wild Flower

The First Law of Love

Until Tomorrow

The Way Back

Return to Yesterday

Forbidden

 The Dove Series

Heart of a Dove

Soul of a Crow

Grace of a Hawk

Until
Tomorrow

a
SHORE LEAVE CAFE
novel

Abbie Williams

central
avenue
publishing
2018

Published by Central Avenue Publishing, an imprint of Central Avenue Marketing Ltd.
www.centralavenuepublishing.com

UNTIL TOMORROW

978-1-77168-126-1 (pbk)
978-1-77168-029-5(epub)
978-1-77168-059-2 (mobi)

Published in Canada

Printed in United States of America

1. FICTION / Romance   2. FICTION / Family Life

UNTIL TOMORROW,
WHEN I CAN FIND YOU IN TIME, WAIT FOR ME...

Chapter One

Jalesville, MT - August, 2013

At some point that night, a dream assaulted me. Later I was to wonder if the quiet sounds of a trespasser had crept into my unconscious mind, triggering the nightmare. What if I'd woken just minutes earlier? Could I have stopped what happened next?

· I would never know.

In the dream I was back at my older sister Camille's wedding, which had taken place in October of '06. Fiery autumn colors decorated the trees ringing Flickertail Lake that bright, sunny Saturday; I'd been eighteen years old and home from the university I attended in Minneapolis. The reception appeared in my dreamscape exactly as I'd witnessed it seven years earlier – everyone gathered in the grand ballroom of White Oaks Lodge, our family and friends, not to mention most of the residents of Landon, eager to celebrate with the happy bride and groom. Champagne and twinkling lights, live music, merry laughter from every direction – but a small knot of unease in my chest. I observed the ongoing festivity from a slight distance, as though sequestered in a dim corner.

Join them.

But I couldn't walk forward.

I didn't know exactly how much time had passed before a man appeared at my elbow. I looked up at him, confused; it seemed I should know who he was but I couldn't remember. I opened my mouth to ask him his name – I *knew* him, there was no doubt, but why couldn't I think of his name? His gaze held mine, the lights glinting in his red-gold hair, and my heart increased its speed.

Patricia, he murmured. A smoldering grin lit his eyes and traveled to his lips.

This was all the invitation I required. I leaped into his arms, clinging to his neck; how could I have failed to recognize him? I spoke his name against the warmth of his skin, joy sparking a fire in my blood that heated my entire body.

Where have you been? I demanded.

Looking for you, of course, my sweet, sweet heart.

His arms crushed me close and I burrowed against his strong chest. A strange crackling noise, one I could not place into context, began to drown out the sounds of Camille's reception, slicing cleanly through the bubble of my happiness; I went rigid, tense with increasing dread.

Do you hear that? Ax, do you hear that sound?

Hear what sound, love?

Realization scalded my senses before I could respond – someone had lit White Oaks on fire. Beyond his shoulder I watched flames streak across the ballroom floor as though alive, consuming everything in their path. I was shouting then – begging people to run, to save their lives, but no sound emerged from my throat and no one was listening. Wild with fear, I tried to drag him outside with me but my fingers passed through empty air.

Axton! I screamed, steeped in terror. *Where are you?*

Brilliant orange light seared my eyeballs; flames licked at the hem of my scarlet bridesmaid gown, scalding my bare legs…

I gasped to consciousness, thrashing upward with such violence that I almost tumbled from the bed. Heart clobbering my ribs, short of breath, I reached for the reassurance of Case, grasping his warm, nude body as my sleep-drenched brain staggered to comprehend reality.

Tish, calm down! It was a nightmare. It was only a nightmare.

Why, then, was the scent of acrid smoke heavy in the air?

I blinked, then blinked again.

It occurred to me I could see not only Case but the interior of our bedroom with much more clarity than this hour of the night should allow. The air was glowing red, as though lit by...

"Fire," I breathed, and my heart liquefied. Naked, I kicked from the covers and sprinted into the living room, almost tearing the screen door from its hinges.

"*Case!*"

He was already at my side. "Oh Jesus, oh God, *the horses*," and we fell over each other, grabbing clothes, flying outside, straight into the belly of the nightmare. Our barn had morphed into an inferno against the black sky, a writhing, crackling blaze a thousand times larger than any bonfire I had ever witnessed. Temporarily mesmerized by the preposterous sight, we stood frozen in place; I shielded my eyes with a forearm, exactly as I would have upon looking straight into the noontime sun. When I stumbled forward, Case grabbed my arm and put me firmly behind him. The sound of the fire was like that of a strong wind, its heat reaching us from a good fifty yards away.

"No!" he ordered, refusing to allow me any closer to the fire.

"Cider," I sobbed. "Buck! They're in there!"

Case retained his calm while I shredded to pieces. He gripped my shoulders, leaning close to hold my gaze and speaking loudly enough to be heard. "Tish, go inside and call 911. Right now."

I clutched at him. "What are you going to do?"

"I know what to do," he assured me; reflections of the enormous leaping flames were visible in his pupils. "Call 911 and whatever you do, do not go near the barn! Tish! Do you hear me?"

I nodded like someone jerking a puppet's strings, tears streaking my face. Case leaned in and kissed my mouth, hard and possessive, and then I raced inside the trailer, made a frantic, messy search for the cordless phone, and dialed the emergency number. When dispatch answered, scant miles away in downtown Jalesville, I cried breathlessly, "Fire! There's a fire at our place, *Case Spicer's on Ridge Road!*"

And then, through the windows of our little trailer, I saw what Case was doing outside; the phone fell from my numb fingers, clattering to the floor. I bounded through the screen door, running full-bore for the spigot, where Case had ripped off his t-shirt and drenched it. I realized, with nightmarish clarity, that he intended to enter that monster of a fire.

Of course he would. Of course he would risk himself for something he loved.

"*NO!*" I screamed, tripping over a rut in the yard and landing hard on all fours. Case appeared as a charred stick figure against the blaze, maddeningly far away from my arms that would have prevented his forward motion at all costs, even the demise of our beloved animals; he had no more protection than his wet shirt wrapped around his head. I knew he was going to try to save our horses, Cider and Buck, and our rabbit and chickens. Mutt and Tiny were huddled near the trailer; I could see their jaws snapping with barks but couldn't hear a thing besides the fire.

I scrambled to my feet. Case had disappeared around the back of the barn and I floundered, panicking, before realizing what I must do. I ran inside and tore a blanket from the bed, then raced to the spigot to soak it, slopping water everywhere. The entire structure of the two-story, pitched-roof barn was engulfed; burning wood, hay, and manure polluted the air with a choking black smoke. I ran in Case's footsteps, shocked by the intensifying heat. The fire's roar was unbearable but I pushed on toward the double doors in back, driven by terror and determination, in equal parts.

Oh God, why did you just have to talk about dying?

Oh, Case, why?

I saw him as I rounded the corner; he burst free of the rolling smoke with Cider in his grasp. His shirt was over the mare's head and she was wild with fear, bucking his hold. Once clear of the smoke, Case let her free and Cider galloped into the night. Case's head and bare chest were black with soot. He didn't see me, single-minded with purpose, saving the animals. He disappeared back inside; he'd told me not to enter the barn and trusted that I would heed his words, but damned if I was going to let him do this without help, and maneuvered the sopping-wet blanket over my head like a cloak. The double doors looked like something straight out of hell, gaping like a broken mouth, smoke tumbling in dense, undulating waves.

Without hesitation, I ran through the doors.

The going was slower than I'd imagined, once inside; the smoke embraced me as if alive, jamming its caustic taste deep into my lungs. The heat was indescribable, burning through the soles of my flimsy tennis shoes, blasting my nostrils. I thought the skin might very well be peeling back from my face. I had a vague sense that I was steaming, the water on my blanket-cloak being cooked away, but my thoughts narrowed, along with my stinging eyes – I had one purpose here and that was to find Case.

Cider is already out.

Buck. He'll get Buck next.

The stalls are straight ahead.

I blundered forward, crashing against the edge of the chicken coop; the gate was open there, which meant Case had already let them free. A high-pitched wail pierced the chaos, a shrill cry of a horse in pain. I turned toward the sound just as a chunk of debris crashed no more than five feet from my body. My throat was too clogged with smoke to scream. As though moving underwater, dense and onerous, I peered upward from the edges of the blanket.

Jesus Christ, the loft!

The boards above gaped with charred holes. Before my eyes, another section of the loft buckled, unable to resist the onslaught of heat.

"CASE!" I had never been so frantic. I ran, heedless of the flames, in the direction of Buck's stall.

The blanket is on fire, it's on fire, oh sweet Jesus, it's on fire…

Buck's galloping body filled my vision as he suddenly bolted in my direction. Instinct was all that saved me as I darted aside, avoiding his panicked flight. His tail swooped against my face as he passed.

"CASE! Where are you?" My voice was ash. I pawed viciously at the air as though this might dissipate the clouds of bitter smoke. What was left of the blanket fell from my shoulders. My lungs were about to explode. And then I stumbled and went to my knees, realizing I had just tripped over Case. Adrenaline shrieked through my limbs, disabling the fear. I fumbled for the pulse in his neck, finding it. In the concentrated orange light he appeared surreal, covered in layers of soot. The smoke would kill us both in another minute, I was certain.

He's unconscious, oh God, he's unconscious…

In that moment there was only one thing I could do, and so I did it; I bent and scraped my arms along the floor, anchoring beneath his armpits, and then I hauled him out of there.

I came to in a room lit by a low-watt green light. Bizarre, disconnected images floated through the oozy haze in my skull as I drifted along. Every internal sound was amplified, as though I was locked in a womb.

Where am I?

I want…

I need…

Remembrance impacted my brain and I tried to sit, unable; something inhibited my movements and blocked my mouth and nose.

Case is hurt! Where is he?

My heart responded and there was a whirring array of mechanical noises, beeps and hisses. Voices lifted in alarm. My eyes wouldn't open all the way; through a slit in each eyelid all I could see was that dim green light. Something tethered my arms and I struggled against what felt like thin tubes attached to the undersides of my wrists.

"Hold her, get her down!"

Fast-moving hands were all over me in the next second. My throat was too parched to protest.

"Five milligrams, *now!*"

Velvet darkness encased me.

Time must have passed. My perception was muddy, clogged. Words floated across my view as though they were tangible objects, constructed of white feathers. I tried to reach for the word *horse* but couldn't elevate my hand.

"Tish, can you hear me?" My mother's lips were near my ear. I smelled peaches, and the scent of her hair.

I tried to articulate affirmation.

"I love you so much," she whispered, and I heard tears slipping down her face; I could actually hear the little wet tracks they were making, the soft plops as they struck the sheet beneath me. "I'm right here, honey, I'll be right here."

And then I was gone again, gliding away with the white feathers.

When I surfaced at last to full consciousness, my eyes opened all the way. I lay in a dimly-lit hospital room and my mother and Camille were both sleeping in chairs positioned near the bed. This time there was nothing inhibiting my nostrils and I drew a single shallow breath. It hurt like hell; pain penetrated the depths of my chest. I could still smell the fire.

"Mom…" I was unable to force more than a rasp from my scorched throat; my tongue seemed five times its usual size but Mom heard my plea and woke at once. Witnessing the naked distress on her face caused the solid world to drop from under my inert body; I knew I was going to die when I heard the answer to my question. My heart would simply give out and I would die.

"Where's Case?" I could hardly speak, weak as a newborn kitten, but anger and desperation lent me strength. "*Tell me.*"

Mom cupped my shoulders and brought her eyes close to mine. I began to cry in dry, rattling huffs. Camille appeared beside Mom and their expressions conveyed such grief that I yanked free, tearing at the tubes connected to my arms, determined to climb from this bed. Mom was breathless with concern; she clutched my shoulders again, stalling my frantic movement.

"Tish, *stop it!* Listen to me. You're in the hospital in Bozeman. You've been here for two days now."

"Where is Case?!"

"He's in critical care. He's been unconscious since he was brought here."

Tears wet Camille's face. "You pulled him from the fire, Tish, you saved him. They found you collapsed beneath him."

I couldn't bear to be in this fucking bed without real answers. "I have to go to him, *he needs me*…"

"Sweetheart, they don't know if he's going to make it," Mom finally admitted, and I could see what it cost her to tell me this. I wilted, curling inward like something already dead. I covered my face with my forearms, IV needles jangling all over the place; I'd succeeded in disconnecting myself from the slender tubes and pinpricks of blood appeared on my arm. Mom kept speaking, low and pained. "He needed emergency surgery on a heart valve. His lungs are compromised right now…"

I moaned, feeling these words like physical blows. I begged, "Take me to him."

"Tish, you're injured. Your lungs are burned."

I closed my eyes, unable to comprehend a thing besides the fact that Case was in critical care, far away from me when it seemed as though we'd just been snuggling in our bed. I could not relent to this weakness; I had to be with him. "Mom, oh God, *please help me*…"

Camille gently caught one of my fluttering hands. "We'll get you there as soon as possible."

"*Now.*" My heart was galloping, fueling my desperation. I realized something was missing and my free hand darted to my scalp.

Mom's eyes filled with fresh tears. "Most of your hair got burned away, sweetie…"

"Now," I whispered. Because I was no longer on oxygen and considered out of danger, the decision was made to properly remove the tubes which had been pumping my veins full of pain medication and salinized water. Camille stayed with me while Mom went to pick up Aunt Jilly, Ruthann, and Clint; my family had arrived from Minnesota late last night. Clark had called them with the terrible news; I knew the Rawleys were here in Bozeman, too, along with my dad. I should have been more grateful for their supportive presence but my thoughts would not widen enough for anything other than getting to Case's side.

Alone for the moment, pale evening light falling through the lone window as I stood on unsteady legs, I leaned against my older sister and wept uncontrollably. Camille held me close, kissing my cheek, her pregnant belly buffered between our bodies.

"He'll be all right," she murmured, again and again. "He loves you so much, Tish, he'll be all right."

In the bathroom I could hardly believe the person in the mirror was me, but I wouldn't waste time worrying over how I looked. I needed to get cleaned up so I could go to Case and put my eyes on him. I needed to tell him I was here and that he would be all right. There was no other option. I focused on that thought as water ran down my skin; despite its warmth, I couldn't stop shivering. Afterward, I sat on the bed and Camille knelt behind me; I felt her baby pushing against my spine as my sister tenderly combed my short, ragged hair. She had procured a pair of scissors to trim what was left but I was too impatient, sick with need to get to Case. And finally, they let me.

He was stationed in the intensive care unit. He lay motionless on a narrow bed, the top half of which was elevated to forty-five degrees. He was drugged, intubated, and tethered to oxygen, a clear-plastic ventilator covering his mouth and nose. They had bathed him and treated his burned forearms; from knuckles to elbows he was wrapped in white gauze. His torso was also swathed in bandages, lacerated from being dragged across hot wooden boards. A doctor assured me that the repair to his heart valve had been relatively minor surgery and that it was good we caught it now, as it may have progressed into something more serious down the road; far more concerning, she explained, was the smoke Case inhaled while saving our horses.

It was brutal to observe him this way, unconscious, with machines breathing and swallowing for him, a screen monitoring his vital signs. I put my hands on his chest with utmost care, wanting him to know I was here; I would not leave his side until he awoke. His skin felt cool beneath my fingertips as I stroked his forehead, his ears; most of his beautiful, red-gold hair had been burned away and hysterical sobs threatened my control.

No. You have to be strong, Tish, now more than ever.

The on-duty nurse finally abandoned her insistence that I leave the room (I refused to listen, telling her she'd have to remove me by force), at last agreeing to let me sleep on the small vinyl chair; my family and the Rawleys spent that night in the waiting room while I dragged the chair beside Case's bed, well away from the side with all the machinery. I fell asleep with my forehead resting on my folded arms and dreamed wretched things – we were back at Camille's wedding reception and Case was telling me he loved me but I wasn't listening. In the dream I could see his heart inside his chest, bright red behind a cage of white ribs; I witnessed it crack to pieces and drain away, helpless to stop it.

In another fitful dream he climbed on his horse, a solid gelding named Ranger, and galloped away, even as I screamed after him to come back. And then suddenly the scene changed and we were deep in the foothills, me bent over his inert body, cradling his head and shoulders. He was dying – a bullet had torn apart his stomach. His blood soaked my lap. I screamed until my throat bled, unable to prevent this from happening, and woke with a choked cry, the nightmare still churning in my mind. It took me a moment to realize that the warm, gentle hand on my back belonged to Aunt Jilly, who was in the room with me; she must have slipped past the nurses' station.

"Tish," she whispered, smoothing her palm between my shoulder blades. "It's all right."

She was standing and I collapsed against her; she cradled my head against her stomach and curved forward to kiss my burned hair.

"Shh," she soothed.

"Will he be all right?" I begged, quiet and devastated. Maybe she'd had a Notion; maybe she would tell me she'd seen his full recovery.

Reading my mind, Aunt Jilly murmured, "I can't make a Notion happen. Oh Tish, honey, I wish I could."

I shook my head, wanting to deny everything but the hope that Case would be all right.

"There's something…" Aunt Jilly kept her voice low and I knew her well enough to sense the speculation in her tone; I held my breath so I wouldn't miss a word. "There's something from the past, just like I told

Camille years ago. I can't see all of it, but there's something you have to understand."

I knew she was right; though I'd never experienced a Notion – the name Aunt Jilly had long ago adopted for her precognitive flashes – I had sensed this truth about past events. Not 'past' as in my own lifetime; the past to which we referred had occurred in another life altogether. A part of myself I was learning to trust, a part long buried beneath the weight of skepticism and doubt, had already recognized that Case and I had been together before now.

"I don't know where to start," I admitted in a whisper, drawing back. In the dim, sanitary room, I studied my aunt's familiar features. Aunt Jilly was my mother's younger sister and I knew her face almost as well as Mom's. Her golden hair was cast in a surreal greenish glow from the tiny lights on the medical equipment, her blue eyes serious and intent as she traced the perimeter of my face with her fingertips. She bit down on her lower lip as though to keep it from trembling.

She acknowledged, "You love him, don't you?"

Spikes seemed to form in my aching throat. "So much I can't even explain it."

"I can tell," she murmured, her fingers lingering against my cheeks, sending small shivers along my skin; her touch was, as always, full of an electric energy. "You've changed this summer, Tish. Grown up." A tender smile shone in her eyes. "I was so happy to hear you'd decided to take a job in Jalesville, with Al Howe." She paused, her smile fading. "Your dad would disagree."

I could not deny this; Dad had arrived unexpectedly in Jalesville a few days ago to inform me – apparently a phone call would not suffice – that he believed I'd thrown away a golden opportunity at a law career in a top Chicago firm. I was willing to concede that it had been a shock to my father, Jackson Gordon; he had funded my seven years' worth of education, including three years of law school at Northwestern College, with the expectation that I would fulfill his idea of my destiny, working as a corporate lawyer at Turnbull and Hinckley, a formidable firm in downtown Chicago. Ron Turnbull, senior partner at Turnbull and

Hinckley, had once been a man I'd longed to impress, let alone work for; I supposed if I considered the fact that part of growing up included the shattering of naïve illusions, then Ron Turnbull's presence in my life was a fantastic example.

I thought, *I have to tell Dad what I know before he leaves.*

I turned from Aunt Jilly, back toward Case; he'd not shifted position since I'd fallen asleep and been swept away in nightmares. He was unchanged: supine, bandaged and stationary, the lower half of his face obscured by the ventilator. I clenched my jaws, hoping they would act as a floodgate against the urge to weep. Unable to resist, I touched his forehead, letting the feel of his skin reassure my fingertips. His closed eyes frightened me to the core but I pushed the fear aside, concentrating all my will upon the positives. Case was alive. He was receiving medical care. His heart valve had been repaired – and neither of us had even realized it needed repairing.

"I'll be right here, sweetheart," I whispered. "I won't leave your side."

"And we won't leave yours," Aunt Jilly assured me, and though I didn't voice it in that moment I knew she understood the depth of my gratitude; I had always understood, from the time I was a young girl in a family comprised of strong, compassionate women, how much we mattered to one another.

Chapter Two

THREE DAYS PASSED.

I refused to leave Case's room and everyone knew better than to attempt to make me, including the hospital staff. Though he hadn't stirred, I spoke to him constantly, wanting him to know I was near; he'd already lived through enough lonely pain for two lifetimes. My family, Case's little brother, Gus, and the Rawleys all took turns sitting with me long after visiting hours expired; necessity had forced Dad's return to his job in Chicago, but not before we'd spoken alone together. I told him everything I'd learned, desiring his perspective on the matter.

"Ron's sub-company buying up an inoperative power plant and its surrounding land is hardly criminal," Dad had pointed out. "Though, I find it odd that Ron failed to mention this detail when he knew you'd ventured to Jalesville specifically to counteract Capital Overland's activities."

"That's just what I mean, Dad," I'd said, forcing a deep breath; my burned lungs could not handle any sort of agitation. "There's more to all this than we ever guessed. Ron never suspected I would stumble onto the fact that Redd Co. is part of his holdings. I never *would* have known if I hadn't seen that document a few summers back, during an externship at Turnbull and Hinckley, remember, like I told you?"

My father had been a lawyer for over two decades and was capable of maintaining a solid poker face when he chose; he was not the sort to be caught off guard but I'd succeeded in doing just that. Dad didn't want to believe Ron Turnbull had ulterior motives concerning my presence in Jalesville; any inference that Ron might have taken advantage of me would raise the ire of not only the lawyer in my father, but his paternal protectiveness. I'd arrived in the small town in central Montana at the beginning of July, ready to assist a local lawyer, Al Howe, in rallying the residents against an out-of-state company, Capital Overland, intent on buying up acreage and clearing out the town.

The company's front man in Jalesville was Derrick Yancy, the younger son of a Chicago businessman – and acquaintance of my father and Ron Turnbull – whose company, Yancy Corps, maintained holdings both powerful and far-reaching. Turnbull and Derrick Yancy were each dangerous individuals, of this I was certain; I had yet to discover their motives or collect enough evidence to prove criminal activity in conjunction with one another, but I would do so if it killed me, if it was the last thing I ever accomplished as a lawyer.

"I'll keep my eyes and ears open," Dad had promised, studying my face, reading the stubborn intensity there. "Tish, keep your head low until I can sort out a few things." He paused for a beat, his cheekbones appearing prominent as he clenched his jaws. "You think the fire wasn't an accident, don't you?"

Our conversation had been last night. I hadn't slept more than a few hours in a row and my worst thoughts were hammering at my ramshackle defenses with more frequency; my insides ached as though scrubbed with a sanding brush. The only thing that helped me cling to sanity was imagining how Case would respond if he could hear me talking to him. I sustained myself with memories of being held in his arms at night; I always rested my cheek just at the juncture of his neck and left shoulder, where I could feel his heart beating. After we made love but before we fell asleep, he stroked his fingers through my long, curly hair, our legs braided together, and we would whisper about our future.

Now my hair was burned away and he was unconscious, a ventilator breathing for him, shifting his chest at evenly-paced intervals. If anything happened to him, if he didn't make it, as I'd been repeatedly warned was a possibility, I would be finished; trying to avoid the thought only seemed to increase its power. The intubation had been removed from his trachea and he'd been carefully weaned from the drugs sedating him – the nurses warned me if he came awake with the breathing tube in place the natural reaction was panic and he would attempt to pull it out. All we could do now was wait; he would either waken – or he would not.

I felt each and every labored breath as I watched his chest rise and fall, plagued by these odds.

Wake up, Charles Shea Spicer. Come back to me, please come back to me. I'm here and I need you so much.

It's all right, sweetheart, don't worry so. I could hear his deep voice so clearly. *My sweet Patricia, it's all right.*

I held his right hand between both of mine; it was well into evening and I hadn't eaten all day, despite several attempts. My stomach was knotted into little bundles of unyielding tension. I had not returned home to Jalesville since the night of the fire; Clark and Al kept me informed of any developments. The Rawleys were caring for all of our animals – our horses, our dogs, our two cats, three chickens, and one rabbit; all of them alive because Case loved them. He was a man who would risk himself, unconditionally, for those he loved. I studied his familiar handsome features, the sounds of the medical apparatuses having long since faded to the background.

What if the past few weeks are all the time we're allowed together in this life? We've been so completely happy. I didn't dare to take it for granted. Oh God, don't let this be all the time we're given. We just found each other.

Determined to banish my terrible thoughts, I tightened my grip and whispered, "I still haven't heard how you got your nickname. Remember, you promised to tell me?" The lifeless slack of his hands was unbearable – his tough, long-fingered hands that found no task too demanding, which cradled his fiddle with graceful expertise and called forth music and joy; hands that so tenderly stroked my bare skin. I steeled my resolve, kissing his knuckles, one by one. "Sweetheart, you saved all of them. Cider and Buck are all right. You saved all of our animals. Now you just have to come back to me. Please, Case, come back to me."

I thought of all of the years he had loved me when I'd been far away, oblivious to the strength of what he never stopped feeling. It was back in 2006, at Camille's wedding, that Case first gathered the courage to confess that he believed we were connected, that I was the only one for him. I'd been young and arrogant, unimpressed at the time by his earnest words; it wasn't until this past summer, seven long years later, that I came west to his hometown for a summer job and fell in love with him. I was fortunate enough that despite the passage of many years, his feelings for me had remained as powerful as ever.

Because you've been together before now.

I knew this to be true. Logic was normally applied to my thought processes but in this matter I relied on instinct and simply *felt*. The past life I could recall most clearly, revealed to me in snippets of dreams and flashes of events I had not experienced in my current life, was perhaps the last time we'd found one another, when we believed Case's name had been Cole Spicer, a man with whom Case was also related by blood. The Spicer family had migrated from Iowa to Montana in the late nineteenth century, settling on the homestead where their descendants had lived ever since.

I vowed silently, *I will find out who did this to us. If it was Derrick, I will personally nail shut his coffin.*

Derrick, the second of the Yancy sons and possessed of a carefully-masked inferiority complex, had spent the past summer living in Miles City while working his considerable wiles on nearby Jalesville, a place I now called home. He'd been far more successful in making sales before I'd arrived to oppose his interests; I knew he hated me, though this hatred was tinged with something Derrick could not explain even if he tried. He and I were also connected by a past life, whether I was willing to admit it or not.

You were once his wife.

This assumption made my stomach curdle because I suspected it was true; Derrick and I had been married at some point in the past. And, based on my graphic, recurring nightmares, it had not been a happy union.

"I wish I could sing for you," I told Case, trying to steer my thoughts in a better direction. "I know if it was me lying there and you sitting here, you'd be singing for me. The sound of you singing makes me feel safer than just about anything in the world, did you know that?" I reached to stroke his shorn head, with utmost care, imagining the thick, beautiful auburn hair he'd inheirited from his mother. Melinda Spicer had died long ago, but first gifted her son with her gorgeous coloring, her sweet, tender nature – and her ability to sing. "Maybe if I sang it would wake you up. Because it would be so terrible you'd have to tell me to shut the hell up and quit ruining the song."

Tears dripped from my chin and I swiped them on my shoulder, unwilling to remove my hands from Case.

Please let us have our lives together. Oh God, please. I will do anything. This can't be all the time we'll have together.

Maybe it's all that you deserve.

The horror was creeping back. My chest erupted with a panic attack; I felt once-removed from reality, as though I was sitting next to my own body rather than inhabiting it. But I would not let go of Case. I could not. I clung to my point of contact with him.

"Hey," someone suddenly said, as though speaking from deep inside a cave. I felt hands around my shoulders and recognized Marshall's voice. He implored, more sharply, "Hey! Tish, it's all right."

"It's not…all right," I gasped, teeth chattering.

Instead of freaking out, Marshall drew a chair near mine and pressed one hand firmly to my back, rubbing in small, brisk circles. He kept talking, low and quiet, in a way that reminded me of how Case spoke to our horses when they were restless, and at last I regained a tentative hold on my emotions.

"Tish, stop this. You're exhausted. You gotta get some sleep," Marsh instructed in his usual blunt fashion. He was one of Case's best friends, and I knew he and Case thought of each other as brothers; Case considered all five of the Rawley boys his brothers. Clark Rawley and his late wife, Faye, had helped raise Case and Gus; their biological father, Owen Spicer, had been an incapable parent and often violent drunk, whose behavior deteriorated after Melinda's death.

"I can't sleep," I mumbled miserably. "I'm so scared…"

"It's worse because you *aren't* sleeping," Marsh bitched, however gently. "Tish, you look like shit, I'm not gonna lie, like somebody punched you in the eyes."

"I don't care what I look like!" I snapped, or would have snapped if I had even one-tenth my usual energy. I croaked, "I will be *right here* when he wakes up. I won't have it otherwise."

"I know," Marshall acknowledged in a quieter tone, his eyes moving to Case. Pain flinched across his face before he composed himself. "I do know that. I'd like to be here, too."

"Thank you," I whispered, tearing my gaze from Case to regard Marsh, who was like my own brother after this past summer. He bore deep shadows beneath his eyes and days' worth of dark scruff on his jaws, appearing tired and haggard, older than his twenty-seven years. Marshall had been here every night, sleeping in chairs during the day so he could stay up with me during the long night hours, both of us skipping work. Other than Ruthann, Marshall had been here the most. Though, they hadn't overlapped much, as Marsh was typically asleep when Ruthie was here during the day.

"I'm not saying it doesn't mean I think you don't need sleep." Marsh plunged both hands through his longish dark hair, roughing it up, before sighing. "God, now I'm barely making sense to myself."

"Did you get some supper?"

"Yeah, and I brought you some, too." Marshall, like all the Rawleys, was tall, wide-shouldered, and lean as a drought year (as my dear great-grandmother would have said, back when she was alive); he moved with agile grace. He said over his shoulder, "I almost dropped it when I saw you freaking out."

"I'm all right now," I whispered, though it was a lie; I was far from all right.

"Here, eat this and don't complain," Marsh instructed, handing me a burrito wrapped in wax paper. I could not have asked for a better, more vigilant companion at this moment. He was reassuringly calm and his frank, sarcastic sense of humor kept me level.

I freed the burrito from its greasy fast-food paper and took a single nibble, resisting the urge to spit it out. But I knew Case would hate that I wasn't treating myself with more care; my stomach lurched at the food but I forced another bite down my throat.

"Everybody already left?" Marsh asked quietly.

I nodded, letting the burrito drift toward my lap; Marshall narrowed his eyes.

"Eat!"

"I am," I whispered.

"I wonder if he's dreaming," Marsh murmured after a spell.

"I wonder that, too. I haven't noticed any R.E.M. sleep." And I'd been watching like a hawk; to me, this would signify a grain of hope.

"I think he can hear us," Marsh said. "I believe he can."

I whispered, "How did Case get his nickname? It's one story I haven't heard yet."

Marshall laughed, reaching to put his hand on Case's leg, gently patting him; the loving gesture tore at my heart.

"Buddy, do you care if I tell that story?" Marsh asked, his voice low and hoarse. "I can't fucking wait to see you up and about again. It's making us all crazy to see you like this, you know. Your woman, especially." Marsh looked my way and smoothed his free hand over the back of my ragged, shorn hair, with tender concern. He returned his gaze to Case. "I've known from the first how much you love Tish. God, that night at The Spoke when you saw her picture for the first time. We couldn't tear it from your hand. Tish loves you so much, and I know you finally know that."

Fresh tears ran down my neck and wet the collar of my grungy t-shirt. Clark had brought me a change of clothes and a pair of my tennis shoes, but I was still an unwashed wreck.

Marsh continued the story, subtle humor in his tone. "Case passed out that same night he first saw your picture but he kept it right next to him, against his heart. I tried to sneak it away, because I wanted to see Ruthann in it. I claimed her for mine the same night, as you know, but Case told me he would break my arms if I tried to take the picture away again."

"You guys are such romantics," I whispered. I knew this particular story well; I'd heard it told many times.

"Shit, when you know, you just know," Marsh murmured. "I believe that. But Case was crazy about that damn picture. He had it with him from that moment forth. When he wrote your song that August, he planned to play it for you at Carter and Camille's wedding."

"He did?" I had been so cruel to him that night, had totally disregarded his words. I choked, "Oh, Case…"

Marsh said, "Hey. Shit. It's all right, Tish."

But it was beyond my control; sobs assaulted and liquid flowed from my eyes and nose. I wept, "I just had my period. I'm *not pregnant*. Oh God, if something happens I *won't even have a part of him with me…*"

To his credit, poor Marshall didn't squirm at my bordering-upon-hysterical words. He only patted my back. And then, inexplicably, I felt Ruthann behind me; she must have slipped in without us hearing. She curled her hands over my shoulders and bent to press her lips to the top of my head, something a mother would do – but that was Ruthie's way. Marsh let his hand drift back to his own side. I was embarrassed at losing such control when it was the least helpful thing I could do. I scrubbed at my eyes and turned to hug Ruthie around the hips.

"What are you doing here?" I mumbled, the words muffled against my little sister's stomach. I probably sounded ungrateful, which was the last thing I intended to convey; I was just confused, since I thought she'd left with Mom and everyone over an hour ago.

"I couldn't sleep, so I came back. I was worried about you." Ruthie's gaze flickered to Marshall and she murmured, "Hi."

He nodded hello.

"Marsh, you remember my sister." I leaned back from Ruthie and rubbed my aching eyes.

"Of course I do." Marshall spoke in a tone of voice unlike any I'd ever heard him use; at the same second Ruthie said, "We talked for a second yesterday."

"Good to see you. Again," Marshall muttered, and then cleared his throat. I peeked sideways at him; he was sitting very still, somber gaze fixed on Ruthann, and he seemed ill at ease, which was strange. I'd seen Marsh operate around women and normally they all but ate from his hand. Not that this situation was normal, but he hadn't behaved like this around Mom, Aunt Jilly, or Camille; with them he'd been his usual charming self.

Ruthie stepped toward the third chair in the room, intending to drag it to the bedside to join us; at the same instant Marsh stood up with that very intention in mind. They bumped into each other and Marsh twitched as if her touch burned his skin. Ruthie dropped her chin, clearly flustered; her hands had made inadvertent contact with his waist. This interplay between them was odd enough that it distracted my attention.

"Here, I got it," Marsh said, speaking decisively; he collected the chair without further ado and positioned it on the other side of mine.

"Thank you," my little sister said, fidgeting with the long braid that hung over her shoulder.

Marsh reclaimed his seat without another word and I couldn't help but shoot him a look; he met my gaze and glared menacingly, and I almost smiled.

"It's hard to sleep at the Carters' house," Ruthie said as she took her seat; my family was staying with relatives of Camille's husband, Mathias. She was quick to add, "I don't mean to complain. It's just that their house is so crowded with all of us. And since Milla is pregnant and Clinty is too big to sleep on the loveseat, that's where I keep ending up…"

"It's all right to complain," I assured her, as I had countless times over the years. "You're too nice."

Ruthie laughed a little, but she seemed tense. She'd never been a complainer. It simply wasn't in her sweet nature. She conceded, "I know. But it was a good excuse to come back over here." She rested one hand on my thigh. "Are you all right? Tish, I'm so worried about you…"

"Thanks for being here. You guys just being here helps me more than you know."

We sat in companionable silence for a few minutes; I finally said, "I talked to Grandma and Aunt Ellen for a while today."

"They miss you so much. Grandma always says the cafe is too quiet without you."

I had to smile at this statement; Grandma had always been the first to tell me to pipe down. I missed her and Aunt Ellen all the time.

"They're such great ladies," Marshall remarked. He sat with his fingers linked over his lean belly, long legs stretched out and crossed at the ankles; he wore dusty work boots and probably hadn't been out of them in the past five days. "I remember when we came to Landon that summer they were like the two sweetest grandmothers anyone could hope for."

"That was fun," I whispered, remembering how Marsh and Garth had played music every night, out on the porch at Shore Leave. We'd all sung along, the notes dancing through the darkness and carrying over Flickertail Lake.

"Yeah, it was. I wanted to stay longer than two weeks." Marsh slouched in the chair, bracing his spine low on the seat.

"Good thing you didn't," Ruthie surprised us by saying. I had the feeling she'd surprised herself as well. She hurried to explain, "I was about ready to drown you in the lake."

Marshall looked her way, one dark eyebrow cocked.

Ruthie twisted her braid in her right hand and justified in a rush, "Well, you wouldn't quit pestering me. I mean, you kept putting ice cubes down my shirt. And you untied my bikini top about a hundred times…"

Now that sounded more like the Marshall I knew.

A wry half-grin tugged at his lips as he muttered, "Yeah, I don't think your boyfriend appreciated that very much."

Ruthie was still dating Liam Gallagher, the guy in question, and had been for the past four years. She smiled a crooked little smile and affirmed, "He was ready to kick your butt back to Montana."

"It's not like he let you out of his sight all that much," Marshall went on, and my gaze darted his way at the none-too-subtle ire in his tone. I tried to send him a telepathic message. *This isn't the way to earn points with my sister!*

"What's that supposed to mean?" Surprise and defense mingled in Ruthie's voice. Since they sat on opposite sides I felt like a spectator at a volleyball game, glancing one way and then instantly the other.

"You were practically attached at the hips." Marshall's tone bordered on outright confrontational.

"Marsh, you were about to tell me that story," I interrupted, hoping to redirect him. I had the sense he was picking a fight with my sister, and I didn't understand why.

"I'll be right back," he said instead, rising and disappearing from the room without a backward glance.

What in the hell?

I looked over at Ruthie, who had leaned forward to stare after him. She jerked her gaze back to me and raised both eyebrows, muting her voice. "He was *such* a pest that summer. A few times I was tempted to flash him, just because." This was a wholly unexpected comment; Ruthie acknowledged my surprise and rolled her eyes, tucking loose wisps of curly hair behind her ears. She said, almost wickedly, "Just to *torture* him."

"God, I can't reconcile that attitude with the little sister I know," I said, in all honesty. Ruthann could easily be queen of the goody-two-shoes, if there was such a thing. Scouring my not-inconsiderable memory, I couldn't recall even one time in all of her twenty-two years she had been in trouble – with friends, with Mom, with anyone. She was simply the definition of kindness. I studied her guileless face. "Maybe I don't know you as well as I think I do."

Ruthie said with a sigh, "Oh, *Tish*."

I reached for her hand. "Tell me it's going to be all right, please. I can't hear it enough."

Ruthie scooted closer. "It's going to be all right, *it is*." She squeezed my hand to convey her certainty. "I'm so happy you found Case, and that you love him. It just feels *right*."

"It's *so* right. I fought it for a long time, but in my heart I always knew the truth."

"Aunt Jilly said there's something from the past you have to understand." Ruthie searched my eyes. "Do you know what that means? It has to do with Cole Spicer and that man you think you were married to, right, that Yancy guy?"

I'd briefly explained my theory to Ruthann, but there was so much more to tell. "Do you want the long version, or the short and sweet?"

Ruthie gave me a withering expression, dark eyebrows pulled low. She murmured, "I'm not going anywhere. I want to be here. Plus," and she smiled, "it means I don't have to sleep on that tiny loveseat. My back is all cramped up."

I slogged a hand through my hair, wondering where to start.

Ruthie studied me and then gently suggested, "You should take a quick shower. I'll stay right here, I promise."

The bathroom was only steps away and I had new clothes folded on the counter in there, courtesy of Clark. There was no logical excuse to refuse; I sighed and relented, mumbling, "Fine."

The warm water felt good, I had to admit. I scrubbed thoroughly, shampooing twice, still unaccustomed to my much-shorter hair. As a teenager I'd preferred keeping it short but had let it grow since college. I retained no memory of my hair burning away; the images from inside the blazing barn were scattered across my mind like jumbled puzzle pieces. What I clearly remembered, knew I would never forget, was the sight of Case lying unconscious on the wooden floor between two stalls. He would have died if I hadn't raced into the barn after him, if I'd obeyed his order to stay back and simply call 911.

I bent forward in the shower, curling around the pain in my gut at this thought.

Had that been the intent of the person responsible for starting the fire? Derrick Yancy was my prime suspect, but had he actually intended for us to be killed? The fire hadn't originated in the trailer, where anyone trespassing would have known we lay sleeping, but instead the barn, leading me to believe that the arsonist's primary purpose had been to warn rather than kill us. No matter; I was murderously angry and Case lay unconscious because he refused to let our animals die in the blaze.

I heard Marshall return; the hushed sound of him speaking to Ruthann floated through the bathroom wall. I hoped he intended to be a little more polite. I knew he was tired and worried, at the end of his emotional rope, but there wasn't any excuse to provoke her that way. Still, I hurried to dry off and dress in my jeans and a much-too-big shirt (I'd requested that Clark bring me one of Case's). When I emerged from the bathroom Ruthie and Marshall sat in taut silence, my empty chair between them, Marsh crunching through a bag of chips.

Before either of them could speak, I asked, "Marsh, will you play for a while? That makes me feel a little better."

"Sure thing," he said agreeably, to my relief; he set aside the chips and retrieved the guitar he'd propped against the wall.

Ruthie folded her legs crosswise, shifting position so that she could watch Marsh as he played.

"What would you like to hear?" Marsh inquired, his gaze alighting briefly on her as he strummed a chord. This past summer I had grown to understand that Marshall possessed a deep well of sincere sweetness beneath the immature, pesky-kid-brother attitude he so often fronted. I peeked at Ruthie from the corner of my eye, hoping she noticed this, at least a little; he hadn't exactly been displaying his best manners this evening.

Ruthie wore an old Landon Rebels t-shirt, white with blue lettering, one that fit a little tighter across her breasts than I remembered from high school, along with faded jeans and well-worn purple tennis shoes. Her lovely face was free of any cosmetics, her golden-green eyes, exactly like Mom's and Camille's, remained fixed on Marshall as he waited for a response. Her brown hair, long and thick and curly, as mine had been a week ago, hung in a single braid. She clutched the braid in a gesture I recognized as self-conscious.

I looked back at Marsh, who was studying her through his enviable long lashes as he pretended to regard his guitar. His dark, wavy hair fell along the sides of his forehead and he hadn't shaved in days, but it suited him well and spoke of his worry over Case. He had eyes of slate-gray and a nose just a little too long and dominating for his handsome face. Like Case, he possessed strong hands that handled a guitar with ample ability and grace.

"How about some Waylon?" I suggested, knowing this would nicely showcase his voice.

He nodded agreement and began strumming the chords to the *Dukes of Hazzard* theme song. He offered us a sheepish grin. "Case loves this one."

"It's one of his shower favorites," I confirmed.

Marsh's expression grew fond and he shifted his right shoulder toward the instrument as he played the song, singing softly and with perfect pitch; as the drummer, he was usually relegated to harmonizing when Case and Garth played but he had a great singing voice, low and throaty. Marsh let the last chord fade on the strings and then gave me a wink. He did so almost unconsciously and I was pleased to observe Ruthie studying him with subtle admiration; he didn't know her well enough to notice this, but for whatever reason it made me glad.

"That was really good," she murmured, and Marsh lifted his eyebrows in a modest 'thank you.' He was too accustomed to playing it cool to really react but I noticed the hint of a smile he couldn't quite contain as he strummed out the first notes of "Luckenbach, Texas," which was another standard he and Case performed. He didn't make it to the chorus before a nurse stalked into the room.

"This is unacceptable," she said without preamble, hands on hips. "People are trying to *sleep*."

"I apologize, ma'am," Marshall said at once, his tone laced with contrition. He set the guitar beside his chair and offered the nurse his most innocent and charming smile; he really was an expert at that particular combination.

Though I understood the nurse was in the right, I glared at her and she glared right back.

"Case likes the music. And it wasn't that loud."

"Just keep it quieter in here, Mrs. Spicer," she said before retreating, and I loved being referred to as 'Mrs. Spicer' so very much I didn't offer any barbed parting comments; I hadn't corrected the staff's general assumption that Case and I were married.

Once the door had closed Ruthie released a huff of laughter, nudging my shin with her toes. "Tish, you'll get us kicked out!"

"I'd like to see them try to kick me out," I muttered.

"Yeah, I'd kinda like to see that, too." Marsh offered up half of a grin.

"You guys!" Ruthie admonished.

"She's not much of a rule-breaker," I explained to Marshall.

Ruthie sat straighter. "I've broken rules!"

Marsh allowed, "Yeah, I guess you were drinking beer that summer we were there. And you weren't twenty-one then."

Ruthie angled me a look that clearly insisted, *See?*

I mumbled, "You're a total criminal."

"So, you're still dating that same guy?" Marsh asked, even though he already knew the answer; he'd asked me that very question about Ruthann the first night my family arrived.

Ruthie did not offer an immediate response and I could see the confusion in her eyes; again Marshall didn't exactly convey polite curiosity. At last she said, "I am," and her tone subtly suggested, *What's it to you?*

Oh, he said, with no sound.

Tonight was not the first time I'd heard Marshall say he'd claimed Ruthann all those years ago when he'd first seen her picture, quite by chance, that night at The Spoke; the wallet-sized image was one Camille once carried in her purse, and featured not only Ruthie and me, but Camille's daughter, Millie Jo. Case had taken one look at that picture and known I was the woman for him, and had kept it in his possession until his angry former wife tore it to shreds to punish him. But I had never really taken Marshall's claim very seriously; I was too accustomed to him joking and exaggerating. Now observing his too-neutral expression, I reconsidered the depth of his sincerity.

I wasn't used to being the peacekeeper; ironically, that had usually been Ruthie's role in our growing years. Maybe it was time I shouldered arms. I poked Marsh and complained, "Hey, you still haven't finished that story."

Chapter Three

Tish had no idea how much I missed her, how much I longed to see her on a daily basis. Ever since Camille had first discovered she was pregnant with Millie Jo, way back in 2003 and a good ten years ago, Tish and I began to hang out more often. Before that summer I was always the baby sister who tagged along, crazy to be acknowledged; Camille's pregnancy and sudden advent into adult responsibilities changed the dynamics almost overnight. By the time we were in high school Tish turned to me for advice or opinions before any of her other friends and I'd been quietly joyful of this fact, never letting on how much I valued the newfound attention.

In this cramped little hospital room, hundreds of miles from home and many years later, I was struck by the realization that I still longed for her attention. When Tish left Landon for college, back in August of 2006, I'd harbored a secret wish that she would decide she disliked Minneapolis enough to move straight home. Earlier that same summer, Clint had decided against attending college and still lived in town to this day, working as a firefighter for the township; he shared a tiny second-floor apartment in downtown Landon with my boyfriend, Liam Gallagher.

But Tish had entertained grander expectations of life, and did not return home. Once she started school we rarely saw her and for the first month I had cried every night with missing her. It seemed a bright and glimmering light was suddenly snuffed from my existence. Not that I didn't find a great deal of joy in the rest of my family; in fact, Camille and

I were closer now than we'd ever been. But I missed Tish to the point that my heart ached, even if I wouldn't admit this for fear of seeming like a weakling. Besides, I was so proud of her for accomplishing what she'd set out to do in the first place, which was to earn a law degree.

I studied her profile in the light cast by the bedside lamp, her features so familiar, one of the faces I'd looked to for my cues since I was a little girl. Her formerly long hair was now short, reminiscent of our teenage years. Camille had trimmed away all of the burned ends, and without her curly mane Tish appeared younger than ever. My older sisters were both beautiful; I had always admired them so much it overrode most of my envy. Even now, as exhausted and hollowed-out by fear as I knew she was, I thought Tish was gorgeous.

My heart cramped up all over again, with worry; her agonized concern for Case Spicer was so apparent that it hovered in the air all around her, a devastating rain cloud she could not escape. My eyes moved to Case, his tall, strong body motionless on the bed, his hands lying palms up, fingers curled inward. His chest rose and fell at regular intervals, but not of his own power. I couldn't claim to know him well but he was my sister's true love and for that I loved him, and silently pleaded with him to come back to her.

Wake up, please wake up, I begged, studying his face behind the oxygen mask. *Please. My sister needs you.*

On the far side of Tish, Marshall Rawley leaned and rested his forearms on the metal bed railing and at this movement my heart contracted, which I didn't understand at all. I didn't understand *him* at all, truth be told. Despite adoring the rest of the Rawley family, I wasn't overly fond of Marshall. Three summers ago, when the Rawleys drove from Montana to Minnesota for an extended visit, he'd teased me relentlessly, much to Liam's annoyance – and Liam was not a person easily annoyed. In four years of dating him I'd never witnessed Liam get upset about anything.

Anything other than Marshall Rawley, that is, who slipped melting ice cubes down my shirt, who tugged the back ties of my bikini top so the entire thing fell forward and left me half-naked. Thinking back on it now, I supposed I should have traded that particular swimsuit for another; it wasn't as though I didn't own any one-piece suits.

But why give him the satisfaction?

It only would have proven to him just how much he upset me; instead, I'd done my best to ignore him. As a final insult, Marshall pitched me in Flickertail Lake on the last night of their visit after I'd made it clear I didn't want to get wet again; not to mention the fact that I'd been holding my cell phone. Even though Camille, Mathias, Tish, Clint, and the Rawley boys were all swimming and splashing under the starry sky, I'd been content to relax on the glider at the end of the dock that night, just watching. But Marshall had climbed from the water and scooped me in his arms before I could think of escaping, right against his dripping bare chest, before executing an energetic leap into the water.

I'd been so upset with him, especially after two solid weeks of teasing, that tears filled my eyes; he was lucky Liam hadn't been there that particular night. Even though Marshall apologized, his laughter doubled him forward. He only laughed harder and pretended to cower when I punched his shoulder before storming out of the lake, wet sundress slogging against my thighs. Everyone whooped and hollered at the fact that I'd actually hit Marshall, and I'd been tempted to call Liam (though I would have had to use the phone in the cafe, since mine was now lost in the lake) and demand that he drive over to Shore Leave and take care of a certain someone. And by *take care* I meant beat to a pulp.

But of course I hadn't done such a thing; I would have felt terrible, even as steamed up as I'd been. Liam was broad and barrel-chested, strong as any two men. Aunt Jilly joked that Liam had been carved from the trunk of an oak tree; Marshall had referred to Liam as 'Paul Bunyan' multiple times during those two weeks – in my hearing but not Liam's, leading me to believe that he did indeed possess a small sense of self-preservation. Though Marshall was tall and built with wiry muscles, he was pretty darn slim, and I figured he'd be no match for my firefighter (lumberjack – *haha*) boyfriend.

All of these thoughts were in my mind as I sat here beside Tish, and indirectly beside Marshall, whom I hadn't seen since that summer until just yesterday evening, here at the hospital. He had taken me by surprise, coming around the corner from Case's room like someone on a mission. At first I didn't recognize him; he'd been completely clean-shaven when I'd last seen him.

"Ruthann," he'd said yesterday, before saying anything else.

I'd had to lift my chin in order to meet his gaze. I'd been walking quickly and we'd crashed into each other; Marshall had reached to prevent me from stumbling, grasping my elbows. I felt a fluttering at the base of my throat, my pulse having taken unexpected wing. I hadn't known how to respond as our gazes held.

"It's been a while," he finally said, hands falling back to his sides.

I nodded silently, agreeing that yes, it had.

"You still look just like an angel," he stunned me by saying next. My eyebrows lifted almost to my hairline at these words.

"Your sister is in there," he said, when it was apparent I was embarrassingly tongue-tied, indicating with one thumb over his shoulder. "She's glad you're here."

"Thank you," I whispered, not sure if I was thanking him for the compliment or for telling me Tish was nearby. For some reason my gaze felt trapped by his. I had never noticed his eyes were so gray, the slightly dangerous shade of an August thunderstorm about to roll over the lake. I blinked and Marshall flowed into motion, stepping politely to the side so I could pass him and enter the room.

"It's good to see you," he said quietly, and I looked over my shoulder but he was already headed down the hall. I stood at the entrance to Case's room, gripping the doorframe, frozen in place for the second time, watching Marshall walk away.

He'd been wearing a gray t-shirt and much-used jeans, over which my eyes roved as though with their own agenda. I saw the lines of his shoulder blades beneath his shirt, the muscle definition along his arms. At the elevator near the end of the hall he stopped and pressed the down arrow, unaware I was observing; he plunged both hands through his hair, grinding the base of his palms against his eyes, shoulders hunching forward. My heart lurched in concern at this sight and he straightened abruptly and glanced over his shoulder, right into my eyes, as though prodded by some instinct. Even though yards of linoleum flooring separated us I imagined I could still see the stormy color of his irises. The elevator doors slid open and I all but leaped into the room and out of his line of sight.

That had been last night; I wouldn't even have seen him today if I hadn't left the Carters' house to come back to the hospital, borrowing Mom's car to do so. Camille and Mom were sharing a bed in the Carters' guestroom, Aunt Jilly and Clint another, while I was relegated to the loveseat in the living room, partially because I was the youngest family member on the trip, but also because I was the least likely to complain. Of course Camille, nearly eight months pregnant, couldn't sleep on such a small couch and Clint was way too tall, and I would have felt terrible making my mom or my auntie sleep there.

And so here I was.

I was especially glad to have shown up tonight, when Tish was sobbing hysterically and needed me, both the late hour and the strain of sleepless nights taking its toll. Marshall hadn't seen me enter the room, intent as he was upon comforting my sister, but he hadn't seemed surprised when I'd appeared behind Tish. Instead, though his face had not altered in expression, I thought something in his eyes conveyed gladness.

Probably he was just relieved that someone other than him could now deal with Tish's weeping.

"You're right, I was about to tell that story," Marshall said in response to my sister's request.

Despite everything I found myself caught up in studying him, as though my eyes didn't have the sense to stay away; not that he'd noticed. I'd had a good excuse when he was playing his guitar and singing in a surprisingly true voice. It was an unexpected treat to hear him sing, to watch him handle the instrument. He seemed very *into* the music, playing and singing with eyes closed, his fingers shaping to and flowing over the strings. I vaguely remembered him making music that summer back in Landon but I'd been too focused upon being irritated with him to appreciate his talent.

Marshall was wearing the same gray t-shirt from yesterday, and the same pair of jeans; there was the narrow rip in the denim across his left knee, which I'd noticed yesterday. He was unshaven to a degree that within a day he would have an actual beard, not just scruff. I knew from Tish he usually spent every waking moment outside; his resultant deep tan created a contrast with his gray eyes. His hair was a brown so dark it was almost black, the color of the antique walnut bed in which I slept back home, and needed scissors and comb applied to it; though, I reminded myself, he seemed nearly as worried about Case as my sister. I knew Case was like a brother to the Rawley family.

Marshall placed a hand on Case's leg and patted him a couple of times, elbows braced on the edge of the bed railing. He had strong-looking forearms, covered in dark hair, and wrists with knobby bones on the outer edges. I blinked a couple of times, wondering at my sudden fascination with him; I exhaled slowly and focused on Tish, who sat with her forehead resting on the edge of the mattress beside Case, holding fast to his hand. I reached to rub her back, which she acknowledged with a soft little sound.

"Well, let's see. Case is actually named after his great-grandfather, Charles Dalton," Marshall began, his gaze shifting upward as he related the story. I noticed this from the corner of my eye, *not* because I looked over at him. "Charles Dalton was a preacher, and old Charles's son, Edwin, also a preacher, was Melinda's father. And Melinda, as you know, was Case's mother. So anyway, Case's dad, Owen, and Melinda were over in Billings that December day Case was born. They'd settled on his name ahead of time but when Owen held his son for the first time he made some joke that the boy was too tiny, that he'd expected him to weigh at least as much as a case of beer. And that's what he called his boy from that moment forth. My mom, who told us the story, said Melinda wasn't happy about the nickname at first but eventually it grew on her."

Tish uttered a small huff of air, nowhere near her usual good humor. "Owen sounds like he was a piece of work. What an asshole, to say such a thing about his newborn baby."

"Oh, he could be as mean as a wolverine," Marshall agreed. "My mom hated him, I know, even if she never said it outright. But I could tell. She worried so much about Melinda."

"No wonder he's been reluctant to tell me that story," Tish murmured, stroking Case's hair; she whispered, "I love you so much. Do you hear me?"

"He hears you," Marshall said, calm and reassuring, and there I was staring at him again. "Don't you worry. He knows."

Tish nodded, then rested her cheek on her bent arms.

"You need to sleep," Marshall ordered, leaning past her to click out the bedside lamp. "Do you hear *me*?"

"I do," Tish mumbled. The room was plunged into semi-darkness; meager light continued to trickle in from the hall.

"Would you like to take a walk?" Marshall startled me by asking; I had been planning to stay at Tish's side.

"Sure," I whispered, and the next thing I knew he and I were in the hallway together.

"Let's go outside," Marshall decided. He nodded in the direction of the desk, where the nurse who'd told us to quiet down was eyeballing us with her lips pursed up in annoyance.

"Good idea," I agreed.

We maintained an awkward silence in the elevator and I was acutely aware of Marshall as he stood beside me in the small space; breathing became an act of will and I fidgeted with the hem of my shirt. He extended his hand in a polite gesture when the elevator doors opened, allowing me to lead the way. We ventured across the small lobby and then out into the night.

"I wish she'd sleep more," Marshall said, indicating with a tilt of his head a small bench beneath a group of trees, to the left of the hospital entrance. It must have been cloudy; not a star was in sight and the air felt dense, the same way it did before a storm broke over the lake. A breeze lifted strands of hair from my braid and blew them across my face.

"You can't make Tish do anything," I responded, sitting on the bench, experiencing a heated rush of nerves as Marshall sat beside me, though he left a good eighteen inches of space between our hips. He immediately leaned forward, forearms to thighs, while I hunched my shoulders;

it was chilly in the breezy night air. The hospital seemed peaceful under the starless, flat-black sky in the middle of the night.

"That's the truth," Marshall muttered, and I realized he meant it was true you couldn't make Tish do anything. I was having trouble concentrating and my gaze kept sneaking back to him. He rubbed his eyes and bent his head forward, rolling it side to side as though to ease a muscle ache. I curled my fingers around the hard edge of the wooden bench beneath my thighs.

"I miss her so much," I said to fill the silence in which we were submerged. "I know it's been a long time since she moved out of Landon, but I've missed her every day she was away."

"I'd miss any of my brothers if they moved that far away." Marshall sat with his fingers laced, studying the distance. "So I know just what you mean."

I shivered.

Marshall looked over his shoulder. "You're cold. We can go back inside. I just wanted Tish to have a second to fall asleep." His gaze was unwavering, his expression serious; he'd spoken with such concern and my heart responded to this by accelerating, even more so when he shifted position and offered, "Here, I'll grab you my sweatshirt from the truck."

"You know what I should probably get back before Mom wakes up and worries." So saying, I stood in a rush, so abruptly that Marshall twitched and sat straight, surprised by my sudden decision to leave. The lights from the hospital sign bathed his face in a bluish glow, leaving mine in shadow. I studied him with my pulse clicking along, as though I'd just sprinted around the parking lot.

"Will you tell Tish I'll see her in the morning?" I asked, the first to break our gazes, digging Mom's car keys from my pocket.

"Of course," Marshall responded, and his tone conveyed what sounded like mild confusion. He added as a farewell, "Until tomorrow, then."

"See you," I mumbled carelessly, and hurried across the parking lot.

I drove over what had become familiar streets in the past few days, back to Harry and Meg Carter's house, where my family was all still asleep. I crept inside, to the little loveseat couch in the living room, beside which my overnight bag was propped. Because it was dark and no one was about, I slipped out of my shorts and into my pajama pants, then curled up beneath an afghan that smelled faintly of lavender. My phone was tucked in my bag and I fished it out, only to see three more missed calls from Liam. I supposed I better send a text; I knew he was worried and I hadn't been the best about responding since we'd arrived in Montana. I tapped my phone and wrote, *Hey there. I was with Tish most of the day. I'm so glad to be here to help her. How's everything back home?*

A few minutes later Liam wrote back, *Good here. Miss you.*

He was a man of few words, which I knew. I imagined him sitting on his bed in the little apartment where he and Clint had lived for the last two years. Though I'd hung out there countless times, I never spent the night; maybe if Liam rented his own place I would have considered doing so, but it was just too awkward with my cousin always present. We were all adults, and Liam and I had been having sex since the first month we'd started dating, but I still preferred to return to my own familiar bedroom in Mom and Blythe's cabin near Shore Leave.

I tapped my phone's screen to send one last message – *I'll let you know how things are going tomorrow.*

Sounds good, sweet pea, I'm excited for you to get home, Liam responded, using his favorite endearment, and I set my phone aside and drew both knees to my chest, closing my eyes.

I thought, *I'm not.*

A backlash of guilt brought my teeth together on their edges; how could I not be excited to return home? What was I thinking?

I cared deeply for Liam Gallagher; we'd been dating since the summer he first asked me out, over four years ago. He was kind and complimentary, sweet to a fault. He never forgot holidays or anniversaries; he gave my mom a birthday card every year, without fail. He knew I loved snuggling as much as I liked having sex, and behaved accordingly. Who could ask for more from her boyfriend? Liam never got upset, never raised his voice unless he was joking about something, and was attentive to my every need. He treated me with absolute tenderness at all times, no exceptions. Aunt Jilly teased us that if there was a trophy for being nice enough to occasionally induce vomiting she didn't know if Liam or I would take first place.

I knew my family adored him and assumed our eventual marriage was a foregone conclusion.

I also knew that the idea of marrying Liam should fill me with certainty and happiness.

Except…it didn't, and a familiar, reprimanding voice swelled inside my head.

What is wrong with you? Liam loves you. You love him!

Maybe after he proposes you'll be excited. Maybe once he gives you a ring and it seems more real.

But what if it doesn't?

What then…

Doubts had plagued me on an increasing basis; because I couldn't reach a satisfactory answer to the question I avoided it, troubled and depressed, lonely in this dark living room in Montana. I closed my eyes, rolled to the side and fell into a doze, tired enough to conjure up a dream…

A forest path strewn with dead leaves and broken twigs, sharp beneath my bare feet. The surrounding trees had blurred with the advance of dusk, enveloping me in a spectral, dark blue light. Urgency compressed my lungs. There was something lurking just ahead but I couldn't see through the gloom…

A cold bead centered on my nape a split second before I perceived the danger. The low voice taunted from somewhere within the tree trunks, hidden from view.

I see you, Ruthann.

I spun around, peering through encroaching darkness, but could not spy him.

My own voice next, a pleading, weakling version of itself – *Who are you?*

A woman's voice clanged in my ear, high with fright.

Run! Run, Ruthie, get away!

There's no time!

Footsteps crunched the dead twigs, first a walk, then gaining speed…

He's right behind you!

I jerked awake and tumbled headlong from the loveseat, gulping for breath. Head swimming and heart like a boiling kettle, I huddled on the floor in a dark, unfamiliar room, eyes darting, wracked with terror – it took precious seconds to recognize that I was alone, and safe, in the Carters' living room; it had been a nightmare, nothing more. After everything my family had been through this week, it was no wonder. Minutes ticked past before I was able to unclench my rigid muscles and roll to a sitting position. I cupped my temples and squeezed shut my eyes, peering into the shifting blackness on the backs of my eyelids, trying to understand why I was so frightened. Frightened down into my bones.

Something I knew I should remember nagged at the edges of my awareness but the images from the nightmare had already dissolved and begun sinking away. When it was apparent I would glean no information from my memory, I climbed back atop the loveseat and gathered my blankets extra tightly around my body.

Chapter Four

MARSH RETURNED TO CASE'S ROOM AT SOME POINT. I MAN-
aged to snag a few hours of sleep and it was edging past dawn when the
day-shift nurse stopped by to introduce herself. I eased straight, feeling
about eighty years old, bleary eyes sweeping Case from head to toe, making sure nothing had changed while I slept, for either better or worse.

"Good morning," I whispered, leaning to kiss his forehead.

Marsh had fallen asleep, his head lolling against the back of a chair,
feet propped on another. Ruthie must have driven back to the Carters'
house; I had no memory of her leaving and hoped Marsh had been polite on their walk. Ruthie was just not equipped to deal with negative
attitudes. As though my gaze or thoughts possessed weight, Marshall's
eyelids fluttered; he groaned, thumping to his other side and grumbling,
"Did you sleep?"

"Maybe you should go smoke another pack of cigarettes," I responded, just as evil-tempered. He opened one eye to question what the hell I
meant, so I clarified, "That's how your voice sounds right now."

"Oh," he grunted, unconcerned, and then mumbled, "I talked to Dad.
He's bringing Wy over this morning. Garth and Sean and Quinn are
working out at your place again. I should get my ass out there, I suppose."

Tears thickened my voice. "That's so amazing, what you guys are doing. Al told me all about it. And I'm so glad you've been here with me,
Marsh, truly. You've kept me sane, for real."

"We love you and we love Case." He referred to the entire Rawley
clan and my heart was warmed for the countless time, so grateful that

Clark had been allowed a hand in raising Case, that Case had been adopted by such a loving family. Marshall pinned me with an unexpectedly earnest gaze as he said, "I was going to drive home later today to change clothes and shower. I thought, maybe…" He paused and his eyes dropped to the floor; at last he mumbled, "Maybe Ruthann might want to ride along and meet the horses."

"You weren't being a jerk to her last night, were you?"

Marshall regarded me with legitimate surprise, eyebrows arched. "Of course not."

"Well, you were being rude when she first got here. What do you care that she still has the same boyfriend, anyway?" I knew, or at least *thought* I knew, but I wanted him to admit it.

Marsh plunged both hands through his tangled hair and looked momentarily agonized. "No reason," he muttered, clearly lying, but I let that go.

"She'd love to meet your horses. She can meet Cider and Buck, too, since they're in your barn. As long as you promise to be nice to her."

"Jesus *Christ*, Tish," he nearly growled. "Of course I'll be nice to her. Thanks a lot."

I smiled at his irritation before turning back to Case and murmuring, "I think our Marshall has a little crush on someone."

"You don't know the *half*," Marshall muttered acidly.

A few hours later Clark and Wy arrived from Jalesville, and Ruthie, Clint, and Camille from across town. Marsh had disappeared, probably to sleep somewhere for a few more hours before heading home. I made a point of mentioning to my little sister that Marshall thought she might like to accompany him to their ranch in Jalesville and meet the horses.

Instead of smiling with her usual enthusiasm, as I'd been anticipating, Ruthie chewed her lower lip, appearing to fish for an excuse. Plucking at her shirt she mumbled, "I'm not really dressed for it."

I glanced at her worn t-shirt and faded jean shorts, ratty purple tennis shoes and anklet socks, the kind we'd always worn in the summer while waiting on the busy dinner crowd at Shore Leave. "You're dressed just fine. Maybe not for horseback riding, but I don't think that's the plan anyway. It might do you a little good to get out of the hospital for a while."

"I *would* like to meet the horses." Her eyes roved to the door as she spoke, clearly in search of something. Or someone. Hoping she sounded casual, I could tell, she inquired, "So…where is Marshall?"

"Sleeping somewhere. He's beat. But he'll show up any minute."

Thirty minutes later he did; Ruthie, Wy, Clint, and Camille were playing cards in the waiting room at the end of the hall, while I chatted with Clark at the bedside. Clark, who sat with his cowboy hat on his lap, let me know that the official cause of the fire had been determined.

"It started in the loft. No appreciable accelerant." Clark studied me with his bushy white eyebrows pulled together. Neither of us knew what to make of this finding; I understood this information would work against me when I pushed for an investigation into an arson claim. Referring to the township fire chief, Clark added, "Marv ruled that a lantern tipped. Could that have been possible, hon?"

"Absolutely *not*." I spoke with complete certainty. "Case is the most careful person I know." Although we did occasionally make love in our haymow we had never been so careless as to burn a candle lantern up there, let alone *leave* one burning unattended. I gripped Clark's hands, speaking intently. "Someone crawled up there to plant a lantern and light the hay on fire that night."

"Do you think it can be proven?" Clark asked. I knew he believed me; the problem was proving it to anyone else.

"I'm going to try my damnedest," I said with angry passion, just as Marshall appeared in the doorway.

Claiming the last chair in the room, he said, "If anyone can prove it, you can. We'll help you. Whatever it takes."

I was immeasurably grateful for their support. "Thank you. I know you guys will. As soon as Case wakes up and we get the hell out of this place."

"You think Yancy?" Marshall asked, keeping his voice pitched low. "That's where I'd put my money."

"Yes. He was paid, or paid someone, to start the fire that night, I know it."

Marsh suggested, "What about that little piss-ant from the city, you know…"

"Robbie?" I clarified, with some surprise. Rob Benson, who had attended Northwestern College with me for all three years of law school, was staying in Ron Turnbull's vacation cabin at present; though Robbie had been absent from the hospital this week, he'd texted me numerous times to express his concern. Robbie had accepted a job offer at Turnbull and Hinckley, despite what I'd told him about Ron Turnbull's connection to the closing of the power plant in Jalesville and its subsequent disabling of local income. Though, it was no surprise to me; Robbie was a career ass-kisser, an opportunist for sure, but not a criminal. I said, "No. Robbie isn't a lowlife in that sense."

"I don't like the look of him." Marshall used his thumbs to drum a staccato beat on the arms of his chair. "Bad vibe."

"Believe me, if I suspected Robbie I'd tell you. I have a few questions for Derrick once we get out of here." Anger heated my chest. "Has he been around town? Have you seen him since the fire?"

Clark said, "No. And as much as I admire your spirit, honey, I don't like the idea of you questioning Derrick Yancy."

"At least, not alone," Marshall followed up.

I was about to insist that I was not afraid of anyone when Camille stuck her head in the room. "Tish, I need your phone. I left mine at the Carters' and I want to call home."

"Here, take my chair," Marsh said at once, leaping up and presenting it to my very pregnant sister. Camille beamed and he helped her to sit, teasing, "You and Carter planning to stop at ten kids, or go for a full dozen?"

"Depends on which of us you ask." Camille fanned her flushed cheeks.

"We'll give you some privacy," Clark said, resting a fond hand on Camille's shoulder. "We can continue this conversation later."

"Tish, I'm gonna head home but I'll be back later this evening," Marshall promised. He drew a slow breath, avoiding my eyes as he said, "I'm gonna go ask Ruthann if she wants to come with me."

"She said she did," I informed him, and was heartened to see a flash of what appeared to be pure joy cross his features, though he didn't so much as smile, typical Marshall. I added, "We'll see you later."

Marshall loped away, Clark joined the card game down the hall, and I repositioned in my usual spot beside Case; two feet away, Camille spoke on the phone with Mathias and I reflected that privacy was a relative concept when it came to sisters. I hardly heard what she was saying anyway, thinking of what Clark had just told me regarding the cause of the fire.

Who crawled up into our haymow and planted a lantern that night?

Derrick wouldn't risk getting caught, would he? But if not Derrick, then who? Who would he trust with such a heinous errand? He has no friends in Jalesville, at least not any I know about. And someone from around here wouldn't do such a thing to Case...

I scurried through a mental list of Jalesville residents but could think of no one locally allied with Derrick; the only person with Chicago connections (at least, of which I was aware) was indeed Robbie Benson, but my gut instinct did not suggest Robbie was responsible. Robbie was the arrogant only child of a very privileged family and prized himself on his model-caliber good looks, which had served to open almost as many doors as his parents' fortune, but I'd known him for years and did not believe he would purposely hurt or betray me.

Unless...

What if Ron issued the order?

Would Robbie act on Ron's orders?

Ron Turnbull held the keys to the figurative kingdom from a young lawyer's perspective, my own once included. He was powerful, wealthy, and potentially more dangerous than I could ever have guessed. My skin began to crawl with horrible little gnats of awareness. Perhaps the real question was would Derrick act on Ron's orders? Did Derrick *take* orders from Ron? I had no idea but it seemed plausible; their families were business allies. Christ, my own father was in their social circle. My mind spun through possibilities, an unwitting rider on an out-of-control carousel. Even if I succeeded in driving out Derrick's investment in Jalesville acreage, what harm could I, with my limited power, lack of experience, and nonexistent funds truly cause him? Why not shift focus to another small town with beautiful, rugged surroundings perfect for vacation property?

What am I missing? Why Jalesville?

Derrick mentioned a land claim, remember, back in July at the council meeting? He said an ancestor had been cheated out of land, maybe even murdered for it.

And where did Ron fit in to all of this, assuming he *had* issued orders to Derrick to destroy our barn? Ron boasted a decades-long law career and undoubtedly knew every legal loophole in existence. Shit, he had probably created his *own* loopholes. I knew he owned acreage in the Jalesville area – his property butted up against Case's land. Why target me, or Case? Ron would only lock us in his crosshairs if we posed real, legitimate danger to him or his plans. Money, land deeds, investment stocks…criminal activity? Maybe I'd stumbled upon a hornet's nest the size of Illinois. Was Ron involved in something in which even he could not buy his way out, if caught?

What is he hiding? How are Case and I a threat?

But, then again…

Maybe I was considering the wrong angle.

Derrick had been the one to deliver a veiled warning earlier this summer, in the parking lot of my old apartment at Stone Creek, suggesting that accidents happened to people we love.

Had he intended even then to take drastic measures, aiming for the one person whose pain would most annihilate me? Was it Derrick's subconscious attempt to personally cause me devastation, as perhaps I'd once caused him? Had he suspected, or even hoped, that Case would *try* to do something like save the horses? Setting our trailer on fire would have been a bolder gesture and could easily have killed us, if killing us had been the original intent; was Derrick astute enough to presume that Case would risk himself by running into a burning barn and subsequently die in the blaze, leaving me forever without him?

Cold sweat prickled my hairline.

Jesus Christ.

I have to figure this out.

There's so much at risk and we're trapped in this fucking hospital…

"Mom's here," Camille was saying, pulling me from the dark, frightening trench of my thoughts; she'd ended her phone call and nodded toward the hall, where I could hear Mom and Aunt Jilly. My sister looked more closely at my expression. "Tish, what is it?"

"I'll tell you later," I whispered, resisting the urge to curl up in a self-protective ball, knees to chest.

Clark offered to take everyone for a late lunch, including me. But I couldn't bear to leave, as they all understood, and Camille stayed behind too. Mom and Aunt Jilly sandwiched me in a hug and I clung, imbibing the familiar peach-and-honeysuckle scent of my womenfolk.

Mom kissed my hair. "What can we bring you? What are you hungry for, honey?"

"Nothing," I mumbled.

"We'll bring you a taco salad," Mom said as though I hadn't answered.

Clint held me close and knuckled my scalp, like the old days, though in those days he would not have been gentle. "I wish I could make things right for you, Tisha. I'm so worried about you."

I drew back and studied my good-looking cousin; growing up, Clint had always been my best friend in Landon. I remembered I had something to tell him and elbowed his ribs. "One of the nurses asked me for your number, Clinty. She's really pretty, maybe twenty or so."

I'd once prided myself on my ability to embarrass him. I had tortured him during my law school years; my college roommates in Chicago had been wild about him (or, at least, the photographs they'd seen) and relentlessly begged me to invite him to Chicago for the weekend so they could seduce him. I'd told them only catastrophe could force him from Minnesota, which further demonstrated my family's concern for me; here was Clint, far from home because I needed him.

Clint, however, did not appear embarrassed; his knowing half-smile meant he was already well aware. "Danielle, right, on the morning shift? I already got it, *thank you* very much."

I elbowed his ribs again. "I should have guessed."

I hugged them all one last time and then reclaimed my chair in the room near Camille, who took my hands in a gesture both protective and maternal. Her gaze was unrelenting. "Tell me. Why did you go so pale a minute ago?"

"You know what we talked about a few weeks ago, about how Case and I knew each other in another life?"

Camille nodded, taking this in stride; she and Mathias believed the same thing about themselves. There was even mounting evidence to suggest that we'd all known *each other*, the Rawleys included. Years ago, before they were married, my sister and Mathias had road-tripped to Montana on a quest to find answers about Malcolm Carter, Mathias's ancestor. They'd possessed very little hard evidence – a couple of letters and a telegram – but they trusted their instinct and journeyed west. Fate was a concept I shied from; I hated believing that our collective destiny was somehow beyond our control, but *something* compelled my sister and Mathias that long-ago summer, pointing them toward both Jalesville and The Spoke, where their paths collided with Case's, and with Garth and Marshall Rawley's.

If not fate, then what?

I shivered and Camille squeezed my hands.

"And in that other life, I believe I was married to Derrick Yancy." Speaking this aloud left the bitterness of ashes on my tongue. "I think he senses it on some level because he was drawn to me when I first moved to Jalesville, for deeper reasons than opposing my opinion. He may have started the fire because he wants to punish me, since I once hurt *him*. In the past life, I mean, I did something that hurt him." I paused for a breath, almost cringing at the inanity of what I was suggesting; the lawyer in me craved solid proof. "But based on my dreams, Milla, Derrick *deserved* it."

Camille held my gaze, a frown creasing her forehead. She was in her third trimester of pregnancy, in no condition to be further agitated by the potential dangers here in Montana. She wore a sundress of ivory cotton, her skin petal-soft and her figure as rounded as a marble sculpture honoring motherhood. Her dark curls were contained in one long braid, reminiscent of Ruthie, and despite the fire burning in her eyes, the one that told me without words she would help me no matter what it took, the word 'vulnerable' filled my head. I pictured my strong, handsome brother-in-law, Mathias, who possessed more vitality and energy than any three men; Mathias would take one look at Camille and she would be in the shelter of his protective embrace before I could blink.

"You think you've lost Case before now," Camille whispered, and I knew she understood better than anyone the ache of ancient loss; I thought of what she'd once told me about Cora and Malcolm, and what she believed about them…

I gritted my teeth; staked out in my mind was the dreadful vision of Case shot in the gut, dying with his head on my lap. Tears burned my eyes and nose. "I can't lose him again. I can't *let it* happen again…"

Camille held fast to my hands. "Tish, *focus*. What else?"

"There's so much…"

"I'm not going anywhere."

I related what Clark had told me regarding the lantern in the hay-mow and then explained my current theories about both Ron and Derrick, keeping my voice low. There was a lull after I finished speaking; my throat ached with repressed tears. I concluded miserably, "I feel so helpless, Milla. I don't know where to start."

Camille would not let me flounder. "You know your enemy, that's something. Dad is looking into things on his end, in Chicago. And hey, I almost forgot. I have a bunch of letters for you to read."

"What letters?" I wiped my nose on the back of my wrist.

"Meg Carter has had them for years, the ones that Mathias and I originally came out here to get, seven years ago. Remember, we never made it to Bozeman on that trip?"

I nodded, remembering well.

"They're written between Malcolm Carter and a woman named Una Spicer. Does that name sound at all familiar?

Sparks stirred in my chest, beating back some of the paralyzing fear. "It does. That's Henry Spicer's wife. Una was Cole's mother."

"Then you start with those," my sister said.

Chapter Five

Marshall asked if I wanted to ride to Jalesville with him to meet the horses and just like that I found myself agreeing to go. We walked together across the hospital parking lot under the hot melt of afternoon sunshine, the impressive mountain peaks ringing the town highlighted against the upturned blue bowl of the sky. Wy tagged along with us like an adorable puppy (though I had the impression Marshall was not of exactly the same opinion about his youngest brother's presence). It was Wy who darted ahead and opened the truck door for me; I smiled and thanked him.

Marshall's black pickup was old and dusty, decorated by scallops of rust. What appeared to be a banded strip of heavy-duty wire held up part of the back bumper, which also sported a red sticker advertising a Jalesville restaurant, The Spoke, and an orange one for a radio station, *Z96.1 – Mountain Country*. The interior was clean but smelled faintly of tobacco, and maybe a hint of cologne. The seats were upholstered in material that reminded me of a print you might see painted on old pottery; white, black, and red, with a repetitive geometric pattern. Wy clambered into the cramped back seat as Marshall walked around the hood to the driver's side; the boy explained, "It's over two hours to get back home, Ruthie, so we'll probably stop and get some food on the way."

"That sounds good," I said, falling silent as Marshall entered the same space, and though he barely glanced my way my chest grew tight and it became harder to breathe. I shifted on the seat, unduly warm and wracked by nerves, which was ridiculous. It wasn't as if Marshall was going to slip an ice cube down my shirt or try to unhook my bra; I choked on a nervous laugh and both of them looked in my direction, clearly wondering what was so funny. I gulped back additional giggles, embarrassed, and quickly explained, "Sorry, I'm just tired."

"Yeah, there is *absolutely* no laughing allowed in this truck," Marshall said in a tone that conveyed severity, but I understood he was teasing me. I risked a glance in his direction; he sat comfortably on the bench seat, a half-smile gracing his lips, left hand hanging from the top of the steering wheel. His eyes crinkled at the outside corners, conveying the amused look I recalled well from three years ago; this seemed much more like the Marshall I had once known. He slowly shook his head, smile widening to a grin, and shifted to first gear, taking us out of the parking lot.

"And absolutely no making out, I'll bet," I threw right back, speaking the first thing that popped into my mind.

Marshall laughed, though I could tell he was outright surprised, and Wy hooted, "You're right about that!"

Marshall drawled, "No laughing, no making out, and absolutely *no touching* at any time."

Wy reached and put the tip of his finger on Marshall's right shoulder, which is exactly what I would have done to Tish had she declared such a thing. I giggled again, prompting Marshall to threaten, "That's two strikes for you, Ruthann, and Wy…I didn't say there was a rule about severe beatings."

"That would violate the *no touching at any time*," I pointed out with maybe a little too much syrupy-sweet emphasis, and Marshall sent another smoldering grin my way.

"You're right," he agreed, just as much honey in his tone. He murmured, "But I don't mind violating that rule, now and again."

A hot, vibrating beat passed from his eyes to mine, causing my pulse to spike, and I realized he was back to his old ways in full force, teasing me with the hope of provoking a reaction. I supposed I should have figured; at least this time I could dish it back.

Before I could respond, Wy said gleefully, "Ruthie, *everyone* knows Marsh hasn't kissed a girl since the seventh grade, back when he had braces."

Both Marshall and I laughed at this statement; Marshall shook his head again, muttering, "Oh, *Jesus*."

Wy was on a roll, continuing the tale with gusto. "See, her braces got all tangled with the rubber bands in his, and they were stuck as good as if they'd been glued together. They had to get someone to unhook them!" And then he yelped and evaded, as Marshall reached backward as though to clamp a hand on Wy's leg. Wy giggled and ducked away and Marshall left off, since he was driving.

"Keep it up," he told his little brother, eyeing him in the rearview mirror. "We have to stop eventually."

In a stage whisper, Wy insisted, "Everyone knows it's true, Ruthie."

Marshall rolled his eyes and relented to the story. "Yes, the fire department had to come and untangle us. It took hours. It was very romantic. No kiss has ever quite lived up to that."

I was laughing long before he finished speaking.

"Marsh, can we get lunch, please?" Wy begged a second later.

"Are you kidding me? Do you have money?"

"Some. But it's at home. I'll pay you back, I swear." Wy leaned between the seats and implored, "Ruthie, I bet you're hungry."

"I could eat," I agreed. "I didn't really have breakfast."

"There's a drive-thru!" Wy pointed to the right. We were almost to the interstate exit that would take us east to Jalesville.

"Fine," Marshall grumbled as though truly annoyed, but I knew better by now. Beneath, I could tell he really loved his little brother. Just like with Clint and Tish, bickering was how they demonstrated it best.

Ten minutes later we were cruising along the four-lane and I found myself irritatingly aware of Marshall, just a few feet to my left as he drove. He was kind enough to pay for my lunch (I'd forgotten everything but my cell phone back at the hospital) and we all sat munching burgers and fries; the cup holder in the middle contained two chocolate shakes, one for me and one for Wy, while Marshall (strawberry for him) simply held his cup in his right hand, driving with his left loosely gripping the bottom of the wheel.

From the corner of my eye and though I honestly wasn't trying, I saw him. I saw the way his jaws moved as he ate, all of us content for the moment, occupied with chewing. I saw the dark scruff that was nearly a beard, the way his cheekbone created an angle on his lean face. He did have a long nose, straight as the blade of a knife, but it suited him. I saw the sinewy, wiry muscles that made up his forearm, his long fingers holding the strawberry shake, the way his lips (which I'd watched while he sang last night) pursed to sip from his straw.

I saw the curve of his shoulder, the bulge of his bicep, just as leanly sculpted as the rest of his body; I saw the way his jeans shaped to his thighs and was shocked by my increasing desire to touch him, right where that faded denim stretched tight across his lap. We spoke not a word for miles and even though Marshall had slipped on a pair of aviator-style sunglasses, I sensed he was also noticing me, every bit as intently.

Wy finished first and leaned forward again, wadding up his hamburger wrapper, mustard on his chin. "I just want Tish and Case to come home. It's so weird not to have them around all the time. Marsh, will Case wake up soon?"

Marshall glanced back at his brother. On a soft sigh, he murmured, "I hope so, I sure hope so, buddy. I know, it is weird. I hate it, too."

"But you should see how much stuff Dad and Garth and the guys have already cleared away from the old barn," Wy said, sounding more optimistic. "Marsh, you gotta come check it out. Everyone is working so hard and it looks a shit-ton better already."

"I will. I was planning to tomorrow, or the next day. I'll come work my ass off, but right now I feel like I need to be at the hospital more than anything."

I found my voice. "Tish really appreciates you being there. She's told me that about ten times since we got to Bozeman."

"She's like my little sister," Marshall acknowledged. "And I know Case would appreciate me being there for her. God, I miss him. I miss hearing his voice. I know it's worse for Tish, but still."

"Let's sing for a while," Wy insisted, leaning to turn up the radio; his elbow bumped my arm and he apologized before saying, "Singing always makes me feel better."

"Same here," Marshall agreed. He looked my way. "You aren't getting out of this, you know."

His eyes were still hidden behind his sunglasses; I could see my surprised reflection on their mirrored surface. "You want me to sing?"

A smile elongated his lips and my heart went out of control. Maybe I was just nervous to sing in front of them...or maybe it was because I liked the way Marshall smiled. Instead of replying, he simply nodded.

"Here, this is a good one, everyone knows this one," Wy said of the current song, and Marshall began tapping out the drumbeat with his thumbs on the rim of the steering wheel. Both he and Wy took up the chorus. I liked country music and knew the song – and there was no good excuse not to join them.

So I sang, at first tentatively, then with a little more heart. When a set of commercials came on after the first few songs, Marshall said, "You're pretty good."

To anyone else I would have responded with a polite 'thank you,' but instead I heard myself snap, "*Pretty* good? I was in concert choir in high school and we competed at State *all four years*."

Marshall was unruffled by my tone. Amending only slightly, he repeated, "Pretty *damn* good." Before I could reply he added, "Concert choir, huh? You know what they say about those concert choir girls..."

I probably should have smacked his arm instead of laughing; to make matters worse, Wy wondered with true curiosity, "What's that?"

I angled Marshall as scathing a look as I could manage. "Yes, tell us, what *is* that?"

Without missing a beat he replied, "They hit those *incredible* high notes. You know, the ones other girls can't touch..."

"*Oh my God*," I groaned, tipping forward I was laughing so hard. I knew it probably wasn't the time or the place; I could blame the sleepless worry of the past few nights, the need for stress release, but when it came down to it Marshall really was funny. Even if he was just trying to provoke a reaction, it was good to laugh.

"You *wish*," I cried when I could catch my breath.

We sang for the next sixty miles and I found myself hard-pressed to recall when I'd had a better time in the recent past. Marshall had a beautiful voice, sincere and true, shifting effortlessly to the background to harmonize with mine when the song featured a woman on lead vocals. Wy was a good sport, singing both male and female parts with equal enthusiasm. We passed the exit to Billings, and many smaller towns in between, before coming upon a road sign indicating that Jalesville was twelve miles away. It seemed as though we'd just started driving.

"I'm so excited to see the town," I said as we rolled ever closer, and Wy reached to turn down the volume for the first time in over an hour.

Marshall grinned. He said to Wy, "It's barely a speck on a map to anyone else but we love it, don't we, buddy?"

"We do!" Wy agreed, all but bouncing on the seat. "I can't wait to show you all the animals, Ruthie. We have all of Case and Tish's animals right now, too. They're staying with us until they get home."

"That's what Tish told me. How nice of you guys."

The foothill country was breathtaking. I cranked down the window (no automatic power buttons in this truck) and simply admired the view as Marshall exited the interstate and took a left, down a steep hill bordered on both sides by towering, long-needled pine trees and scrubby bushes; the truck jounced over a set of railroad tracks and at last entered the town.

"The Spoke!" I cried as we rolled along Main Street. I'd heard so much about the little bar from Camille and Tish that I felt like I'd already been inside.

Marshall promised, "We'll take you there."

A few blocks down Main Street, Wy indicated a small brick building. "There's where Tish works," he explained. The modest law office was a far cry from what Tish once envisioned for herself, a gleaming Chicago high-rise where she would skyrocket through the ranks, but as we drove past Howe and James here in Jalesville, a poster featuring a local rodeo taking up the bottom quarter of the front window, I understood this was where my sister truly belonged.

"This is where you guys live?" I asked, with sincere awe, a few miles later as Marshall turned into a long gravel driveway.

"This is the homestead," he affirmed, and I leaned to peer out the windshield at the gorgeous two-story log house nestled within view of the mountains on the western horizon. There were two barns on the sprawling property, one appearing new and the other much older, constructed from wide wooden boards, with a steeply-pitched roof and encircled by a split-rail corral; a couple of horses stood there, eyes closed against the low-slanting afternoon sun.

"But the original homestead was west of here, right?" I heard myself ask as Marshall parked the truck. Loud barking came from the direction of the barn, followed by bounding dogs; two horses nosed up to the fence as though to welcome us. I was oddly certain about the old homestead's location; I battled a sudden urge to climb from the truck and walk toward the western horizon.

Marshall didn't move to open the door; he sat quietly watching me. "Tish must have mentioned that, huh?"

"Yep, it's out where there's some old caves in the foothills," Wy affirmed, lightly thumping his fists on the back of my seat; he couldn't get out until I did.

Good guess about the homestead, I thought, and suppressed a shiver.

The warm sun felt like a blessing on my face. It seemed as though I'd been inside for weeks straight. I inhaled the dry air with its faintly herbal scent, distinctly different than the humid lakeshore of home; wilder, somehow. Wy immediately appropriated my elbow and hauled me to the corral, first indicating a lovely auburn horse. "Look here, Ruthie. This is Case's sorrel, Cider. And this other guy is one of ours, Gunpowder. He's a pinto. My horse is his mother."

Marshall called over his shoulder, "I'm gonna go shower. I'll be right back."

"Good, you smell!" Wy hollered.

Marshall disappeared inside the house; I realized I was staring after him and snapped my gaze back to Wy, who was hanging on the fence and giving some love to Gunpowder, rubbing the horse's neck, kissing him between the eyes. Wy invited, "C'mon, let's get the dogs."

Wy walked me around the property, pointing out details with the eager diligence of a tour guide. We were tailed closely by five big dogs, two of which belonged to my sister and Case; as we stood in the backyard, where the view to the mountains was unimpeded, Wy pointed north and said, "That's how you'd get to Case's house. It takes about fifteen minutes on the horses. You want to meet all of them?"

"Of course," I said, even though what I really wanted was for Marshall to rejoin us; I found my gaze returning time and again to the front door of the house, impatient for him to emerge.

Wy added, "One of the cats just had a litter up in the haymow. I'm gonna go see if I can find them. C'mon!"

He ran ahead and a minute later his head popped out the loft window.

"Ruthann, come and see!" he called, hanging over the edge to wave.

"Be careful!" I cried.

Wy giggled and disappeared; from right behind me, Marshall drawled, "Aw, he's fine. He knows better than to fall out."

My spine twitched at the sound of his voice so nearby; after all of my obsessive watching, I hadn't even heard him come back outside. I turned to spy him standing with his thumbs caught loosely in the front pockets of a new pair of jeans, dark hair clean and damp, though he hadn't shaved; my eyes, which seemed out of my control when in proximity to Marshall, detoured briefly to his mouth. I turned back toward the barn and struggled to breathe in a normal rhythm.

"Ever been in a barn?" Marshall asked, coming to a halt on my left side; he was tall enough that my forehead was on a level with his shoulder. He glanced down at me, with a grin. "That sounds like the first line of a joke."

Playing along, I asked, "As in, were you born in a barn?"

Without hesitation Marshall replied, "Nope. Conceived in one," and I nosedived from fairly composed to flustered and flushing in less than a second; his grin deepened. "God, you're cute."

Cute.

He was in his element teasing me and here I was, predictably riled up. But – *cute?* How condescending. What about *you still look just like an angel*? Had that been a joke, too? I decided it probably had and hated that I cared.

Wy hollered, "Come meet my horse, Ruthann!"

I brushed past Marshall without a word, finding Wy hanging over a stall door on the left side of the barn.

"This is Oreo!" Wy held my elbow as though he thought I might not listen unless forced.

"I've heard about her from my sisters," I acknowledged, reaching to pat the mare's glossy black nose. "You're a beauty. Wy takes good care of you, doesn't he?"

Wy's brown eyes shone with pride. "I do. She's one of our best breed mares."

"How many horses do you guys have?" I asked, refusing to look in Marshall's direction as he grabbed a pitchfork from a hook on the wall and began doling out hay.

"Six are ours. There's eight total right now, including Cider and Buck. Buck had some burn welts on his hide but Doc Tomlin said he'll be all right. Case saved him." Wy's expression changed. "I love Case like a brother. He's just like a big brother to me."

My hands fell still on Oreo's neck and she made a whooshing sound, nudging her nose against my armpit to encourage further attention, but I focused on Wy, wanting to gather him close in a hug but afraid he'd be embarrassed. "He'll be all right. We have to trust in that."

Wy nodded and swiped at his nose with a knuckle; he was fifteen but sometimes seemed younger, and tenderness overtook me. I couldn't resist patting his head, cupping my hand around the back of it the way I did back home with my nieces and nephews; I baby-sat them all the time and was accustomed to consoling. Redirecting his attention, I indicated another horse. "So what's this guy's name?"

Wy led me down the row, his natural cheer restored, and I felt an increasing bond with him; he was the youngest in a large, outspoken family and craved any amount of attention, which I understood well.

"This is Arrow," Wy announced at the last stall in the row, and the horse within stomped its back hooves and tossed its head.

"He seems a little wilder than the others," I observed, not reaching to scratch this horse's neck as I had with all the other animals. Arrow was a gorgeous creature, muscular and sleek and silver-gray, his hindquarters flecked with dark, circular patches; his mane and tail were as black as a new moon night. I murmured, "You know it, too, don't you?"

"He is pretty wild," Wy agreed.

"Aw, he's a good boy," Marshall said and my spine twitched; for the second time I hadn't heard him approach. He added, with clear affection, "He's mine."

"Marsh has had him from a yearling," Wy chimed in. "He got bucked a bunch of times before Arrow would let him ride."

"Well, we had to figure each other out," Marshall said, scratching Arrow's big square jaw. Arrow nickered and exhaled a noisy breath; I noticed how his ears turned toward the sound of Marshall's voice.

"You cried the first time," Wy remembered in a singsong, and his eyes danced with teasing.

"You see how great it feels to get bucked, buddy, and then you can crack all the jokes you want," Marshall responded, with a touch of humor. "Besides, that was over twelve years ago. I was just a kid."

Again I was caught up in watching Marshall; his eyes were as gorgeous a variation of gray as Arrow's hide. Marshall alone possessed gray irises; Clark and the rest of his sons were all brown-eyed. I wondered about their mother, who'd certainly been the one to gift Marshall with those eyes, including the long, mink-dark lashes, though these in no way detracted from the air of self-confident masculinity he exuded. Despite Wy's silly story about braces and rubber bands and no kissing since the seventh grade, I was sure reality included dozens of beautiful women in Marshall's past, women with more experience than I could even conceive.

What do you care?

It's not your business!

And you have a boyfriend!

But as our gazes held, the smile slowly disappeared from Marshall's face. I was close enough in that moment to see the grain of his skin, the crisp outline of his lips, which had a lot of natural pigment. There was a little indentation in the exact middle of his top lip, which Grandma would call an angel kiss, and a sudden, bursting desire to feel it beneath my tongue struck at my senses. I looked immediately away, cheeks torching.

Oblivious to any undertones between his brother and me, Wy invited, "Come see the new kittens, they're up in the loft."

I trailed Wy to the haymow ladder, self-conscious of my dirty jean shorts and tattered t-shirt as I sensed Marshall following close behind; at the ladder, constructed of narrow wooden beams, which Wy had scaled with as little effort as a monkey up a vine, Marshall warned, "Careful now."

I stood grasping the outer slats of the ladder, poised to climb, but hesitated at these words, unsure if he was teasing, and spied his gaze flicker to my breasts. My lungs emptied of air; my heart churned like I'd been jogging in place for the past half hour. Just his brief glance in that direction made gemstones of my nipples.

To say the least, I was not used to this feeling. *At all.*

Marshall, probably able to read every thought flooding my mind, spoke with an overly-innocent tone. "Don't worry. I'll be right behind you. If you stumble, I mean."

He was *so* naughty. And here I was, reacting like a flustered teenage girl. Marshall loved every minute of tormenting me, I could tell, just like he had that summer in Landon.

Well, two can play at that game, I thought grimly. I may not know much about seduction, but I did have a boyfriend. I wasn't *totally* clueless. And I knew I had a nice body – not that this should matter in the whole scheme of things, I realized, but a devil took up sudden residence on my shoulder and jabbed its pitchfork tines into my skin. Besides, I'd never used my considerable curves as a ploy before.

So maybe it was about time.

"Are you *sure* it's stable?" I asked, infusing my voice with concern. I navigated the first rung, pretending to be uncertain, squaring my shoulders so my breasts thrust forward and taking care to arch my hips *just* enough in his direction. From the corner of my eye I saw Marshall's throat bob as he swallowed, and felt a hot surge of vindication.

"It's stable." He sounded slightly hoarse. "Trust me."

Marshall waited until I was a couple of rungs up before following, and then I lost all my false bravado and raced to the top. The haymow was sweetly scented, long beams of afternoon sun decorating the stacks of bales, gilding them with angelic light. Marshall cleared the final rung but I focused on Wy, who lay on his belly in the far corner.

"See, here's where she hides them," Wy murmured.

I knelt to join him, the floorboards and loose hay prickling against my bare knees, peering into the nest the mama cat had made in the hay; four little kittens mewled at her belly. They were just old enough to have fur, tiny tails sticking straight up.

"Oh, wow," I breathed. "They're so little."

"Aren't they cute?" Wy reached a tentative finger.

Marshall crouched beside me. "Don't touch them, buddy, she'll nip you."

As much as I wanted to deny it, I could not; I was vividly aware of Marshall at my side. My senses seemed sharpened by his presence and I noticed every detail, from the soft sound of his breath to the abundance of dark hair on his forearms to the knobby bones on the outsides of his wrists; his callused and capable-looking hands, his hair still damp from the shower, the faded patches on his jeans, the way he knelt with one knee on the floor. I swore I could even smell him, the scent of his skin and the soap he'd used, and all these things made me itchy and restless; my nipples swelled again, rubbing the inside of my bra.

I don't understand this at all.

I don't even like him!

Wy asked, "Marsh, what if Case doesn't wake up?"

The boy's voice was low and rough, and the heartfelt question snapped me from my irritated self-absorption. Wy's dark eyes were full of tears and Marshall gripped his little brother's shoulder and squeezed. "*Hey.* He will. We can't think otherwise."

"Tish won't let anything happen to him," I said softly. "That's what I keep telling myself."

Marshall laughed a little at my words, agreeing, "Damn right. That woman is a force to be reckoned with."

Wy nodded, knuckling away his tears.

"Come here," Marshall muttered, and then bear-hugged his brother. Despite the gravity of the situation I found room to wonder what it might take to be afforded the same privilege, that of being held close to Marshall Rawley. He roughed up Wy's shaggy hair and then asked, "You two ready to head back to the hospital? Everybody is fed for the evening."

I was reluctant to leave but there was no excuse to stay; besides, Tish needed us. "Thanks for bringing me with you guys."

"Our pleasure, ain't it, Wyatt?" Marshall said, looking at me as he spoke.

Wy surprised me by moving from Marshall's embrace and hugging me around the neck. The boy smelled of sweat and dust, of hay and horses, but I hugged him right back, rocking him side to side. Wy shifted to kiss my cheek and landed the smooch pretty close to my lips (his breath smelled like the chocolate shake he'd been sipping and his mouth left behind a sticky spot), prompting Marshall to mutter, "Sweet *Jesus*, you're pushing your luck, kid. That's no way to get your first kiss."

I giggled and so did Wy; he released me and bounded for the ladder, leaving Marshall and I momentarily alone. Our gazes held for a beat, and then another; maybe eighteen inches of empty air separated our bodies.

Not a question so much as an observation, Marshall whispered, "You said your boyfriend wanted to kick my ass back to Montana?" Without waiting for an answer he added quietly, "He'd want to kick it a lot farther than that for what I'm thinking right now."

I inhaled a sharp breath before I could compose myself; he got me *every* time. Anger rose in my chest. "*Very funny.*"

"You think I'm kidding?"

Without saying another word I followed Wy, who was already on the ground; I could hear him murmuring to his horse.

Marshall said, "Ruthann," in a tone of voice that made my heart throb with painful staccato beats, but I ignored this request for my attention, descending the ladder and stepping outside into the late-afternoon sunlight.

Chapter Six

Don't give him the satisfaction. He's only messing with you.

But it was no use. Marshall was *all* I could think about, and had been since I'd arrived from Minnesota. I would be lying if I pretended otherwise.

I considered what Tish had once said about the air in Montana being different than back home; she was right. There was a wild tinge in the breeze, a suggestive whisper that stimulated my senses. I turned my face westward, letting the warm, falling light bathe my skin and paint the world scarlet. When Marshall touched my shoulder blade, my eyes flew open. I looked up at him in angry confusion; all I really wanted in that moment was to study his face to my heart's content. And still that wouldn't be enough to satisfy the longing.

"Hey," he implored. "I didn't mean to offend you. Please don't think that."

His light touch seemed to burn through my t-shirt. I muttered, "Just forget it, all right?"

His eyebrows drew together, creating a small, vertical crease between them; I realized he was just as confused by my attitude. He insisted quietly, "I really didn't."

Before I could respond Wy came out of the barn. "We better get back, huh, guys? We gotta drive two hours."

Marshall inhaled a deep breath, reluctant to leave words hanging between us, I could tell. He looked toward Wy and ordered, "Lock up the big doors, all right, buddy? I'll check the house. And we'll get going."

We were all hot, dusty, and tired. At the truck, Wy made a scene about not riding in the backseat. He whined, "But I get carsick, Marsh, you *know* I do."

Marshall ran both hands through his already-wild hair, clearly frustrated; he grumbled, "Quit being a baby. Ladies get the front seat."

Standing near the open passenger door, I said, "You can have the front seat, Wy. I'll ride in back."

"My head hurts," Wy complained.

Instead of looking concerned, Marshall looked ready to bite his brother's head clean off. Speaking through his teeth, he ordered, "Then stay here! There's no reason for you to drive all the way back if you're not sleeping over anyway."

Wy's shoulders slumped with relief while my pulse slid into a nervous rhythm; it wasn't that I was *afraid* to ride all that way alone with Marshall…

"Are you sure you're all right?" I asked Wy, as Marshall thumped into the truck and started it up.

Wy nodded, hair flopping over his forehead. "I'm fine. I'll just take a nap."

I walked him to the front door, stalling; as Wy disappeared inside I half-expected Marshall to beep the horn a couple of times, but he didn't. He was wearing a black cowboy hat, which he'd collected from the barn, and his sunglasses, so I couldn't tell if he watched me walk to the truck or not; somehow I was sure he did. He leaned and opened the passenger door and then offered his hand to help me in, as though I was climbing onto a wagon seat. I couldn't resist the temptation; his warm fingers closed around mine and the contact of our skin felt so good I almost shivered. Far too quickly he released my hand to clutch the gear shift, reversing the truck.

"Is Wy gonna make it?" His tone was tinged with humor again, rather than frustration.

"You could be a little more patient with him," I nagged. I loved how Marshall looked in his cowboy hat; something resonated deep inside me as I studied his profile. I could not deny he had a way about him that made me feel dangerous and hot – physically and emotionally broiling-hot.

It's wrong to feel this way and you know it.

Besides, he'd just laugh at you if he knew you thought that. What a victory for him.

And so I looked away.

"I know I could be more patient," he acknowledged, driving us west toward the interstate. He sighed. "And I know it's not an excuse to say that I'm tired."

"We all are," I allowed, lacing my fingers, fitting my thumbnails together.

"I'm just not a very patient person," Marshall continued, as though this was some big revelation.

"Like that's a secret?" I was smiling and he looked my way, with a crooked smile of his own.

"Thanks," he muttered drily, smoothing both palms over the top curve of the steering wheel. The truck was back in the foothill country now as Marshall accelerated to take us onto the four-lane, turning to look over his left shoulder as he did so, and my traitorous gaze leaped to the fly of his faded jeans. Temptation pelted me. I imagined what would happen next if I leaned and cupped him in that exact spot.

Ruthann!

My blood sizzled. I tore my eyes away from his zipper, cheeks afire, thankful he could not read my mind. Then again, hadn't he just told me that what he was thinking, back in the haymow, would make Liam want to kick his ass?

So what was it he was thinking?!

"You hungry?" he asked as the truck flew along in the dazzling evening light. The wild beauty of its jeweled tints and the way it washed over the landscape made my heart almost ache.

"Kind-of," I mumbled, distracted by my spooling thoughts.

"What does that mean? That doesn't help me," Marshall complained. His tone bordered on moody, but for whatever reason it only made me want to smile. He required a little sweetening up; wasn't I the perfect person for that?

But not like that!

You cannot under any circumstances reach over there and unzip his jeans.

Even if you want to so much it hurts!

Matching his tone, I demanded, "Well, what *would* help you? *Jeez.*"

From the corner of my eye I saw the flash of his grin. He muttered, "I just meant it doesn't help me decide where to get us dinner, that's all." And then he reached and flicked his finger against my bare left knee, not hard; more as though to get in the last word, nonverbally.

It was strange to be engaging in this sort of banter. And enjoying it. Liam never teased me. Liam knew all the foods I liked, but then again we'd been together for four years. Of *course* Liam would know where to take me for dinner without any sort of confrontation. And Liam would never dream of flicking my leg like that; he would consider it impolite, and if there was one thing I knew about Liam, he would never treat me impolitely.

"You're such a *baby*," I told Marshall, venting, leaning across the bench seat to flick his right earlobe, *not* gently. He laughed and evaded. I aimed again, giggling, this time connecting with the side of his neck. I kept after him, jabbing his ribs as I pestered, "I thought *Wy* was the youngest in your family. Maybe not, maybe *you're* the baby..."

"I am not a baby!" he insisted, laughing, blocking his ribs with his right elbow; our squirreling around knocked his sunglasses to his chin. I made a triumphant sound, snatching them from his face and putting them on mine.

"Thanks," I said, as he regarded me from under the brim of his black hat. I liked that my eyes were now hidden and his were not.

"Don't make me pull over," he warned. "Because I will."

"I'm *terrified*," I mocked, and he laughed all the more, slowly shaking his head.

He reached with deliberate intent and hooked his right hand over my left thigh, just above my knee. It was the most ticklish spot on my entire body, not that he could have known such a thing. I froze, thrilled that he was touching me. A giggle escaped my lips and he smiled smugly.

"You should be," he muttered. His strong, long-fingered hand appeared very tan against the fair, freckled skin of my thigh.

"You're not getting them back," I challenged, but my voice gave me away; I wasn't doing a good job of disguising the breathlessness.

"Really?" he asked, and gently squeezed.

I bit the insides of my cheeks to keep hysterical giggles from flying forth. My skin blazed beneath his touch, incinerating a path straight to the juncture of my thighs. He squeezed again, with just slightly more pressure, and it was either relent or have a heart attack. I twisted away, gasping, "Here!"

I was such a chicken.

"Thought so." His voice was ripe with satisfaction as he reclaimed his sunglasses, slipping them into place with a wink.

I licked the end of my index finger, getting it really wet, and then stuck the tip right in his ear. He yelped, using his shoulder to swipe at the wetness.

"Take that!" I cried, and he went after my leg with a vengeance.

I shrieked, laughing too hard to breathe as he tickled me.

"Shit, this is…dangerous," he acknowledged, laughing so much he could barely speak the words. He quit tickling and replaced both hands on the wheel; his sunglasses had fallen again, this time to his lap.

"Maybe you need a pair that actually *fit*."

"Maybe I need to pull over right now and teach you a lesson."

I wasn't brave enough to call this bluff though I longed to ask, *Would this lesson involve your hands all over me?*

"Chicken," I announced, giggling at his surprised expression. I explained, "That's what I feel like eating for supper."

Marshall settled his sunglasses back in place. "Well, that helps me a little."

"*Glad* to help," I said breezily.

"I know a good place just off the interstate in about twenty miles. Is that all right?"

"Oh, *now* you're being considerate," I muttered, feeling another hot jolt between my legs as I studied him, which was *so* disconcerting; he looked unimaginably sexy with his hat pulled low and all that scruff on his jaws, his wide shoulders and the irresistible fit of his worn jeans over his long legs, inundating me with pure, aching *want*; instant guilt followed in its wake.

"I'm not especially considerate," he replied, sounding contrary.

"That's a shame. Your dad and your brothers are *such* gentlemen." Somehow I knew that beneath this fronting Marshall was every bit as much one.

"I didn't say I *can't* be. When I want to."

"Typical man."

"What's that mean?" he demanded.

"When you *want* to be?" I asked pointedly, repeating his phrasing. "As in, when you're trying to get laid?"

Dang, where did that come from?

I bit down right on the middle of my tongue.

"*Ouch*, woman!" he cried, but we were both laughing again. "That hurt a little, I'm not gonna lie. Unless that was some kind of invitation, because in that case…"

I smacked his shoulder. "I have a boyfriend."

"That Paul Bunyan guy, right?"

"*Liam*, you mean."

"Right. Paul. Guy with the big blue ox, planted all the apple trees in Minnesota...what?"

I was laughing so hard I almost couldn't reply, "That's *Johnny Appleseed*, dummy…"

"Oh, sorry," he said, not sounding at all sorry. "*Paul* was the guy who chopped down all the trees with his *big, huge ax* and wouldn't let his girlfriend out of his sight."

"Just because I can't kick your butt doesn't mean I won't try," I warned.

"Oh, you go right ahead and try," Marshall invited, wickedly. "I'd love every last second of that."

"You *wish*," I mumbled, my laughter stamped out beneath a rush of sudden angst; I was shamelessly flirting and enjoying it way too much, and that was borderline slutty, in my opinion.

Marshall saw the change in my expression; shifting the subject, he gently nudged my upper arm with his knuckles, indicating that I look out the window to the right.

"A prairie falcon," he said, his voice laced now with awe. "Isn't she pretty?"

He looked back at the interstate while I leaned to keep watching the bird, soaring with wings spread wide.

"She is pretty," I agreed softly. "How do you know it's a female?"

"Females are always bigger than males, plus her coloring is a little more muted. It's pretty lucky to see a female. You don't see the falcons quite as much as, say, hawks."

"You like being outside, don't you?"

"I do. You too, I'd wager."

"I do. That's the hardest part about winter for me, being stuck inside."

I knew he was referring to Mathias as he said, "Carter says the winters in Minnesota are pretty tough. Same out here, but I don't think we get quite such cold temps."

"But I'm sure you get as much snow. I mean, with the mountains."

"We get a fair amount. I drive over to go to college in Billings all winter, or at least I have for the past couple of years, and I haven't been snowed out more than once or twice."

"You don't live on the campus?" I hadn't realized he was a student and was curious to know more. About everything involving him, if I was honest.

"I could live in a dorm, I suppose, but I like living at home, plus it saves money. I usually only go three days a week. I'm working toward a bachelor's in environmental science. I should have finished it years ago but I wasn't mature enough back then." He looked my way. "Not a word."

"Hey, at least you're going to college. I haven't yet and I don't have any excuse. I like living at home, I guess, working at the cafe. I'd miss my family if I moved away to school."

"I thought for a long time that I'd make a living making music," Marshall admitted. "We put some effort into it and we're local celebs, Garth and Case and me, I mean, but it's not steady money. My plan is to work for Montana Fish and Wildlife, as a game warden. Sean already works for the parks department in our county, as a water surveyor, and Quinn is planning to do the same, once he gets his ass in gear. I'll graduate by twenty-eight, which isn't terrible, I guess. God, it's weird, though. I mean, thirty used to be so far away." He paused. "I guess for you thirty is still pretty far away."

"Eight years," I acknowledged. "But I know what you mean about time flying by. It seems like we just moved to Landon, but that was ten years ago now."

"What about…" He paused again; I sensed he was enjoying our more serious conversation and so didn't needle me by using the wrong name. "What about Liam? What's he do?"

"He's a firefighter for the township." I gnawed my lower lip, staring out the windshield, a part of me almost expecting to see the prairie falcon continuing to keep pace with us. "He lives with Clint, in Landon. I suppose that when…" I trailed to silence; I hadn't intended to steer the conversation this direction.

"When?" Marshall prompted.

At last I muttered, "I was going to say that when we get married…"

"You're engaged to him?" he interrupted, and it sounded like there was something lodged in his windpipe.

"No!" I said at once, and Marshall's shoulders visibly relaxed. "No, but it's where we're headed."

"You love him, then?" His voice was hardly a whisper.

"He's the first guy I ever loved." I spoke quietly, aware I wasn't exactly answering the question as he'd framed it; right now I was having trouble picturing Liam's face. I looked over at Marshall and just that fast I was swept from solid footing, tugged away from what I knew as real. And I was equal parts thrilled and terrified.

What's happening here?

Marshall didn't respond to my words, instead signaling with the right blinker as he muttered, "There's the place," and I spied a diner just off the interstate, its red-and-pink neon sign glinting against the violet breast of the evening sky.

"The place with the good chicken," I murmured.

"How could you tell?" he asked, still slightly gruff as he pulled into the parking lot beneath a giant neon bird, complete with pink feet and a red wattle, the neon rippling as it appeared to flap its wings.

"Here, you wait," he ordered after he'd parked. "I'll be damned if I let you think I'm only a gentleman when I want to get laid. *Shee-it*."

He rounded the hood while I watched, so drawn to him I could hardly sit still. Hat and sunglasses in place, he swept open the passenger door and helped me down, again just the briefest of touches before releasing my hand as we walked toward the entrance. I wanted to grab his elbow and press my breasts against his arm, but of course I didn't do that.

He made a show of holding the front door and I giggled at his efforts, entering the diner to the mouthwatering scent of frying chicken. I didn't realize I had moaned a little, in pure anticipation of eating, until Marshall said, "Ruthann. *Dammit*, woman. You can't make sounds like that because I can't promise I'll keep acting like a gentleman. It's tough enough as it is."

He had removed his hat and sunglasses and my heart flapped around behind my ribs at both the expression on his face and the urgency in his tone. He winked then, all heat and subtle suggestion; fast as quicksilver, he was back to teasing.

"Two?" asked the host, a boy about Wy's age.

"Yes, please," I said, knotted with confusion, and Marshall and I followed him to a booth near the windows. I scooted to the middle of the red vinyl seat and Marshall sat across from me. Our faces were about three feet apart; less than that as I leaned forward, pretending to regard the single-sided menu.

"There's hay in your hair," he observed.

"Yours too."

"People might think we were rolling around in it," he murmured.

And then, like a sudden, stinging blow to the head, I realized he wasn't just messing with me; the truth was, at long last, beginning to dawn.

Wake up, Ruthann.

He likes you.

My heart caught as though on the edge of something sharp.

And you like him.

Don't deny it.

"What'll it be, kids?" asked a woman at our elbows. Her sudden appearance made me startle, and Marshall smiled.

"We'll share a number six and whatever the lady would like to drink," he said.

"Yes, I *hate* ordering for myself," I complained, trying to locate number six on the menu.

The server shifted to the opposite hip and tapped her pen. She eyed Marshall with open appreciation and joked, "Hon, you could order for me *all* you want."

The number six was a whole fried chicken, with fries, coleslaw, and cornbread on the side; it sounded perfect. I requested, "And a root beer, please."

"Same here," Marshall said as the server collected our menus. "It's the best thing on the menu, trust me."

And for whatever reason, I did trust him.

"So where will you work, once you graduate?" I asked.

"In the local area, hopefully. If you don't mind working solo there are quite a few options, and I don't mind that one bit. Our house is crowded enough that I appreciate the solitude. Besides, you're never really alone in nature. I suppose I'll get my own place once I graduate."

"By twenty-eight?" I teased. "I don't know…"

With a touch of self-deprecation, he agreed, "Right. I know my brothers and I fight all the time but I would miss the shit out of them if they weren't around. And I hate the thought of Dad being there alone, once Wy moves out."

"You guys are close, aren't you?" I found I didn't much like the thought of sweet Clark being alone in that big house, either.

He nodded. His gaze skimmed out the window to the parking lot and then to the sunset beyond, where the horizon scattered beams of peach and violet light. "We were always close but when Mom died we really learned to count on each other. That's never changed in all this time."

It was an invitation to tell me more as I admitted, "Tish has told me some about her."

Marshall released a slow breath, his eyes lingering on the sunset, hunching his shoulders a little before relaxing the posture. His forearms lined the edge of the table, hands stacked atop each other, thumbs linked. At last he murmured, "She died a long time ago. But I still miss her."

"How old were you?" It hurt to imagine him abruptly motherless.

"I was a senior in high school. I had just turned eighteen." His eyes came back to mine as he explained, "She died in the autumn. A truck driver went over the yellow line on the highway and hit her car."

"I'm so sorry."

"I remember her best when I'm outside," he said, as though I hadn't spoken. "She loved being outside, rocking on the porch, working in the yard. Garth and me used to pick flowers out in the foothills for her. Bitterroot was her favorite. She always said the best presents were the ones that didn't cost anything at all." He closed his eyes for a second. "She's buried out near the old homestead on our property, beneath her favorite tree."

My throat felt raw; the sensation of being swept from solid footing yanked at me again and it was only his presence that kept me from being seized away forever; his presence kept me anchored. "What was her name?"

"Faye," he whispered, and in his voice was an ancient ache, one that would never fully heal despite the years separating this day from that one. "God, my dad loved her with all his heart. In all this time he's never found someone else. And he won't, I know. He wouldn't do that to his memory of her."

"Wouldn't she...don't you think she would want..." I faltered, concerned that what I was trying to say would be offensive.

Marshall knew what I meant. "She would want him to be happy, you mean?"

I nodded.

"She would, I truly believe, but it doesn't mean he agrees. I can't imagine Dad with anyone but her, even after all this time."

This close to him, and allowed the excuse to study his eyes under the diner lights, I could see flecks of secondary colors in his gray irises, deep indigos and clear greens, radiating outward like thin spokes on a wheel. A smile nudged his mouth at my prolonged, silent perusal, and he murmured, "What?"

I flushed, dropping my intent gaze to the tabletop as I admitted, "Your eyes are a very unique color."

"I was just thinking the same thing about yours. They're beautiful. Green and gold, like treasure." His smile widened as my flush spread, sending heat down my neck.

"Thank you," I whispered. Our root beers arrived while we were talking, but I hadn't noticed. Marshall took one of the straws and ripped the paper from the top, then pulled it out with his teeth; for a second I thought he would place it in my drink, so our mouths would touch the same spot, but he didn't. Just now, talking about his family, he had seemed vulnerable and I battled the need to grasp his hands and thread our fingers; I opened my straw, forcing my thoughts, and the conversation, to safer terrain. "That was fun singing in the truck today. And I liked hearing you play last night, too."

"I just hope Case can hear it. I haven't been gone longer than a few hours since he's been in there." His eyebrows drew together, the worried crease again forming between them.

"Tish really appreciates that. I'm so glad you've been here for her." Guilt poked its cold fingers into my conscience yet again – how could I be enjoying myself in any capacity when Tish was hurting so much? "We should hurry and get back."

"You're right," Marshall agreed. "God, I hope Case wakes up soon. I've never seen him as happy as he's been in the past few months." He studied me as though debating whether to continue. "Tish thinks it was an arson fire, has she told you about that?"

"She's told me some." I had been shocked at the news; all the way from Minnesota, crowded in the car with Mom, Aunt Jilly, Clint, and Camille, we assumed the fire was accidental. I was still grappling with the idea that someone could want to harm my sister. I thought back to the first night in the hospital as I swirled the straw in my glass, stirring up root beer bubbles; I wanted to ask Marshall's opinion on a few other things Tish had told me, but wasn't sure how much information she had trusted him with – especially concerning what she and Case believed about past lives. Finally I voiced my worst fear. "Do you really think someone is trying to kill them?"

Marshall's shoulders squared, conveying protective defiance. "They'd have to get through all of us first, Dad and Garth and me. Gus, Sean, Quinn, even Wy." He touched my bare forearm, just briefly, rubbing my skin with his thumb. "To answer your question, I honestly don't know. Tish thinks if that was the case the fire would have originated in the trailer, not the barn. Destroying the barn was a message to them to back off, to quit investigating Capital Overland. But your sister is stubborn as hell and Case is even worse. They won't back off, especially now."

"But *why* is this company so worried? What are they hiding? What do they think she knows?" I hated the lack of knowledge.

"I will do everything in my power to help them figure it out," Marshall said, studying my face; he'd withdrawn his touch but our fingertips were only inches apart on the table. "I love them both, I hope you know. Case is my brother, even if we don't share actual blood. He's my best friend. And your sister is his true love."

His use of this phrase struck me, deeply. I whispered, "I want to be here. I want to help, however I can."

There was no mistaking the quiet joy in Marshall's eyes. He was someone who was rather good at underreacting when he felt the situation required it, I already knew, but my words impacted him, I could tell.

"Then stay," he implored softly. He was serious, almost stern, and my heart throbbed in response.

Our food arrived at that second and the server clacked the overflowing plastic basket on the table, effectively cracking the intimate little bubble surrounding us. She ordered, "Enjoy!"

"You choose first," Marshall said graciously, having regained his composure; he nodded at the food.

"Thanks," I whispered, and dragged my eyes from his. The chicken was fried to a perfect golden crisp and I snagged the first piece I saw.

"Breast," he observed. "Good choice."

He made me laugh so effortlessly. I made a show of biting into it; mouth full, I said, "It's *delicious*."

"Oh, I believe it," he replied, with relish, lips shiny as he dove into the chicken along with me.

"Thanks for asking me to come with you today," I said after we'd eaten in silence for a minute. "It was good to get out of the hospital. I feel guilty for wanting to get away. Tish is there all the time…"

"If I could make her take a break, I would. But you know as well as me that she won't."

"Mom tried to get her to go to the Carters' and sleep for a few hours yesterday. But Tish just about bit her."

Marshall snorted a laugh. "I admire her for it, though. When Case wakes up she's the first person he wants to see, trust me. I have a feeling he will soon, I just do."

"I hope so, oh, I hope so. It's killing Tish to see him this way and I hate it."

"I know. We'll finish up and get back there, what do you say?"

"Yes," I agreed, suddenly exhausted.

The air had cooled with falling night and we hurried to the truck. I was shivering as I climbed inside and Marshall turned up the heat, inviting, "If you want to sleep, go ahead. We have another hour to drive." He reached into the backseat and pulled out an old flannel blanket. It smelled a little like motor oil but I was chilled enough that I didn't care. "Here, use this. I don't have a sweatshirt, I'm sorry. You're not really dressed for the cold…"

"Thank you," I whispered, wrapping into the blanket, drawing my knees to my chest. My skin rippled with goosebumps and I shivered again.

"Just don't unbuckle the seatbelt. It's too dangerous."

"You're tired, too." I studied him, overwhelmed by tenderness. He'd started the truck but hadn't put it in first gear, sitting there behind the wheel with his eyes on me. I wanted to slide straight across the seat to his arms; I knew he would be warmer than any ten blankets.

Marshall cleared his throat and reached for the gear shift. "I'm fine, don't you worry. I'll get us there."

And so I snuggled against the seat, instead; my belly was full and I was warm, and Marshall was nearby. Close enough to touch, even if I couldn't touch him. My eyes drifted shut. My last conscious thought was, *I wish I could lean against his shoulder*.

Chapter Seven

I LAY IN A FIELD OF FIREFLIES, OVERCOME WITH AWE, A prairie somewhere at dusk. My shoulder blades resting on warm summertime earth, both hands stacked beneath my head, I admired the glinting insects against the backdrop of an ash-purple sky, smelling the sweetgrass, the scent of which always seemed most potent at night. I heard Ranger, our horse, grazing somewhere beyond my line of sight. I was anchored to this gorgeous place by contentment, happiness so profound that my heart could hardly bear the fulfillment. I heard his footsteps and rolled to one side, parting tall stalks of grass so I could watch him approach. As always, the sight of him filled me with wonder and joy.

Sweetheart, he said. *My sweet Patricia.*

He knelt to cup my face and I gasped, waking to the reality of the hospital room in Bozeman.

Wait –

Disoriented, ripped from the prairie in my dream, I teetered in a murky space between two realities – and finally realized Case's hand was resting on my cheek. I sat straight so fast the chair tipped over. Case's eyes were open. *They were open.* Relief pummeled me like a warm, drenching rain.

"I'm here, Case, I'm right here." Words poured, along with tears, as I touched his face. "Oh God, *you're awake.* Oh sweetheart, I've been *so scared…*"

He tried to answer, unable to speak around the ventilator, but I understood what he wanted and leaned closer, peppering him with soft kisses. He cradled my jaws with both hands and a sound of deep relief emerged from his throat. For the first time in days, I felt like I could draw a full breath.

"You're all right, sweetheart, it's all right. We're at the hospital in Bozeman. Cider and Buck are safe. You saved them." As I spoke he caressed my cheekbones, my lips, tracing gentle fingertips along my eyebrows and down the sides of my face, and I felt washed clean by the love in his eyes. I was whole again.

"Oh Jesus, *oh thank God*," Marshall said from behind me, suddenly appearing in the room from out of nowhere. He rushed to the bed and put both palms on Case's chest, unashamed as tears trickled over his cheeks. "We've been so worried, Case, *Jesus Christ*. Tish saved you, she dragged you out of that fire!"

"I didn't get hurt," I was quick to insist, answering the first of many questions I could tell Case wanted to ask; he made another low sound, brow wrinkling, and engulfed my hands within his, the gesture both protective and possessive. I brought them to my lips and kissed his knuckles, tasting the warm salt of my tears.

Marshall said, "Jesus, bro, we've been so fucking worried. Tish hasn't left your side."

Hoarse with emotion, I ordered, "Don't *ever* scare me like this again. I've been out of my mind."

Case reached and simply tugged the ventilator from his face. His skin was raw-looking, his lips chapped and stubble thick on his jaws. He inhaled a painful breath, and then another.

"Tish," he rasped, and clutched my wrists. It cost him to talk but he demanded, "Tell me…you're not hurt."

"I'm not hurt, I promise you. You're awake." I was so grateful my limbs felt weak. "Nothing can hurt me anymore."

His voice was sandpaper on scarred wood. "I dreamed of you…all this time, sweetheart."

"I kept talking to you. I was so scared. I tried not to be, but I was." Now that he was conscious I was ready to collapse, to simply let him comfort me. I choked on another wave of sobs. "I'm so happy to see your eyes open, you don't even know."

"Come here," he whispered authoritatively, and I wasted no time climbing onto the bed beside him, as carefully as I was able, staying clear of the monitors connected to his body.

"You're gonna get in trouble," Marsh warned.

Case wrapped me in the blessed security of his embrace; I clung, shuddering with sobs, as he stroked my shorn hair, kissing my forehead, my closed eyelids. When I shifted, concerned that I was putting too much weight on his arm, he whispered, "Don't move, love, you're not hurting me. I need to feel you."

A nurse bustled into the room, making concerned clucking noises.

"Mrs. Spicer!" she squawked.

"He's awake," Marshall explained.

"It's all right," Case assured the nurse. "I'm just fine."

"It's wonderful that you've woken but you're far from fine," she badgered. "And right now we need to do a full examination." I imagined her standing with hands planted on hips. "Mrs. Spicer, you need to get up!"

Marsh helped me from the bed and the nurse told Case, "Your wife is a stubborn woman, Mr. Spicer, no offense."

He grinned. "That is a fact."

Marsh and I were forced to leave the room while the nurse and an on-call doctor did their work; we leaned against the wall outside the door, both of us emotionally and physically depleted, in nearly equal parts. The window at the end of the hallway showed a sky black with nightfall.

"Ruthann is going to be so happy," Marshall said. "She's here with me, she just had to go to the bathroom," and as he spoke the elevator doors opened to reveal her.

"Is everything all right?" she asked immediately, fear in her voice; she saw the tears on my face.

"Case is awake," Marshall explained.

"Oh, thank goodness!" she cried, grabbing me in a hug. "I've been so worried."

I wilted against my little sister, crying all over again. When I felt capable I drew away, swiping at my leaking eyes, and Ruthie smoothed damp strands of hair from my face. Her expression was vibrant with relief, her curls arranged in a messy bun with small pieces of hay sticking in it; her clothes seemed unduly wrinkled and I couldn't help but notice that Marshall, who was also decorated with bits of hay, was studying her as though he wanted to eat her up in one bite.

Holy shit – did they –

Marshall caught himself staring at Ruthie; he ran a palm abruptly over his face, shoving away from the wall and then touching my upper arm. "I'll be right back. I'm gonna call Dad and the guys."

Marsh kissed my cheek before loping down the hall and my thoughts darted like minnows; did I question Ruthie about just what exactly had occurred between her and Marshall tonight? It wasn't *technically* my business, but as I observed my little sister staring after Marshall just as intently as he'd been studying her, my curiosity spiked.

As though sensing I was about to commence with a cross-examination, Ruthie took my elbow, leading me to a grouping of chairs. "When did Case wake up?"

"Just before you guys got here," I said, searching her face for clues without appearing to be doing so; Ruthie held my steady gaze, her expression as ingenuous as always. I thought, *They didn't have sex, at least not yet. But they will soon, especially if I know Marsh.* New happiness bloomed in my heart; maybe this meant Ruthie would stay in Jalesville. Maybe she and Marshall had a future together. *Hold on, don't get ahead of yourself. She'll feel guilty about Liam…*

She squeezed my forearms. "I'm so happy. Marshall had a feeling when we were eating dinner. When will they let him come home?"

"No one has said yet. Hopefully soon. I haven't even been back out to our place!"

"I got to meet your horses today. Cider is so sweet. Buck is still being treated for his burns but Wy said he's healing as well as can be expected."

"Oh, I'm so glad to hear that. I miss them so much!" I suddenly realized Wy wasn't with. "He must have stayed home?"

Ruthie nodded and a flush began creeping upward from her neck, infusing her cheeks with hot color; I hid a smile, watching as her eyes moved again in the direction Marsh had disappeared. She was saved by the door to Case's room opening.

"Your husband is asking after you, Mrs. Spicer," the doctor said.

Case was sitting up in the bed. I flew to his side and the same nurse barked, "Not on the bed!"

"Yes, on the bed," Case contradicted in his raw, hoarse voice. He grinned, entwining our fingers as I perched near his hip, unable to take my eyes from his face.

"I can go home later this week," he said, and my shoulders drooped with relief.

"We'll have you return for follow-up appointments in the next month," the doctor said. "And the less you talk for a few weeks, the better. You're going to be healing for quite some time. We'll check in before morning."

As the door clicked shut, leaving us alone, I slid my arms around his neck, glutting myself on the sight of him awake.

"Mrs. Spicer," he murmured, tracing a thumb over my bottom lip. "Did we get married while I was unconscious?"

"I wish." I leaned a breath closer and kissed his mouth, nuzzling his skin. "You taste like mint."

"They helped me brush my teeth. I think maybe moss was growing in there." He paused to inhale, a painful, wheezing sound that hurt my chest to hear. "And my heart valve…Jesus, baby, that scares me. The doc explained what they did."

"They said it was good we caught it now, that's the blessing in disguise here." Brushing his thumbs across the shadows beneath my eyes, he whispered, "You haven't slept, baby." He held my face, speaking around a lump in his throat. "The doctor told me what the EMT said that night. You dragged me from the barn. You went in there and risked your life."

"You went *back into the fire*. I saw you get Cider out and then *you went back in*…"

"You risked your life," he repeated. His hoarse words flowed with mounting emotion. "If something had happened to you I'd be destroyed. It would fucking destroy me for good and I would die."

"You would have died *anyway!* You were *unconscious* in a burning barn!" I hadn't intended to allow my anger to surface but it surged all the same. "You shouldn't have gone in there in the first place! I know you wouldn't let them die but you could have been taken from me. *Forever.* Do you know what I've been through this week, thinking you might not survive?"

My tirade broke off as I choked on a sob. He was anguished at my words, I could clearly see; he whispered, "I wasn't thinking straight that night. I should have considered you would come after me." He ran both hands down my shoulders, my ribs, anchoring around my waist. "I love you, Patricia Gordon. Oh God, *I love you so.* You have my heart. You've always had my heart but I want to give you my name. I don't want one more night to pass without you being mine in every way."

Within five minutes we had assembled Marshall, Ruthann, and the hospital chaplain; the on-duty staff was confused, since they thought Case and I were already married. Ruthie was startled but Marshall proved tranquil and smiley, his eyes brimming with quiet satisfaction.

"Don't you think we should call Mom and Aunt Jilly?" Ruthie kept asking, fluttering about the room like a nervous little fairy; she wouldn't quit smoothing her fingertips over my hair, concerned I wasn't properly outfitted as a bride. "What about Milla and Clinty? They'll be so upset that they weren't here…"

"They'll understand," I promised. "You and Marsh will be our witnesses. We'll have a big party at Clark's later this month, when we get home."

"But, Tish…" Ruthie grew teary-eyed. Her sweet voice quivered as she said, "But you don't even have a *veil*."

Before I could reassure my little sister I didn't care about a veil or a dress, Marshall, quietly watching, moved to her side and took her right hand, cradling it between both of his. This gesture was endearing and unexpected enough that her nervous fluttering stilled.

"Are we ready to proceed?" the chaplain asked. He stood waiting at the foot of the bed, an older man with narrow-rimmed glasses and a simple clerical collar. He held a small bible in his hands, and his eyes were both patient and kind.

"Wait!" Ruthie cried. "What about a ring?"

"That's a good point." Marshall gently released her hand. "Here, I have an idea. I'll be back in a minute. Less than that."

He disappeared and Case said, "I'll get you a beautiful ring, baby, don't you worry. I just don't have it tonight."

"I don't care about any old ring. You know me better than that. I care that you're here with me and I am never going to take another day for granted. I am going to cherish every moment we have together. Every last second."

Marshall burst back into the room, out of breath. He explained, "I ran outside," and presented the ring he'd constructed of a dandelion stem as proudly as if it were a two-carat diamond on a filigreed platinum base.

"It's perfect," I whispered, just as Case said, "Thank you, little bro."

The chaplain glanced with subtle amusement at Ruthann. "Are we ready to proceed?"

She flushed as she nodded; I saw her reach for Marshall's hand as he hurried back to her side.

"We are," Case said, and the gravity of the moment caused everyone else in the room to fade to the background.

We had requested short and simple, desiring to be joined as husband and wife as quickly as possible. The chaplain checked his watch. "It is just after midnight. On this fine early morning the two of you wish to be married. And so I ask, do you, Charles Shea Spicer, take this woman, Patricia Joan Gordon, to be your wife, for better or worse, in sickness and health, forsaking all others, as long as you both shall live?"

These words, so traditional, so formal; all I could see was the joy in Case's eyes. Death had come far too close to parting us and his fingers tightened around mine, acknowledging this, as he said, "With all my heart, I *do*."

The chaplain instructed, "Then place your ring upon her finger," and Case lifted my left hand to his lips and kissed my knuckles before he slid, with only a little difficulty, the dandelion-stem ring into place on my third finger.

"And do you, Patricia Joan Gordon, take this man, Charles Shea Spicer, to be your husband, for better or worse, in sickness and in health, forsaking all others, as long as you both shall live?"

"Until the end of time, I *do*," I whispered.

"Then by the power vested in me by the great state of Montana, I hereby on this eleventh day of August, two-thousand-thirteen, pronounce you husband and wife."

Ruthie was sniffling and swiping tears, leaning against Marshall's chest; holding her close, one arm locked around her waist, Marsh's grin was about as wide as the Montana sky. Case and I were kissing long before the chaplain invited, "Son, you may kiss your bride!"

"Damn right!" Marshall cried, sweeping us into an exuberant hug. "Congratulations, *Mr. and Mrs. Spicer.*"

Ruthie joined the hug, kissing my hair. "I'm so happy I got to be here."

Marshall grabbed his guitar, which was waiting faithfully in the corner, and began to strum the opening notes of "I Knew the Bride."

Ruthie held out her hands. "May I have the first dance?"

"Of course," I said, laughing, and we waltzed in an uncoordinated fashion around the cramped little room. For sure we were going to get kicked out now.

"You're *married*," Ruthie said, her left hand clasped in my right as she took the man's part. "I love you, Tish. I'm so happy for you."

"I love you, too." I thought of how she had reached for Marshall's hand.

Maybe…

Just maybe…

By the time we'd calmed down it was after three in the morning. Two other patients, both of whom were able to leave their beds under their own power, had stopped into the room to congratulate us. One of the nurses presented us with champagne (she'd called her husband at home to deliver it to the hospital). Marsh popped the cork and all of us sipped straight out of the bottle, giggling; Ruthie spilled some down the front of her t-shirt.

I could not have asked for a more beautiful or perfect wedding.

Chapter Eight

"WHERE SHOULD WE SLEEP?" I WHISPERED TO MARSHALL as we crept out of the hospital in the wee hours of the morning, leaving Tish and Case happy as clams in their room. The sky glowed with dawn, the first streaks of yellow stretching through a low cloud bank, creating the illusion of inverted ocean breakers above the mountain peaks. The clouds were backlit in bright saffron. I trembled, with both happiness and early morning chill, and when Marshall wrapped his arm around my waist and drew me to his warm side, nothing had ever felt more natural.

"I just don't want you to be cold," he explained, his low voice close to my ear. "That's all. I'm not trying to be ungentlemanly."

Allowed this unexpected pleasure of being tucked against him, I snuggled close as we walked, my arms encircling his lean ribcage. Both of us slowed our pace so we wouldn't reach the truck so quickly and therefore be forced to separate. I whispered, "I know. And thank you."

"I'm just so happy right now." He spoke with hushed wonderment. "That was the most beautiful wedding I've ever had the privilege of attending."

"It was. I'm so glad we were there." I paused, swamped with guilt, which had assaulted me so much in the past few days. "But Camille will feel bad. And so will Mom…"

"They'll understand, don't you worry. I was thinking about Dad and Gus, and everybody who probably should have been there, but they'll understand. They'll all see what matters most, which is how perfectly happy those two are, just you wait."

"You're right," I acknowledged, reassured. Marshall's beat-up black pickup loomed in front of us. My heart plummeted with regret; we'd reached it so fast.

Neither of us released our hold on each other. Marshall's thumb traced a slow pattern on the side of my waist and I felt that light touch thundering at every pulse point. My left breast was cradled against his side; my heart was drumming so hard I was sure he could feel it.

Marshall leaned down and kissed the top of my head. He murmured, "All right, I admit I just took advantage there."

Without questioning why I turned and slid my arms around his neck; I had to stand on my tiptoes. Marshall exhaled a swift breath and his arms swept around my ribcage, crushing me to his chest. He pressed his cheek to my right temple; my face was at his collarbones and he smelled so good that hot little thrills erupted in my blood. I curled my fingers into his wavy, uncombed hair and his strong hands spread wide-fingered on my back.

I fit so wonderfully against this man, as though his body curved and shaped to accommodate mine, flowing effortlessly around me. When I hugged Liam it was like I was hugging a tree trunk (Aunt Jilly's words certainly played into that image), but never once had I experienced this sense of blending together with Liam so that our bodies seemed part of the same entity. With Marshall, holding him and being held, I didn't know exactly where my body ended and his began.

I understood, *This is how it's supposed to be.*

"Don't stop," he murmured when I shifted just slightly, intending to draw away, guilt driving the motion. Guilt, and fear – that what I felt was too strong to deny.

"Marshall," I implored, tightening my hold instead. He cupped my shoulder blades and then ran his palms along my waist, up and down, with an urgency just barely held in check – my body responded to this caressing in bursts of onrushing heat. My chin jerked upward, instinctively seeking his mouth, and he bracketed my neck, tracing my collarbones with his thumbs while his gray eyes poured into mine in the early-morning light.

"Ruthann." He whispered my name like an incantation, like a prayer. I could feel the powerful thrusting of his heart; he sought assurance that I wanted this, too. Without hesitation I pulled him close, answering his unspoken question, and our lips met with a soft breath caught between, the sound of surrender and need –

His tongue claimed the interior of my mouth, tracing its contours with voluptuous caresses, hot, supple kisses that would have taken me to my knees if I hadn't been clinging to his neck. The ground fell away and I was seized in a rapid current, kissing him with an abandon never before known to me. His mouth and the sensations it awakened became everything that mattered. I held his jaws, feeling them move as we tasted each other both shallow and deep. He licked my lower lip, with sensual slowness, then the upper, before parting them anew and finding the tender skin of my inner lips with the tip of his tongue. I shuddered with pleasure and his hands swept lower, hauling me flush against his hips.

A car entered the parking lot no more than twenty feet from us, forcing an abrupt return to reality. Trembling and lightheaded, I tumbled into a hushed giggling fit, hiding my face against the warmth of Marshall's chest. He kept me close, chin braced on the top of my head, just as revved up; he rocked us side to side.

"You taste like fried chicken and root beer," I mumbled, teasing him, inhaling his scent with my nose against his shirt.

He tucked hair behind my right ear so he could press his lips there. "You taste like heaven."

Another rush almost took me out at the knees. I shivered, giddy with happiness, kissing the indentation between his pectoral muscles – and just that quickly guilt backhanded my face.

What had I done?

What had I just let happen?

I drew away – it was the last thing I wanted to do but I was falling back to earth, fast now.

Witnessing the signs of sudden retreat, Marshall took my shoulders in his hands. "Hey. You haven't done anything wrong."

"I have…" I gulped, stalling, my eyes darting to the bright yellow clouds as if seeking answers there.

What would Liam say? How would he feel about what you just did?

To his credit, Marshall took the situation in hand with admirable calm.

"C'mon, it's all right," he murmured, leading me to the truck, opening the door and helping me in, all with touches gentle and sweet. I watched him round the hood to join me inside, palpitating with desire and disbelief and wonder. He started the truck and I tucked my hands beneath my thighs to keep from reaching for him as he shifted into first and headed out of the lot.

I knew I had to say something; I couldn't sit in silence like a child. "I'm sorry…"

He touched the brakes, halting the truck and pinning me with his eyes. "Don't be sorry. *I'm* not sorry that just happened."

I stumbled, "I mean…it's just…"

He nudged my leg with his knuckles, interrupting my nervous blathering. "I have an idea, for today. They've been barn-raising at Case's, like Wy was talking about yesterday. I've been at the hospital every day so I haven't had a chance to help, but I know Dad and Garth and everybody have been busy this week. They've been cleaning and hauling. I bet we're close to being able to get a barn going."

The calmly-delivered words achieved Marshall's intended effect; I released a breath and regained the ability to speak in coherent sentences. "I'd love to help. Where are the supplies coming from?"

"Donations, mostly. And Al. Don't tell Tish, but he's been heading all of the rebuilding efforts. Dad won't accept any money, of course, but Al has been buying food and beverages, all that, while everyone works. It is amazing. Half the town is pitching in. What do you say we go there today?" I sensed him grin, further easing my throttled-up nerves.

"Don't you need to sleep?" I asked, not yet daring a full look in his direction. If I looked at his mouth – with its beautiful, sensual shape – I would be a goner. "You haven't slept since yesterday."

"I think I feel a second wind coming on," he said easily, resuming driving. "I'll crash really hardcore later today."

I knew it was pointless to wish myself curled up with him when he finally did get a chance to sleep, but I did wish it – deeply. Pondering the reality of a barn-raising, I said, "I don't know how much help I'd be doing carpentry, but I can clean up their house. How is it?"

"A mess. Both of them are crappy housekeepers, I'm not gonna lie."

I giggled. My hair was still tucked in a sloppy bun and I eased it out of the rubber band, letting it fall down my back, rubbing my sore scalp.

I felt Marshall's gaze as he asked, "Are you hungry?"

Thinking of our conversation last night I replied, "Yes. For a powdered donut and a cup of coffee, with two creams. Is that helpful enough?"

He grinned anew. "Hell yes, and then some."

There was a filling station in sight. Marshall topped off the gas tank and then we went inside and loaded up on breakfast; he made a point of handing me two mini-cups of half-and-half from a bucket near the coffee machines. He grabbed two bacon sandwiches and a box of powdered donuts and paid for everything.

"Thank you," I told him, back in the truck, where I busied myself arranging the food on the seat between us, pulling out the retractable cup holder for our coffees.

Marshall sat with both hands resting on the wheel, watching my frenetic movement. He spoke with unruffled conviction. "I really like being around you. I can't pretend otherwise. I'm not sorry we kissed back there. I just want you to know that."

I fell still, studying his somber eyes. The sun had cleared the eastern horizon, glinting inside the truck the same way his words pierced light directly into me. A smile grew on my face and was immediately reflected on his; I admitted in a whisper, "I'm not sorry, either. And I really like being around you, too."

"I'm glad," he said simply, and then took us east toward Jalesville.

His phone rang a minute later and he drew it from his jeans pocket. He observed, "It's Tish," and then answered by saying, "Good morning, Mrs. Charles Spicer."

I heard my sister giggle. "Can I talk to Ruthie?"

"Sure thing." Marshall passed me the phone.

Tish said, "Your phone keeps going to voicemail, that's why I called Marsh. I wanted to tell you I talked to Mom and Aunt Jilly just a second ago, and they're not mad about missing our wedding. I told Mom you were headed back to Jalesville with Marsh." She paused. "Camille is upset, though."

"Told you," I muttered, trying not to think about why my phone was going straight to voicemail; I had at least five missed calls from Liam. I wanted to tell my sister that Marshall had kissed me and I would have been rocketing beyond the clouds with elation if I wasn't so guilty, but of course I bit my tongue. "It's like Marshall said, everyone will be happy because you two are so happy. You know?"

"I do," Tish whispered, then released a soft laugh. "Before Case fell asleep we were joking that we didn't get to consummate our marriage. I plan to make up for every second of that when we get home. We're going to consummate the *shit* out of our marriage, just wait."

Marshall started laughing; he could hear every word.

I told her, "I'll see you later, all right? You go and dream about what you just said."

Tish hung up and I passed the phone back to Marshall, realizing most of my things were still in Bozeman.

"I don't have any clean clothes. Shoot, I should have thought of that."

"You want me to turn around?" Marshall asked, even though we were already flying along the interstate beneath the bright morning sun.

"No, that's all right. It would just waste time. If we're going to work all day it doesn't matter if my clothes are clean."

"You can shower at the house. I'll lend you a shirt, if you want."

His words sparked intense visions of everything I wanted from him – none of which I could confess, especially not just now. Instead, I whispered, "Thank you."

We hadn't traveled another mile before I fell asleep. I didn't realize until we were already back in the Rawleys' yard and Marshall nudged my shoulder. I opened my eyes to his smoldering grin and my heart stormed and surged behind my ribs, like a prisoner demanding release. Marshall looked so good, so effortlessly inviting, it was torture to deny the urge to grab his shirt and yank him down on top of me.

"Hey, we're home." His eyes glinted with teasing. "You want me to carry you inside?"

My cheeks torched and I sat straight. "I think I can manage."

The whole Rawley family met us at the front door, crowding around for hugs, and I thought of what Marshall and I had discussed at the diner yesterday, about how close they were. Clark's sons all looked like him, tall and wiry, with cocoa-brown eyes, easy grins, and long noses. Marshall alone possessed gray eyes and though his brothers resembled him closely, I thought he was by far the most handsome. Sean and Quinn looked enough alike that I commented they could be twins.

Clark laughed. "They were born in the same year, nine months apart. I don't know how Faye and I managed those early days. Garth and Marsh were both little holy terrors of mischief and Sean was only a month old when we discovered Faye was pregnant again."

Marshall's brothers teased me about having to spend the night in his less-than-worthy company while Clark poured coffee and dished up eggs for me, letting Marshall fend for himself, which he did, leaning against the counter and crunching a slice of bacon, smiling to observe his father and brothers tripping over themselves to wait on me. They demanded details about the wedding and Marshall let me tell the story. He was disheveled and unshaven, hay on his clothes and sleepless smudges beneath his eyes; I couldn't keep my gaze from him, smiling as I related the part about the dandelion ring he'd made for Tish.

"Dad said we'll have a big party when Case and Tish come home," Wy said as soon as I'd concluded the story.

"But first we have to get their place in shape," Clark said, ruffling Wy's shaggy hair.

"How's it going out there?" Marshall asked.

"They lost a great deal. We cleaned up more scrap than I'd like to think about but it does my heart good to see everyone pulling together," Clark said. "Things have improved daily. It's like the old days, everyone pitching in."

"I'm gonna go clean up," Marshall said, wiping both hands on his jeans. Through the noise and bustle of his dad and brothers, he leaned close to me. "We'll head over there as soon as you get ready, how's that sound?"

"Good." I tried not to appear short of breath as our eyes held, nor to feel bereft as he left the room.

Clark said, "There's clean towels and shampoo in the guest bedroom upstairs. Wy, you show the way as soon as Ruthie finishes eating, all right, son?"

Marshall had disappeared up the same set of stairs just a few minutes earlier but we didn't see him as Wy led me along the hall to a wood-paneled room decorated with black bears. He showed me where the bathroom supplies were located and seconds later I was alone. I turned in a slow circle, noticing the tall windows through which sunlight created hot rectangles on the floor, the little twin-sized bed and nightstand, the carpet and quilt, all patterned with bears. After locking the door I stripped free of my dirty clothes, hearing a shower running in another part of the upstairs, knowing very well that Marshall was in it; I pictured the hot water coursing over his lean, naked body.

Thoughts of Liam instantly jammed my guilty head, my boyfriend of the past four years who expected me to return to Minnesota with my heart intact. Liam, who was strong and hardworking, whose devotion to me would never waver. Whose phone calls I was avoiding.

You cheated on Liam. He doesn't deserve that.

I'd told Marshall just last night that I wanted to stay in Jalesville, and this was the truth. But to consider not returning to my life in Minnesota, the sweet, simple life I'd never questioned, seemed almost unthinkable by the light of day.

You have to go home. You know you can't stay here.

But in my mind I was already back in Marshall's arms in the dawning light, held so perfectly close to him. I touched my parted lips, caressing with increasing pressure as I replayed our kisses. My knees began to shake. The remembrance so affected me that I sank to the edge of the bed and cupped my breasts, bending forward at the waist. My nipples swelled as I swept over them with my thumbs – and, *oh dear God*, how I wanted Marshall's touch there instead, my own a sad substitute – but it would have to suffice.

I needed to be touched and I needed it *now*, shocked by this urgency. I stumbled to the shower and let scalding water turn my skin crimson as I plied my fingers over my wet, stimulated flesh, gasping as I shuddered at last with a small but intense orgasm, resting my forehead to the damp blue shower tiles and attempting to regain my breath.

Concerned that I was taking too long – *if they knew what you were really doing in here, Jesus Crimeny, Ruthann!* – I turned off the water and climbed from the steaming shower stall, seeking towels and clothing. Both were folded on the counter and I knew Marshall had been the one to place them there for me, before taking his own shower. I lifted the shirt and my face split with a smile as I observed his not-so-subtle stamp of possession; it was from his high school days, a white, much-worn team shirt with M. RAWLEY printed in green capital letters across the back.

I dressed in my jean shorts (foregoing yesterday's underwear), my bra, and Marshall's old t-shirt, which I saved for last, slipping it over my head with a distinct thrill. It was snug enough across the front that I had to stretch it out with both hands, but otherwise fit perfectly. The medicine cabinet revealed three toothbrushes in store packaging and so I brushed my teeth, braided my damp hair, and called it good. I let my braid fall over one shoulder, angling my back toward the mirror so I could see Marshall's name between my shoulder blades.

He was in the kitchen when I clattered down the stairs, leaning backward against the counter with the base of his palms caught on its edge behind him, talking to Wy. He paused in whatever he was saying to his brother, watching me with subtle, heated admiration. He had combed through his dark hair and shaved since an hour ago. I hadn't seen him without his dark scruff since I'd been in Montana; he looked younger, and more handsome than ever. He was wearing work clothes – worn jeans and a faded green t-shirt, heavy-duty work boots, and he said, "Good morning. Again."

"Thanks for the shirt." I was grateful beyond belief for my bra, which disguised the hard pearls my nipples had become.

"Of course." He was smiling now, dropping his right shoulder forward. "Yours, I'm guessing?"

"In school there were so many of us in a row we just got used to having our first initial on everything." He glanced down at the shirt, and subsequently my breasts, before he concluded innocently, "It seems to fit you pretty well."

Wy, drinking a glass of milk, watched us with ill-disguised interest.

"You guys ready, or what?" Sean appeared at the back screen door, which opened into the garage. Catching sight of me, he offered, "Ruthanna-banana, you wanna ride over there with me and Quinn?" He was wearing huge black sunglasses and a black ball cap, plus a black t-shirt and dark jeans, and had adopted Tish's old nickname for me.

"You gonna rob a bank on the way?" Marshall asked, indicating Sean's clothes.

"Nope, already got lucky last night." Sean grinned like a jack-o'-lantern.

"*Liar*," Wy said with certainty, backhanding a milk mustache from his top lip.

"Thanks, but I planned to ride with Marshall," I said.

Marshall sent his brother a smug smile.

"Hey, it's your nose. See y'all there!" Sean headed back outside.

I giggled. "What's he talking about?"

Wy supplied helpfully, "Farts."

Marshall shoved away from the counter with both hands, roughing up his brother's hair. He promised, "I'll try to control myself."

Outside under the hot sun the guys had their trucks running; Marshall explained, "Sean and Quinn share the work truck, that's the green one over there, and Dad has the dually for hauling the horse trailer." He indicated Clark's enormous diesel, which Wy was learning to drive. "And I managed to scrape together enough cash to buy my own. It's a beauty, as you already know."

I eyed his rusted-out truck. The twisted wire holding up the back bumper wouldn't last much longer. I'd discovered yesterday that the passenger seat had a loose spring, which I'd sat upon for hours. But best of all, I got to ride in it with Marshall, alone.

"I like your truck a lot," I told him honestly.

"I like *you* a lot," Marshall returned, grinning as he settled his black cowboy hat over his dark hair, and I glowed. I absolutely felt myself glow.

"We'll see you over there!" Wy called from the driver's seat of the diesel.

"You'll need sunscreen," Marshall said as we pulled out behind Sean and Quinn. "There's some in the glove compartment."

"Thanks, I try not to forget that."

I fished out an orange plastic bottle and spread sunblock on my forearms. I was about to replace it when Marshall reached and flicked my knee with his finger, like he'd done last night. "Don't forget your legs."

"Don't you flick me," I complained, even though I was delighted that he'd done so.

"You gonna lick my ear again?" he asked, holding his curled finger aimed at my leg, a little higher up my thigh this time. I giggled and evaded.

"I didn't *lick* your ear," I corrected. "I gave you a wet willy."

Both of us were laughing and he demanded, "A *what*?"

"What do you call it?" I used the edge of my hand to block his attempts to flick my leg.

"If it was any of my brothers, I'd call it worth a beating. But from *you*…"

I caught his wrist as he went in for the kill but before I could tighten my grip he slipped free with one effortless motion and aimed for my upper arm; it wasn't his fault I shifted to avoid him and he ended up flicking the side of my breast.

"Ow!" I yelped, though it didn't hurt as much as startle me. I knew it was an accident and I was laughing, but Marshall looked legitimately shocked.

"Oh God, I so did not mean to do that…"

"I get a freebie now," I insisted, with glee. "And you have to take it!"

"That's fair," he agreed, lifting both hands as though I'd pointed a gun at him, before reclaiming the wheel with his left. He implored, hamming up the pleading, "Remember that it was an *accident*…please, Ruthann…

sweet Ruthann…"

"I'm not that sweet," I muttered, pretending to peruse him for a vulnerable spot. If I was possessed of a much braver soul I would aim for the fly of his jeans, but no way was I that bold. We had arrived at my sister and Case's place and I was momentarily distracted, looking out the windshield at the rebuilding efforts, well underway. Marshall took advantage of my distraction, parking across the street from the yard and hurrying from the truck, slamming the driver's side door. I chased him, the prickly roadside grass scraping at my calves. He had a head start but didn't exactly try to evade me; I caught the back of his t-shirt before he'd even cleared the gravel road.

I cried, "Freebie! Take it like a man!"

Marshall laughed, head tipping back, holding his hands up and out to the sides. He offered, "Take your best shot."

He waited until I'd taken careful aim before twirling me around, lifting me against his chest with my spine to his front, his arms as strong as steel bands around my waist. He proceeded to carry me over the driveway toward the action while I spit loose strands of hair out of my mouth; my elbows were effectively pinned and I was laughing too hard to really struggle.

"You *owe me!*" I gasped, bouncing along in his arms as he walked, my knees bent like I meant to push off the nearest solid object.

"Oh, I always pay up," he murmured right in my ear, his husky voice sending shivers down my spine, hat brim bumping the side of my forehead. I thought if I didn't kiss him again before this day was done, I may very well die.

"You are an evil, *evil* man," I grumbled, only provoking more laughter. Curious stares were being directed our way. Sean and Quinn jogged to catch up with us.

"What's going on here?" Sean demanded, resetting his ball cap so it was backward on his head. He caught the end of my long braid and twirled it like a jump rope. "You need us to kick Marshall's ass?"

Quinn assured me, "We'll take care of him, Ruthie, don't you worry."

"This is the second-best thing that's happened to me just today,"

Marshall announced, squeezing me even more tightly to his chest. I knew I should probably be upset with him for this kind of manhandling, but I wasn't.

"What's the first-best?" his brothers questioned, in perfect unison.

"Oh, *no way*, that's for me to know." Marshall grinned like a little boy with a secret.

"Look out, it's the rest of the Rawley boys!" called a woman's voice. "Hide your daughters!"

There was good-natured laughter from all parts of the big yard, a sense of flowing movement as people came to greet us. Marshall set me on the ground, curling his hand around my braid for just a second before fully releasing me. I tugged down the hem of my shorts and straightened my t-shirt, warning Marshall in an undertone, "I'm not forgetting anything."

He winked, all lazy confidence.

A short, balding man wearing khaki dress pants and a button-down shirt that had wilted in the heat sought me out. "You have to be one of Tish's sisters. My dear, I'm Albert Howe. I've heard so much about you girls from Tish. Welcome."

"Ruthann Gordon," I said, shaking his hand; Al Howe was part of the reason Tish had decided to stay in Montana. "I'm happy to meet you. I've heard a lot about you, too."

"And she and Case were married this morning, is that right? Oh, I couldn't be happier," Al said. "I knew Spicer was in love with her even before Tish did, I do believe."

"What do you think of what we've done here?" asked Garth Rawley, the oldest of the brothers, swiping sweat from his forehead with the back of one wrist. He was tanned and shirtless, sporting a thick beard and full mustache, and instead of a hat wore a red bandana tied over his dark hair. He added, "Little Ruthie, good to see you, hon."

"This will make Tish *so* happy," I rejoiced, looking beyond Garth toward what had been the barn. Of course I hadn't seen it before it burned, and could only imagine the destruction, but there were at least two dozen people here now, working on the rebuild. The yard was scorched black in an enormous, vaguely circular shape and the air still held the lingering scent of char, but there wasn't much other evidence of the old barn.

"Holy shit, you've been busy," Marshall said, eyebrows lofted as he scanned the yard. "Shit, tell me what to do and I'll get right on it."

There was a skeletal frame in place already. Al appropriated my arm, leading me on a tour. I met other residents of Jalesville and more than one person told me how much they adored Tish, how she was part of the reason their town hadn't been completely lost to Capital Overland. The only other person I already knew was Garth's wife, Becky, who had been to Landon three years ago, on their summer visit.

"Marsh got you into one of his t-shirts, huh?" Becky said after she'd hugged me and kissed my cheek. She was pretty and soft-looking, all abundant curves, with eyes the blue of aster blossoms and blond hair in a loose ponytail. "That Rawley charm is tough to resist, I know. I hope Marsh doesn't care if his shirt gets dirty as hell today."

"Please, put me to work," I offered, grinning.

"There's more work gloves on the steps there," Becky said, indicating. "I've been weeding the flower bed but their house is…well, let's just say it needs some help."

I took stock of the yard as I made my way to the little green-and-white trailer where Tish now lived. It was undeniably rundown but I'd witnessed my sister's happiness; I supposed she would be content to live in a refrigerator box, as long as Case was with her. I peeked across the street where Marshall and his brothers were unloading their tools, including an aluminum folding ladder; Marshall knew I was looking his way, somehow, and used his free hand to tip his hat brim. I tore my eyes away and entered the trailer, which was stuffy with the scent of leftover smoke.

First, I opened windows.

Then I located a sponge and a bottle of spray cleaner, and made myself useful. Two hours later the place was sparkling; I was pretty darn pleased with my efforts. Someone's truck radio had been playing all morning as men crawled over the slowly-growing structure of the barn, tuned to a local classic rock station, and in addition to hammers clanging and buzz-saws whining, there had been plenty of singing along. I recognized Marshall's voice among a dozen others; I'd been keeping an eye out for that black cowboy hat, those faded jeans. He'd rolled his sleeves over his shoulders and was sweating profusely, just like all the men. From time to time they climbed down ladders and gulped from plastic cups at the water cooler.

At one point Marshall dumped a cupful over his head, shivering at the welcome chill before using the bottom edge of his t-shirt to wipe his face, exposing his lean-muscled belly. I just *happened* to be on the lawn as he did so, shaking out the kitchen rug, and he'd paused for a second, letting his damp shirt fall slowly back into place. He'd grinned. If he'd opened his arms just then, I would have knocked people out of the way to jump into them.

It was mid-afternoon when Becky came inside to wash her hands.

"Any chance you want to come clean my house next?" she asked, scrubbing dirt from her wrists and fingernails. The next thing I knew she bent forward over the sink. I flew to her side.

"I'm all right, hon," she murmured, turning off the faucet. "I'm pregnant. Just had a little dizzy rush."

"You are? Congratulations! That's wonderful."

"It was a little unexpected," Becky confessed, drying her hands. I hurried to pour her a glass of iced tea before pouring one for myself. We sat at the kitchen table, now adorned with a canning jar overflowing with wildflowers, which I'd picked from the yard on the far side of the trailer.

"Well, Tommy isn't even a year old yet." Becky fanned her face and took a long sip, the ice cubes clinking in her glass.

"You guys planning to have a bunch of boys in a row, too?" I asked, smiling, thinking of what Clark had told me this morning.

"That's Garth's hope, but he doesn't have to carry each baby for nine months so it's a little easier for him to say he wants seven or eight kids." She looked past my shoulder. "Speaking of the devil."

Garth thumped up the steps and stuck his head in the trailer. He was still shirtless, his bandana dark with sweat all along his forehead. He was as good-looking as ever (he looked a lot like Marshall, I couldn't help but notice), and Becky was already smiling adoringly at him.

"Hi, honeybunch," he murmured to her, and then asked, "You guys ready for lunch? Food's here."

I looked out the front windows to see a van rolling into the yard, the words *Trudy's Diner* painted on the side.

"Oh yum," Becky said. "Trudy brought lunch yesterday, too. C'mon, Ruthie, ladies first."

I followed her out, but not before fishing two big, clunky ice cubes from my tea glass, hiding them behind my curled fingers. The sun was a hammer straight overhead. There were two collapsible tables set up beneath the lone cottonwood on the property, covered with tablecloths; a woman I assumed was Trudy was unloading food from the van as a bunch of hungry men descended on the tables. Clark and Becky were helping carry food containers and I supposed I should offer to help, but the ice cubes in my hand were melting fast. I spied Marshall headed my way, just as I'd been hoping.

"You've been working hard all morning," I greeted, trying to appear innocent, keeping my hand hidden behind my back. There were sweat rings decorating his shirt at the neck and armpits, sweat trickling down his temples to his jaws as he grinned from beneath the brim of his black hat.

"You too," he said.

"Hey, what's that?" I pointed behind him. He turned at once and I was already laughing as I reached up and slipped both of the ice cubes straight down the neck of his shirt.

He sucked a sharp breath as he whirled around. "Damn, one went *right* down my jeans."

"Ha, *ha!*" I cried, evading as he tried to grab me around the waist. "Serves you right!"

"You want a really, really sweaty hug?" he demanded. "Is that what you want?"

Wy saved me, jumping up and hooking an arm around Marshall's neck, whooping, "Double chicken-wing!"

Marshall shifted and caught Wy in a loose stranglehold. "Not exactly, buddy."

I darted away to help unload food and that was when Al Howe caught me by complete surprise, offering me a job at the law firm. I stood in the hot sun, holding two containers of potato salad, and he recognized that he'd rendered me speechless.

"I've been pondering all morning what to do about the fact that Mary Stapleton, my dear secretary, who's been with the firm for decades, just informed me she plans to retire to watch her great-grandkids. Threw me for a loop until I realized the answer to the dilemma is right here under my nose. Now, I know from Tish that you intended to return to Minnesota but she hinted you might be interested in a change. Is that so?"

I studied his serious face, at last finding my voice. "Yes. Thank you for the offer. Can I let you know by tomorrow?"

"Absolutely." With a twinkle of good humor, he added, "But let me know that you've agreed!"

I followed Al to the tables, thinking of my mother, who would arrive in Jalesville to collect me by tomorrow at the latest, ready to drive home. Back to Minnesota and the life I'd never considered changing, at least not this drastically.

What is happening to me?

The truck radio continued to blast classic rock; the current song was "The Power of Love" by Huey Lewis. Marshall had saved me a seat at one of the tables, which he indicated as I approached; the side of my hip bumped his left shoulder as I slipped beside him. Marshall sat with his forearms surrounding a plate piled high with food. He'd removed his hat at the table, like all the men, dark hair flattened to his temples with sweat. He seemed to sweat more than any man I'd ever known; still, the urge to hug him was almost overpowering. I craved the way his body meshed with mine, as it had this morning. He watched me sit, grinning like he knew a secret.

"I just thought some ice would help you cool off," I said sweetly. "You look like you might need it."

His grin became wry as he muttered, "You have *no* idea," and my eyes were drawn to his mouth, his beautiful mouth with its angel-kiss indentation. I turned away, knocking my fork to the ground in my haste to appear preoccupied; my face was afire as I bent to retrieve it.

"Isn't this great?" Marshall was waiting to dish fruit salad onto my plate. I knew he meant how everyone was pulling together here.

"It is," I agreed, scooping a heaping portion of bacon-laced macaroni noodles. "It would be like this in Landon if someone needed a hand. Small towns, you know, everyone helps each other."

Marshall nodded. "And it's great to be outside on such a gorgeous day. Sean and I are building stalls right now, that's what we've been doing all morning." He peered upward between the cottonwood boughs and reflected, "I'd hate to be trapped in an office all day. How do people do it?"

"That would be all wrong for you," I agreed. I couldn't keep my gaze from him and gave up trying. "Tish told me you do construction jobs all summer."

"I do. Garth does a lot of contracting work these days, with Becky's dad, and I help them if they need it. I make some good money doing construction, and I try to get a music gig now and then, with Case. I miss it when we don't play on a regular basis."

"When's the next time you play?"

"Around the fire this Friday, I expect, now that Case is all right. I won't be on my drums, but I'll have my guitar. And our old fiddle. Case has always been the best on the fiddle, but I know a few songs on it."

I desperately wanted to be at the fire with him this Friday; the desire centered as a burning ache in my chest.

Marshall seemed to read my mind, pausing in his eating. "I've been trying not to think about this, but I suppose your family is planning to head back to Minnesota now. Camille is in a hurry to get home to Carter and their kids, she was saying so earlier this week."

My heart fell, striking individual ribs on the way down.

"You're right," I whispered.

He studied me in silence; he didn't appear to be breathing.

I admitted, "Al just offered me a job in the law office," and Marshall's eyebrows lifted.

"What did you tell him?" he asked, keeping his voice neutral.

"I told him I'd let him know tomorrow." I could not have looked away from those somber gray eyes, not for anything. "I'd like to tell him I'll take it."

"Then that's what you should do."

"It's not that easy."

"Why not? What's stopping you?"

"Plenty of things." But right now I was struggling to recall exactly what these things were.

"If you didn't have to worry about what anyone else wanted or expected, what would you do?" he pressed.

"It's not that easy," I said again.

"Just try," he insisted.

"Then I'd stay." My heart battered my ribs.

Relief and happiness and joy crossed paths on his face. He murmured, "Well, then."

Because I couldn't handle my surging emotions, instead of answering I reached and flicked his bicep. He nudged my arm and indicated beyond my opposite shoulder, murmuring, "Would you look at that…"

I turned to look and just that fast an ice cube went down the front collar of my shirt. He couldn't have aimed better; it glided wetly into my right bra cup and even I had to laugh at my own gullibility.

"*Darn you*," I nagged. The ice puddled against my sweaty skin and I was wearing his threadbare white t-shirt. "You are in *so much* trouble."

"Sorry, I couldn't resist. I can't believe you just fell for that. I have to teach you a few lessons."

We'd caught Sean's attention and he leaned over the table. "I'll hold him and you can have a free shot, Ruthie."

I hunched my shoulders in an attempt to dislodge the ice cube, a wasted effort at this point. I punched Marshall's arm but he only laughed harder, ducking his shoulder to avoid further blows, eyes detouring to my chest. "Oh God, I *am* an evil man. I own it, I admit it."

My nipple was round and evident, chilled from the ice. I leaned my elbows on the table so it wasn't so obvious, muttering, "Just you wait.

When you *least* expect it…"

Garth came up behind his younger brother, affectionately knuckling the top of Marshall's head. "C'mon, you little shit, quit pestering Ruthie. Free time's all through."

I giggled as Marshall was almost literally dragged from my side. Lunch was ending and I helped clean up as the men returned to work. Becky, Trudy, and I packaged up leftovers and loaded the van; I folded the tablecloths.

"Ruthie, I'm heading out," Becky said after Trudy had driven away. "Will I see you later this week? What's your plan?"

"I honestly don't know." I stood holding a stack of linen against my belly. I thought about how she'd told me she was pregnant, flattered that she trusted me with the news.

"Well, it would be great if you stuck around for a while." Becky nodded toward the men. "Marshall is smitten with you, like nobody's business. But I suppose that's pretty obvious." She caught me in a hug before I could reply. "Just in case I don't see you before you go."

After Becky left I remained rooted in the yard, beneath the whispering leaves of the tall cottonwood. I confessed to the tree, "I'm pretty smitten with him, too."

I spent the afternoon washing clothes. Tish's machines were old, loud, and clunky, stacked on top of one another, and there was a waist-high pile of laundry waiting beside them. I stood folding towels, humming along with the song on the radio outside, "Run to You" by Bryan Adams, when I caught sight of Marshall jogging across the yard toward the trailer. I flew to the screen door, holding it open with my forearm. He stopped at the base of the cement steps leading up to the door, standing with a dusty boot braced on the bottom one, using his knuckles to knock back his hat brim. Grinning up at me, he drawled, "Hi, there."

"There's an entire tray of ice cubes in here, with your name on them." The trailer was in the shade now, as well as the lower half of the emerging barn.

"I'm sorry I got your shirt all wet," he murmured, a smile playing over his lips as he eyed mine.

"What do you want?" I pretended to nag, but my tone was more inviting than the sight of Flickertail Lake on a humid day.

He climbed one step, which put his nose on a level with my breasts. Our eyes locked.

When he spoke, his voice was low and hoarse, any hint of teasing having vanished. "Aw, Jesus, Ruthann, I want to kiss you again. I can't think about anything else…"

"Marshall…" His name rose from my lips in equal parts yearning and invitation.

He grasped my right hand and bent to kiss it, his sweat-stained shirt straining across his wide shoulders. His lips met my flesh and heat blazed between my legs. When he lifted his head, both of us were breathing hard. I twined the fingers of our joined hands and stepped backward, into the empty kitchen, and he followed as though magnetized. The screen door clacked shut. The radio kept playing, hammers panging and saws scraping – but we heard none of that, too busy claiming each other with arms, hands, mouths.

My tailbone was braced against the sink before I knew what had happened, as we kissed open-mouthed and reckless. His hat hit the floor. I dug my fingers in his thick hair and he groaned deep in his throat, clutching my ribs, thumbs sweeping the lower curves of my breasts. I hadn't kissed anyone but Liam in years and Marshall was a different kisser all around, intense and heated, his tongue pelting my willing mouth. It was so incredibly good – lust and need gripped me in a stranglehold of intense proportions. My thighs curved to accommodate his hips as I arched my pelvis, grinding against him, mindless with desire.

With one fluid motion he hauled me atop the counter and threaded my calves about his waist, kissing my neck, my ears, taking my chin between his teeth as his lithe hands claimed the fullness of my breasts. He kneaded my flesh with an expert touch – my head fell back as I panted in response, gripping him with arms and legs, his hard, lean body that fit so perfectly against the soft curves of mine. I ran my palms down his torso, greedy to touch, and over the fly of his jeans at last, which covered a rigid, bulging column of flesh. He groaned as I stroked with increasing pressure, closing his teeth on the side of my neck, both of us shaking, aware of nothing but each other.

Except for a faint sound, growing louder –

"Ruthie, you in there?" It was Wy, coming closer.

Sweat trickled down Marshall's temples and his eyes appeared almost black with desire; my heart jolted all over again, flooding me with an agony of passion and angst. There was no choice and he exhaled in a rush, planting one last kiss on my lips before lifting me from the counter to solid ground. I reeled, bracing on his chest, and he said in my ear, "I could kiss you until the end of time, angel, and it still wouldn't be half enough."

Tears gushed to my eyes and Marshall saved me from discovery – he went to the door, outwardly calm, to meet Wy before the boy could enter. I dabbed at the wetness in my eyes and raced for the bathroom, where I could not meet my own gaze in the mirror. I was radiating heat, my thoughts pinwheeling, shying away from any sort of accountability. I wanted Marshall with a feverish, single-minded insanity of wanting. And now that it had taken root, it would not be denied. Denial was no longer an option.

You are behaving like a slut, I thought, punishing myself.

Through the bathroom door I could hear Wy as he spoke excitedly. "I want to show Ruthie the new stalls! Is she in there?"

I splashed my face with cold water; Marshall said, "She'll be right out, buddy."

Just the sound of his voice sent my blood pumping.

I dried my skin and straightened my clothes. Wy was walking on his hands in the front yard; I could see him out the windows. Marshall, who'd replaced his hat, stood on the steps, arms folded, watching his brother and offering commentary; he turned to look over his shoulder as I opened the screen door and stepped outside, and the smile that overtook his face was the only answer I needed.

"I'd love to see the new stalls!" I called to Wy, and together the three of us walked to the barn, Wy between Marshall and me, chattering with typical enthusiasm.

Within the emerging wooden structure sun fell in crisscrossing patterns on the cement floor, creating stripes of light and bars of shadow along all surfaces. Sweet-smelling sawdust frosted every horizontal plane. Sawhorses were bridged by sheared wooden planks; I'd heard the whine of an electric blade intermittently all day. Sean and Quinn both knelt nearby, wielding sanding brushes. Clark and Garth, and a few other men whose names I could not recall, were perched on ladders, working on the arch of the structure high above. The sight of bare wooden beams against true-blue patches of sky was an unexpectedly pretty one.

"The cement floor stayed intact, fortunately," Marshall explained, indicating it. He spoke with such composure all while an undercurrent flowed between us, a swift river of unspoken words, and the promise of more.

Wy led me around the space, just as he had when showing me around his family's barn yesterday – *had that only been yesterday?* – pointing out details large and small. Marshall leaned on a stall to speak with Sean and Quinn but I felt his eyes on me as I followed Wy, admiring all the work that had been accomplished in the past week.

"This is amazing," I told Wy, who beamed.

We ended up back where we'd begun, at the first set of stalls where the guys were still wielding sanders, and Wy hung over the top edge alongside Marshall, letting his arms dangle down the front. I hooked both hands on my hips, all of us covered with stripes of sunlight.

Clark called down through the wooden skeleton of the ceiling, "Ruthie-honey, would you be willing to mix up a new pitcher of lemonade?"

"You need any help with that?" Marshall asked, with just a hint of wickedness.

"I think I got it, but thanks," I murmured, though the sight of his eyes with that expression made me weak all through my lower body. I may have put a little more sway than usual into my hips as I walked out of the barn. And I made sure to tug my braid over one shoulder so Marshall had a nice, clear view of his name between my shoulder blades.

Shameless.

That is exactly what I had become.

Dinnertime eventually rolled around and men began collecting their tools and leaving; Wy helped me fold up tables and chairs, which we propped against the back of the trailer for tomorrow's use. I called good-bye to people as they headed home before resuming weeding the flower beds, having taken up Becky's work. There were patches of wildflowers blooming throughout the yard but no one had tended them in a long time. My knees and hands were black with dirt, the back of my neck sunburned. I eased to my heels as another truck rumbled away, lifting gravel dust, searching for a sight of Marshall.

Sean and Quinn were carrying a ladder to the work truck, Wy following with a toolbox dangling from his right hand. I smiled a little at the sight of Wy without a shirt; here was evidence of what Marshall had surely looked like as a teenager, tall and gangly, ribs like a marimba. I quit with the weeding, brushing both hands on my shorts, and jogged over to the barn, which appeared serene in the setting sun. Clark was talking on his cell phone, the last person in the barn. But where was Marshall? His truck was still here. I knew he wouldn't possibly leave without me but it wasn't until I reentered the trailer that I stumbled upon him. A slow, tender smile overtook my face.

You poor baby, you were so tired, weren't you?

I felt my heartbeat all the way to my feet and fingertips. Unable to resist, I crept to the couch where he lay sprawled and simply indulged in studying him, clutching my braid in one hand. He was on his back, one knee drawn up against the back of the couch, the opposite arm hanging off the edge. His left hand rested lax upon his chest, long fingers spread like a starfish. He snored at a low grumble, lashes soft on his tanned, angular cheeks. His hair and shirt were still all sweaty and his feet were bare. It took every iota of willpower I possessed to keep from curling up beside him on that couch. The evening sun was lazy and mellow, casting long beams through the open windows. I heard the last of the work trucks growl to life as a man called good-bye to Clark.

I went back outside, stepping into the wheat-tinted light like someone in a dream. I didn't know exactly what my intent was; I didn't realize until Clark caught sight of me and called, "I talked to your mother just now, Ruthie-honey, and she's planning to drive over from Bozeman in the morning."

My heart seized at these words but I tamped down my distress. I told Clark, "I'll call her a little later."

"You must be starving," he said. "How about we run into town and grab some dinner? Wy is just getting the truck going…"

It took some courage, but I steadied my voice. "I'll wait here, if that's all right. Marshall is sleeping on the couch and I don't want to leave him alone. Plus, I still have some work to do in the trailer."

Fortunately Clark was only listening with half an ear, I could tell, as he yelled across the street to Wy, "Boy! Don't clip that mailbox!" He looked my way. "That's fine, Ruthie. Marsh can run you home when he wakes up, the lazybones."

"He's had a long day," I agreed, working hard to continue sounding calm.

And within two minutes there was nothing in the yard with me but dust motes, resettling over the gravel road that led back to town in a thousand rainbow flickers.

Chapter Nine

Now that I was alone with Marshall, albeit a soundly-sleeping Marshall, I was as nervous as I'd ever been in my life. I paced outside for a while, actually paced, until I gathered enough courage to enter the space where he lay asleep, oblivious to my machinations. It took three tries before I was able to set foot inside, easing shut the screen door so it wouldn't sing on its hinges. I was *that* terrified for him to wake up, even though I had so craftily orchestrated being left alone here, with him.

With Marshall.

Oh God oh God, oh my God…

Within the trailer the light had grown dusky as the sun disappeared behind the ridge. I clicked on the bulb above the stove. Marshall continued snoring. Probably he would sleep until morning and I was a moron, so agitated that remaining stationary became impossible. I tried to sit at the kitchen table but the sound of the chair scraping over the floor seemed as loud as a fire alarm. I was starving but too worked up to cook something; using the stove would be noisy. When I lifted my arm to peek in a cupboard, hopeful of finding a box of crackers, I realized I smelled. And not at all good.

In the bathroom a minute later, no more than fifteen steps from Marshall, I stripped from my dirty clothes; though safely hidden behind a closed door I felt more naked than ever as they fell at my bare feet. With trembling fingers I un-braided my hair, my chin bent as I stood in front of the mirror, nipples aimed straight at its reflective surface.

My breasts were round and pale, dusted with tiny freckles. For all my sunscreen efforts back home there was still a clear demarcation along my upper body, showcasing my bikini line; freckles descended over the tops of my thighs. I climbed into the shower and cranked the faucet to the right. The pipes groaned and I might as well have used a tire iron to pound upon them. I closed my eyes, seared by embarrassment, even though there was no immediate sound of footsteps from the direction of the living room.

Ruthann.

What have you done?!

What in the hell were you thinking?!

I scrubbed my long, tangled hair, using Tish's shampoo, her favorite strawberry-scented brand. I used her body wash next, coconut-y sweet, and the warm water felt good on my skin as I stood in its spray for long minutes, stalling; I'd worked myself into a state resembling terror. I had just leaned back to rinse the last of the conditioner when there was a knock on the bathroom door, two soft raps, and Marshall's voice, conveying clear confusion as he asked, "Hello?"

My heart fell to the shower floor and almost went right down the drain. I was hardly in a position to ignore him and of course he wondered what in the hell, not knowing who was currently in Case's trailer with him, taking a shower. I could be a burglar, or worse, and then I was overcome by the hysterical desire to laugh.

"It's just me," I called, in a remarkably steady voice.

I could feel his surprise like an entity that popped into the shower along with me. He stood there rendered speechless for a moment in which I hugged my torso, bending forward in pure, ecstatic agony.

At last he asked, "Ruthann?"

"Yes." I remained bent double in the spray, my voice slightly muffled. "You were sleeping."

He didn't say anything else. Minutes ticked by and the water began running cold. I couldn't hide in here like a child, as much as I really longed to, so I shut off the showerhead with a thunk-clunking of pipes and then listened intently for any hint as to what Marshall was doing.

"Hey, I'm making us some supper," he called from the kitchen, sounding typically at ease, and I could also hear the sound of something frying; my anxiety level cranked down a few notches. I combed through my hair, trying to remember if the bathroom was in sight of the kitchen. It wasn't, I decided; I needed to sneak over to my sister's room for some clean clothes.

"I'll be right there," I called, double-wrapped in a towel as I darted across the hall. I closed the bedroom door and located a pair of Tish's jean shorts and a clean tank top; I found my bra but still had no panties. No more than a minute later I emerged into the kitchen, trying to pretend nothing was out of the ordinary.

Marshall stood at the stove, frying eggs. He glanced my way and I could tell he was keeping his face carefully expressionless, gauging my mood. "Thanks for waiting with me. Guess I was pretty tired."

"Everyone else headed home." As if he wasn't well aware of this fact. My heart was about to shred apart. Marshall was still barefoot. Somehow this made me ache even more fiercely with wanting him.

"I figured." There was something in his voice I couldn't interpret. He continued studying me. I was frozen at the edge of the kitchen, watching him. I could smell frying eggs and the scent of my clean hair. I felt as tensile as a soap bubble, just as likely to shatter at the faintest touch. A deep indigo cloak had overtaken the sky while I'd showered.

"Are you hungry?" he asked, low and quiet.

"Yes," I whispered; the word scraped my throat. "But not for…eggs…"

"Ruthann." My name sounded almost like a warning. He drew the pan away from the burner and clicked it off. The tension in the air was so concentrated I couldn't catch my breath. He stood only a few paces away and I sensed he was waiting for even the slightest hint of invitation to make his move. I thought if he did not put his hands on me I may very well implode.

I whispered, "What?"

The gray in his eyes resembled a storm, clouds backlit with lightning. "I'm not going to play fair," he warned quietly. "I don't care that you have a boyfriend. I will do whatever it takes to win you, do you hear me?"

I could see the way his pulse beat at the juncture of his collarbones. And suddenly I was licking him in that exact spot. Marshall hauled me into his arms, my legs circling his waist as he clutched my backside with both hands. My heart thrust so hard I was surprised it wasn't visibly displacing my ribs. His eyelids lowered slightly; he sensed my desire to allow him to have his way in every regard. He brought his lips to within an inch of mine and breathed, "Oh holy God, Ruthann, I want you so much. I have for so long."

The only light in the room came from the small fixture over the stove. My hands had come to rest on his collarbones and I could feel the thunder of his pulse, matching mine. I grasped his jaws, as I had earlier today, brushing my thumbs over the sweet fullness of his lower lip as I whispered, "I want you, too."

His eyes flashed with a hot, satisfied joy. He carried me to the couch, where he knelt before me, my thighs cradling his hips. He took my face between his palms and leaned closer, tasting my lips with one soft sweep of his tongue. A pleading sound rose from my throat as I clutched his shirt, arousal stampeding my blood; I was so wet my jean shorts were damp, my body rioting in response to him.

He leaned back so he could see my eyes. "I've never seen anything more beautiful than the way you look right now. You look like an angel, Ruthann. I've always thought so, but never more than this moment."

I felt drunk on his words and his touch, clinging to him as his strong fingers followed a path down my ribs. I couldn't speak but he understood anyway, easing free the button on my shorts as he whispered, "Let me go down on you. Will you let me do that?"

Yes, I tried to whisper, trembling and ablaze, tugging at his shirt; I wanted no more barriers between our skin. He grinned, yanking it over his head, tossing it to the side. His torso was lean and suntanned, his chest covered in dark hair. His eyes flashed fire as he slid the jean shorts down my legs.

"No panties?" he murmured, peppering little kisses low on my belly. He made a hot spot near my navel with his tongue. "I wondered how far down your freckles went…"

"*Oh,*" I moaned as he guided my legs apart. "Marshall…*oh my God…*"

He eased two fingers inside, stroking as he whispered, "I want to make this so good for you."

"*Yes,*" I panted, each breath falling over the next, my head arched back. Nothing had prepared me for this intensity of feeling. I was so wet I could feel it along my inner thighs as Marshall teased my clit with his tongue, circling and caressing; gasping moans burst from my lips. His mouth was hot and sleek at the juncture of my legs – I lost all sense of time, crying out his name, quaking beneath him – at last he gently pressed the base of his palm just where his mouth had been, carrying me through the most powerful orgasm of my life.

I lay quivering, flat on my spine on the couch, forearms crossed over my eyes; sensation continued to flare along my nerves, sizzling after-shocks of pleasure. Marshall moved to cradle me to his bare chest, displacing me toward the back of the couch; full-length he was much bigger and longer than me, and curled protectively around my body. He kissed my damp hair and murmured, "I'm pretty proud of myself right now, I have to say."

I uttered a soft laugh, slipping my arms around his neck and only then daring to meet his satisfied eyes. I couldn't believe after what we'd just done that I was a little shy to look at him. He was smiling, gray eyes crinkling at the outside corners.

I blushed all the way to my toes as I whispered, "Thank you for that."

He laughed and I flushed brighter, heat devouring my skin. He was warmer than a winter furnace, his shoulder muscles lean and hard beneath my hands. "It was my great pleasure, I can assure you. I've never been so turned on in my life. But I've always known it would be this way with you."

I pressed my nose to his neck, hiding my face. "It was *so* incredible. I've never…I can't even…"

"You've never?" he repeated with quiet disbelief, lifting my chin with one hand. "You mean…"

"Never like that," I whispered, not wanting to think about Liam right now.

There was no challenge in his voice, only a desire to know the truth as he asked, "He doesn't make you feel this way?"

I slowly shook my head. Marshall's jeans brushed my bare skin and I tightened my arms around his neck in a manner that could only be interpreted as possessive. I latched a knee over his hip, eyes closed, and the heat of his mouth meeting mine was almost shocking in its immediate intensity. He plied his tongue over my lips and lightly bit my chin, murmuring, "Then I bet you never knew you could feel the same way again, right after…"

My eyes flew open.

"Let me show you," he whispered. "But let's get you naked first, you beautiful, sexy woman. I want your nipples in my mouth."

Five seconds later they were, my fingers buried in his dark hair. Wordless, mindless, I had become a creature of pure desire. He lavished attention on my breasts before lifting his head. "That summer…you wore that tiny little…*green bikini*…"

He was short of breath and I smiled at his words. He grinned widely in response and I couldn't resist teasing him, catching hold of his ears as I pressed closer, my nipples gleaming-wet. I murmured, "You thought about us doing this?"

He nuzzled his chin between my breasts, with a low, heartfelt groan. "Only every *second*. You have no idea how much I thought about us doing this."

"More," I insisted in a whisper, blushing all over again, and he obeyed at once, opening his lips over my nipple, running one hand down my belly and then lower, caressing the slick wetness he'd created there. I'd known it would be this way with him – somehow I had always known, too.

"*Marshall*," I gasped, and he grinned as my hips jerked in adamant invitation.

"I like hearing you say my name that way," he whispered. "I like it very much."

His wide shoulders arched over me as he worked his way down my body with hungry kisses. I allowed him every access and the throbbing pleasure built to a soaring height and shattered me yet again as I writhed beneath him on the couch cushions, my thighs bracketing his head.

"I need you *inside me*," I begged, shivering so hard I was surprised my teeth weren't chattering.

He was full-length above me in a heartbeat and I twined my arms around his shoulders and my calves his waist. Both of us were glossy with sweat, his eyes onyx arrow-points in the lamplight. I bit his neck, urging with my hips, and he groaned, "Oh holy Jesus, angel, don't do this to me. I don't have a condom with…*oh God…*"

"I don't care," I moaned.

His voice shook. "We can't risk it, I don't want to get you pregnant. Not yet, anyway, and I'm about to come really hard…oh God, Ruthann, *touch me…*"

I shifted and frantically unbuttoned and unzipped, freeing him from his jeans. He was huge and rigid in my firm grasp, burying his face against my neck, shuddering as he spilled over in a hot, creamy rush. I held tightly as he collapsed on top of me, both of us shaking, giddy with bliss. I was naked; Marshall's jeans were bunched at his knees. He smelled faintly of cologne, of sweat and sawdust and wood shavings, and I inhaled his scent like I would the clear mountain air; nothing had ever felt more right than our naked bodies tangled together.

After a time I whispered, "When can we get some condoms?"

He rumbled a laugh, tightening his embrace. "As soon as I can stand upright again, I will find us some. But right now I don't want to move because I'd have to let go of you."

I went all to pieces at this statement. I loved the way he said such tender things, and already anticipated hearing them.

"Marshall," I whispered, and tears spurted into my eyes, startling me as much as him.

He rolled us to the side, leaning on his elbow so he could see my face; he brushed damp hair from my cheeks. "Ruthann. You haven't done anything wrong."

I closed my eyes, moisture leaking over my temples as the impact of what had happened between us began to strike, pulling no punches.

Furious with myself, I swiped at the tears, contradicting, "But I have. What about Liam…"

"How long have you been with him?" Marshall asked, though he answered his own question right away. "A long time, haven't you?"

"Since I was eighteen."

"Have you ever been with anyone else?"

"Not that way. And *never* like this. The way you make me feel, Marshall…I can't even describe…"

"It's the same way you make me feel. You have to know that."

I touched his face, seeking my bearings, trailing my fingertips over his eyebrows, his long, knife-edged nose, tracing the shape of his wide, sensual mouth and the slender curve of his jaws, dark with stubble. He watched me watch him, the storm gathering again in his gray eyes. And I knew, deep in my soul and however inexplicably, that somehow I had always known this man's face.

"Your eyes are so beautiful," I whispered, and immediately amended, "*You're* so beautiful. Everything about you."

"Thank you," he whispered.

"What we did in the last hour…" I drew a fortifying breath, sheltered in his arms, and reframed the point I was attempting to make. "In four years, I've never done such intimate things with Liam." Heat rose from my chest as I stumbled over the words. "I didn't…I didn't even know it was possible to feel like this."

Marshall's expression was one of tender sincerity; he spoke with quiet conviction. "If I lived to be a thousand I could never be thankful enough for the past hour. Holy God, sweet woman, I've never felt like this, either."

"But you've been with other women," I argued. The thought hurt like a physical blow, I could not deny.

Marshall pinned me with a direct, unavoidable gaze. "I've been with my share of girls. I'm not gonna lie to you, not ever. Ladies *do* like the drummer." I flicked his chin in response and he laughed and caught my hand, bringing it to his lips, gently biting my index finger. "But tonight goes so far beyond anything I've ever done, anything I've ever felt. Years ago, on the night when Garth, Case, and I first met Carter and Camille at The Spoke, the night we all sang together, she showed us that picture of you and Tish. I saw your face and felt this rush of awareness. I knew we'd be together, some way, somehow. Here was Case claiming Tish as his woman, holding nothing back, so I kept what I thought to myself. But I felt the same about you, Ruthann. I still do, it's never stopped in all this time."

"What about when you guys came to Landon that summer? Why didn't you tell me then that you felt these things for me?! Why did you let all this time pass?"

He laughed, half-ruefully. "Yeah, when you were attached at the hip to Liam." He all but growled, "I want to kill him just thinking about him touching you in the past."

I shook my head. "I'm the one in the wrong. He deserves better than this. He's a good man and he would never dream of hurting me." I wanted to huddle up with guilt. "He's expecting me to come back to Minnesota this week."

Marshall cradled my face in both hands. "This has been the most beautiful twenty-four hours of my life, being near you since yesterday. Driving with you, eating dinner with you, watching you sleep beside me in the truck. Being at Case and Tish's wedding together. Seeing you wear that t-shirt with my name on it all day." His eyes implored me to understand. "If I've made you feel guilty, that would kill me. I didn't take advantage of you, if that's what you think…"

"I don't think that, I promise you I don't." Tears stung my eyes once more; I had to tell him the truth. "You understand me, Marshall, in ways I can't even explain."

"I want you to stay in Jalesville," he insisted. "I want you to take that job with Al, and stay here."

Despite everything I felt a welling of panic, of unsteady ground. I wanted this – I wanted *him* – but I was reeling from everything that had happened since yesterday.

"I just need…a second…" My voice trembled.

Marshall was very still for a moment; at last he said, "I understand.

C'mon, I'll bring you home."

He helped me to my feet and then to locate my clothes; we were all but wordless. I gathered up the things I'd borrowed from Tish and stuffed them in the laundry, promising myself I would take care of them tomorrow. I decided it would look too suspicious to show up at the Rawleys' house wearing new clothing and so I slipped into my dirty shorts and the M. RAWLEY shirt, hands trembling as I stood at the bathroom mirror to braid my hair.

Marshall was cleaning burned eggs from the pan as I returned to the kitchen, wearing his dusty jeans and sweat-stained green t-shirt. I wanted nothing more than to race across the meager space separating us and get my arms around him. He looked my way and I could sense his extreme reluctance to leave things hanging, but he finished what he was doing and only asked quietly, "You ready?"

I nodded and he clicked out the light above the sink, leaving the space in dimness. I heard him fumbling with something near the screen door and seconds later there was a red-orange glow from a string of chili-pepper lights hanging outside.

"There," he murmured, and I could tell from his tone he was trying to put me at ease. "Case always has these going."

The night air was chilly and we hurried across the road to his truck, Marshall opening the door for me. I clambered inside and he followed, starting it up and making a U-turn. I could sense his growing concern but he remained wordless, allowing me a little space. It wasn't far to his house, I knew, and I was so tense, so tightly-strung, we hadn't driven more than fifty yards on the deserted gravel road before I burst into choking sobs. Marshall pulled to the shoulder and killed the engine. Without a word he scooted over and collected me close. He smoothed a hand over my hair and then gently bracketed the nape of my neck, beneath my braid, while I sobbed, ambushed by a wild rainstorm of emotion.

"It's all right." He pressed his lips to my temple.

I gripped the front of his shirt until my knuckles hurt, soaking it with my tears. I didn't know how much time passed before I could draw a full breath and I gasped, "*I'm so sorry,*" before being overwhelmed by another bout of weeping.

"You have nothing to be sorry for. Not one thing."

I shook my head against his chest. It took another few minutes before I was finally able to speak, and then words spilled like water from a tipped bucket. "I'm not sorry for what happened between us, Marshall. It's just that I can't avoid hurting Liam, not now. He has never been anything but kind and loving our entire relationship. He expects me to come home and marry him. He's been talking about it for the past year." I inhaled a shuddering breath. "Then we got here and it's all been so crazy, with the fire, and everything with Case. And *you,* Marshall. I didn't expect to feel any of this, but I do feel it and I can't deny it. I've never felt something so strong, that just *overtook* me so fast. With Liam, everything is so safe…so comfortable…" I trailed to silence; my hands remained fisted around Marshall's shirt.

"He knows you, but he doesn't truly understand you," Marshall supplied quietly.

"I told you that you understood," I murmured.

After a moment's pause he asked, "Do you know how happy I was when you reached for my hand at Case and Tish's wedding, after I went and made that dandelion ring? It felt so right, the two of us being there with them."

"It did," I whispered. "I didn't realize how much I wanted you to hold my hand until you did, there at the bedside. You knew I needed that."

"C'mere, angel." He tugged me into his full embrace and said at my ear, "I wanted to kiss you last night after we ate at the diner, there in the parking lot. But I didn't want to scare you off. I didn't want you to think I was being too…forward."

"Yes, too *forward,*" I muttered, and smiled, despite everything. "That was very gentlemanly of you."

"Let me tell you something," Marshall said then, my cheek against his chest; I could feel the vibrations of his heated words as he delivered them. "Liam might be the nicest freaking man in the world but if he is too goddamn dense, too goddamn clueless, to know what you really need, to know who you really are, then he has never deserved you and he never will. Your sisters talk about how sweet you are, how innocent, and you are those things. But there is a deep well inside of you, of heat and strength and sensuality, in addition to your sweet innocence. And I see it. I've *always* seen it, and now I know it. It's part of who you are and I *see you*, do you hear me? I see you, Ruthann."

His words pierced my heart; I whispered, "I do."

He kissed my lips, lingering there as he whispered, "Let's go home."

The Rawleys' big yard loomed into view much too quickly; I didn't want to go inside and attempt to act natural around everyone. I was terrified of having nothing more than the memory of Marshall to hold close and increased my grip on his hand, our fingers latched on the seat between us.

I whispered, "Will you come tonight…"

He knew exactly what I meant. "Of course I will. You didn't think otherwise, did you?"

Inside the house it was pure chaos. Music played on the kitchen radio while Sean and Wy battled it out on some racecar video game, bashing each other's shoulders as they shared the couch in front of the living room television set. Quinn was making root beer floats at the kitchen island. Clark sat at the table with a newspaper and an ashtray; he was the only one who actually looked up as we entered the kitchen, though everyone called out some form of greeting. The house smelled of root beer, recently-baked pizza, and cigar smoke. And just slightly of dirty socks, but I supposed that couldn't be helped in a household of five men.

Marshall said cheerfully, "Hey, everybody. Did you save us some supper?"

I thought Clark's eyes swept between us with a little too much certainty, but maybe in my paranoia I was just imagining that; he said, "There's pizza on the stove, you two."

Marshall rested a hand on my lower back to usher me forward and even this light touch made me come all undone.

"Wasn't it a wonderful day?" Clark reflected. He invited kindly, "Ruthie, come join me."

As I sat across from Clark I thought, *It was more wonderful than any day I've ever known.*

My eyes went straight to Marshall, who had continued to the kitchen where he stood talking with Quinn, both of them nabbing pepperoni from the remaining pizza on the stovetop.

I said to Clark, "Yes, it was."

Marshall joined us at the table, setting a plate with two slices in front of me and then claiming the chair on my left, dragging it closer; Clark's mustache lifted with a fond smile.

"It was a beautiful day," Marshall agreed softly; it took everything we had not to steal a look at one another. "In every possible way."

I was so aware of him I seemed to be audibly resonating. Marshall leaned on his forearms, our elbows just a few inches apart.

Quinn called from the kitchen, "You want a root beer float, Ruthanna-banana?"

"Sure, thank you."

From the couch, Sean yelped, "*Goddammit*, Wy!" as the video game made a loud, rude noise and Wy laughed, socking his brother's shoulder. Clark shook his head and snapped the edge of his newspaper, cigar caught between the first two fingers of his right hand.

In the bustle, nobody noticed me reach beneath the table to grip Marshall's knee, communicating everything I could with a single touch. That I loved what had happened between us, both the physical and the emotional, that I wanted and needed him, and was overjoyed and slightly terrified by these truths. Quick as the flash of a firefly he put his hand over mine and returned the gentle pressure, and in his touch I felt both an acknowledgment and a promise for later.

And then we let each other go.

Chapter Ten

Later, as I lay curled in the twin bed in the black bear guestroom, my phone vibrated with a text; it was from Liam and my heart squeezed inward like a piece of ripe fruit in a tight fist. First I had avoided Mom's text (*See you bright & early in the morning, sweetheart!*) and now I was avoiding my boyfriend's. Because, despite all of the incredible, earth-shattering things I'd experienced with Marshall in the past twenty-four hours, Liam Gallagher was still my boyfriend. And Liam would never fully understand me, that was true, but he deserved better than what I'd done to him (however indirectly), and I felt sick with shame for that.

Liam's text inquired, *Are you doing all right?*

I closed my eyes and thought, *Liam, why do you have to be so kind? Why haven't you ever been an asshole to me, in all these years?*

Downstairs the house was settling into quiet as the guys all headed to bed. I was aware Marshall intended to sneak to this room once the coast was clear and even my guilt over Liam was not enough to quell my anticipation of his arrival. And so I set aside the phone without responding.

Time passed and my agitation amplified.

What if he fell asleep?

What if he doesn't come?

But I should have known better than to worry.

Even before there was the faintest indication, I sensed Marshall moving toward me. I threw off the covers and rolled to my knees, naked beneath an unbuttoned flannel pajama shirt. I met him at the door as it slid inward and he moved soundlessly into my open arms, closing the door behind him, his deep kiss stealing my murmur of welcome. He carried me straight backward to the bed, lowering me upon it and bracing above. My thighs cradled his hips and his hands were busy seeking out my bare skin while I freed my arms from the long-sleeved pajama shirt.

"Naked," he whispered against my lips, his hands full of my breasts, and I could tell he was grinning even though I could hardly discern his features in the darkness of the room.

"Yes, naked," I giggled, returning kiss for hungry kiss, breaking the contact of our mouths only to strip him of his shirt. I demanded in a whisper, "Did you bring a condom?"

"I stashed some in the drawer in here. I had to steal them from Sean's supply…oh my God, angel, *that feels so good…*"

He was already as hard as a telephone pole against my pelvis and I was grinding against him, his lightweight pajama shorts the only thing remaining between our flesh.

"Good thinking," I murmured, latching myself all over his strong, wiry body. His tongue plundered my mouth and our kisses became words that became kisses as we struggled to get closer, to devour each other and savor every second of this stolen time.

"You taste so good, angel, come here…"

"Don't stop…"

"I won't stop, I swear to you…"

"I love your chest hair…"

He snorted a laugh at my heartfelt declaration, rubbing it against my swollen nipples as he suckled my lower lip, cupping a hand between my legs and deepening each subsequent stroke, arousing me to the point of crying out.

"You're so hard…"

"*I need to be in you…*"

"Get these shorts off…"

I bucked against his hand, my shoulder blades driven into the mattress with the force of our kissing, relinquishing my hold only to allow him to grab a condom from the bedside table. The little drawer slammed and I clambered to my knees, breathless and shivering, running my hands along the tops of his shoulders.

"*Hurry,*" I implored, biting the nape of his neck. My hair was a humid, tangled mess, falling over us as I pressed my breasts to his sweating skin.

"For the love of all that's holy, get back in my arms." He lunged and I muffled a giggling shriek against his neck as we rolled across the bed, my hair caught between our mouths.

We ended with Marshall on top. He braced on his forearms, poised just at the juncture of my legs, and studied me at close range, our hearts throbbing with an accelerating rhythm; darkness robbed us of color but I imagined the stormy shade of his eyes. Just as before, I didn't know where my body ended and his began. I could smell his breath and taste him on my lips, and exhaled in a rush, so full of joy I almost split along the seams as I lifted my hips.

"*Ruthann,*" he groaned, sliding fully home.

I clung to his shoulders, my thighs tight around his waist. "You feel so good…*stay still for just a second…*"

He obeyed, holding himself deep, as I shuddered and came in an unexpected rush, overwhelmed by the solid length, round and hard as a fence post, filling my body. Quivering, soaked in our mutual sweat, I closed my teeth on the side of his neck, electric aftershocks continuing to pelt my flesh. He was taut with restraint, lips against my temple as he murmured, "Holy *shit.*"

My flesh was so sensitive to him I felt another one building between my legs already, and begged, "*More.*"

Marshall's husky voice was at my ear as he took up a steady rhythm, my hipbones clasped in his broad palms. "That's it, angel, come again. Come all over me, I love it so much…"

I lost all sense of time and space as our bodies flowed together, our unceasing motion creating a powerful, intensifying wave that was about to crest. I felt in danger of being ripped apart by its force but Marshall held me secure, my gasping cries muffled by our joined mouths. At last he could no longer hold back and shuddered violently, burying his face against my neck to contain all sound.

Sometime later he mumbled, "Thank you, oh dear God, thank you for that."

Our bodies remained linked and I wasn't sure if I could manage standing upright; at this moment, I felt scarcely capable of lifting my arms. I was crushed beneath him but I didn't want him to move. I kissed his chin and couldn't resist the urge to tease, whispering, "*What* a gentleman."

His low huff of laughter tickled my ear. "What I am is thankful, angel, beyond all earthly measure, thankful for *you*. I never knew two people could *make* love like that."

"It was so right," I murmured, utterly replete in his arms. I opened my eyes, which had adjusted to the dark, seeking his in the gloom. He rose to one elbow, hair falling over his forehead, his long nose casting a shadow over his cheek. He caressed my jaw and bent to kiss my lips, but softly this time.

He whispered, "I feel like I was made just for you. I don't know how to say that any other way."

His words were soft pleasure that dusted every inch of my skin. Stroking his hair, I whispered, "I feel like anything I want to do with you is right, that you would never be shocked."

"Amazed, for sure, but never shocked." He pressed a warm kiss to the base of my throat; there, he lingered, inhaling. "You smell so damn good. Oh my God, so good. Your whole body smells like heaven to me."

I bit his earlobe. "You smell amazing to me, too. And you sweat more than any man I've ever seen!"

We were both muffling laughter; Marshall growled against my neck. "Well, you got me all worked up, beautiful woman. What do you expect?"

"You've been sweating *all day* like that," I contradicted, giggling, shivering as he closed his teeth over my right nipple. "But I think it's sexy."

"You've been wearing those tiny little shorts for the past three days," he said. "Of course I've been sweating. Watching you climb the loft ladder was like being tortured alive."

I repeated, "Tortured alive? There's no such thing as being tortured *dead*."

We were wrestling now, kissing and laughing and gasping, by turns;

there were no sheets or blankets left on the twin bed, which was barely big enough for the both of us. I pinned his wrists, but only because he allowed it, and then took advantage of the position to lick his nose. He sputtered a laugh, flipping me beneath in one fluid movement.

"*Ha*," he said, and I twisted to evade as he went for my ear, almost falling off the bed. He wrapped me in his arms, preventing me from tumbling to the floor, and I commandeered his jaws and tugged him close for another kiss.

"More?" he whispered against my lips, and I was laughing and nodding and kissing him all at the same time.

"What's your middle name?"

"Marie. What about yours?"

"Augustus."

"Marshall *Augustus* Rawley," I whispered, trying out his full name, liking its taste on my tongue. I lay naked in the crook of his left arm, lax and languid; we'd used up every condom Marshall had earlier stashed in the drawer and dawn was rapidly approaching, but neither of us wanted to lose time sleeping. We drifted now in a sweet, soft lull.

"It's after my mom's granddad."

I thought of what we'd discussed at the diner off the interstate. "Thank you for telling me about her."

"It's good to talk about her. I'm so afraid to forget her voice. I mean, it's there in my memory, but sometimes I can't hear it until I think of her singing. I can always hear her singing voice. She sang to us all the time."

I rearranged position to hug him as hard as I could, with arms and legs.

"She was everything in our family, Ruthie, our anchor. Dad was like a ghost after she died. If not for us I think he would have died the next day, I really do. He loved Mom so much." The rasp in his voice nearly killed me. He rested his mouth to the top of my head, as though gathering strength. "And she was gone so fast. The last time I ever saw her was at breakfast that morning. If I could just go back to that one morning and see her again…"

I covered his face with little kitten-kisses, tears flooding my eyes.

He drew a slow breath, chest rising like an inflating life raft. On the exhale, he murmured, "I know Case loved her with all his heart, too. Mom was like his mother after Melinda Spicer died. That's part of why we all love playing music and singing together. We feel closer to her that way."

I whispered, "I don't know exactly what I think heaven is, but wherever it is your mom is there. She listens when you guys sing and it makes her happy. That's what I believe."

"Do you think her soul is waiting somewhere for my dad? For all of us? Do you think we'll see her again?" His voice was very soft.

"I do. I don't have any proof but I believe souls wait for each other, or try to find each other, somehow. I've talked about it with my sisters. Camille and Mathias were together in other lifetimes…you know that story, right, about Cora and Malcolm?"

"I do. And it just proves there's no guarantee that souls are allowed to be with their mates. I hate to think of it as some sort of celestial crapshoot. What a horrifying thought."

I countered, "But it makes sense if you think about it. If we lived, say, a hundred and fifty years ago and were supposed to find each other in that life, and then I died young –"

"Ruthann! Knock on wood. Jesus, don't say such a horrible thing."

"I'm just saying, *theoretically*…" I began to explain again but Marshall took my hand, curled my fingers into a fist and lightly rapped it on the edge of the nightstand, effectively knocking on wood for me.

"Sorry, I'm too superstitious to let that slide." He kissed my knuckles before gathering me back in his embrace.

"No, you're right, my Aunt Jilly would scold me." I was deeply touched by his action. "But I meant, say a terrible thing like what I just said *did* happen to me, just like Camille believes happened with Cora, and then you lived out your *full* life, say eighty or ninety years. What if I was reborn, or returned to Earth, or however it happens, when you were still living the earlier life…what then?"

"We'd have to catch up somewhere along the years," he recognized. "It makes my head swim a little, but I know what you're saying. It could take generations. But I do believe that all of us – Carter and Camille, Case and Tish, you and me, my brothers – we've all been together before now. Finally, we've all caught up again."

"Then there must be a reason. Aunt Jilly said there's something from the past that we have to understand."

"There's plenty we have to understand right here, in the present. Tish was just talking about confronting Derrick Yancy, after Dad told her they'd ruled the fire as accidental." He stroked my hair with a gentle, repetitive motion and my eyelids grew increasingly heavy. We hadn't scratched the surface of what needed discovering, but sleep was drawing me under.

We lay in soft silence for a time before Marshall whispered, "I like how your curls wrap around my fingers. It's like your hair is holding onto me." He pressed a soft kiss to my mouth and spoke more quietly still. "I want you to hold onto me."

I tightened my grip in response, my nose resting against his chest. Sated and near sleep, I whispered his name on a slow exhale – and then jolted as if struck by lightning as my phone, abandoned on the night-stand, flared to buzzing life with an incoming call; the room glowed as though fireflies had been released from a hundred jars.

"It's Liam." Marshall caught sight of the display screen before I did and I heard the fire in his voice even though he attempted to downplay its presence. The phone continued vibrating, insistent as a tornado siren; I could not bear to answer it, naked in Marshall's arms.

"Did you talk to him last night?" Marshall controlled his tone with effort but he was jealous, as I well understood.

"No," I mumbled, willing Liam to hang up before I screamed. At last my phone went dark and I turned away, covering my face; I was worse than any girl I'd ever judged.

"Ruthie, it's all right. Tomorrow you can call him and tell him you're breaking up."

"So now you're telling me what to do?" Ashamed of my behavior, the default emotion became anger. Marshall seemed too far away; I longed to roll toward him and be enfolded in his warm strength, but I didn't dare.

He spoke with a biting edge. "Of course not. But I think I have the right to expect something from you after last night."

My phone interrupted us again, this time with a text message.

Dammit, I thought, applying pressure to my forehead with all eight fingertips.

Marshall moved without asking, reading the text before passing it to my hands.

Liam had written, *I'm worried. Call me, sweet pea.*

I cringed beneath the whiplash of guilt; there was no way to avoid hurting someone who didn't deserve it and the blame rested solely on my shoulders, I could not pretend otherwise.

Tension crackled like static electricity. Marshall asked, "He calls you 'sweet pea?'" This could have come across as deriding but I heard only his barely-controlled pain.

"It's from a movie he likes," I whispered.

"It suits you." Marshall's throat was raw as he acknowledged, "He loves you."

"He does," I whispered. Suddenly I couldn't bear to be facing away from Marshall, and flipped over. He sat cross-legged a few feet away, forearms braced on his bare thighs, wide shoulders slightly hunched, as though anticipating a blow. In the gray light of early morning his features appeared shaded by pencil strokes. I cupped his knees; he immediately placed both hands atop mine, squeezing gently. I held his gaze, needing him to set aside his jealousy and understand. "I'm not in love with Liam but I do care for him. I hate the thought of hurting him. It will hurt him so much when I tell him we're over."

"You need to tell him the truth."

"He's been my boyfriend for the last four years. I owe him more than this."

"Such as what? Such as, you owe him *yourself*?" Marshall demanded. "You don't owe him anywhere near that much! Besides, I won't allow it!"

"*Allow* it?" I rolled to my knees, temper rising like a springtime river.

"Call him *right now* and tell him it's over!"

"Don't tell me what to do!" A small part of me acknowledged and marveled at Marshall's ability to rouse me to intense emotion. Prior to the past forty-eight hours, I had considered myself dependably calm.

"Then everything we've said and done tonight is bullshit, is that it?"

"NO!" I throttled down my volume and hissed, "None of it was bullshit! It's more real than anything I've *ever felt!* You *know* that! You're being deliberately mean!"

Marshall inhaled an angry breath, taking his temper in hand with real effort, I could tell. He plunged his fingers through his hair and at last admitted, "I'm just so fucking scared. I'm scared you'll feel bad enough to go back to him."

"I'll tell him but I'll do it my own way, all right? And you can't get so upset with me. I won't have that, do you understand?"

"Ruthann." The bite in his voice had washed away. "Come here. Please, come here. I do have a terrible temper, I'm sorry."

I could no more refuse than I could stop the sun from cresting the eastern horizon. I lunged gladly into his arms, widespread to receive me, burying my face against his neck. I clung and he held; a soft, low sound of relief issued from his throat.

"I know you didn't expect this, but it happened," he murmured, caressing my hair, my spine, my shoulder blades and hips, his fingers seeming to trace the bone structure beneath my skin.

It struck me what he'd said. "Do you mean *you* expected it?"

"I've known we'd be together since I first saw your picture, seven years ago now."

I whispered, "I never get mad. I was *yelling* at you."

"Maybe it's about time you actually *got* mad once in a while."

I flicked his earlobe. He snorted a laugh, catching my hand before I flicked an even more sensitive spot.

"Got you," I muttered, my hair tangled between us.

"Stay here," Marshall whispered.

"I wish it was that simple."

"It is," he said. "Now that you're in my arms, it's that simple."

Chapter Eleven

WE SLEPT FOR AN HOUR, BRAIDED TOGETHER. I STIRRED before Marshall, alerted by the brightening window; dawn had arrived. Clasped to his chest, back to front, his wrists crossed atop my belly, I imbibed the pleasure of this moment, making note of each detail as though for the last time. I was agonized; within a few hours my family would be headed east on the interstate to collect me for the return trip to Minnesota.

What will you do?

Aunt Jilly would tell me to listen to my gut.

What do you want?

The answer was obvious; my entire body pulsed with the awareness.

Marshall. I want Marshall.

But doubt crept in along with the dawn, rendering me terrified. When it came down to it, I had only known Marshall for a few weeks, counting the summer three years ago. I could not deny that our physical connection was something I'd never realized two people could share; I felt fragile and naïve, besieged by my feelings, now traveling in uncharted territory with this knowledge. Our attraction was overwhelming but felt entirely natural; the more I received of Marshall, the more I wanted. If I was back home in Landon, immersed in my old life and with distance between us, would I slowly forget how I'd felt here, in Jalesville?

And a far deeper terror gripped me.

I don't want to forget, not ever. I don't want it to stop.

I edged closer to the man behind me, whose arms held me securely even in sleep, who'd understood more about me in a week than Liam would understand in a lifetime. I released an anguished breath, imagining leaving Montana and never seeing Marshall again. Almost against my will I thought next of Liam; everyone back home expected us to get married, including his parents. Liam would do anything I asked, would never think of fighting with me, would cherish me all our lives. I knew this, and felt sicker than ever at the thought of hurting him. Guilt crawled over my skin and itched along my scalp. In a hundred years, Liam and I would never achieve the level of intimate intensity that had sprung to life between Marshall and I in mere hours.

I knew this, too.

Marshall breathed my name as though caught up in a dream. I rolled to face him and he murmured in happiness, eyes still closed as his hands spread across my tailbone and drew me flush against his naked body.

"Good morning," he murmured sleepily.

"Good morning," I whispered, curving my thighs around his hips in the oldest and most natural of invitations between a man and a woman.

His eyes opened and drove into mine.

"No more condoms…" he whispered, though this protest was noticeably without conviction.

"Just don't come inside me." I was breathless now, shifting to engulf him, gasping as he slid inside, where I was hot and wet, more than ready.

He grasped my hips, tipping me into his thrusts, studying my face, his quiet voice laced with husky desire. Between kisses, tasting my skin, he murmured, "I can't believe how beautiful you are. You're like an angel in my arms."

"Marshall," I panted, overcome, my palms on his collarbones, feeling the lean muscles of his chest tightening with each movement of his lower body. I bit his bottom lip and he pressed my shoulder blades to the mattress as my breaths became moans, which he collected with his kisses. I shuddered as he rocked into me, taking me past all reason.

"You feel so good," he gasped. "Oh God…*oh God…Ruthann…*" His teeth were bared with his fierce breaths and he trembled in my arms. I muffled a sharp cry, shuddering as I came all over him. Not five seconds later he pulled out, collapsing atop me with a deep groan. I locked my ankles around his waist.

The room shone with advancing day; sun gleamed like spilled copper on the floorboards and inched a slow path up the wall.

"Marshall, I'm so scared." Daylight had already stolen too much time. He lifted to his forearms. "It will be all right, I promise you."

"How?" I whispered desperately, gorging on the sight of his face; it was more than bright enough to discern the secondary shades in his gray irises, to imbibe his expression of passionate tenderness. Possessiveness tore furrows in my heart; I grasped his ears, fingering his wild hair and pressing both thumbs to the dark, sleepless smudges under his eyes. His lips appeared slightly swollen; a bite mark the size of a silver dollar bloomed on the top curve of his shoulder and another, even larger, graced one of his chest muscles. There was no way in hell we could disguise what we'd done; how could we hope to pretend nothing had happened between us?

"It will," he insisted softly, studying my eyes, dusting soft kisses along my cheekbones. "Trust me. I want that. I want you to trust me."

"I do," I whispered.

"I hate sneaking out and leaving you alone in here. But Dad would skin me alive if he caught me taking advantage of you this way." Subtle humor glinted in his eyes but I could not muster up a return smile, and caught his wrists in my hands.

"I don't know what to do," I whispered miserably.

"Stay here with me." He kissed my lips, with utmost gentleness. "Please, Ruthann Marie."

"Thank you for last night. For everything." My voice wobbled. I pressed my thumbs against the knobby bones on his wrists.

"It's just the beginning," he whispered.

There was definite activity from other parts of the house and Marshall was forced to hurry, donning his abandoned shirt and pajama bottoms, collecting the sheets and blankets from the floor. I felt a cold twisting of nausea now that he was at the point of leaving this bedroom, ending what we'd shared within these four walls. At the last second he darted back to the bed and scooped me close, kissing my lips, my neck, my breasts and belly, before enfolding a blanket over my shoulders.

His eyes burned into mine. He implored, "Please don't go," and then he was gone, closing the door silently behind him.

I crumpled, physically hurt by his absence, naked in the bed in which we'd made repeated, uninhibited love. I pressed both hands to my pelvis, closing my eyes and reliving everything Marshall had made me feel in the last few days.

What should I do, oh God, what should I do?

My phone vibrated as though in response, a buzzing, censuring reprimand. Liam was calling again and I could sense his concern two states away. No more delaying. I pressed the icon to answer, my throat tight with guilt and the crushing weight of responsibility.

"Hey," I said, answering on the fifth or sixth ring.

"Ruthie, I've been so worried." Liam's familiar voice loomed in my ear and my stomach clenched.

"I'm fine. Everything is fine."

"You sound funny, are you sure you're all right?"

"Yes."

"I talked to Clint last night." I could picture Liam combing one hand through his blond hair, roughing it up as he did when agitated. I knew all of his mannerisms, down to his habit of chewing the skin around his thumbnail when he talked on the phone. "He told me about how Tish got married. Why didn't you call me? Are you *finally* coming home now?"

I drew a determined breath. "I'm sorry I didn't call you last night. I was just so tired." I closed my eyes and saw nothing but Marshall. I whispered, "Tish and Case got married in his hospital room in Bozeman. I'm so happy for her." Tears burned in my eyes and throat.

"I wish I could have been there," Liam said.

I curled around my stomach, ashamed; I recognized that even if I had the power to go back in time and prevent the past few days from occurring, I would not. I breathed shallowly, trying not to think about Marshall's tongue on every inch of my skin; trying not to think about his eyes and the way he tasted, the sensitivity and strength of his hands, of being enveloped in our passionate intensity. In time would that fire burn away, leaving me wrecked? As destroyed as Case's barn, charred and hollow and requiring massive rebuilding?

"Ruthie, are you there? We must have a bad connection."

"I'm here." My heart insisted, *Tell him. Do it, tell him the truth and be done with it.*

But I could not yet summon the wherewithal to annihilate him. Sunlight sifted across the bottom edge of the bed, golden and benign, seeming to promise renewal, but I could not rally my courage. "I'll call you later today," I promised, and hung up before Liam said another word.

A sudden knock on the door sent me jerking so hard the phone flew from my fingertips and clattered to the wooden floor. I scrambled beneath the tangled sheets, tugging them to my nose, still naked.

Wy called, "Ruthann! You awake? It's breakfast pretty quick here."

My nerves refused to settle. "I'll be down in a little while!"

"It'll get cold if you don't hurry," he pressed, not to be deterred.

"Buddy, leave her alone!" I heard someone call, probably from the foot of the stairs. It wasn't Marshall; maybe Quinn?

"Give me just a minute," I told Wy.

I realized I couldn't hide out in here in this bed that was full of the scent of Marshall, and of our lovemaking, but before I crept to the tiny attached bathroom I held the sheets to my nose and inhaled repeatedly, until I felt lightheaded. I showered, letting the steaming water turn my skin red. I pressed my palms flat to the wet tiles, then my forehead, reliving last night without letup, my stomach occupied by a thousand half-panicking birds.

What should I do, what should I do?

Oh God, what should I do?

What if you're pregnant?!

You're not pregnant. Stop freaking out.

What should I do…

I finished showering and wrapped in a towel, realizing I didn't have any clothes. I paced the room, growing ever agitated, but fortunately Marshall had realized the same thing; Wy knocked a minute later, calling, "Ruthie! Marsh gave me a shirt for you!"

I tightened the towel and stepped with damp toes to the door, easing it open.

Wy announced, "Room service!"

I said, "Thanks, buddy," and accepted the clean clothes. I still didn't have any panties and would have to wear my dirty jean shorts again, but Mom would be bringing my things today.

And she'll expect you to be ready to go home.

My heart and gut both twisted. Back in the bathroom, I slipped into my bra and inspected the new t-shirt, smiling despite everything as I read the maroon words printed on gray material: RAWLEY FAMILY REUNION, JALESVILLE, MT, 2008. I dressed and then stripped the bed, hearing activity from the direction of the kitchen, male voices talking and laughing, singing along with the radio; I could smell coffee and breakfast.

My internal radar was firing on all cylinders as I descended the stairs, zeroing immediately upon Marshall, who was dressed in faded jeans and a pale blue t-shirt, freshly shaved and hair still damp as he poured cream in his coffee. The air between us crackled and sparked. I felt blinded, lightning searing my retinas, everything else receding to the distance; Marshall's very presence was like an arrow fired between my ribs. With concentrated effort I tore my gaze from his because Clark was welcoming me to breakfast. The other sounds in the room rushed back to my ears – Wy laughing with Sean, Quinn asking his father when in the hell some insurance check he was waiting for would arrive. Marshall brought the coffee mug to his lips, watching me over the rim as he took a sip; his gray eyes were deep with unmistakable concern.

Someone stuck his head in the front door – Case's little brother, Gus Spicer – and hollered, "Wagons are rolling out, guys, c'mon!"

"The boys are heading to Case's," Clark explained. "I'll wait here with you, Ruthie, until Joelle arrives."

Sean, Quinn, and Wy grabbed travel mugs and surrounded me for farewell hugs; as far as they knew, I was leaving within the hour. Marshall moved more slowly but he was clearly heading out along with his brothers. I tried to continue breathing as he came near, unable to drag my eyes from him. Desperation rammed my breastbone. He paused at my side, resting gentle fingertips on my forearm; in the bustle of everyone heading for the door, he leaned close and asked, with as casual a tone as he could manage, "Will you walk me out?" There was a palpable undercurrent of distress flowing from him.

Yes, I said without sound.

Under the brilliant midday sun I was surprised to see an actual horse-drawn wagon waiting at the edge of the old barn, piled high with hay bales and upon which the guys were all climbing to hitch a ride – everyone except Marshall, who drew me to the side of the door and ignored his brothers, even though no one was paying attention to us.

Without preamble he said, "Dad just told me your mom is headed from Bozeman to pick you up. I feel like I'm dying, Ruthann, I can't breathe." His eyes were haunted, a hollowed-out gray as he stared down at me. "Tell me you're staying here."

He was holding my left elbow and I clutched his forearm with both hands.

"I *want* to stay here."

"Then stay," he implored, and my heart ached with each new beat. He ran his index finger over the word RAWLEY printed on my shirt. "I love seeing you in this shirt with my name on it…"

"You'll be at Case's?" I asked, wracked with tension.

"Just minutes away." Pain flinched across his face but he collected himself, requesting hoarsely, "Let me hold you, before I go."

Without hesitation I wrapped my arms around his waist and clung, pressing my cheek to his collarbones. My tears wet the neck of his blue shirt. Marshall crushed me closer and kissed my temple, and then he drew a ragged breath and stepped deliberately away. His eyes were wet and I could tell he was having just as much trouble as I was, holding it together. He swallowed hard and whispered, "Okay, then," and walked toward the wagon.

I stood motionless in the bright sunlight, arms folded and digging into my ribs, watching the distance between us increase. His brothers, loaded on the wagon, were staring unashamedly, mouths all but gaping, but I didn't care. Marshall paused at his truck to grab his cowboy hat from the driver's seat and as he settled it over his dark hair he looked back. Just seconds, and then he continued to the wagon.

I watched until it disappeared from sight along the dusty road.

Tish, I thought, spurred to furious motion. I dashed inside to find my phone, the door slamming behind me; Clark looked up from the paper he was reading.

"I have to call Tish!" I cried and flew back outside without further explanation; the dust stirred up by the grinding wagon wheels hadn't yet settled.

"Ruthie, I didn't even get to hug you good-bye!" Tish complained upon answering. She sounded tearful. "Mom and everyone left about an hour ago. God, it was so good having you guys here."

I blurted, "I'm staying in Jalesville!" And just like that, the decision was made.

"You are? That's wonderful!" Good old unflappable Tish. "I had a feeling you might! Is it because of Marshall?"

I whispered, "Yes. But also because I want to help you. I've missed you so much."

"I've missed you, too! Oh, this is such great news, Ruthie, I can't wait to tell Case. Speaking of that, have you told you-know-who?"

"Do you mean Mom or Liam?" I paced alongside the corral fence; three horses had emerged from the barn to bask in the morning sunshine and they studied me with curiosity, tails flicking.

"*Liam,* of course," Tish verified. "Shit, he's the one who's going to have a problem with this, not Mom. Well, maybe Mom a little…"

Cider stuck her long nose over the topmost beam of the fence and nickered, I cupped her square jaw with my free hand. "Your horse is letting me pet her. She's so pretty."

"Kiss her for me," Tish ordered. "I miss her so much! I can't wait to see everyone. How're the dogs? How's Buck? Is he healing up all right?"

"He is, the Rawleys are taking good care of all of them." I smiled just speaking their surname. Elation swelled in my chest. "I want to help you guys figure everything out." I damned it all and confessed, "I want to see Marshall. And there's something I need to tell you…"

"Did he kiss you?" Tish demanded and I stifled the urge to laugh. My sisters really did think I was completely innocent, at all times. She carried on, "I've known how much he likes you for a long time now and it wouldn't surprise me if he tried something. He must have. And you must have liked it."

Oh, had I ever liked it.

Deciding I didn't need to tell the whole truth to my lawyer sister at this second, I admitted, "He did kiss me." My cheeks scorched. "There was a lot of kissing."

Tish giggled. "I'm *so* happy. Call Mom and then call me back. And you can live with Case and me, for now."

"No," I said at once. "I mean, thank you for the offer, but I can't impose. I wouldn't do that to you. And Al offered me a job."

"Good, he said he intended to. I'll call him and tell him you're taking it."

"No, I can do that." My phone beeped; Mom was on the other end. I told Tish, "I'll call you back in a minute." I straightened my spine before answering my mother's call, gathering my resolve like bundles of scattered twigs.

"Hi, love." Mom sounded like her usual cheerful self. "We've left Bozeman, honey, and we're heading straight home. We'll be there to pick you up in less than an hour."

Her long nose near my waist, Cider made a companionable whickering sound, nudging my ribs. Wy's mare, Oreo, clomped to the fence to join us and the presence of the horses offered me comfort. "Mom, I'm going to stay in Montana."

There was a pause. "Wait, did you say you want to stay in Montana?"

"I did, Mom." Exhilaration sang in my blood; I was doing something for myself for once.

"But how in the world will you get home?"

"I can always buy a plane ticket, later," I hedged. "Will you come and drop off my things at Clark's? I'm out of clean clothes to wear."

"Ruthann, hold on a second. How long are you planning to stay?" Mom sounded as though she'd forgotten I was no longer twelve years old.

"I'm not entirely sure. I promise I'm not going crazy. I really miss Tish. I want to live close to her again. I want to be somewhere new. Al offered me a job here." I paused, hearing Camille and Clint in the background. I implored, "Mom, you understand, don't you?"

I pictured my mother's beautiful face; I'd never doubted her love or devotion. I did, however, doubt her capability to regard me as a grown woman, able to make decisions without first consulting her.

"But what about your things?" Mom asked, and I heard notes of both confusion and doubt.

"I have everything I packed for the trip here. Can you mail me a box with the rest of my clothes?"

It wasn't like I owned much, anyway; I didn't even have my own car back in Landon. When it came down to it, my life revolved primarily around other people – the family I dearly loved, but who struggled to see me as anything but sweet Ruthann, always there when needed. Whether it was to pick up a shift at the cafe or watch the kids, I was the one they depended upon. It wasn't that I begrudged this fact, not truly, but it was frustrating.

"But, honey…" Mom sounded at a loss.

"Jo, let her be," I heard Aunt Jilly say. "Ruthie needs a change of scenery." She raised her voice. "Ruthann, do what you need to do. We'll send your things to you, babe."

"What about Liam?" Clint sounded mystified. "Let me talk to her."

Mom passed him the phone and a second later my cousin's familiar voice was in my ear. "Ruthie, what's up? Have you talked to him today? He thinks you're coming home. Did you guys…did you guys break up?"

"I'll see you in a little while." I was unwilling to answer any more questions.

"I think you should probably call him," Clint insisted.

"I will," I promised, and hung up. My blood burned swift in my veins as I stared up at the bluest of blue Montana skies. I let my phone fall to the earth. I hugged Cider's neck, with pure, bubbling joy. With a growing sense of excitement, I announced, "I'm staying here, girl. *I'm staying in Jalesville.*"

Oreo nickered and delicately side-stepped as another horse ventured from the barn. Arrow was gorgeous in the sunlight, watching me but not advancing to the corral fence. I studied the beautiful animal; he was almost exactly the color of Marshall's eyes.

"I have to tell him," I said aloud, heart clattering. Though I'd never ridden before, I addressed Marshall's horse. "Maybe we can ride over there right now! What do you say, boy?"

Arrow snorted as if he understood, pawing the ground, wide nostrils flaring. Behind me, the front door to the house opened.

"Ruthie, hon, is everything all right out here?" Clark asked.

When I turned around my smile was so wide that Clark's brows lifted and he smiled in response. I flew to wrap my arms around Marshall's father's waist; my voice muffled by his worn work shirt, I murmured, "It is now."

Becky drove me into town after Mom, Aunt Jilly, Camille, and Clinty had dropped off my things and resumed their drive home to Minnesota – Mom was tearful and Clint remained confused, but Aunt Jilly and Camille understood, I knew, even without words. Camille studied my eyes and smiled as she tucked hair behind my ears; she whispered, "Keep me posted on what's going on here, promise?"

Aunt Jilly gathered me close and her soft voice in my ear gave me a shiver. "He's the one for you, love, I can tell. Don't let anyone tell you otherwise."

Marshall Augustus Rawley.

I wanted to text him, call him, ride one of the horses over to the barn where they were all working to tell him I was staying – but I was determined to accomplish a few things first.

As we drove to Jalesville, baby Tommy in his car seat, Becky said, "I'm so glad you decided to stay. If you'd only seen the way Marsh pined for you when we visited Landon that summer. We'd get back to the Angler's Inn in the evenings and he'd sit out on the balcony porch and just stare into space. I know he comes across like nothing bothers him, but he's pretty tenderhearted beneath it all. I'm not saying he's any saint, and I know because I've known him forever, but if you could see the difference in him now that you're here. It's significant."

"I wish he would have told me how he felt back then." I recalled that particular July, imagining Marshall at the familiar hotel in my home-town. The thought made me all the more determined to get my arms around him – which I intended to as soon as I secured my job and a place to live. And it occurred to me that I needed birth control pills as soon as humanly possible.

I admitted to Becky, "I had no idea that summer. But he *did* try to show me. He just used the wrong tactics."

Becky giggled. "Garth tried to tell him the junior high routine was *not* a good plan. Poor Marsh was so jealous of that big blond guy you were dating. But you're here now and that's what really matters. I can tell really you like him and it makes me so glad, Ruthie. Garth said the same thing after he saw how the two of you acted around each other at Case's. We got home that night and he said, 'Yeah, they've got it bad for each other.'"

Our first stop was Howe and James, Attorneys-At-Law, where we found Al out front on this early Monday morning, scraping paint from the window with a flat-edged tool. As Becky parked, Al jogged to the passenger door. Opening it, he heralded, "Good morning, ladies! I just heard the good news! Tish called to tell me Jalesville has a new resident."

"Hi, Al," Becky said. "Isn't it exciting?"

"I would like to accept the job," I said, attempting to use my most formal tone.

"In person, no less." Al beamed. "I couldn't be happier, nor could your sister. Tish also said you need a place to stay. Just so happens one of my rental properties is across the street, above Trudy's Diner."

I should have known Tish would be unable to contain my news. "That would be wonderful, thank you. I don't really have many things…"

"That's for the best because the place is miniscule. We'll get you squared away with some furniture." Al put me immediately at ease; he seemed the type to confront challenges with nothing but calm. He gestured at the front window of the law office. "I'm just readying the glass for a new paint job. *Attorneys Howe and Spicer*, from this day forth. I thought Tish might appreciate her new name front and center. Come along, my dear, I'll give you a quick tour."

Inside the office it smelled pleasant, of books and ink and coffee; I recognized Tish's things on the desk to the right of the entrance, near the wide front window. An elderly woman with carnation-pink glasses and matching lipstick gathered up my hands. "I'm Mary Stapleton, dear. I was just your age when I started here. What a darling you are. Look at those curls. I would have known you for Patty's little sister anywhere."

Patty? I wondered. "Thank you, ma'am."

"Let's say Wednesday?" Al asked. "You can use these two days to get settled and then Mary can show you the ropes."

Al dug keys from his desk drawer and led us across the street to the diner, where we followed him up an outdoor flight of wooden steps to a narrow landing on the back of the two-story building. The apartment entrance faced a tiny parking lot; the town of Jalesville, roughly the same size as Landon, stretched beyond that. In the distance the foothill country shone under the vivid sun in hues of brown from honey to walnut. A sudden shiver along the spine, a cold pulse of energy, caught me unaware; I had the odd feeling that if I'd looked a second faster I would have spied someone out there in the distance, watching us.

"As you can see, it's rather cramped," Al said, guiding us inside, and I followed, grateful for the distraction. The space consisted of a living room, a kitchen, a bathroom with a shower stall, and a bedroom in which I could probably touch all four walls at once. "But it's a good price and it will be all yours."

"I don't care that it's tiny. It's perfect, thank you so much, Al." I addressed Marshall's nephew, who peered at me over Becky's shoulder. "What do you think, little guy?"

Becky bounced her son and responded, "He thinks you'll love getting to decorate without anyone else's suggestions." She giggled. "C'mon, I hear Trudy's truck. We'll go ask her for some cleaning supplies and scrub up that cute little kitchen, what do you say?"

Al made sure the electricity was on and the water running, gave me two keys to the front door, and then returned across the street to the law office while Becky and I worked together cleaning my new apartment. I enjoyed Becky's easygoing company; it was like having one of my sisters in the room.

I told her, "I'm dying to see Marshall. He doesn't even know I'm staying yet."

"I don't have my phone or we could call him," Becky said. "I don't know Marsh's number by heart. Stupid cell phones. You don't have to memorize anyone's number anymore! I could recite all my friends' numbers when I was a kid and now I don't even know my own brother-in-law's."

I paused in my industrious scrubbing. "Would you mind driving me out there after we're done here?"

"Sure thing, Ruthie. I'm going to run downstairs to Trudy's and grab a couple of muffins before we go. I'm starved. You want anything?"

"No, thank you." There was something else I needed to do before we left, without chickening out; my stomach was in tangles at the thought of talking to Liam but I could not be such a coward. Left alone in my new apartment, still marveling that I had a place to call such, I walked to the window above the sink, bare feet dragging, and braced my hips against the creamy-white counter. I knew I was doing the right thing but my heart shrank into a nervous, regretful ball at the thought of hurting Liam.

It would be far worse to stay in a relationship that isn't right.
You know this, Ruthann.

The problem was, Liam didn't know. Nor would he share this opinion.

I scrolled to his name and pushed the icon to call him, my chest hot with nervous tentacles. He would probably be at work; I was afraid he wouldn't answer and I would not under any circumstances leave a message to tell him the news.

"Ruthie, where are you?" Liam answered on the very first ring and I realized I had Clint to thank for his accusatory tone; my cousin had obviously called ahead.

"Hi." My voice was thick. Without relenting to the urge to stall, I said, "Liam, I'm staying in Montana. I decided to stay out here and help Tish."

"Without calling me first? Had you already decided this when we talked this morning?" Liam sounded livid, at least as livid as he was capable. He cried, "When were you planning to tell me?"

I cupped my forehead, grinding my teeth. "I decided I need a break. I'm so sorry, Liam. I need a change. From Landon and from–"

"From me, just say it," he challenged, the words grating in his throat. "You need a break from *me*."

"I'm so sorry. I can't be your girlfriend anymore. Please understand…"

"Understand *what*, exactly? Out of *nowhere* you decide this? Clint said you just up and decided to stay there, with no warning. This isn't like you at all, Ruthie. Your mom is devastated."

"She's not devastated," I disagreed. "Clint is exaggerating."

"What about me?" Liam whispered. "*I'm* devastated. I don't understand this one goddamn bit."

My chest clenched to hear him restraining tears. He never cried, never cursed.

"I'm so sorry." I knew it was meaningless to keep saying so, but I was at a loss.

"I love you, Ruthann." He was choked up. "Just tell me when you're coming home."

"I don't know."

"But I *love you*," he pressed.

"I have to go," I whispered.

"This is bullshit!" he yelled.

"I'm so sorry to hurt you." And I hung up.

I released a tense, painful breath. I heard Becky climbing the back steps. She called, "You ready, hon? I got us each a blueberry muffin."

You did the right thing. You did something that you should have done a long time ago.

It was shitty to spring it on him like that.

But would it be better to let him think differently?

No. Truth is better every time.

And the truth is Marshall. It's always been Marshall.

You just had to realize it.

The intensity of my need to see him grew to bursting, even as the goody-two-shoes part of my mind kicked in with reproachful vengeance —*You need to get back on birth control before anything else.*

No touching until then.

But…

None, Ruthann.

I want Marshall to court me. The old-fashioned word resonated in my heart. *I want that so much.*

I locked up my new place and Becky drove us through town, out over the gravel roads to Case's new barn, where the crew was working in the deep golden gilt of the summer afternoon. I spotted Marshall instantly, perched up high on a ladder; he wore his black hat and his faded jeans with the rip in the left knee, his pale t-shirt darkened now, with sweat. He looked over his shoulder and seemed in that moment suspended against the blue sweep of the big sky behind him, perfectly silhouetted, watching as I flew from Becky's car. This picture of him would remain etched in my mind, of Marshall waiting for me to come to him.

Later in my life, when missing him threatened to wrench apart my soul, I would find this picture in my memory, Marshall stark against the cloudless Montana sky on the day I told him I was staying.

He sprang to motion, hurrying down the ladder and sprinting across the yard, and I leaped into his embrace; he caught me halfway between the barn and the gravel road, lifting me straight off the ground; I felt the tremor that passed through his body. We were both breathing hard. His hat fell off and rolled away. Against my neck he rejoiced, "*You stayed.*"

I laughed a little, happy tears gathering. He heard me sniffle and sought my eyes; his expression was of terror. "Tell me you're staying."

"Come here," I ordered, half laughing, half choked up. I stroked the hair falling along the sides of his forehead and then gripped his ears, for emphasis. "I'm staying here. Don't make me flick you."

"I'm shaking," he said, and he was. "That's not very manly of me, but

I don't give a shit. I've been so scared all day I couldn't think of anything else. I couldn't eat. I'm weak with hunger. But I'm so goddamn happy right now, I can't even explain in words."

"So am I, oh Marshall, so am I."

I hugged him close, kissing his jaw, his ear, the side of his forehead, all with exuberant joy. Marshall let my feet slide back to the ground and kissed my lips, a soft, worshipful kiss that spoke of his extreme relief, and then rested his forehead to mine. The sunlight struck our faces, glinting in our eyes, which were already dazzled by each other.

"I had a plan all set if you decided to go back to Minnesota," he confessed. "I was planning to pack up my truck and come after you. Steal you away."

"You were?" I whispered, overcome with emotion, with the sight of his eyes and the scent of him, the feel of his arms encircling me. This was why I had stayed here. This man.

"Of course I was."

"I couldn't have left, not after last night." I stroked my thumbs over the angles of his cheekbones. "Not after this morning."

"I was scared, though," he whispered. "I was so scared today."

"I should have called you right away but I needed to get some things figured out first. Plus, I don't have your number." I kissed his chin just as he went to kiss my lips, and we clocked noses.

"Did you?" he murmured, kissing my nose, rocking us side to side. "Get some things figured out?"

"Yes. I have a job and an apartment, courtesy of Al. It's tiny but I don't mind. I told Tish I'll stay at the trailer until she and Case get home. Becky is helping me to round up some furniture. Mom is going to send the rest of my clothes." I admitted, "I'm exhausted."

"I'm bringing you home right this second and we'll have supper and sit by the fire." He curled both hands around my loose, tangled hair, gathering it at the nape of my neck. "I'm going to play songs for you all night. I'm going to sing for you, my sweet angel-woman."

"That sounds so wonderful. But, Marshall…" I drew a fortifying breath, not sure if I could go through with this or not. I reminded myself

I'd decided to stick to my guns. I explained, "I want us to take things slow. No touching until I can get on birth control here, at the very least."

Because we remained wrapped together as I spoke, it seemed a very idle threat. Marshall tightened his arms and grinned. "Starting when, exactly, with the no touching?"

"Soon," I whispered, but our lips were only a breath apart.

"I just want you here," he said seriously, all teasing vanishing from his face. He removed his touch and stepped back one careful pace. "If that means I can't touch you for now, then I promise I won't. I respect your wishes."

I was already unduly cold and empty without his arms. I insisted, "But I want to see you every day. Every evening. I want…" I implored him with my eyes, begging him to understand.

He whispered, "Me to court you."

That he recognized this brought tears surging. He had even used the same word. He knew, *he saw*. Marshall saw me. A lump grew in my throat. "Yes, that's it. That's it exactly."

He dropped to one knee with characteristic grace and brought my knuckles to his mouth. His lips were warm and soft and I knew what they were capable of upon my skin, as my rushing bloodstream attested. He whispered, "Because you are a lady."

From the direction of the barn there arose a flurry of whooping and clapping – my gaze darted that way to spy everyone watching us with rapt and undivided attention. I giggled and Marshall surged to his feet and scooped me in an exuberant embrace, spinning us in circles. He said in my ear, "I'll stop touching in just a second, I promise." To everyone observing he yelled, "C'mon guys, let's finish up! We're celebrating tonight!"

Chapter Twelve

AT THE RAWLEYS' HOUSE HOURS LATER, I WAS BUNDLED IN a thick sweater of Marshall's, a pair of my own jeans and fuzzy wool socks (also courtesy of Marshall), curled up in a lawn chair. The merriment around the bonfire was infectious and riotous. It was what Clark called a full house, all of his boys and their womenfolk crowded around, with the exception of Case and Tish, who wouldn't be home until tomorrow. There were either musical instruments or beer cans in everyone's hands. Wy, on my left, played his harmonica, staying on pitch with the little instrument as Garth and Marshall strummed tune after tune, everyone singing.

I felt sure that happiness radiated from me like rays of dawning sunshine. I could not deny this truth, even as the thought of Liam stung like a jagged cut at the back of my mind. I tried to soothe this ache, reminding myself it was far worse to continue a relationship that wasn't right for either Liam or me; the worst part was the knowledge that while I felt this way, Liam did not. He loved me, as he'd reminded me this very afternoon, and had not seen this coming.

Why does it have to be this way – why do I have to hurt someone, no matter what choice I make?

But I was honest enough to acknowledge if I had to hurt Liam to be with Marshall, I would make that choice every time.

My gaze was never far from him; Marshall was absolutely giddy, his gray eyes alighting on my face time and again, unable to keep from smiling. He had remained every inch a gentleman through dinner, withdrawing my chair at the table, not so much as brushing his finger-tips on my hand. And yet the heat that flowed between us required no physical contact for us to feel the impact of its intensity.

It would be far more cowardly to go home and refuse to acknowledge what's between you and Marshall. You belong here.

At dinner Marshall had explained to his family we were now court-ing, which was met with general enthusiasm and much teasing.

Wy cried, "Can I *finally* tell Ruthann how much you like her?"

"It's about damn time," Garth said, with a grin.

Sean agreed, "I'll second that!"

"Your mother was Ruthie's age when we got married," Clark said, soft with remembrance. "I knew I would marry Faye from the moment I clapped eyes on her." He indicated Marshall. "My boy has had his heart set on you for a long, long time now, little Ruthie, and it makes me so happy to see the two of you together at the table."

I thanked Clark and violated my own rule by linking my fingers through Marshall's; he enfolded my hand within his.

Becky said, "Marsh, you better count your blessings," to which Marshall responded, "Believe me, I am."

Much later Marshall drove me over the gravel roads to the trailer; we were accompanied not only by Mutt and Tiny, Case's dogs, but also two of the Rawleys' labs, intimidating animals with deep-voiced barks that suggested they were more than willing to take chunks from any intruder; all four dogs were going to stay with me, at Marshall's insistence, as he was not too fond of my lack of proper protection.

"If there's any noise within a hundred yards, these guys will go nuts and then you'll call 911 and then me, in that order," he said, as the dogs bounded from the truck bed and galloped around the yard.

We'd reached the trailer and Marshall's truck was idling. I was having acute difficulty recalling my self-imposed no-touching rule, given that just over twenty-four hours ago we had been touching and then some, right inside the trailer.

"I will," I promised. "If I was scared I wouldn't stay here alone."

"I'm so happy you stayed, angel. I can't describe how happy I am, because it wouldn't come close to being descriptive enough."

"Marshall Augustus Rawley." I loved the sound of his full name. "I'm so happy too. Because of *you*."

He took my left hand in his right and brought it to his face. He closed his eyes and kissed my palm and I couldn't contain a small sound, it felt so good. His lips lingered on my skin and I was about to lean over and wrap my arms around him when he opened his eyes and kissed my knuckles before releasing hold. I sensed his desire to respect my wishes about taking things slow.

"Will you be out here in the morning?" I asked.

"Wild horses couldn't stop me." Our eyes held fast, anchored to each other. "And tomorrow night...wait." He resituated position on the seat and started over. There was not one hint of teasing in his voice as he asked, with formal intonation, "May I pick you up for dinner at six?"

"Yes," I whispered.

He grinned. "Let me get these guys rounded up for you. And then I'll go."

Out under the night sky, Marshall yelled for the dogs. When they raced up to us, wiggling with pure joy at the attention, he made them sit and then said in a no-nonsense tone, "Guys, you watch over Ruthann tonight. I'm trusting you. If anything happens to her, if she gets so much as a splinter, I'm holding you all personally responsible." All four animals listened, their eyes bright in the moonlight, tongues hanging as they panted. He informed them, "This woman is my sweet angel and I'm dying to touch her right now, truly dying, you guys, to kiss her soft mouth and taste her, and feel her hands in my hair and her breasts against my chest..."

I started giggling at this heartfelt speech while the dogs continued watching Marshall, rapt with attention.

Marshall went on addressing them. "I respect that we're taking things slow. Maybe you guys don't believe me, but I *promise* I do. However, it doesn't change the fact that I want to touch her so much I actually am in some physical pain right now. But I'm courting this woman and I have resolved to keep from caressing her beautiful angel face and her sweet, luscious, curvy body until I am begged to do so…oh *Jesus*…"

"*Marshall*," I chastised, laughing too hard to flick him.

He kept talking to the dogs, concluding, "And so I'll say good-night and force myself to leave, and remind you all again to watch over her with your lives. I'm dead-fucking-serious, guys."

He looked at me then and he was so handsome and sweetly adorable, teasing me and yet completely serious at the same time. Still giggling, I stood on tiptoe and hugged him with all my strength. "Thank you for the compliments, by the way."

"I'm shaking again," he said, as I drew away. "Thank you for the hug. It'll help me through the night." He drew a deep breath. "Until tomorrow, then."

"Goodnight," I whispered as he headed for his truck.

Marshall opened the driver's side door but didn't climb inside. "Make sure you get in all right. I won't head out until you do."

I unlocked the door with no trouble and ventured inside, along with four excited dogs, clicking on the light above the stove; its particular tint and the sight of the couch made my stomach woozy with vivid remembrance of what we'd done there.

Willpower, Ruthann.

I returned to the screen door and blew him a kiss.

Thirty minutes later I was curled up on the couch in pajama pants and one of my M. RAWLEY t-shirts (Marshall had gifted me with about a dozen of them, at my request), squeaky-clean from a scalding shower, eating straight from a jar of fudge sauce I'd found in the cupboard. I knew I could have slept in Tish's bed but I wanted to be on the couch, where I was inundated with the sense of Marshall.

You're here! You're really here.

You did something brave and listened to your own heart for once.

"I wish Marshall was here," I confessed to the dogs. Three of them sprawled on the living room rug while the fourth, Bender, stretched out on the cooler kitchen floor; their heads lifted at my words, ears perking. Gesturing with my spoon, I continued, "We're courting. Isn't that romantic? Even the word 'courting' is romantic. I wonder what he's doing right now."

I jammed the spoon in the fudge jar and set it aside so I could grab my phone. I knew I could not be so fickle as to text Marshall that I wanted him to come back to the trailer immediately (even though I knew he would and that we would be naked and wrapped together in probably less than five minutes) so instead I scrolled to his name and the number he'd given me earlier and texted, *I can't wait for tomorrow.*

I'm glad. You're not the only one, he responded less than a minute later, and I smiled, wide and warm, curling up with the phone.

The dogs are keeping me company. They said to tell you hi.

Remind them they better be protecting you or else.

They are. I wish you were here.

I wish so too.

But thank you for understanding everything.

You know I understand. I can't help wanting to touch you but I am capable of holding back. At least a little.

I wrote, *XOXOXOXO.*

He texted back, *XXXX. And you know right where.*

Kisses or hugs? Which is which?

X = kisses. X marks the spot. XXXXX.

I love your kisses.

I'm the happiest man alive, he responded, and I imagined him reaching over to the nearest wooden surface to knock his knuckles upon it.

I can't stop thinking about you.

He wrote back instantly, *I'm so glad. And likewise.*

I called him then, needing to hear his voice, and he answered on the first ring. "Hey there. I was just about to call you."

"I'm lying here on the couch and thinking about everything that's happened today."

"I'm sitting on the back porch and wishing we were stargazing together. It's so beautiful out. Tomorrow night we'll do a little stargazing." He paused and acknowledged softly, "It's been a hell of a day for you, hasn't it? We didn't really get a chance to talk alone since dinner. You said you talked to Liam. How did that go?"

I sensed his concern, the careful way he asked the question. I admitted, "He was shocked. And he was sad, Marshall, I can't deny that. He was so sad, and I hate that. It's my punishment, I suppose, to know I hurt him. That hurts me. I mean, I'm not fishing for sympathy, it just does."

"I know, angel, I didn't think that at all. I wish it didn't have to be that way, I really do."

"I've known for a long time Liam and I should go our separate ways." I stretched flat on the couch and propped my bare feet on the back cushions. "I first knew when he started talking about marriage and instead of feeling excited, I just felt empty. But everyone expected us to get married." I sighed and reflected, "That's the downside of small towns. People have expectations of you that are hard to shake."

"I know exactly what you mean. Families do the same thing. Your family is one of the most loving I know and they still have a view of you that isn't totally accurate. I can see that."

"You're right. I love them all so much and I know they love me, but they don't completely see me. I mean, I'm sure I don't see them exactly as they are, either."

"That's a good point. You kinda get into a role in your family. Like in mine, we pick on each other so much I forget that my brothers are grown men, good, decent men who have adult concerns. I just tend to see the same guys I've fought with and beat on, and who've beat on me my entire life."

"I love being around your family. Your dad is such a sweetheart. He loves your mom so much, even still."

"He does," Marshall agreed softly. "When he was talking about courting her this evening, you can tell it's like yesterday for him. He lets himself be content with memories and won't move on. It's not healthy, but I get it. She was the one for him, the only one."

"I'd like to see a picture of her. I feel like I know her a little, from what you've told me, but I want to know so much more. I'm so sorry you guys lost her. You were so young."

"It'll never completely stop hurting, I realized that a long time ago. But at least I was old enough that I can remember her pretty well. Wy was so young, he doesn't have the memories of her that the rest of us do. She was part of my life until I was nearly an adult and I will forever be grateful. I had her for eighteen years and two days."

"It's so good to talk to you," I whispered. "I love flirting with you, and teasing you, but just to talk…"

"And know that I can be serious?" I could tell he was smiling.

"I knew you could be serious. And it's what I need right now. But I also love that you tease me, that you…play with me. I'm not up on some pedestal with you."

"It doesn't mean I don't worship the ground at your feet. Because I do. But I know what you mean. I'll treat you like a woman. And a lady. And a sweet angel. You are all of those things, and so much more."

"Marshall," I whispered, overcome with emotion.

"I'm right here," he said, and my belly went weightless at the tone of his voice.

"I'm so glad," I whispered. Bender lumbered over from the kitchen and began licking the jar of chocolate sauce; when I snatched it away the big lab climbed onto the couch, nudging me aside with his nose to steal a better position on the cushions.

"Bender just climbed up here with me. I think he thinks he's smaller than he is."

"He's a lover. He'll manipulate you into petting him all night. Now I'm jealous as *hell*…"

"Oh man, here comes Howler," I said, giggling; the second lab discovered a dollop of fudge on my shirt and began licking industriously, resting an enormous paw on my belly. It tickled; I was laughing as I scolded, "No, *get down!*"

Just that fast all four dogs sprang to alert, noses lifted to sniff at the air. Their sudden wild barking caused my heart to stop and Marshall to demand, "What is it? Ruthann, what's wrong?"

I flew to the screen door to spy a car approaching. It took a second to realize it was my sister; I wilted against the door frame, with relief. "It's all right, it's just Tish driving up."

"*Jesus*," he breathed. "I'm having a heart attack. I'm halfway to the truck. It's just Tish?"

"Yes, she's parking right now. I'm surprised she didn't call." I let the dogs out and they mobbed my sister as she climbed from her Honda.

"I'll let you go then. I'll see you first thing in the morning."

I whispered, "Good-night, sweetheart," overwhelmed by the desire to lavish upon him every tender endearment I knew.

He marveled, "You called me 'sweetheart.' My knees just went weak. You think I'm kidding, but I'm not."

Tish spied me at the screen door. "Hi, Ruthie! Get off the phone, I have to talk to you!"

Using his words, I told Marshall, "Until tomorrow, then."

"I'm counting the seconds, angel."

Tish bent down, hugging the dogs as they licked her face. "I'm sorry I didn't call! I was *so* excited to get home. Gus and Lacy brought my car to Bozeman."

I jogged to her and she stood to hug me. Rocking side to side we clung, gathering strength from one another. At last Tish murmured, with awe in her voice, "Look at that."

She was facing the barn. Even in the dark it was an impressive sight. The work accomplished over the week was a testament to the love of the Rawleys and others who cared deeply about Case and my sister.

"I can't believe it, I just can't believe it…" Tears streamed over Tish's face, wetting my neck.

"We've been working hard," I murmured, keeping my arms tight around her. "Isn't it wonderful?"

"I have such a horrible picture in my mind, Ruthie, of that night. Of our barn burning and Case running back in there…"

"Get rid of that picture. Let it go away forever."

She heaved a shuddering sigh, wilting against me. "I'm so glad you're here."

"Same here, you don't even know. Can I help you carry anything inside?"

"No, I don't have much. I'm going back right away in the morning. I just wanted to come home and shower and change, and grab Case some new clothes. I'm so glad to see Mutt and Tiny." She crouched down again, hugging them close. "*And* Bender and Howler? Protection, right?"

"Yes. Marshall brought them over when he dropped me off."

Tish regarded my shirt as she rose slowly to her feet. "I see you're wearing his clothes. *Hmmm.*"

I giggled, insisting, "We're taking things slowly."

"Uh-*huh.*" Of course my older sister saw straight through me. "I don't know if taking it slow will help. I mean, the way Marshall looks at you is probably enough to get you pregnant anyway. C'mon, let's go talk."

Tish marveled at the spotless appearance of her place; once she'd showered and changed into clean pajamas we sat together at the table in the quiet kitchen, the glass jar of wildflowers centered between our hands. I opened two beers and we sipped with pleasure; beer always brought Shore Leave to mind, its yeasty scent as deeply ingrained as fried fish and perking coffee.

Tish fixed her blue eyes on me. "Let's hear it."

I traced a fingertip along the phlox blossoms in the jar, sending pale petals drifting to the tabletop like sweetly-scented snow, avoiding her gaze.

She smiled. "I *knew* it."

"Knew what?" I demanded, but my scorching cheeks were a dead giveaway.

Tish lifted her right eyebrow, a perfect, ironic arch.

"He's so…he's just so…" My face was a thousand degrees.

Tish giggled, teasing softly, "Way to *go*, Marsh."

"I never knew it could be this way." I caught hold of her free hand and squeezed, and her amused expression dissolved. "I feel like I've been going day to day with my eyes closed, until this past week. He *sees* me, Tish, Marshall sees who I am. Making love with him was so…it was just so beautiful it's hard to put into words."

"He's in love with you," she whispered, returning the gentle pressure on my hand. "This place is where we're supposed to be. I've felt that since I first arrived in Jalesville and now you understand it, too. We belong here with Case and Marshall. They've been waiting for us for so long now."

Her words triggered a jolting shiver, an acknowledgment of something deep in my bones; maybe it had always been there, dormant, awaiting the moment of recognition. Tears blurred my view of Tish's face. I whispered, "But they've been waiting longer than we know." I struggled to explain what I meant. "It's almost like…"

"They've been waiting beyond this lifetime," she finished quietly.

I nodded.

"Camille and I were talking about it before she left," Tish said and her eyes caught fire, burning anew with sincerity and determination. "Aunt Jilly said we have to understand something from the past. But… *what*? And how would it help us *now*, with all the things we need to understand in the present? Oh God, Ruthie, there's so much I don't know." Tish scrubbed both hands through her hair. "Al said he hasn't seen Derrick since before the fire, like he's laying low. Not that Derrick would willingly divulge anything, but last month he wanted to tell me something. He said I was in danger if I stayed around here, in those exact words, and he was right. I have to figure out what he knows, how to get answers from him." She paused to take a long swallow of beer. "The fire was ruled as accidental, did Marsh tell you?"

"Yes. So where does that leave us?"

Tish straightened her spine and I was relieved to observe her usual resolve settle around her. "I have a few ideas. First, finding a way to approach Derrick. I can't just stalk him down and demand answers. He's on guard. He has to know I suspect he's responsible for the fire. Maybe the better question is did Derrick act on his own? Or did Ron Turnbull contact him that night?"

"What are they trying so hard to hide?"

"That's exactly what we have to find out. Tomorrow, I'm making a list of what we know and what we need to discover. I'm too damn exhausted to write lists right now."

I voiced one of my worst fears. "Do you think whoever started the fire will be back?"

Tish gritted her teeth; her cheekbones appeared hollow as she fought for control. "We have to assume it's a possibility. Oh God, Ruthie... does Derrick despise me enough to figure Case would be the one to run into a burning barn to save our animals, that there was a good chance he would die? That's exactly what *would* have happened if I hadn't followed him..."

"We'll figure this out, I swear," I promised, alarmed by the terror in her eyes. "We will."

Tish nodded slowly, gaze fixed on a point beyond my shoulder; I knew she wasn't seeing the inside of the trailer. At long last she murmured, "I almost forgot. Camille gave me a couple of old letters before they left for Minnesota and I haven't had a chance to read them yet. I don't know if they'll help, but it's a place to start..."

"You mean the ones Una Spicer wrote to Malcolm Carter?" I interrupted. "I was just talking about those with her at the Carters' house the other night, but I didn't get a chance to read them."

"They're right over here..." Tish found her purse and extracted several pieces of paper, tucked carefully between the pages of a cookbook. She explained, "Camille didn't want them to get ruined."

"These are from...1882." I peered at the date as Tish gently unfolded the first letter. "Wow. Look at that cursive handwriting. It's so perfect."

"These are from Cole Spicer's mother to Malcolm," Tish said, scanning the letter as she spoke. "The Spicers have been here in Montana since the 1880s, along with the Rawleys. What Case and I have pieced together, with help from Clark, is that their two families knew one another and in turn knew the Carters, who might have known *our* family, back in Minnesota."

"Isn't that wild? Camille was so happy to learn Malcolm was still alive in 1882." It had been an old photograph of Mathias's ancestor, Malcolm Carter, tucked in a trunk in our grandmother's attic, which initially led Camille on the path to discover more about him.

"Malcolm was in communication with Una Spicer that spring. Case's family is descended from Una and her husband, Henry. Clark told us so few documents exist from those days that he doesn't know the names of most of the original Rawleys in Montana, other than his great-something grandfather, Grantley, and another brother, Miles, who died young."

My brow furrowed with concentration, my eyes roving the cursive words on the yellowing paper as I peered over Tish's shoulder; she was still talking.

"I want to see if Una mentions Cole. Here, you take this one, Ruthie, see if anything stands out."

The letter she passed to me was dated Sunday, May 14, 1882 and the greeting contained a name I already knew – *Dearest Malcolm, We received your latest letter with feelings of great relief.*

"What a treasure these are," I mused, smoothing the paper with a reverent touch. As I did, I swore I could see Una Spicer; overwhelmed by the strange sensation, I squinted, leaning forward to watch as she bent over the very letter now before me, pausing in the middle of a sentence because her neck ached. She rolled her head side to side before resuming her writing.

I heard a sound – the echo of distant wind, growing stronger –

I yanked my fingertips from the page.

Tish looked up. "What is it?"

"Nothing," I mumbled, distracted by a particular word further down the page; it took me a moment to realize in what context Una was using it as I read her words – *I harbor such concern for the marshal. I have from the first. He is a kind and capable man but there exists a deep chasm of sadness in him. His circumstance is so lonely and I find it terribly disconcerting how closely he resembles our dear, lost Miles. When he and the boys play that old fiddle Henry lent them, I find it nearly too haunting to bear.*

I touched the word 'marshal', unduly troubled; I understood Una Spicer was referring to a lawman from her own century, not *my* Marshall–

Why, then, did desolation seep into my heart?

Why did I feel such concern over a man I'd never known? A man with a deep chasm of sadness, *who played his fiddle...*

"The marshal," I whispered, studying this word on the page; the word appeared to grow darker, rising to meet my fingertips, and I pushed back from the table. My chair clattered to the floor but the entire kitchen suddenly seemed very far away –

The marshal…

"Ruthie!"

Tish called to me from the other side of a windswept prairie.

He's in danger, I whispered.

I was only vaguely aware of Tish grabbing me around the waist. The dogs were going crazy. Tish's arms kept going, like scissor blades through gauze, closing around nothing more than empty air. My skull hummed and the world disappeared in a single blink.

Chapter Thirteen

SOMETIME LATER – OR MAYBE JUST SECONDS, I HAD NO sense of time – my eyes opened to find Tish hovered over me, tearful and stricken, reduced to babbling. "*Oh my God*, you scared me to death. Ruthie, are you all right? Oh God, what just happened? I don't know what in the hell just happened…"

I clenched hold of her forearms. She felt solid and substantial, and I craved reassurance that I was actually still here in the trailer, in one piece. For a second, I hadn't been. I'd been…somewhere else entirely.

Tish. My lips moved but I couldn't manage words.

She enclosed me in her embrace and I clung; wracking shivers claimed my legs. Her voice wobbled. "Ruthie, I could hardly believe my eyes. I swear you started to…this sounds *so insane*…I swear you started to *disappear*. I grabbed you and then you…then you *came back*…"

I tried to shake my head, wanting to deny it. I croaked, "I just need to rest…"

What I needed was Marshall but I didn't know how to explain to him what had just happened without running the risk of sounding crazy. I wanted to believe my senses were wrong, that I was so tired I'd misunderstood. There was no way I'd "disappeared" from the kitchen; things like that simply weren't possible.

Marshall would want to know you're in distress. You know this.

Tish held me until my trembling subsided. Drawing away, she put her hands on my face and an understanding passed between us, with no words; we would not discuss this tonight. She whispered, "It's all right. You're all right. Here, I'll get you a glass of water. Maybe you'd like a warm shower…"

Tucked together in the full-size bed in her room a little later, our backs touching beneath the covers, she murmured, "It's been such a long time since we've talked in the evenings. We always used to back home."

"Those were good old days," I whispered, edging closer to her warmth. The window was open just enough to allow a faint, sagebrush-scented breeze into the dark bedroom, and I was chilled.

"How did Liam take everything?" Tish asked. I heard her rearranging her pillow.

"I hurt him. There was no way around it. He doesn't understand why I couldn't be his girlfriend anymore."

"He will in time. He wasn't right for you. There would always have been something lacking between the two of you."

"You're right. I've known it for a long time. I do love Liam in my own way but I understand now that I've never been *in* love with him. There's a difference. I just never admitted it to myself."

"And once you know it, you can't live without it," Tish whispered. "Or at least, you can't live with a substitute for it."

"I shouldn't have let it drag out this long. I hate hurting him this way."

"He'll be all right. The distance between you two will help."

My eyelids felt weighted; Tish's warmth and the layers of blankets had helped settle my nerves. "I'm so glad you understand."

"Of course I understand." A soft sound, almost a laugh, accompanied her words. "I'm much more romantic than I used to be, in case you hadn't noticed."

"This just adds to what Marshall and I were talking about tonight," I mumbled, nearly asleep.

"What's that?" Tish wondered.

"That you really don't know your family members as well as you think you do."

The last thing I heard was Tish murmuring, "But probably well enough."

Deep in the night I woke – *or was I still sleeping* – to hear Una Spicer. I lay with eyes closed, Tish breathing evenly alongside my body in the waking world while Una's voice, urgent with tension, reached me from the dream world.

Wake up, Ruthie, Una insisted, and my spine jerked. *He's coming. He's more dangerous than you could know.*

Who? I whispered, drifting somewhere between the two worlds.

A forest path bathed in the hues of sunset appeared before my closed eyes, beckoning me forward. Broken twigs and dead leaves dug into my bare feet as I stood rooted, unwilling to advance, muted auburn light flickering over my head and dappling my shoulders; beneath the sheets, my knees jerked. I knew, beyond a shadow of a doubt, that something terrible, worse than any nightmare conjured by a tired brain, lurked at the end of this path.

Ruthann, he's coming!

Wake up!

Wake up!

Out in the dark living room Bender issued a deep, hair-raising growl.

I jolted as though electrified, throwing off the covers and bounding from the bed. The trailer suddenly exploded with violent barking.

What's wrong, what's wrong?!

The presence of danger loomed, blindsiding me.

"Ruthie!" Tish cried, yanked from sleep as I raced for the kitchen.

Growling, jaws snapping, all four dogs crowded the screen door and I fumbled with the lock to let them free. Sacrificing all sense, I followed as they bounded toward the barn like wolves on the hunt.

"Stop!" I screamed, but I didn't mean the dogs. "Stop, you *fucking son of a bitch!*"

I ran, heedless of my vulnerability. Gravel sliced my bare feet. Clouds had blotted out the stars, leaving little illumination to aid my vision. Paces ahead, the dogs were snarling so furiously they sounded rabid. Behind me, the screen door banged open.

Tish screamed, "Ruthann!"

I reached the barn, assaulted by certainty as plainly as the scents of cut wood and sawdust; a new set of double doors had been constructed but not yet hung and I entered the echoing space with nothing impeding my flight.

"Get him!" I shrieked to the dogs, maniacal with fury. "Get that fucking bastard, hurry! *He'll get away!*"

The dogs had cornered a man at the back of the barn; I was no more than thirty feet away and I saw the tall outline of him against the wall boards, heard his low, vicious voice. I could not discern his features in the dark but felt the returned weight of his gaze, dense with mutual hatred.

My fingers curled, becoming claws that I would use to tear out his throat –

I was almost upon them –

The dogs lunged.

I stumbled over a low stack of boards and fell hard on the cement, scraping palms and shins and knees; painful seconds passed before I realized the dogs were scrabbling and clawing at the wall boards and that their muscular, tensile bodies were the only others in the barn.

Tish reached my side, barefoot, gasping and short of breath.

I screamed, "Get him! *He's getting away…*"

I scrambled to my feet, disregarding her cries to stay put, and sprinted out the back entrance, which gaped wide, exposing the dark night. My eyes had adjusted and I looked wildly in all directions, seeing nothing. No telltale outline of a running body, no one crouched to spring; the dogs had not given chase.

Maybe he's hiding nearby.

The hair on my nape stood perfectly straight.

Tish clamped hold of my pajama shirt and gasped, "What…*in the hell*…is going on?"

"There was a man here! Didn't you see him?"

The land beyond the back of the barn faced east and stretched for miles with little to mar the view – the mountains lay to the west. Someone at a running pace could have easily disappeared into the foothills and therefore from sight under cover of darkness. I bent forward, hands to thighs, trying to catch my errant breath, to reassert reality into the situation. My palms were raw, my knees bleeding.

"I'm calling the police!" Tish was livid. "Come inside, right now!"

"I'm calling Marshall," I whispered as the dogs swarmed our legs, panting with exertion but otherwise silent.

Whoever he was, he was gone.

Within fifteen minutes the trailer was bursting with bodies. Marshall was the first to arrive, and he hit the ground running; I met him halfway to the truck, shuddering at the depth of relief, the welcome security, his arms offered. Face against my hair, he demanded, "Are you all right?"

I nodded assurance, tucked against him. He cupped my head with one hand and inhaled a huge breath, chest expanding. "I'm so glad you called me."

"I'm so glad you're here."

He caught sight of the bandages crisscrossing my palms and I sensed his concern double. "What the hell happened, angel?"

"I fell," I explained, and was spared further explanation by the arrival of Clark's diesel truck.

Clark had hauled along Sean, Quinn, and Wy, each armed with heavy-duty flashlights. They immediately began prowling the barn, looking for any sign of intrusion; though reluctant to leave my side, Marshall joined them. On their heels was Jerry Woodrow, the local sheriff, who detoured to the barn before taking a seat at the kitchen table to speak with me while Tish talked on the phone with Case. Marshall sat in an adjacent chair and I was relieved to observe that Tish had put away Una Spicer's letters; in light of everything else, I didn't want to deal with those. I reached for Marshall's hand and felt measurably better.

"Why don't you tell me what happened, Miss Gordon," Jerry invited. All the lights in the trailer were blazing and the elderly sheriff appeared somewhat haggard in the bright glow; he'd removed a wide-brimmed cowboy hat once inside, which he placed on the tabletop. He smiled encouragingly; a gray handlebar mustache obscured his top lip. Beyond his shoulder, the small clock on the stove read 2:48.

"Tish and I were sleeping. I woke up because the dogs started barking." I squeezed Marshall's fingers, interlocked with mine. "This was about an hour ago now. I ran for the kitchen and let the dogs out, and they ran for the barn so I followed them…"

"You *followed* them?" Marshall's brow furrowed; the worried crease appeared above the bridge of his nose.

"I know it was dangerous," I admitted, speaking now to him rather than Jerry. Marshall wrestled with several strong emotions, each of which wanted to gain the upper hand, but he choked back additional words, letting me continue. "The dogs ran inside the barn and there was a…" I gulped, struck all at once by the irrationality of what I'd done. I'd been armed with nothing more than fury – inexplicable fury that burned even now at the base of my gut. I felt like a fool; I'd acted with no concern for my safety and could barely find words to justify my actions.

"Yes?" The sheriff prompted.

Marshall squeezed my hand; consternation radiated from him like heatwaves.

"There was a man in there," I said, infusing my voice with confidence. I'd *seen* him. I wasn't wrong. I could not explain where he'd gone but I was sure he'd been there. "The dogs had him cornered and they were barking like they meant to tear him to shreds."

"And then?" Jerry remained calm.

Marshall appeared stricken. I gripped his hand like it was a tow rope on a life boat, keeping me afloat.

"Then I fell over a pile of boards. When I looked up, he was gone."

"Were you carrying a flashlight? A lantern?" Jerry pressed, and I knew where he was going with these questions.

"No, but he was there, I'm sure of it. I saw the shape of him against the barn wall. I could hear his voice." I restrained a shudder, with titanic effort; Marshall was about two seconds from completely losing his cool.

"Did you address him? Was he speaking to you?" Jerry pressed.

I struggled to recall those adrenaline-charged seconds. My memory had already begun to stretch gauze over them, leaving behind a spider's web of uncertainty. I admitted, "I couldn't hear over the dogs."

Tish came to stand beside Jerry; she had ended her call with Case.

Holding my eyes, she quietly spoke one word. "Bull."

Too engrossed in what I'd been relating, Jerry didn't hear her. He asked, "Then what happened, Miss Gordon?"

"The dogs were clawing at the wall but no one was there. I ran out the back and looked all around, but he was gone."

Jerry sat back from the table and smoothed his mustache with a thumb and forefinger. He nodded toward Marshall. "When did you arrive, Rawley?"

"About five minutes before you," Marshall said, not taking his eyes from me.

"Did you find anything in the barn?" I asked Jerry. Clark and the rest of the guys were still out there; I could hear them through the open windows.

"There are plenty of footprints but there have also been dozens of people working here this week," Jerry said. He lightly rapped the table with both fists. "I'll return in the daylight but I'm not hopeful of finding much." He rose and nodded at Tish. "Case'll be home tomorrow, sounds like?"

She nodded. "Thanks for coming out, Jerry."

"Anytime," Jerry said. He replaced his hat and tipped the brim, then bid us farewell. The screen door sang on its hinges as he went outside, where Clark emerged from the barn to speak with him. Their low voices seemed to fill up the kitchen, even from a distance.

Marshall and Tish spoke simultaneously.

"I feel like someone just punched me in the goddamn chest. You put yourself in danger!"

"It's just like that night with Mathias!"

I focused on Tish, because Marshall's worry over my wellbeing was manifesting as anger. I whispered, "The man Bull was fighting in the woods…"

"Disappeared before his eyes," Tish finished, sinking to a chair. Exhaustion painted bruises beneath her eyes. Fortunately Marshall was distracted by our words and his anger lowered a notch. He leaned forward, strain creasing his forehead.

"The night Mathias was walking his trap lines, years back?" Marshall clarified; he knew the story, from either Mathias or Camille. It was one of two unexplained acts of aggression on members of my family, both having occurred in 2006; Mathias had been struck and dragged while walking his winter trap lines, and later that year, in the summer, Aunt Jilly was attacked by a man named Zack Dixon.

Neither incident had been resolved; we were no closer to understanding who had tried to kill Mathias that cold February night, and Zack Dixon had never been apprehended. *Still at large* was what the Landon police had said, a sickening phrase to haunt all of us. My mind snagged on the idea and then streaked, lightning-quick, through a thousand horrible possibilities. Had Zack returned? Had it been *him* cornered in the barn less than an hour ago? I struggled to reform the picture in my head. Zack had been tall and athletic; the man just now had also been tall –

"Ruthann." Marshall's voice sent my half-panicked thoughts scattering.

"You don't think…" I looked between Tish and Marshall.

"No," Tish said, with certainty. "It's not Zack Dixon. But someone was out there, I believe you, Ruthie. I could tell Jerry was skeptical, but I believe you."

Marshall seized on this angle, his temper rising all over again. "You should have called 911! You ran out there with nothing to protect you! What if –" He choked on the words and ran a hand over his face.

"Marsh," I whispered, and moved to sit on his lap. He sheltered me in his embrace; I could feel the taut edges of his tense muscles.

"You shouldn't have done that," he whispered.

"Case was upset, too," Tish acknowledged, scooting her chair closer to us, resting a palm on my back; I knew she was thinking of what else had taken place tonight – right here at this very table. I sent my sister a silent plea not to mention it just now.

"Don't ever do something that dangerous again," Marshall implored, his voice raw with emotion. "Please, Ruthie."

"Stay here tonight," I whispered, my hands in his hair.

Marshall slept on the couch and I returned to the bed with Tish; we all needed rest but when daylight began poking fingers in my grainy eyes, I hadn't slept more than twenty minutes in a row. Tish rose early and showered, intending to drive to Bozeman to pick up Case. I knew I'd imposed the no-touching rule but I couldn't resist the temptation of Marshall out there on the couch. He lay on his back in the golden dawn, rubbing his eyes; he was disheveled, jaws and chin bristling with thick black stubble. He'd shucked his boots and socks but nothing else; catching sight of me, he made a sleepy sound of happiness and reached with both arms. I dove for him.

"I'm doing the best I can with the no-touching rule, I promise you, angel," he murmured, hands all over me as I burrowed into his warmth.

"I know," I whispered, thinking of what Tish had said last night; *he's in love with you.* Joy soaked into my heart like warm, wet rain into dry earth. I was in love with him, too; no doubt about it. I wanted in that moment to confess but held it back, content to study his handsome face at close range in the morning light.

I thought, *There's time. We have nothing but time together.*

I was a fool.

Marshall gently collected one of my hands and ran a thumb along the wounds at the base of my palm. Bandages covered the gashes. He kissed each one, with characteristic tenderness. "I'm sorry you got hurt."

"I'm sorry I made you worry. I know what I did was dangerous."

"Did you see someone in the yard before you ran to the barn? Was the door locked last night when you and Tish went to bed? Oh Jesus, that door is never locked…"

"We locked it last night. And no, I didn't see anyone in the yard. I woke up because I was having a nightmare." I struggled to remember its contents but nothing sprang forth – even still, I shuddered. The shower pipes clunked, signaling Tish's imminent appearance in the living room; Marshall withdrew his hands from my loose pajama shorts, where they'd been curved around my backside, and we shifted to a less intimate position as I continued explaining. "I was disoriented because it was so early in the morning. And then Bender started growling." My skin prickled, just recalling. "I let them out and they rushed for the barn. They knew someone was there, they were going crazy. I didn't think about what I was doing in that moment, I just chased after them."

Tish, wrapped in a dark blue robe about five sizes too big, appeared in the kitchen in time to hear my last comment; she said, "You were screaming and swearing, Ruthie." She perched on the arm of the couch, near our heads. "I've never heard you swear like that. My heart about stopped when you ran outside."

"What was I saying?" I demanded.

Tish's eyes lifted toward the ceiling as she recalled. "You yelled 'stop' and then something about a fucking son of a bitch."

"I did?" My memory of chasing the dogs was nothing more than a reddish-tinted blur. I sat straight, rubbing my eyes in hopes of forming a clearer picture. "I remember being angry. I think…I must have figured whoever was out there was responsible for the fire. The dogs had surrounded him. I couldn't see his face, but he was tall…"

Tish was paler than ice. "Was it Derrick?"

"I don't know what he looks like, I've never met him," I reminded her. Resolve welled in my chest. "I want to see if he left anything behind, come on."

Tish needed to finish getting ready but Marshall joined me in the barn, which possessed half a roof; I skirted the boards that had tripped me last night, thankful the section I wanted to explore remained open to the morning sky, and therefore ample light.

"Right here," I said, running both hands over the wall; long, narrow ruts had been torn in the boards. "See, the dogs saw him, too. They wouldn't have clawed the wall if there hadn't been someone there."

Marshall knelt to inspect the ground along with me; I could tell he believed what I said, which warmed my heart anew. I'd recognized the slightly patronizing air surrounding Jerry Woodrow while he'd questioned me; certainly the sheriff wanted to assume that I'd misinterpreted what I'd seen, my imagination stirred up by the week's tumultuous events.

"I don't see anything." Disappointed, I sat on my heels and drummed my thighs with both fists. "*Dammit*."

"Let's look outside," Marshall said.

The air was chilly with morning; goosebumps broke over my skin. A breeze ran its fingers through our hair as we peered eastward. I jogged a few paces ahead, into direct sunlight, scanning the ground, poking at the grass with the toe of my tennis shoe. It was impossible to determine if someone had crossed this ground at a run a few hours ago.

"I wish I could say I was an expert tracker." Marshall hunkered near my knees. He cupped a handful of dry soil and let it trickle between his fingers. "I could follow a reasonable trail, but damned if I can tell if someone passed this way last night. You know, though…" He paused, looking east, the sun creating copper threads in his dark hair. "My gut says he didn't run in this direction."

I nodded slowly, frowning at the blue-washed horizon. "I agree. But how could he have disappeared so fast? I was only a second or two behind. He really did just seem to vanish." My gaze backtracked to the barn. "Unless he ran around front. I figured he ran into the foothills, but maybe he doubled back."

Marshall rubbed a hand along the back of my left leg. "We better get moving, angel, you're cold. And it's gonna be a busy day."

He stood and took me in his arms; I tugged his head down toward mine but two inches from my lips he halted. A smile glinted in his eyes as he murmured, "I don't know if courting allows for a kiss before we've had our first official date."

I giggled, pressing closer. "Just one…"

"No touching," he reminded, caressing my hipbones with slow, circular movements of both thumbs, each circle edging slightly closer to my pelvis.

"*Marshall…*"

His smile became a grin; he placed a feather-soft kiss at the outer corner of my lips and my knees all but buckled.

"I can't give in so easily," he murmured, kissing the other side of my mouth, just as softly, leaving me quivering and wet.

"You're right," I whispered, calling his bluff. It took every drop of my willpower to release him and step back. "We shouldn't kiss until *after* our date."

His grin deepened as he nodded agreement, adjusting the front of his jeans. "I deserve a medal. C'mon, angel, let's get breakfast."

Chapter Fourteen

By evening I was established in my tiny new apartment above Trudy's Diner. The rooms smelled a little like bacon grease, a little like coffee and fried fish, but I had grown up at the Shore Leave Cafe so these smells were familiar and I felt at home. Tish left for Bozeman after eating breakfast with Marshall and me, and Clark and the crew from Jalesville arrived to work on the barn, a final flurry of effort before Case and Tish arrived home this afternoon. It seemed word of last night's intruder had spread like a rampant case of chicken pox; everyone wanted to talk about it and I was glad to beg off with the excuse of heading into town.

Wy and Becky helped me all day; of course they demanded all the details about what had occurred last night, from my perspective. Wy drove us around in the diesel truck and we collected and subsequently unloaded the household things obtained on my grateful behalf; I now possessed a twin-sized mattress, a small, Formica-topped kitchen table and two matching yellow chairs, a cardboard box of kitchen supplies, a set of bath towels embroidered with daisies, an armchair upholstered in faded pink denim (which Trudy's short-order cook helped us cart up the back steps), and a framed picture of two wild horses running against an orange sunset. Wy had painted it with watercolors in the seventh grade and presented it to me as a house-warming present.

I couldn't have loved it more.

I treated Becky and Wy to a late lunch at Trudy's and we sat in the peaceful afternoon light, the diner empty of all but us and the dust motes twirling in the sunbeams, in that daily lull between the lunch and dinner crowds. We ate cheeseburgers and onion rings, and Wy packed away a piece of strawberry pie topped with two inches of whipped cream for dessert. He pretended to stab at my knuckles with his fork as I repeatedly filched strawberries.

"Ruthann, I swear you always put me in a better mood," Becky said, leaning over the table on her elbows. Because she was pregnant we hadn't let her carry anything up to the apartment besides the hair dryer and homemade soap bars she'd brought for me.

Wy, guarding his pie and with mouth full, nodded vigorous agreement.

"Thank you," I said, embarrassed and pleased.

"All of us," she insisted. "I've never seen Marsh so happy. He's glowing like a firefly."

Wy snorted a laugh, reminiscent of his older brothers. "I'm telling him you said that."

"I doubt he'd deny it," Becky said, nudging his shoulder with hers; the motion knocked Wy's next bite from his fork to his lap.

"*Dang it*, Becky," he grumbled. I took advantage of his distraction to steal another strawberry, as Becky offered a giggling apology.

"You can get another piece, if you want," I told Wy; he'd done the bulk of today's lifting and hauling, after all. And besides that, I loved the kid enormously. "I appreciate all your hard work."

"I'm glad to help," he said, with an easy grin.

Becky was reading a text message; she informed us, "Garth said the roof is done and that Tish and Case are about twenty minutes away."

"We better get going!" Wy ate his last bite and backhanded crumbs from his mouth.

"You head back out there, buddy," Becky said. "Ruthie and I have to swing by my sister's to pick up the Buick, remember?"

"Are you sure she doesn't mind?" I asked for the third time. "I can make payments once I start work."

"She doesn't mind at all, and she said you don't have to pay her a thing. It's just been sitting in their sideyard since she got a new car. It needs an oil change but Marsh can do that this weekend."

An hour later I arrived back at my apartment, driving a new-to-me car with a good engine and soft leather seats despite its overall rundown appearance. As it was in Landon, people in Jalesville were chatty and kind, curious to know more about me and just as quick to offer help. I couldn't believe the generosity heaped upon me just today. I parked at the edge of the lot and killed the engine, but didn't climb out. I sat completely still for a moment instead, staring blankly out the windshield; I hadn't fully processed what had happened in the past twenty-four hours. Moving as slowly as someone in a dream sequence I cupped my jaws, pressing against the rounded boncs beneath my skin; I'd not shaken the sense that I'd been in danger in more ways than one last night.

Vanished, I thought, distressed by the word, which swirled through my mind like lazy smoke. Something else danced at the edge of my consciousness. *You almost vanished last night, just like the man in the barn.*

My phone rang and I leaped as though prodded by a sharp point. I saw that Mom was calling, so let it go to voicemail; I knew my family had arrived safely back in Landon because I'd spoken to Mom this morning, a conversation in which she'd encouraged me more than once to call Liam.

"Clint and I talked to him last night," Mom had said. "He doesn't understand this, honey, and you need to explain what's going on. I didn't tell him about you and Marshall but I think you should."

Though I didn't admit it to Mom, I strongly disagreed. Liam already despised Marshall from that summer three years ago; Liam never disliked people and yet Marshall had provoked Liam into wanting to kick his ass back then, when I had done my best to *avoid* Marshall's attention.

"I'll talk to him, I promise," I'd hedged.

Sitting in the driver's seat and battling guilt, the late-afternoon sun hot on my left arm, I scrolled to Liam's number. It rang ten times without an answer but I was not up to leaving a message, and sent a text instead — *I know this is a shock for you and I am so sorry. Please believe me. I needed a change in my life. I started to realize this a while ago and I should have said something right away. I'm so sorry.*

How patronizing, how lame. I felt shallow and small; Liam would probably chuck his phone across the room. But then I thought of what Marshall had asked me the other night, about what I thought I owed Liam. I owed him the courtesy of an explanation but Marshall was ultimately right – I did not owe Liam *myself*. I didn't expect Liam to write back, and he did not. For a little longer I sat without moving, the sun baking my arm, hearing the sounds of the dinner rush starting up at Trudy's; the diner windows were propped open to the beauty of the sunny summer evening, and laughter and chatter, the clink of coffee cups and forks against plates met my ears, as familiar as anything I had ever known. I studied the jewel-toned wildflowers growing tall and thick at the edge of the parking lot.

And suddenly my fingers flew, scrolling to a new number.

See you soon!

Marshall texted an immediate response – *I can't wait! XXOO*

I hadn't seen him since breakfast this morning but we'd been writing intermittently all day, flirty, wonderful, sometimes sweet and sometimes suggestive texts, all of which made my nerves hum with anticipation and happiness; I'd learned he was fond of endearments.

O & then XX, I wrote back.

Hell YES, my sweet darling angel baby.

Remember first date = one kiss.

Can I choose placement/duration of kiss?

My fingers trembled as I texted, *Hurry.*

I'm coming baby! XXXOOO

I raced up to my apartment, ignoring the mess as I changed into a soft ivory sundress with a short skirt and lace-trimmed edging, one that Camille had lent me. I shook out my hair, brushed my teeth, did a quick mascara job, and had just applied lip gloss when I heard someone thundering up the outside steps. My heart exploded like a firecracker. Seconds later I flung open the door to find Marshall standing with his right hand poised to knock. He grinned widely as I leaped into his arms; fortunately he compensated for my weight and we didn't go tumbling down the flight of stairs.

"You're here!" I cried.

Marshall rocked us side to side, his mouth against my temple. "Of course I am."

"I loved texting you all day," I murmured, running my hands over his back.

"I must be dreaming," he whispered. "You know how many times I've imagined taking you on a date? And here you are in my arms."

"If you were dreaming I wouldn't do this," I said, licking his nose, and he snorted a surprised laugh. I shrieked and giggled, trying to evade his tongue as he went for my ear. He got me just as good and I was weak with laughter.

"More?" he demanded.

"Yes, more," I begged.

His eyes drove straight into my already-besotted heart. He stroked my loose hair with both hands. "It's impossible for me not to touch you. Look at you. You're so beautiful I can hardly believe you're real."

I pulled him closer. "One kiss."

His eyes caught fire as instantly as a struck match, lashes lowering. "Shouldn't that be at the *end* of the evening?"

Breathless and shivery, I shook my head, pressing my breasts against his chest.

"I don't want to be accused of disappointing a woman who looks like an angel." He gripped my waist and curled his fingers possessively around the material of my sundress. "Especially *my* angel. But I don't know that I should give in just yet…"

"Kiss me *right now*," I whispered; his mouth was less than a breath away.

"How much do you want it?" His lips brushed mine.

"*So* much." I was trembling openly now, my body a tuning fork vibrating in response to his proximity.

"*How* much?" He licked my lower lip.

"With *all my heart* much."

"Say my name, just like that."

"Kiss me first," I demanded.

He slowly shook his head, gray eyes afire with both teasing and arousal.

I thumped my fists against his ribs. "*Please*, Marshall…"

Before I could blink he parted my lips with his and gave me what I'd asked for.

"How's that?" he whispered and if not for his arms I would have melted onto the floorboards.

"My sweet Ruthann Marie," he murmured, grasping my jaws to reclaim my mouth, and all I could think of was making love in the guestroom bed, when he'd kissed me this deeply. Marshall made a throaty sound and drew slightly away. "Angel, I'm gonna lose all control here and I made you a promise. We're courting. And besides, I have a surprise for you in the truck."

"You do?" I smoothed dark hair from the sides of his tanned face, admiring him anew. "You look so handsome."

He grinned. "I *did* shower. I was a mess after shingling the barn all day. You guys were busy, too, Wy was saying."

"Yes, come see! I can't believe all the things Becky rounded up for me. I can't thank her enough."

"She adores you," he said, as I led him by the hand on a tour of the apartment.

"I like her, too. Her sister even let me use her old car."

"I'll get it tuned up for you this weekend."

We'd reached the doorway to the bedroom, where the bare mattress was covered by haphazard piles of clothes, bras, underwear, and the daisy-embroidered towel set; a small lamp was plugged in beside the mattress and there wasn't an inch to spare between it and the wall. I leaned against Marshall's chest, indulging in his strength and the heady scent of his warm skin. I whispered, "Thank you, sweetheart, for everything."

"No fair," he whispered, tucking his chin over the top of my head; he was so much taller than me the position was a natural fit. "You called me 'sweetheart' *and* there's a bed, right there…"

I giggled, eyes closed against his black t-shirt.

"There's about a hundred quilts and sheet sets in Dad's linen closet," Marshall said. "We'll swing by the house and you can pick some for this little bed." He tightened his arms around me. "Aw, Ruthie, I'm so god-damn glad you're here."

I stood on tiptoe to kiss his chin.

He said, "I almost forgot, Tish and Case invited us to dinner before I left. I told them it was our first date but they insisted. What do you think?"

"I think that sounds good. But then I want you all to myself."

Marshall kissed my forehead, with a small groan. "That may be too dangerous, especially with you in that tiny little dress. Sweet Jesus, I'm already sweating." He grinned at my laughter. "Come on, angel, we'll eat with them and then we're going to ride Arrow and do some stargazing. With *minimal* touching. Speaking of that, you better grab some jeans and tennis shoes."

"We are?" I almost jumped with excitement. "I've never ridden a horse."

"Something tells me you'll be a natural," he murmured, and I flicked his chin this time.

Marshall's truck was decorated with wildflowers. I noticed as we descended the steps in a coppery glow of evening sunshine, and my breath caught. There were flowers tucked beneath the windshield wipers, piled on the dashboard and behind the rearview mirrors; white and yellow daisies, purple phlox, tiger-spotted lilies and lemony bee balm, all long-stemmed and with petals overspilling every which way. I stopped short and put both hands to my mouth. Marshall cupped my shoulders from behind as he said, "I thought you might like it. Wildflowers suit you."

"You just *know*," I whispered. "You picked all these, didn't you?"

"I did. Case and Tish *might* be missing a few dozen flowers from their yard and surrounding areas."

I collected a bouquet from the dashboard and held it on my lap as Marshall drove us down Main Street. The cab of the truck was bursting with the scent of blossoms and I thanked him again, burying my face in the soft petals.

"You are so welcome. I've been thinking of everything I want to do for you, all the sweet and romantic things that courting involves…like flowers."

"It's even a romantic word, *courting*," I reflected.

He grinned. "There's pollen *all* over your nose, angel."

I inspected my reflection in the rearview mirror; my overzealous inhaling of the orange lilies had left behind a similar color on my nose. Rubbing at it only made matters worse.

Marshall offered, "I could lick it away…"

"Good thing we're just going to Tish's," I said, giggling.

A hazy, hot-pink sun was bisected by the edge of the ridge beyond the trailer as Marshall drove along the gravel driveway and parked beside Tish's car. Mutt and Tiny raced to greet us. The scent of hand-hewn wood hung like a fresh breath in the motionless air; I leaned forward to study the new barn against a satiny, peach-tinted sky. It was complete after today's industrious work, with a shingled roof and heavy double doors. Would Case and my sister lock those doors tonight? Would they remain awake long after midnight, awaiting trouble? Would someone risk returning once darkness settled over the foothills? I wanted to tell Marshall we should stay here tonight, to help keep watch.

The screen door of the trailer opened.

"Hi, you two!" Tish called. She was wearing a pale blue denim sundress, her short hair curling around her cheeks. Case was at her side, dressed in jeans and a t-shirt, with bandages covering both his forearms. Though he wasn't fully recovered, and surely exhausted beyond belief, Case appeared nothing but happy.

Marshall and I held hands as we made our way up the path to the door. With quiet sweetness Marshall announced, "Ruthann and I are courting, in case you hadn't heard."

Case teased, "I think you may have mentioned that a time or ten today, little bro." He smiled at us, deep voice still painfully hoarse.

"I know it's your first date but we wanted to see you guys," Tish said. "Supper's almost ready." She peered more closely at my face. "Is your nose orange?"

"I smelled the flowers Marshall picked for me and got pollenated, see?" I indicated the truck.

Marshall ushered me inside, where it smelled like onions and garlic bread and tomato sauce. He wrapped Case and my sister in a double bear hug. "It's so fucking good to see you guys home. You don't even know."

I hugged them both, too, taking a second to study Case at close range, this time when his eyes were open. He was tall and strong, incredibly handsome, and yet so much more than that – kindness and determination, and depth of character, were also present on his face. Driven by instinct, I hugged my new brother-in-law a second time, squeezing hard, overwhelmed with affection and gratitude; I whispered, "Thank you for making my sister so happy."

We drew apart and I could tell my words touched him; tears had formed in both our eyes. He said in his hoarse voice, "Thank you for being here for her."

"It smells great in here, what did you make?" Marshall asked, heading for the stove, lifting kettle lids.

"Spaghetti and meatballs," Tish said. "*And* cheese bread."

"Have a seat, you two," Case said, indicating the table. "I'll grab you a couple of beers."

"This is Aunt Ellen's recipe, isn't it?" I asked, stealing a spoonful from a simmering pan. "Oh, *yum.*"

Case helped Tish get supper on the table as the four of us talked and sipped our beers; I enjoyed this glimpse of him and my sister in their home, working together setting out plates and transferring noodles and sauce to serving bowls, mundane tasks made sweet because they were shared. I couldn't claim to know Case well, at least not yet, but I already liked him tremendously. He and Tish looked so right together; I thought of the way my body blended with Marshall's, as though we were part of the same being, and recognized that this also occurred between my sister and Case. Their every movement spoke of their love and so I didn't have to know Case very well to perceive that he belonged to Tish, and she to him.

Marshall unconsciously followed the direction of my thoughts. Gesturing with his beer bottle, he said, "Look at the four of us. Case, did you ever think we'd see the day when we'd finally have our women in the same state?"

Case grinned in wry acknowledgment of Marshall's words. He rasped, "I still feel the need to pinch myself, just to make sure I'm not dreaming."

Tish latched an arm around his neck and kissed his jaw. "You're not dreaming."

"So, have you two been able to do much consummating lately?" Marshall asked in a curious, conversational tone, provoking everyone's laughter.

Tish cried, "Don't make me pinch *you*, Marsh!"

Case's grin widened. "Well, I'm not a man to speak about such things…"

"But you *do* have a certain glow about you," I teased, charmed to see a flush overtake his cheekbones at my words. All the food was on the table and he and Tish took their seats.

"Speaking of *glowing*," my sister mused, narrowing her eyes as she gave Marshall a shrewd once-over.

"I'm glowing like a freaking bonfire, are you kidding? By the grace of God I have been allowed to court Ruthann. And that means I'm on my best behavior."

Case snorted.

"Marshall has been a perfect gentleman," I said primly, hoping my face didn't appear as flushed as it felt.

"*Riiiiight*," Tish drawled, elongating the word, and we were all laughing again.

We ate as an indigo evening spilled from the west and soaked up the daylight, dipping garlic bread in rich, tomato-sage sauce, spearing meatballs and winding long noodles around our forks; our mouths grew ringed with red sauce. As darkness pressed at the windows our conversation shifted to last night's events; I knew Case had heard the story forward and backward by now, but he wanted my perspective.

"I know there's no evidence that someone was actually out there…" I began.

Case politely interrupted. "You said you saw someone, and I believe you. There's more to this than any of us know."

Warmed by his encouragement, I began again. Case listened with a frown creasing his forehead; we'd all stopped eating. When I reached the part about hearing the man's voice, Tish asked, "Was he speaking *to* you, do you think?"

"I can't remember. I suppose he must have been, he was looking right at me. If I hadn't tripped over those boards…"

"Thank God you did," Marshall said, with quiet vehemence. "I can't bear to think about what might have happened if you'd reached him."

"I wanted to kill him." I'd already told Tish and Marshall this very thing, at breakfast, but it felt no less shocking now. "I have no idea who he was but I wanted to get my hands around his throat."

Case leaned forward. "The last you saw of him was right before you fell?"

"The dogs lunged just before I tripped. It couldn't have been more than two seconds before I looked back up, but he was already gone."

"And the dogs didn't chase him, they were clawing the wall where he'd been standing," Tish said. She held my gaze for a silent moment. "I don't think he ran, I think he disappeared."

I knew she was thinking of exactly what I was just now – last night's other shocking event, the one I hadn't told Marshall about. I meant to tell him, but now wasn't the right time.

"I think you're right," I whispered to Tish, and found room to be heartened by the fact that our men were both supportive of the illogical notion that someone could simply vanish; no matter what, they believed us.

"Disappeared *where*, though?" Marshall said, leaning forward with his elbows on the tabletop. "Are we talking straight-up science fiction, into another dimension sort of thing?"

Case set aside his beer bottle. Both he and Marshall wore expressions of stubborn determination mixed with eagerness; despite the gravity of the topic, there was a certain amount of fascination in it. Tish held my gaze, wanting me to mention Una's letters before she did, but I could hardly bring myself to remember the horrific sensation of disappearing, let alone discuss it when there was another weighty matter already on the table.

With my eyes I implored Tish – *Don't say anything yet, please.*

She responded by lowering her chin a fraction of an inch, indicating that she would not.

"I talked with Mathias today," Case was saying. "He was telling me what his dad remembers about that night back in '06. Bull swears to this day the man disappeared before his eyes. Bull had him in his grasp and yet he just vanished. No explanation, no clues. Just gone."

"Could the guy last night have been the same person?" Marshall wondered.

"Or maybe just someone with the same ability," Tish said, her brow adopting a lawyerly scowl. "Both situations have similarities. Think about it. A man disappeared seemingly into thin air, and both times the man's physical person was threatened prior to disappearing."

Case was nodding, rubbing his chin with a thumb. "You're right. Bull was ready to kill the man who'd attacked his son…"

"And the dogs," I supplied. "Last night the dogs would have torn him to pieces."

"A self-preservation thing. That makes sense," Marshall allowed. "But we still don't have a reasonable explanation for *where* these guys vanished. Across town? Across the country? Back to their beds? Is it controllable or involuntary?"

The word 'involuntary' flashed inside my head.

Headlights cut a sudden swathe through our conversation; outside, Mutt and Tiny began barking. Case rose, Marshall on his heels. Tish, peering out the front windows, observed, "It's Robbie."

Chapter Fifteen

ROBBIE BENSON, TISH'S FORMER NORTHWESTERN CLASS-
mate, climbed slowly from a pint-sized and expensive-looking vehicle,
closing its door with a soft click and then standing alongside it; despite
having taken the time to venture here, he appeared in no hurry to join
us. Tish pushed open the screen and invited, "Come in."

He approached the trailer with obvious wariness. Though there was
nothing to fear, certainly not from this slim, hesitant man, my heart
would not settle. Marshall, sensing my agitation, wrapped an arm around
my waist and drew me close as Tish held open the door so Robbie could
enter.

"I'm sorry to barge in," he said, stepping inside but advancing no farther; his cautious gaze took in Case, who appeared as imposing as a
wrecking ball, glowering at Robbie with wide shoulders squared. At last
Robbie quit stalling and focused on Tish; he spoke quietly. "I'm sorry for
what you've been through this week."

Robbie's skin glowed with the bronze hues of someone accustomed
to spending the summer months lounging on soft beach sand. His hair
was nearly the same shade, highlighted and stylized; he was almost pretty, smooth-skinned as a teenager, with long-lashed eyes of flawless blue.
Wearing fitted dress pants, a crisp periwinkle polo shirt, and a platinum
watch surely worth more than what I earned in a month, he appeared
uncomfortable to the point of nausea; it was, however, obvious he'd
sought out my sister for a specific purpose. He cleared his throat and
requested, "Might we sit for minute?"

There weren't enough chairs at the table, so Marshall and I claimed spots on the couch while Robbie joined Case and Tish. Robbie declined the offer of beer or food, and sat with hands folded; it seemed like a pose designed to keep one's self from fidgeting. I perched on the edge of the cushions, my fingers linked with Marshall's, watching as Robbie inhaled slowly, studying the tabletop. Finally he said, "I've known you for years, Tish. I *know* you, therefore I realize what I'm about to ask goes against your grain." He paused for effect, baby-blue eyes fastened on her face. "You have to let this whole thing with Ron Turnbull and the Yancys go. Please, let it go. As your old friend and former classmate, I implore you."

A mushroom cloud seemed to form over the table, siphoning the breathable air from the room.

Marshall and Case both spoke at once.

"It's because you're in it up to your fucking nose, isn't it?"

"Explain yourself, *immediately*."

With visible effort Robbie remained focused on Tish, who whispered, "What 'whole thing' would that be, Benson? Tell me what you mean."

"For the record, I'm not *in* it, whatever 'it' is. But I do know the Yancys mean business here. They are not to be fucked with. They want this area. For fuck's sake, God only knows *why* they want it, but they do. You already know Ron bought out that power plant so there was less chance anyone would stay around here." Robbie paused, letting this sink in before whispering, "Will you kill me if I tell you something terrible about your father?"

My heart plummeted; the blood drained from Tish's face so quickly that Case put an arm around her shoulders, bolstering her.

"He's screwing Christina Turnbull." Robbie spoke the words as though they tasted bad in his mouth. His gaze dropped to his folded hands as he admitted, "I only know this because…I'm fucking her, too."

"*Robert Benson*," Tish uttered, fingertips at her mouth, creating an arch over her lips.

Robbie inhaled through his perfect little nose, nostrils narrowing. "I'm dead, crucified, fucking *castrated* if Ron ever finds out."

Marshall had been rendered speechless; he searched my eyes,

squeezing my hand, startled by this unexpected news and concerned for my reaction. I demanded, "Who is this woman? Someone at Dad's firm?"

"She's Ron Turnbull's wife," Tish whispered. Some of her shock was wearing away as she regarded Robbie anew; her eyes blazed and color was restored to her cheeks, with a vengeance. "What the *hell* were you thinking? You're telling me you would risk your career that way?"

Robbie lifted both palms like someone proving he wasn't concealing a weapon. "She came on to me, I swear to God. You've seen that woman! You think I could possibly say no? I'm fucking ashamed of myself to the end of time, all right? It's done now, anyway. I was only ever a distraction for her. It's all Jackson, all the time. I'm telling you, Christina is obsessed with your father."

"*Jesus*, Dad," Tish almost growled, grinding her fingertips against her temples.

"You expect us to trust your word with no other evidence?" Case asked, and he appeared so stern I felt a flicker of sympathy for Robbie, who was clearly out of his league.

"I have no reason to lie to you," Robbie rushed on. "I'm trying to *help*, for Christ's sake! The Turnbulls and Yancys go way back. Ron bought that broke-ass plant, like I just said, and paved the way for Derrick to sweep in here and charm the town into easy sales. Not so easy once you arrived, though."

"Then why send me here in the first place?!"

"It was a fluke, Tish. Your dad volunteered you, remember? He's hiding beneath Ron's nose. Jackson suggested to Ron that you might want to work for Al this summer – remember Al and Ron were once friends, in some universe I can't even imagine. Your dad figured it would be good experience for you but also make *him* look good. Less of a chance Ron would suspect anything between him and Christina, and then they could keep up with their secret meetings. Christina is totally hot for Jackson, even I know this. Jesus, it's *so* twisted. I hate myself, I really do. Tish, I'm telling you, your dad is a pussy hound like I've never known, and I thought I was bad..."

"*Enough*," Case ordered, and Robbie fell silent as obediently as if Case had swung an ax blade into the tabletop.

Tish sought my gaze and we exchanged several dozen sentences without a word. When she looked back at Robbie, he was nearly incinerated by the anger in her gaze. She said, "I don't care about that. What I need is something concrete. I need to know who started that fire in our barn. *Who*, Rob?"

Robbie sounded sincere. "I don't know the answer to that, I swear. Ron paid somebody probably, but good luck ever tracing it back to him. I do know Ron ordered Derrick to fuck up your apartment here last month, to scare you away for good. Remember when we were in Chicago to take the bar exam, we were having lunch with your dad and Lanny? Ron and Christina stopped at our table, remember? Tish, *you* were the one who brought up the fact that Redd Co. had purchased the power plant, and it must have startled Ron. And that night you called me, the night of the fire…"

"What?" She spoke through clenched teeth.

Robbie squirmed. "I talked to Christina that night. I told her a little of what you'd told me about realizing Redd Co. was Ron's company. I didn't realize this info could hurt you, I swear on my fucking trust fund."

Tish exhaled through her nostrils; if I was Robbie, I would have run for my life at the expression on Case's face. Tish prodded, "You think Christina told Ron? And he arranged to have our barn destroyed as a warning? Would he have called Derrick that night? Derrick threatened me last month, told me that accidents happen to people we love. And someone was on our property *just last night*, Robbie."

"It wasn't Derrick last night, I can tell you that much. He's in Chicago this week. I can't confirm anything about Derrick starting the fire. Shit, that brings up something else. Someone texted me about an hour ago, from a blocked number. I drove over from Ron's cabin so I could show it to you. Well, and also because I'm leaving for Chicago tomorrow morning." Robbie fished his phone from his pocket and placed it on the table. An instant later, we'd all crowded around the small screen.

The text contained only three words: *Franklin doesn't exist.*

Tish sat back and blinked slowly; only she and Robbie appeared to derive any meaning from the cryptic statement.

"Tish," I implored.

I could nearly see the wheels turning inside my sister's mind. She ran both hands through her hair. When she didn't immediately answer, Robbie seemed to notice me for the first time. He explained, "Derrick's older brother is named Franklin."

"We need this traced," Tish said. Unable to remain stationary, she rose and began pacing. "What the fuck does it mean, he doesn't exist? Franklin *does* exist, I've seen his picture. He lives in Chicago and knows Dad, for fuck's sake."

"I just thought you should know," Robbie said, watching her agitated motion; his expression grew beseeching. "For what it's worth, I think you deserve to be happy. I can't pretend to understand why you'd want to stay in this no-man's land, but you deserve happiness. Please, let all this go. Your barn is restored, you're married now; you have a job. What else do you need?"

Tish stopped pacing and moved to stand alongside Case, still in his chair. She rested her hands on his shoulders and the two of them faced Robbie with quiet stubbornness.

"You wouldn't understand, Benson," she whispered. "It's the principle of the thing. This is my husband's home. This is *my* home. We can't let it go."

"I figured that's what you'd say," Robbie muttered. He rose and collected Tish in a farewell hug. Drawing back, he cupped her shoulders and looked square into her eyes. "I'll be starting work at Turnbull and Hinckley next week. I'll keep an eye out for anything you could use, I swear."

Tish studied him as if to determine his authenticity. At last she said, "Thank you, Rob. I appreciate that. And thank you for everything you've told us tonight."

Case stood and shook Robbie's hand; as an almost comical afterthought, Robbie offered a palm to me, murmuring with mild flirtation, "Unfortunately we haven't been properly introduced. You must be Tish's gorgeous little sister." He squinted. "Is your nose orange, or am I seeing things?"

Tish said, "Take care of yourself, Benson. Find out what you can, especially about that text. Keep me posted."

"I will. I'll be in Chicago by tomorrow night, thank God." He nodded one last time before departing; a hush fell over the room as we stood listening to him descend the front steps and crunch over the gravel to his waiting car. The taillights flashed red as Robbie drove away before anyone spoke – and then it was like an avalanche.

Tish seethed, "I'm going to *fucking kill* our father. I'm calling him right now."

"No!" I cried, ready to restrain her from grabbing her phone. "This isn't the time. It's a shock, I know, but do you really think Dad is going to *admit* to messing around on Lanny? Besides, how would you tell him you found out? If Robbie's your informant now, you can't go ratting him out before he even gets back to Chicago!"

"Jesus, I'm sorry you two had to find out something like that about your dad from a little piss-ant like him," Marshall said; he'd opened the fridge to extract fresh beers for all of us.

"Tish, baby, come sit," Case invited. He withdrew a chair and angled a thigh toward her. "C'mere, let me hold you for a second."

Tish chewed her bottom lip hard enough to make little dents but she couldn't resist Case's open arms, and sank to a seat on his leg. He bundled her close and squeezed, pressing a soft kiss to her bare shoulder. I was relieved to see some of the tension drain from her body; she rested her head on Case and murmured, "You're right, Ruthie, I can't let Dad know that I know. At least, not yet. *Shit*." She uttered a small, low laugh. "There's chocolate pudding for dessert, guys, I almost forgot."

I told her to stay put and served up bowls of pudding, which Marshall topped with whipped cream. It was going on nine by now, crickets singing madly outside.

Taking my seat, I teased, "This has been a pretty exciting first date."

Holding two bowls of pudding, which he placed before my sister and Case, Marshall asked me, "Are you still up for some stargazing, angel?" His tone was of quiet innocence but my heart responded hotly, increasing in speed.

"Of course," I murmured, and he grinned knowingly as he took his seat to my right. Love for him absolutely flooded my senses; love, tenderness, passion...each pounded equally through my body and burst to bloom in my heart. I spooned a particularly large, gooey bite of chocolate and cream. Lifting my spoon toward him, feigning concern, I wondered aloud, "Marsh, do you think this smells weird?"

He leaned closer at once and it was with delight that I applied the pudding to his nose.

"Oh, you are *so* in trouble," he muttered, swiping at his nose while we all laughed uproariously, grateful for the excuse to ease the tension of Robbie's news.

Marshall and I left less than an hour later, after I'd changed into the clothes I'd brought for horseback riding. At the door we hugged Tish and Case, who assured us they would be all right alone; we'd offered to stay and help keep watch.

"You two go and enjoy the rest of your date," Tish said, hugging me one last time.

"I'm sorry about Dad," I whispered, clinging to my older sister. "It was about the last thing I thought Robbie was going to say."

"We'll talk more tomorrow," Tish said. "Do you start work?"

I nodded, smiling as I promised, "I'll see you at the office, then."

There was a bonfire roaring when we arrived at the Rawleys' a few minutes later; Sean and Quinn, along with their girlfriends, were hanging out around it, laughing and drinking beer, a typical summer evening at Clark's. Wy barreled out the front door as Marshall put the truck in park.

"Whatcha guys doing?" Wy asked, wrenching open my door and offering a grin. He peered more closely. "Why is your nose orange?"

"Pollen," I explained, gathering together a bundle of flowers. "Can we get these in some water? I think we can save a few from wilting."

Inside the house it smelled like a bakery; Clark's sister, Julie Heller, whose family owned and managed The Spoke, had stopped earlier for a visit, bringing dessert.

Clark invited, "Pie's still warm, you two. And there's caramel ice cream."

Marshall complained, "We're on a date, Dad. And we haven't really had a moment alone."

Clark's bushy mustache twitched as he restrained a smile. "And so you came *here?*"

I fetched a glass vase from a cupboard, wondering where to put the flowers; Clark always kept potted bitterroot – which had been Faye's favorite flower – on the dining room table, and there were already too many things cluttering the island counter. Then I spied the mantle with its arrangement of family pictures. I settled the vase there and was drawn to the framed photographs. One in particular caught my eye and I lifted it, with care.

"This is you, isn't it?" I asked Marshall, who came from the kitchen to stand beside me, using his knuckles to trace a path between my shoulder blades as I smiled at the image from November, 1990; there was a date stamped in gold on the bottom corner. I indicated the little boy resting an elbow on his mother's shoulder.

He nodded without speaking, his mouth softened by remembrance. I wanted to take him in my arms and kiss away the lingering hint of sadness present in his eyes, though nothing short of restoring Faye to her family could do that.

"You all match," I observed. "Mom used to do that to Camille and Tish and me, too."

The picture had been taken outside this very house and a sunny day gleamed golden in the background, the brown earth of November a sharp contrast to the bold blue of the afternoon sky. Clark and Faye were posed sitting on a quilt spread over the ground, their four sons (Wy not yet born) clustered around them. I could plainly distinguish between the brothers even though they'd been dressed in matching flannel shirts.

"My grandpa took this picture," Marshall explained.

I studied Faye's face, which shone with an expression of genuine contentment; Marshall's beloved mother, a plump, pretty woman with shining hair the color of maple syrup falling over her shoulders. In the picture Marshall was leaning against his mother, her arm around his waist; Faye appeared at ease, surrounded by her menfolk, her abundant love for them making the family whole. She'd been gone for nearly ten years now. The twisting in my heart was strong enough that I lifted one hand, surreptitiously, and pressed against the pain.

"She's so pretty. She looks happy," I whispered, and almost kissed the photograph. "You all look happy. You were five years old?"

He nodded. "I remember that day so well. Grandpa took about a hundred pictures before he was satisfied and then not two minutes after he finally let us quit posing, I fell and chipped my tooth on a rock and broke it almost clean off."

From the kitchen, Clark laughed as he added, "And we didn't end up getting it fixed because it was a baby tooth. You looked like a little reprobate."

"Mom was so worried. I cried like a baby."

"You were always your mama's boy," Clark said.

I replaced the picture on the mantle and wrapped my arms around Marshall's waist from the side, burying my face against his chest. I wished I had the power to erase all unhappiness, all pain, leaving him washed clean. He squeezed me closer, whispering, "Would you like to ride Arrow for a while?" and I nodded, craving the feeling of his body against mine as we rode double.

Marshall and I suffered a great deal of teasing from the direction of the bonfire once we emerged outside but I didn't mind. For one thing, I loved feeling like a real part of the Rawley family. Even the sweatshirt I was wearing was one Marshall had given me, complete with his name across the back, and I smiled up at him as we walked to the barn to collect Arrow; he was swinging our joined hands.

"What?" he asked softly, eyes crinkling at the outside corners as he grinned in response, the firelight glinting over our faces, bathing our skin in a warm orange glow.

Before I could answer, Sean called in our direction, "That's cheap, Marsh, totally cheap!" He warned me, "Be careful, Ruthanna-banana, horseback is the smoothest way to cop a feel on a first date!"

Everyone laughed hysterically at this warning, including me. Marshall called back to his brother, "You're *way* past due for an ass-kicking."

"I'm telling you, little Ruthie," Sean insisted.

His girlfriend, Jessie, called, "I know for a *fact!*"

Quinn said, "Marsh is just playing innocent."

Sean couldn't resist, "Well, it *has* been a while since he's had a woman out here with him. I'd say about fifteen years or so…since junior high, probably…"

Everyone was dying with laughter and Marshall warned his brothers, "Keep it up!"

Sean fired back, "That's *your* job!"

I called over to the fire, "I'll be careful!"

"I'll protect you," Marshall assured me and the next thing I knew I was in his arms and we were kissing, hidden safely between the rows of stalls. Horses clomped and whooshed all around us, though in that splendid moment of kissing him I heard only my racing pulse. I moaned with pleasure; he tasted so good, a combination of flavors as unique to him as the blue and green spokes of color in his irises. I dug my fingers in his hair and pushed my breasts against his powerfully-thundering heart.

"Touch me," I begged against his mouth, grasping his right wrist and hauling it toward my breasts, just in case there was a chance in hell he didn't realize what I meant. Though of course he did; I felt him grin. I licked the sweetness of his full lower lip, lightly biting down, and he groaned and shivered.

"I think first date *actually* equals second base," I whispered between kisses as Marshall unclasped my bra and caressed in earnest.

"We're doing as well as can be expected…with the no touching." He was short of breath, his lips on my neck.

"Come here," I begged, and he surged upward to reclaim my mouth, driving me against the wooden slats of the barn wall. I clung to his shoulders as we kissed open-mouthed, clutching the material of his t-shirt, desperate to tear it from him. Small, intense sounds broke free from my throat, matching the ones from his.

"Oh God…*oh Jesus*," he uttered hoarsely. My legs were locked around his waist, my spine braced against the wall. His eyes burned into mine. I nipped his chin and he groaned again. "We're *courting*..."

"I want you so much," I pleaded, grinding my hips against his with zero restraint. After all my big talk, I was playing really dirty.

His eyelids lowered and a pulse thrashed between my legs. A wild frenzy of kissing, me gripping his head, his hand straight down the front of my jeans, touching and tasting each other, enough could never be enough...

"Holy shit, they didn't even wait to ride Arrow!" Sean yelped, wheezing with laughter from the entrance of the barn. He ordered, "Wy, turn your head, boy, for the love of God!"

I couldn't help but laugh, burying my face against Marshall's chest as he lowered me gently to the ground and then yelled at his brothers, "*Severe beatings* for anyone who's still in my line of sight in two seconds!" He turned us so that his back blocked me from view, allowing me the chance to refasten my bra, whispering in my ear, "I'm so sorry about them."

Sean caught Wy in a headlock; neither of them budged an inch. Wy's voice cracked as he protested, "I don't even know what's happening!"

"I was going to use the pisser and thought there must be a mountain lion in here, what with all that scuffling," Sean said.

"What's going on?" Quinn yelled from the fire.

"There was a mountain lion attacking little Ruthie!" Sean insisted.

"All right, that's it," Marshall muttered, and Sean whooped and darted away as Marshall took off after him, Wy on their heels.

In any event, we didn't get a chance to ride Arrow that particular night. Marshall dropped me off at my apartment hours later, after we'd joined everyone at the bonfire and did our stargazing there, complete with bowls of warm apple pie and caramel ice cream; it wasn't until we were driving across town that Marshall acknowledged, "It's been a hell of a night. We haven't had a chance to talk about everything with your dad."

"I'm at a loss. I can't even begin to understand what he's thinking." I was exhausted and wanted Marshall to come upstairs with me, craving the way our bodies blended together.

Sensing my thoughts, he whispered, "I hate driving away and leaving you here alone."

"I hate it, too. But I'll be all right. Besides, Bender will protect me."

The big lab's tail thumped at hearing his name; he hunkered patiently in the backseat, waiting to accompany me upstairs. I patted Bender's head and Marshall stroked the dog's floppy ears, reminding him, "Buddy, you know your job."

The two of them walked me to my landing while I made sure my key worked in the door.

"Thank you for a wonderful first date," I whispered.

Marshall cupped my jaws and moonlight fell over us, bathing exactly half of his face with light, creating a sharp angle over his cheekbone. "When I look at you, my knees go weak. I feel like someone just punched me in the gut."

His words could not have been more sincere but I gripped his wrists and couldn't help but tease, "You mean it hurts?"

He nodded, exhaling softly. "You're so beautiful that yes, it does hurt a little."

My heart was what hurt then, with need for him, a near seizure of need. I stood on tiptoe to hug close his strong, wiry body as I whispered, "Thank you, sweetheart."

He spread his hands over my back and kissed my lips with utmost gentleness, whispering, "Until tomorrow, angel."

Chapter Sixteen

I WAS SO DEPLETED I SLEPT WITHOUT DREAMING, SPRAWLED atop my narrow mattress, and though Bender started the night lying on the floor, he ended it stretched beside me, pinning me under the covers. The big lab produced so much heat I was sweaty beneath the patchwork quilt long ago pieced together by Faye. Marshall and I had raided the linen closet at his house last night; I had also been gifted with two sets of sheets and an afghan knitted by his grandma. I checked my phone to make sure there were no messages, concerning or otherwise, from Tish.

"*Shoo*, dog," I groaned, and then giggled, since Bender didn't budge. Marshall came to collect him an hour later; he was headed to Miles City with Garth for a siding job and so couldn't linger, though we made up for the separation of the night hours with kiss after kiss, there on my little landing, until Garth, waiting in the parking lot in his idling truck, gave the horn two impatient beeps.

"When will you be home?" I asked between kisses, his forearms anchored around my waist, running my free hand over the side of his face, his hair; I'd tugged the cowboy hat from his head so I had better access to his mouth and it dangled down his back, caught in the fingertips of my right hand.

"This afternoon. I'll come over the minute we get back," Marshall promised. His gray eyes were so full of arousal and longing I knew my heart would continue to throb out of control long after he left. His voice was soft and husky as he whispered, "Come here," and stole one last kiss before I resettled his hat. I leaned my hips on the railing and watched as he headed to the truck, letting Bender climb inside first. Marshall stood on the running board and blew me a kiss before they took off. I watched until the truck disappeared into the dusty distance.

Tish was already at the law office when I jogged across the street fifteen minutes later, stationed at her desk with her reading glasses in place, riffling through a stack of file folders a good four inches thick. She'd been alone, the radio the only other sound in the room.

"Morning, Ruthie," she said as I entered to the tingle of the bell attached above the door. "It's so great to look up and see you coming across the street. How's your place?"

"I love it. I'll give you the tour at lunch."

Our gazes held; Tish removed her glasses and sighed, murmuring, "I didn't call Dad. I thought about it, but what you said last night was right. It's not the time to accost him."

I perched on the edge of her desk. "What do you make of everything? Do you think Robbie was exaggerating any of it? I mean, he called Dad a…" I couldn't speak the phrase, too ashamed that someone had applied it to my father.

"A 'pussy hound?'" Tish supplied somberly. "Yeah, tact isn't Robbie's strong suit. Not to mention that he'd been drinking. Not to excess, but enough that he wasn't watching his mouth. I suppose I could have guessed about Dad and Christina. After you guys left I was telling Case about how when I was in Chicago for the bar exam and we saw Ron and Christina during lunch, I *thought* she sent Dad a funny look. Speculative, you know? It didn't occur to me it's because they're intimate." She winced, as though unwillingly picturing it; I'd never met Christina Turnbull but the mental image of my father with another woman wasn't exactly unknown; after all, Dad's affair with Lanny had been the catalyst for ending my parents' marriage a decade ago.

"I feel like I don't even know who Dad is anymore, Tish. How could he do something like that to another wife?"

Tish tapped her glasses on the stack of files as she murmured, "Mom's never been wrong about him. You know, what I really want is to get Dad's opinion on that text. I couldn't sleep, thinking about it. And because I was listening for prowlers. Case dug out his dad's old shotgun and propped it beside the bed. Thank God no one showed up last night and got blown to bits."

"What if it was just a wrong number? How sure are you guys that it was even meant for Robbie, or referred to Franklin Yancy?"

"Not sure at all. But it's something to go on and we don't have much else at this point. Robbie called me on his way out of town this morning and we discussed it a little more. Robbie's never actually met Franklin but he said his parents move in the Yancys' social circle. He said he'd ask his father about him."

"Same with Dad, right, he knows those people?"

Tish nodded. "I'll ask him about Franklin, too, when I feel comfortable calling him without exploding. Dad promised he'd help me before he left for Chicago. I want to trust him, Ruthie, I can't help it."

"I know," I whispered. "I do, too." I looked around the office, noting that Mary's desk had been cleared of most of her belongings.

Tish followed my gaze. "Mary should be here any minute. She promised to come in to show you a few things. Al's over at the courthouse but he'll be back before noon." She paused and I felt the change in her expression the way I would have a shift in the wind. Her voice was very soft as she inquired, "Did you tell Marsh about what happened with Una's letter?"

I stalled, looking out the window at the brilliant sunny day there unfolding. "I haven't found the right time. I don't want to worry him on top of everything else." I realized I was hugging my own midsection and eased the pressure of my arms. "I don't even know what happened, Tish. I can't get a handle on it. I keep telling myself I was just imagining things, but...I *wasn't*."

"We definitely weren't imagining it." Tish wrapped a hand over my knee, as if to physically anchor me to the here and now. "It was the letters that caused it."

"It was like when I touched the paper, I could actually *see* Una Spicer. I feel like I *know* what she was writing about, like I know the people. The marshal, for instance..." From somewhere distant a vibration reached me and spiraled through my center; the awareness in my spine, at a bone-deep level, was sudden and disturbing.

No, I thought, standing abruptly and turning away, covering my distress with the pretense of checking out my new desk. *You are not going to disappear.*

"You'd tell me if you felt it again, wouldn't you?" Tish was already at my side, having closed the distance between us in point-two seconds.

My throat was dry but I whispered, "I'm all right."

"Here, sit down, Ruthie. I'm worried. You're so pale."

Despite myself I implored, "Does Una mention the marshal again?"

Tish battled the urge to lie; I could read her face like a beloved book. "Please tell me."

She spoke with quiet resignation. "She does. I've read her every word." Of course she had; Tish was a consummate scholar, after all, with a memory like a steel trap.

"And?"

"She doesn't refer to him by name, at least not in any of the letters we have. Case and I thought at first that she might be referring to Miles Rawley, the brother who died young, but then when I reread that part I realized Una said she thought the marshal *resembled* Miles, so it couldn't have been him. This marshal was someone else. Una clearly cared for him, whoever he was. She worried that he wasn't eating properly, that maybe illness was the culprit…"

I ached at this news, almost against my will; the distant vibration increased in frequency. "Is there more? Was he sick? What happened to him?"

"I don't know, Ruthie, I swear. There's nothing more about him. Una was more concerned because Cole, her son, was overdue to arrive home. She'd been writing Malcolm to inquire if he knew Cole's whereabouts that spring." Tish trailed to silence, staring out the front window as though momentarily seized by the images, both imagined and real, of another century.

"Was Cole in danger, do you think?" My voice was hardly more than a whisper but her shoulders convulsed with a shiver.

She turned to regard me, the blue of her eyes almost shocking in its intensity. An understanding passed between us, something deeper than even our connection as sisters – as though the universe itself was attempting to communicate a message to us, if only we were capable of hearing it.

"He was," I whispered, recognizing what she'd already sensed.

Tish closed her eyes and rubbed her forehead. She muttered, "I lay awake at night, worried about him. It's like…"

"Like he's right there, but we can't see him," I finished.

Tish nodded. Asking the question was unnecessary; I already knew the answer.

"We have to keep searching," I whispered.

That evening Marshall gave me my first lesson on how to saddle a horse, and I was glad for the cheerful distraction of animals and the pleasant scent of leather permeating the tack room connected to the barn. Clark made supper for us and after dessert Wy came to hang on the corral fence to watch as Marshall led Banjo, one of their mares, from the barn and looped her lead line around the top beam of the fence. She was a lovely horse with a smoky-gray hide, a dark stripe down the middle of her back, and graceful black legs.

"Hi, pretty girl," I murmured, patting her neck, which twitched beneath my touch.

Marshall cupped her square jaws and kissed her between the eyes. "She's about the most even-tempered of our mares, except for Oreo. You'd never believe she was sired by the same stud as Arrow."

He spoke words like 'sired' and 'stud' very matter-of-factly, noticing my amusement and winking.

"Good to know," I said lightly, continuing to stroke Banjo's neck. Marshall held my steady gaze in the sunset light and I reminded myself that Wy was only a few yards away, observing. Marshall was wearing his black cowboy hat, a pair of worn leather gloves, and his faded, dusty jeans, like he had no damn idea just how incredibly sexy and tempting he looked. My stomach was fluttery and my knees weak; I could have related to anyone who asked the exact number of hours it had been since the morning we'd made love in the guestroom bed.

Marshall moved behind me to grab the saddle blanket resting over the corral fence; Banjo's saddle was positioned beside it. He explained, "The pad always goes first," and passed it into my hands.

I positioned the blanket, which was a fleece rectangle about an inch thick, as squarely atop Banjo's back as I could.

"Now, if you have to adjust the pad, pull it backward or lift it straight up," Marshall instructed. "If you slide it forward along her back, it irritates the hair there. Pulls it the wrong way."

I nodded, absorbing his words, watching Banjo; she stood polite and still as a carving, her sleek black tail the only part of her that was moving.

Marshall grabbed the saddle next, muscles taut, the evening sun highlighting the lines of his body. He looked so *right* in his black hat, handling these tasks with both skill and natural grace.

"You want to approach from the left. This is a western saddle, which means the cinch is permanently attached to the right side. You flip the left stirrup up over the top of the saddle and then settle it squarely over the pad. You want about three or so inches of pad showing in the front. It's not easy at first." He demonstrated, of course making it *look* easy, and then swung it down from Banjo's back. "Now you give it a try."

I accepted the saddle from his arms and was surprised by its heft, but I was determined to do this right. I strained to lift it; Banjo's back seemed higher than a skyscraper but I finally managed, only knocking the pad a little off-center.

"That was pretty good." Marshall was facing away from the sun and my eyes were dazzled by both his grin and the low-slanting beams. "The western saddle hasn't changed much in probably a hundred years." He grasped a raised piece on the front in his gloved hand. "This is the horn and always goes in front. Beneath it is the pommel, and here in back is the cantle. These are the—"

"Stirrups," I interrupted. "Those I know."

"Yes, ma'am," he responded, lifting the one closest to us and settling it over Banjo's back. "Now we buckle the cinch, which was the hardest thing for me to learn, back when."

"How old were you?"

"Probably three or four," he said, in all seriousness. "Dad had us in saddles almost before we could walk."

"What was your first horse's name?"

"Dee," he responded softly. "She was a little sorrel Garth and I both learned on."

My adoring gaze moved between his lips and his eyes.

Both of us nearly forgot Wy until the boy piped up. "I remember Dee! I rode her a few times before we had to put her down."

Marshall resumed the lesson, the picture of patience. "First, reach beneath and grab the cinch. See here? And this is the latigo strap, which has to run through the ring of the cinch." He demonstrated with slow, exact movements. "Then you have to feed the strap through the D-ring, this thing here. What you want is about a foot or so of free strap coming from the D-ring. After that, you tie a western cinch knot."

He demonstrated at least a dozen times before I got the hang of it; by the time the sun vanished, leaving the world in a muted twilight glow, I'd gained a basic handle on how to buckle the cinch and tie the appropriate knot.

"That was not as easy as it looked," I muttered, sweat trickling down my temples, observing as Marshall removed Banjo's saddle for the final time and replaced it in the barn; he emerged and rested a fond hand on the mare's hide, patting her.

"Buddy, will you go and grab us something to drink?" Marshall requested of his brother. My heart began accelerating.

"Sure," Wy said agreeably, hopping down from the fence.

Wy had hardly turned his back and I was in Marshall's arms; he murmured intensely, "I need your mouth, *right now*."

And of course I gave it to him.

By the time the next weekend rolled around I had learned to competently saddle, mount, trot, and dismount Banjo; I'd learned the rudiments of working as a secretary in a law office and my way around a legal file cabinet, and I'd procured and begun taking birth control pills. Clark treated everyone to a celebratory Friday dinner at The Spoke in honor of Tish and Case's marriage, a welcome respite from our collective concerns, the evening merry with music and laughter, food and drinks. Marshall and Garth, guitars in tow, joined a local band on stage and the five of them played a waltz while Case and my sister danced. Marshall also took the opportunity to introduce me to the servers and bartenders, all of whom were his cousins.

No trespassers reappeared on Case's property but an unwelcome figure did return to Jalesville; Al called Tish on a Saturday morning two weeks later to let her know Derrick Yancy was back from Illinois.

That very night Marshall and I took Arrow for a ride after eating dinner with Case and Tish – we'd spent the entirety of dinner discussing Derrick's return and the necessity of confronting him. Derrick had made no attempt to contact Tish since the fire and she was leery of approaching *him* with no warning; she felt strongly, however, that she alone should seek him out, assuming Derrick would be more willing to speak to her with no one else present. And of course Case was adamantly against this idea, leaving the issue unresolved as Marshall and I left the trailer, the two of us headed for the stargazing we'd missed back on our first date.

"I've never seen the stars look like this," I marveled as we left the Rawleys' yard behind, headed west into the foothills with Arrow at a steady walk. Marshall hadn't saddled his horse since it was easier to ride double without one; both of us were bundled in jeans and warm sweatshirts in the chilly night air. Riding this way with him, snuggled against his warm strength, was about the most wonderful thing I'd ever experienced.

"Screw the stars. I've never felt anything as good as you in my arms," he murmured in response, his chin near my temple, and I ran my palms over the length of his hard thighs, braced on either side of mine. He kept me gently anchored with his right hand, holding the light riding rein in his left. Beneath us, Arrow's powerful muscles shifted as he walked with controlled patience. I could sense that the big gray horse wanted to move faster than a walk but he never disobeyed Marshall's commands; his pointed ears were like radar, constantly attuned to the sound of his master's voice.

I picked up our earlier conversation, frustrated by the lack of answers to any of our questions. "I understand why Case doesn't want Tish to talk to Derrick on her own but I can see her point, too. After all, Derrick told her he had something to tell her and she never got to hear what."

"But it's dangerous. If Tish really was married to Yancy in another life, like we were talking about, it's all the more reason to avoid confrontation. Case wanted to kill Yancy months ago, before we'd even found out all these other things. You should have seen the way Yancy looked at Tish at the city council meeting back in July. Case was ready to break his neck *that* night."

"But Derrick knows things. Even if he doesn't always understand what he's knowing." My words sounded almost nonsensical, so I rephrased. "I mean, something inside of him remembers the past life when he and Tish were married. Even if he can't explain it, or would ridicule the whole idea. It's still *there*, somewhere in his head." I paused, my gaze pulled upward as I thought of something entirely new. Studying the stars, I murmured, "I wonder if he was a Yancy *then*, in the past life."

I felt Marshall's slow, thoughtful nod as he considered. "It would be a possibility. I mean, we all believe that Case might have been Cole Spicer. And Cole is Case's ancestor."

"So we could reasonably assume that maybe Derrick's soul has stayed close to the original family, too." I spoke softly, watching the sky. Beneath its vast, unending blackness, I felt no larger than a speck. A tiny dot on a map, a cork bobbing in an ocean. Thoughts of disconnected souls swimming across the night sky, struggling against powerful currents beyond their comprehension, filled my head.

As if sensing my unease, Marshall tightened his arm around my waist. His voice sent the frightening images scattering. "Right. That's why Derrick called Tish a whore back when we played at the Coyote's Den. It's probably a good thing she didn't mention it that night. Case would have dragged Yancy through the bar."

"Tish said those two are spoiling for a fight. And maybe it's a fight that's been brewing for over a century." Even speaking the words aloud felt strange…but I believed what I said.

Marshall gave a low whistle. "This is *so* fucked up. But even so, it doesn't seem farfetched." He paused, searching for a way to make his point, gently smoothing a path up and down my thigh with his palm. "What I mean is that I feel like it's meant to be this way. Ever since that night way back when we met Carter and Camille at The Spoke, our paths have been leading toward something beyond all of us."

"Toward each other," I whispered, renewing my grip on Marshall's legs. "I agree with Tish that Derrick is the key, somehow. He *knows* things. He knows his family's business and why they want Jalesville. If anyone has answers, it's him."

"But will he give them up? He's on guard, like Case said."

"But he's also under tremendous pressure. He's losing business here. He's *failing* his father. According to Robbie, that's a big issue with Derrick."

Tish had spoken to Robbie for almost an hour on Friday afternoon, sitting at her desk in the law office. Robbie's first week at Turnbull and Hinckley proved relatively uneventful; he said Ron had personally welcomed him to work on his first morning and he'd been given the requisite rookie load of paperwork. He had, however, made slight headway on the mysterious text.

"It was sent from Chicago, that's all my cell provider was able to tell me," Robbie had told Tish that afternoon. He also relayed what he'd learned from his litigator father, Asher Benson of Damon and Benson, which was the fact that while Franklin Yancy was well-known in Chicago business circles, he was rarely seen. Asher recalled meeting him only once, and very briefly, during a dinner party hosted by T.K. Yancy, the family's patriarch. Franklin had a reputation for mild eccentricity, Asher explained, and traveled abroad extensively, while Derrick, more than a decade his brother's junior, seemed to be the foot soldier, the one assigned to less-pleasant tasks.

"I knew it!" Tish had crowed. "The chip on Derrick's shoulder must be enormous by this point in his life. His brother gets to travel to places like London and Milan while he wallows in rural Montana. No wonder he's always drunk when he's not working."

"But it still doesn't explain the text!" I'd countered. "Franklin Yancy obviously *exists*. So what did the text really mean? Did someone mistype it?"

It was yet another question we could not answer.

Marshall said, "I'd bet my last dollar those bastards are all criminals. Tax fraud, embezzlement, God only knows what. They want our land, but for what? Are they trying to cover something up? Somehow protect themselves or their interests?" He made a low clicking sound to Arrow, taking the horse around a patch of scrubby brush. We were well away from the house by now, the stars riotous and splendid as they spilled across the night sky with no moon to outshine their brilliance.

"They're basically untouchable, like Tish was saying. They're protected by their wealth and position."

"I'll ask around at college when I start back there next week. Maybe someone from the local Fish and Wildlife chapter has heard something, or has some idea. Maybe there's some environmental angle we haven't considered." Fish and Wildlife was the state organization for which Marshall hoped to work upon graduating next spring.

"No, Marsh, please don't. It's the kind of thing you see in bad late-night movies, when people get suspicious of the person asking too many questions…"

Marshall swept loose hair from the side of my neck so he could press a gentle kiss there. He whispered, "I don't want you to worry, angel. I'm all right."

As he spoke I caught sight of a silver ribbon winding through the tall, rangy grass ahead, and pointed. "Is that…"

"Rawley Creek, we always called it." Marshall's tone grew reverent. "It bisects the old pasture where the sheep used to graze back when we still ranched. The original homestead cabin was built right nearby, I haven't had a chance to show you yet. We can ride over here tomorrow, in the day, so you can see it."

The small creek lay bathed in starlight, a slender, winding mirror reflecting the night sky. It was a beautiful sight and should have conjured feelings of quiet peace, but a strange anxiety grew in my skull. Arrow snorted and sidestepped in response to my increasing tension. Breathing became difficult. I brushed at my face like I meant to push aside a smothering hand. Across miles or centuries – I could not have accurately said – I felt the distant tremor of awareness.

Marshall tugged Arrow back in line with practiced movements and his grip on my waist tightened. "You're shivering. What's wrong, Ruthie?"

I didn't know – I couldn't explain. I only knew the horrible sensation was returning in droves, tearing at the substance of my body. I made a sound, a low whimper that became a grating hiss. I felt the sudden presence of others surrounding Marshall and me, only they were not *here*. I closed my eyes, fighting it, clinging to Marshall's legs. Fear paralyzed my limbs.

Stop, I pleaded, but a picture formed on the backs of my eyelids.

Men and women sat on blankets spread over the ground, while children – all little boys – played near the creek. Laughing, chatting, admiring the sun as it pierced a magenta cloudbank on the western horizon, they were but paces away. *Here but not here.* Rich pink light cast their upturned faces in a radiant glow. Smiling and at ease, they appeared happy. Alive. So alive their warm breath touched my cheek – so close I could have grasped them in my hands. It was the Rawleys, but not the family I loved here in 2013. It was the family from over a century ago, and I knew them.

I knew them.

Me – not some past incarnation of me. And they were just beyond the edges of my perception, just beyond the black, starry night where Arrow, Marshall, and I existed.

What...the hell...

Reality flickered like fireflies at twilight. Time didn't exist and yet it *did* – the magenta sunset became dark night and then flickered back again, like channels being changed. Somewhere in the distance I heard my own voice screaming for Marshall, racing to reach him before…

Before…

My fingers passed straight through his legs. He was shouting my name, feral and frantic –

No!

No, please no.

Don't take me! Not yet!

A vortex of pure energy tore at my body. I was as insubstantial as a sunbeam, a dust mote, *almost gone* –

"RUTHANN!"

Marshall's voice sliced through the roaring nonsense.

Like a taut rubber band snapping to its original shape I was hurled back to myself at the last possible instant, *only a breath from the point of no return* –

All at once the night was quiet and immobile; the Rawleys had vanished.

Marshall swung Arrow sharply about and heeled him to a full canter, riding hard away; we had barely cleared the distant yard before he dismounted with me in his arms and went to his knees on the ground. I understood without words that he'd felt it just as strongly, the imminent danger of our separation. It had almost been too late. My heart would not slow its speed. I clutched Marshall's sweatshirt; his arms were wrapped almost double around my torso. His breath was harsh and choppy and I realized he was crying. The house remained dark except for the lone kitchen light, the bonfire pit silent.

When he'd regained enough control to speak, he whispered one word. "*Never.*"

Depleted, I couldn't even open my eyes.

"It will *never* take you from me." He spoke roughly. "Whatever *it* was…there was some kind of fucking force field out there, oh God, *oh Jesus*, you started to disappear. *Ruthann…*" His voice broke.

"I can't go back there, I don't want to go there," I babbled, recognizing the need to explain what I truly meant; I had to tell him about Una's letters and the marshal, and the vision of his ancestors…

"You're here, angel, right here with me. I won't let you go."

Arrow stood on guard, long neck curved protectively around us, motionless as a sculpture except for his swishing tail. I inhaled Marshall's scent until I finally calmed. And later, in the parking lot at my apartment, Marshall killed the engine of his truck. For the first time, Bender was not with us at this point in the evening.

Marshall said, "I need to hold you while we sleep. Will you let me do that?"

I was so in love with him it was one part pain, a fall I hadn't seen coming, had not expected, but welcomed with quiet intensity. I whispered, "Of course."

It was late. We were silent as we climbed the stairs to the landing; inside, once I'd emerged from the bathroom wearing one of his t-shirts and my pajama shorts, he simply extended his arms, reaching for me. He was sitting on the bed in his boxers and nothing else, sheet drawn up to his thighs, and I admired him in the soft lamplight…this man I loved so much my bones seemed to be resonating.

This man I could not do without.

He whispered, "The way you look right now, ready for bed. I want to see you this way every night for the rest of my life."

Tears hazed my vision. I fell into his embrace and pressed my face to his chest hair, slipping my legs beneath the sheet to twine around his; Marshall settled us on our backs and gently stroked my hair with both hands.

"The lamp," I murmured, unwilling to move.

"I'll get it," he whispered back.

Chapter Seventeen

I WOKE TO THE MUTED CLATTERING OF THE SHOWER AND rolled to my right side, curling around the single pillow on the bed; Marshall was humming in there, just quietly, and I smiled at the sound. After we spent over an hour talking – the primary topic being Una Spicer's letters and what we thought had happened last night – I'd slept dreamlessly, secure in his arms. Even though we hadn't concocted a satisfactory explanation for what had occurred, it was Marshall's opinion that if I avoided the things which seemed to trigger the feeling of disappearing – all of which had a physical connection to an earlier century – then everything would be fine; both of us pretended to believe this.

When the water turned off I called, "Good morning!"

Marshall, dripping wet, stuck his head out the bathroom door. "Morning, angel. I just took the iciest, coldest goddamn shower I could handle. Waking up beside you just a little while ago…"

"*Courting*," I murmured, but it had been weeks. My birth control was working by now.

Marshall grinned. "It seems like I'm usually the one reminding *you* of that."

"You dry off, sweetheart, and I'll make us breakfast."

"It was so good to hold you all night," he said, all teasing dissipating.

"It was so good to be held."

Standing in the kitchen moments later I realized I possessed zero breakfast food. I surveyed the countertop in hopes of spying a stray banana and instead caught sight of my phone, message light blinking. A second later I was slapped by the sight of a dozen missed calls and texts from Liam Gallagher.

Oh no, I thought, sinking fast, wishing I could just delete all of them without having to read or listen, without having to acknowledge the sting of my own culpability. *Stop it, Ruthann. Don't be a coward. The least you can do is see what he had to say.*

I'd heard nothing from Liam since the afternoon I'd texted him while sitting in my car in the parking lot, though I knew from conversations with Mom and Camille that he wasn't dealing well with my absence. Dark, oozing guilt reentered my soul. I hated that I'd made another person feel this way. Gingerly, as though handling a tiny bomb, I read the most recent text message. I pressed my fingertips to my forehead, hard and punishing, just as Marshall came around the corner from the bathroom, dressed in his clothes from yesterday and smelling like coconut body wash.

Whatever he'd started to say, with cheerful sweetness in his voice, changed instantly to concern. He caught my shoulders. "What's wrong?"

"It's all right, I just…" I faltered, uncertain if it was the right thing to tell Marshall about Liam's sudden, obsessive attempt to reach me. I finally muttered, "Liam's been texting me…"

"Do you want me to call him?" Marshall asked after a short, tense silence.

"No. He's hurting right now and I did that to him. If *you* called he would flip out. It would be terrible." Unexpected anger spiked in my belly; without directly acknowledging it, I realized last night's unexplained events were also being given an outlet, fair or not. I flung the phone to the counter, where it clattered, ricocheting to the floor. "You *can't possibly* think it would be all right for you to call him!"

Marshall's jaw tightened. "I can see he's hurting you by doing this and I'd like him to stop."

"I deserve it! I broke his heart and I feel sick about that! The last person he wants to hear from in this situation is you! He *already* doesn't like you!"

Marshall plucked my phone from the floor with a single brusque movement. The latest text was from around five this morning and Liam had written, *Please call me. I need to talk to you. I love you and that is never going to change.*

"This is stopping, now." Marshall set the phone on the table with a deliberate lack of speed, stone-faced.

Guilt hissed in my ears; I would not pretend to ignore my accountability in this situation. I faced off with Marshall. "As though I can help what he writes! He does love me, even if he shouldn't, and it's not like you can just get rid of those feelings so quickly." An angry exhalation interrupted my tirade. "And I told you before, don't tell me what to do!"

Marshall spoke through his teeth. "He's trying to guilt you into feeling hurt and that will stop *today*. If I have to call him to explain this fact, *then I will!*"

"You won't! Liam doesn't deserve that!"

"He's using every tactic he can to make you feel like shit!"

"I told you, I *deserve* it!"

"No you don't! Stop saying that!"

"What do you want me to say?!" I yelled.

"You know what I want?" Marshall yelled right back. "I want to drive to Minnesota and smash my fist straight through *Paul Bunyan's face!*"

"For what?" I demanded, hot and sweaty, thrumming with emotion.

"For thinking he has the right to tell you he still loves you, that's what," Marshall seethed. He turned abruptly away, covering his face. More quietly, he admitted, "And I hate that you're so protective of him."

I yanked at his wrists. "Look at me! *Dammit*, Marshall, can't you see that I'm *in love with you?* Are you *blind?*" Tears surged into my eyes, further infuriating me. "In case you *hadn't realized.*"

There was a crackling moment of silence. He lowered his hands.

"Did you hear me? I'm telling you I love you!" I yelled.

He found his voice, hoarse though it was. "Ruthann. I've been in love with you for so long now I can't remember a time when I wasn't. Oh God, *I love you.*"

"*Marshall*," I moaned, overwhelmed with emotion. "I don't mean to cry, I love you so much...I don't know why you make me so *mad*..."

He used his thumbs to brush aside my flowing tears. "I wish I could promise I won't make you mad ever again, but it would be a lie. I have such a bad temper. I'm so sorry, please don't cry…"

"I'm still mad…" I was laughing and weeping at once, and Marshall was shaking a little.

He implored, "Come here, sweetheart, come here in my arms."

I kissed his mouth, my lips wet with stray tears. I whispered, "You don't have to go anywhere today, do you?"

Curled together on the bed later that same day, Marshall lay with his cheek against my stomach, his thumbs bracketing my hipbones. I played my fingers over his left ear, my other arm tucked beneath my head as we sprawled naked and sublime.

"I love how you smell," he whispered. "Right here, on your sweet soft belly. You smell so good. This is my favorite place on earth."

"That tickles," I admonished as he exhaled against my skin, trailing kisses to the soft triangle of my pubic hair.

There, he rested his face and murmured, "And here. I want to stay between your legs for all time. Will you let me?"

I giggled as he teased with his tongue, and then gasped as his teasing became something else. He shifted and settled me just where he wanted, grasping me from beneath. His intent was serious now and my breath grew short as I spread my legs even farther, falling into the sweet, wet world he had shown me, a world of such sensual pleasure, one I never knew existed. For a time we were safely cocooned within it, this intimate place that witnessed my gasping moans and his panting breath, both of us shuddering with the sacred joy of our lovemaking.

"Yes, you may," I murmured primly, much later, when he had collapsed atop me.

"May what, angel?" he whispered against my neck, hoarse with exertion.

"Stay between my legs for all time," I whispered, shivering as little jolting shocks, afterthoughts of deep pleasure, surged between our still-joined bodies.

Marshall laughed, husky and low. "I love to hear those words come from your sweet angel mouth." He cupped my shoulder blades and nuzzled kisses on my sweating skin. I pulled him closer and whispered something else, and he snorted a laugh and bit my earlobe. "And those words. Though, no one would believe me that an angel talked that way."

I giggled and nipped his chin, urging with my hips, and he bit me again, this time on the side of my neck. "But you're *my* angel, and I love how you talk."

"More," I ordered, smiling into his gray eyes, running my calves along the sides of his lean torso.

Marshall grinned in response, slowly tonguing my lower lip, then taking it between his teeth as he resumed our rhythm. His voice vibrating along my nerves, he whispered, "Yes, ma'am."

"Is it like this for everyone?" I murmured, even though I already knew the answer. He was so very hard, silken and hot within me; I arched into his deep thrusts, quivering anew at each delicious penetration of his flesh.

He shook his head in response. His eyelids were at half-mast, his forearms on either side of my head as he braced above; his voice was a throaty whisper. "It's a gift, angel…"

Sometime later, crushed beneath his exhausted weight, I hugged him as hard as I was able and teased, imploring, "*More…*"

"Even if you beg and *plead*, I gotta rest a minute," he muttered, and I giggled.

I kissed his jaw, where sweat had trickled down from his temple, roughing up his dark hair. I whispered, "You just *know*."

"I told you I see you." He rolled us to the side so I fit against him rather than beneath. Half asleep, he kissed my ear and almost immediately began snoring. I lay awake for another minute, admiring the way the lazy evening sun pouring through the single window shone on the dark hair covering his forearms, crossed like an X beneath my breasts. His hard, tanned skin was such a contrast to the pale, freckled softness of my breasts and belly. Blissfully content in this moment, I pressed my thumbs to his knobby wrist bones and then joined him in sleep.

I didn't wake until my phone buzzed with an incoming call, just after dawn the next morning. It was Monday, and there appeared to be the promise of sun on the horizon. I was reluctant to move, mostly because moving would take me from Marshall's arms and the warmth of his embrace, but partly because I was squeamish about discovering who was calling so early. My phone was out in the kitchen and went to voicemail.

Please don't let it be Liam.

Marshall kissed the top of my bare shoulder and then resumed a light snoring. I muffled a giggle, rubbing sleep from my eyes, and mumbled, "I think there might be someone camping in our bed…"

"Hmmm?" he wondered, still dozing.

I scooted my naked backside closer to his hips and insisted, "Yeah, he's camping out beneath the sheets, I can feel his tent pole," and then Marshall started laughing, shifting over me, the covers still drawn to our waists.

"Woman," he said softly, but with enough intent that my stomach went all woozy with delight. "Might you have a suggestion for where I could…" He was momentarily overcome with laughter. "Where I could maybe pop this tent?"

And then we were both laughing so hard we could barely kiss.

Tish had left me the voicemail, to my great relief, which I realized after Marshall and I dragged ourselves from bed and showered together. Since it was a single stall rather than a showerhead positioned over a tub, the experience was a lesson in body positioning.

Marshall joked, "Good thing neither of us is claustrophobic," sliding his hands up and down my wet body; likewise, I could not keep mine from him, curling my fingers into his chest hair, licking water from his neck, clutching the lean muscles of his ass. Being allowed to touch him with no restraint was sensual and moving in ways I could not articulate; I simply *felt*, and feeling negated the need for any words. The heat of his muscles and his lithe strength, the shape of the bones beneath his skin, the wavy hair that fell to his shoulders when soaked, the look in his eyes – as though he wanted to devour me and yet simultaneously couldn't believe his own good fortune.

"You are *so* sexy," I adored, rubbing my nipples in small circles against his chest; I giggled at the way I could speak and behave so boldly, all while my cheeks flamed.

Marshall twined long strands of my hair around his fingers. "You look like a mermaid right now, a sweet, hot, sex-starved mermaid straight out of my wildest dreams."

He made me laugh so effortlessly; I collapsed against him, demanding, "Wouldn't I have a fishtail in that case?"

"Not if you were out of the ocean," he contradicted knowledgably, one hand gliding along my belly, then lower; I latched a leg around his waist to allow him better access.

"That feels so good…" I clung for dear life as he caressed, my head falling back.

Marshall teased my neck with little wet kisses; his lips on my chin, he whispered, "You know what word I think of when I look at you?"

Our bodies were nearly suctioned together with the steaming water flowing over us. Between kisses, I whispered, "Tell me…"

"'Lavish,' that's what word. I want to lavish you with kisses and with love…plus, you're lavishly beautiful…"

I gripped it and ordered, "Come lavish me with your cock."

Marshall hoisted me against the shower wall; we thrust together so vigorously that he came within a minute. My wrists linked at his nape and my ankles at the base of his spine, I reflected, "It's like we've been deprived for years instead of a few weeks."

Marshall licked a slow line along my jaw, closing his teeth over my earlobe. "We *have* been deprived for years, my sexy little mermaid, of each other. I can't get enough of you. I'm like a starving man."

I roughed up his wet hair and his eyes crinkled at the corners as he grinned. I said, "I promise to feed you. As best I can." I traced the sensitive skin behind his ears and lamented, "But right now we have to get ready for work."

Twenty minutes later Tish greeted me as I entered the law office with, "Did you listen to my message?"

"No," I admitted, straightening the bottom edge of my sleeveless yellow blouse. Mom had mailed me several boxes from Landon, sending my clothes, including all my cold-weather gear; my jewelry (not that I owned much) was contained in a sealed envelope tucked in the pocket of my winter coat. In addition, Mom had included a container of things she thought I might need, such as ink pens, stamps, rubber bands and adhesive tape, cuticle cream and mosquito repellant, some of my old CDs. In the very bottom of one box, Grandma and Aunt Ellen had stashed two covered tin pans, loaded with peanut-butter chocolate-chip cookies and marshmallow brownies, my two favorites.

My family loved me and I knew this to the bottom of my heart.

"Good morning, Ruthann," Al said from his desk, setting aside a document and a pen.

"Morning, Al," I said.

Tish leaned forward over her desk, pinning me with her blue gaze as she said succinctly, "Al knows everything."

He uttered a laugh, rising to join us near Tish's desk, closer to the front windows. "I thank you for the compliment, though I believe Helen Anne would disagree."

I stashed my purse in Mary's former desk, now mine, and then took a chair to my sister's left. Al remained standing, ankles and arms loosely crossed, fingers tapping in a conveyance of excess energy. He nodded at Tish, allowing her the floor.

"For this moment, let's set aside the issue of our father and Christina Turnbull," Tish decided, leaning back, crossing her long legs. She wore nude heels, an apple-green sleeveless blouse, and a smooth beige skirt; the matching linen jacket hung over her chair. Her phone was within arm's reach; I saw her eye it, as though wishing she could call Dad right now and demand answers.

"Duly noted," Al murmured, nodding again.

"We were talking about Derrick just before you got here, Ruthie. I called you this morning to tell you to hurry. Al agrees with my theory about Derrick's inferiority complex. His take on the text about Franklin is that Derrick was drunk and sent the message as a shot against his older brother."

Al followed up. "The message was sent from Chicago, correct? And

Derrick was in Chicago at that time?"

Tish and I both nodded.

"And Derrick drinks to excess, as you, Tish, have unfortunately witnessed on more than one occasion. I see this as a drunken slur. It's likely Derrick wishes Franklin *didn't* exist, and possibly vice versa. Franklin is quite a bit older than Derrick, more than a decade, I'd guess. Perhaps more a secondary father-figure."

"You've met Franklin?" I asked.

Al nodded. "On one occasion, many years ago. I was never well acquainted with the Yancy family. They are…how to put it delicately… quite a few rungs above my own family on the social ladder. Franklin and Derrick's mother died long ago. She was T.K.'s first wife."

"Point being, Franklin actually *does* exist," I said.

"He does. Unless I met a ghost all those years ago. At that time Franklin traveled frequently for the family business, and it seems he still does. What is it that Robbie calls Derrick? The nickname he assigned to him?"

A smile fluttered across Tish's lips, erasing the frown she'd been wearing. "Number Two."

"Indeed. Of course, this makes Franklin 'Number One,' elder brother, the son against whom Derrick constantly attempts to prove himself," Al said.

"Do you think their father favors Franklin?" Tish asked, leaning forward now, knocking askew a stack of files.

"Undoubtedly. Franklin was the one who started up Capital Overland in 1993. He seemed to sense the tech boom in that decade. I'd go as far as to say he has an extraordinary ability for predicting stocks trends and making investments. Surely he's tripled the family's wealth by now."

A shiver chilled my spine, drawing Tish's attention. In the next instant her gaze leaped to the front windows and she stood so quickly her chair flew backward.

"It's Derrick," she all but growled, stalking to the window; Al's handiwork painted on the glass – the new, inches-tall lettering proclaiming *Howe and Spicer, Attorneys at Law* – fell in striped shadows across my sister's face. I skirted Tish's chair to reach her side and peered out at a black SUV rolling slowly past the office. The angle of the sun obscured my view of the man driving but Tish and I were framed in the front windows, staring at him, as he couldn't fail to observe. Despite the bright day a dark, palpable tension flowed between my sister and this man; I imagined the glass between them cracking like an eggshell and shattering to the pavement.

I swore I could hear the enraged challenge spooling through my sister's mind in that moment – *come in here, bastard, I dare you.*

The SUV was crawling, its wheels barely turning. Someone in the car behind Derrick's tooted the horn with two impatient beeps and Derrick accelerated, his vehicle disappearing from our line of sight.

Tish muttered, "There *has* to be a way."

She and Al headed to court not fifteen minutes later; just as in downtown Landon, most people in Jalesville walked to and from any daytime appointments. I sat idly for a few minutes, my chin resting on my knuckles as I watched them amble across the town square. Tish, taller than Al by about four inches, seemed to be listening intently to whatever he was saying. Clutching his briefcase in his left hand, Al gestured with his right, and I hoped he was counseling Tish to avoid a solo confrontation with Derrick Yancy. In the brief time I'd known him, I already liked Al Howe. I wouldn't have gone as far as to say he was a replacement father for Tish, but he definitely exuded a paternal kindness. And our own father had left a lot to be desired, of late.

I turned next to my work, which also included filing, answering the phone, and greeting anyone who entered the office. In addition to people stopping by to make appointments, I was gifted at midmorning with a peach pie baked by Marshall's aunt, Julie Heller, who dropped in for introductions; she hadn't been at The Spoke on Friday when Clark had taken us all out to eat. Julie resembled Clark, her older brother; she was tall and lean, deeply tanned and with the same warm brown eyes. Her long hair was slate-gray, held back with a tortoiseshell headband. She wore small turquoise earrings and minimal make-up; as she placed the covered pie plate on my desk her first words were, "Hi there, hon. I can see why my nephew is in love."

I flushed, standing to shake her outstretched hand.

"Julie Heller." She had a firm grip and a no-nonsense attitude, much like her daughters, Pam, Lee, and Netta.

"Ruthann Gordon," I said, and flushed brighter; I'd been a breath away from saying 'Ruthann Rawley' instead. "I'm glad to meet you. I met your girls at The Spoke."

"They told me all about it. They love seeing Marsh so happy." She latched her hands loosely on her hips and a smile softened her face. "You never saw a sweeter little thing than Marsh when he was a boy. Oh, he could be a devil, but no one could stay angry at him for long. His nickname was 'Marshy.'" She chuckled, leaning back at the waist. "Our little Marshy. Doesn't suit him anymore, but we like to tease him."

I giggled. "I can imagine."

"Well, I won't keep you long. I just wanted to bring dessert and welcome you to town and to our family. Come over for dinner anytime! Especially after you two have a couple of kids." She grinned at my raised eyebrows, that wide, knowing Rawley grin which so often graced Marshall's face. "Not to rush anything, of course. It's just that my own darn girls haven't given me any grandkids yet, so I have to steal Clark's."

Thoughts of the family pictures on Clark's mantle filled my head, of Marshall as a beloved little boy, surrounded by his family. Faye's presence was strong in my mind as I said, "Marshall's birthday is coming up and I want to do something special. I know it's hard for him…"

Julie nodded slowly, her gaze lifting as memory hauled her backward through time. "You're right. Faye died just two days after he turned eighteen." She issued a soft, low sigh, eyes fixed on the ceiling but surely witnessing the past. "That was the worst day of our lives."

"What happened?" I whispered; I knew only the barest of details. We were still standing and so I offered her a chair, wanting to keep talking. I found her presence unexpectedly comforting; she could have been Grandma or Aunt Ellen in those moments, an older woman who loved her family above all else. The office was quiet and peaceful, inhabited only by us and warm sunlight.

"Faye was driving over to Miles City that afternoon, for an appointment. The boys were all in school that day...it was a Friday. Except Wy, he would have been home with Clark. I was sitting at the sewing machine when the phone rang, mending a seam rip in Lee's cheerleading sweater. Lord, I can even remember the song playing on the radio. I had a strange feeling when I heard the phone, like I didn't want to answer. Clark could hardly speak." Tears brimmed in Julie's eyes and then in mine, in response. She had to swallow before whispering, "I remember trying to think of the last time I'd seen Faye, and panicking because I couldn't."

"I'm so sorry." Hearing these details stabbed at my heart; as soon as I saw Marshall I planned to get my arms around him and not let go until tomorrow morning. Something else occurred to me and I spoke before I thought. "Who hit her car that day?"

Marshall had never mentioned the identity of the driver, and I'd never asked; it seemed intrusive, even insensitive. But I felt I could question Julie, suddenly concerned it had been someone local. What if the Rawleys had been forced to see this person every day since? Accident or no, how could you keep from blaming him until the end of time?

"He was a truck driver on a route to northern Minnesota. Claimed he fell asleep at the wheel. Clark would have killed him with his bare hands but it had been an accident, it was plain. After the sheriff questioned him that terrible day, the driver seemed to disappear – at least to my knowledge, Clark has never heard from him since." New tears wet Julie's eyes, which she swiped with her knuckles. "I thought Clark would die along with Faye. God, how he loved her. He wanted to, but he had the boys to think of. Those boys are his saviors. The Spicer boys, too. They kept him going when he wanted to disappear."

Julie had spoken the word 'disappear' twice within a few seconds and it seemed to possess weight, settling over my shoulders and clinging like an unwelcome cloak; my spine twitched.

Julie continued, "It's been ten years now but it's still hard for them. Time hasn't helped much. We all wish Clark would find someone...not as a replacement for Faye, no one could replace her, but for companionship.

I worry so for him, for what he'll do once Wy heads off to college. I know the boys look out for their dad but they have lives of their own, too. I hope they'll settle around here, like Garth and Becky, but it's not fair to expect it."

Studying Marshall's aunt, whose face resembled his, whose brown eyes shone with compassion, I confessed, "I'd love that. I would love to have a dozen of Marshall's babies and live near Clark."

Julie reached to squeeze my hand. "My nephew is a lucky man." Her head dipped just slightly to one side, her gaze deepening; she spoke slowly, almost as though thinking aloud, as she said, "You're special, Ruthann, and I mean that as the sincerest of compliments. There's something in your eyes…something about you altogether. I don't know exactly how to explain it. A sense of…" She paused, peering into my irises as though they contained the answer she sought; at last she whispered, "A sense of destiny."

Destiny…

Didn't I tell you that Rawleys make boys, sweet darlin', my sweet angel?

My father taught me two things, and one of those was to marry a woman for love.

I cannot keep this child…

Don't go, don't leave me here!

Tell me the way back…

I swear to you I will find you, in time we will find each other again. Promise me you'll remember…

I blinked and the voices rippled away, swift waves over a shallow pond. Sunlight stung my eyes.

Someone was saying, "Are you all right, hon? You went so pale for a second there. I didn't mean to startle you. Here, let me get you a glass of water."

It wasn't until then that I realized where I was…*when* I was.

Marshall's aunt was filling a plastic cup at the water cooler. I concentrated on her for a long moment; my head continued to swim with sluggish undulations. As though locked in a silent dream, I noticed Al and Tish across the street, their mouths moving as they chatted, returning to the office.

It's all right, you're all right, I told myself. *You'll be just fine.*

But it was a lie.

Tish was brimming with the good news she and Al had received at the courthouse – according to Hank Ryan, council chairman, Capital Overland had lost so many sales in the past few weeks that Derrick was rumored to be returning to Chicago for good.

"People are losing whatever faith they might have had in Yancy's business dealings," Al said as he settled his briefcase on his desk. "We may just win this fight yet!"

They were jubilant and I tried to imbibe some of the feeling; my mind felt like it had been struck by the equivalent of a heavy object.

"I never doubted it," Julie said, with a grin. "Our lawyers are second to none."

Tish beamed. "I won't rest until he's gone for good, but this is a great sign."

She and I left for lunch a few minutes later, after promising Julie we'd bring Marshall and Case to dinner at her house in the near future. Julie hugged each of us before leaving and I assured her again that I was all right, just tired.

"What did she mean?" Tish badgered as we headed for Trudy's Diner.

I fiddled with my apartment keys, purposely stalling. I wanted to tell my sister about what had happened when Marshall and I were riding Arrow Saturday night, but the words wouldn't come. I felt exhausted deep down in my bones, plagued by an increasing notion that I was going crazy. Hearing voices, seeing people who weren't there; feeling my body dissolve like smoke in a breeze.

"Oh, we were talking about how Marshall's birthday is always hard for him." We stood under Trudy's awning; if I closed my eyes, I might have been standing on the porch at Shore Leave, hearing the sounds of lunchtime in a busy cafe, smelling fried food.

"Case was just saying something about that, too," Tish murmured. "Does Julie want to plan a party?"

"She wants to help. I told her I'd like to do something special." I eyed my apartment windows, a floor above. "I just need to run upstairs quick. I'll be right back. Will you get us a table?"

Inside my place it smelled like coconut body wash. The scent brought this morning's shower to mind and I flushed at the heat of the memory, wishing Marshall was home. As I entered the kitchen I saw that he'd arranged an enormous wildflower bouquet in one of the three water glasses I owned and then positioned this gift on the counter, along with a note. Despite everything, I raced to it with all the joy of a treasure hunter.

The note read, *Hi angel, make your nose orange all you want with these. I can't wait to see you later. Love, M. Rawley XXXX*

I traced my fingertips over the bold strokes of his handwriting, giggling at the signature, reminiscent of his high school shirts I continually wore to bed. I recognized the flowers as those growing along the edge of the parking lot and smiled, imagining Marshall making Garth wait in the truck as he picked flowers and hauled them up here; he was joining Garth on a roofing job today. The note was written on a piece of paper torn from a business pad – the top bore the logo from Becky's dad's construction company.

I pressed the sweet words to my heart, braving my phone to see if there were any messages from Marshall and finding just one, as though he was purposely keeping his to a minimum to compensate for Liam's excess. Over three hours ago Marshall had written, *Just got to the jobsite. I miss you. Wish my face was buried in my favorite place on earth.*

I flushed from hairline to toes. *Thank you for the flowers, sweetheart. They're beautiful.*

His phone must have been in his pocket because he wrote back instantly. *You're so welcome. I can't wait to see you later. I need your lips on mine.*

I braced my lower spine against the counter, hot and melting just imagining his voice speaking those words.

Which ones, exactly?

Naughty woman. My delicious naughty angel baby.

We made it nearly a month.

I'm surprised we had the will to make it 24hrs.

Can we ride the horses tonight?

Of course. I should be done by 5.

I can't wait to see you. I love you so much there aren't words.

"Ruthie, I'm starving!" Tish complained, appearing in the front door and startling me from my absorption with Marshall. "Trudy's saving us a table. What's taking you so long?"

"I'm coming," I whispered, my face about a thousand degrees; it grew even hotter as my phone glowed with a final text from Marshall.

I love you with all my heart too, angel.

Chapter Eighteen

September, 2013

"I'm heading over there right after work," I told Tish on a stormy Friday in mid-September. Rain had been falling since midmorning, at times conveying the sound of gentle drumming and at others, like this moment, gushing down the window glass like water over a dam. Thunder had growled intermittently; for a brief period around noon, lightning had knocked out power to the south side of town – which consisted of about a dozen businesses, including the law office. But there was an increasing band of blue sky along the western horizon, and with roughly three hours until the party was set to begin I was optimistic the sun would reappear.

"I'll be there as fast as I can. I told Al before he left for court that I had to leave early, too. He's so flattered you invited him and Helen Anne."

"He said they haven't been to a surprise party in ages."

Marshall's birthday, which fell on the tenth, was still a few days away and with all the people "in" on the secret I figured there was a good chance he was aware of the surprise, but I didn't care. I'd loved planning a party for him, along with plenty of help from Clark, his brothers, and Julie. It was to be held at The Spoke later tonight; Clark and Julie had spent the day smoking pork ribs and baking bread pudding, both Marshall's favorites. I'd enlisted Sean and Quinn to run interference today, keeping him occupied after he returned from college in Billings until it was time for the party. Tish and the Heller girls were going to help me decorate; Julie had closed the bar to all but party guests this evening.

"I hope he's surprised." It was my desire to reclaim Marshall's birth-date as a day worth celebrating; it was time he had a few new memories to associate with autumn.

Tish smiled and I realized immediately she knew something I did not; I recognized this particular expression – wide smile without her teeth showing, eyes glinting – as one of semi-smug knowing.

"*Dammit*," I muttered. "He does know."

"I didn't say that!"

"I can tell!"

The outer door opened, emitting Case, who was carrying an umbrella but still soaked; his wet jeans fit like a second skin. He flew inside and shook water from his hair, exclaiming, "Shit! I thought it was clearing up!"

I implored my brother-in-law. "Case, what's the secret? Tish knows something!"

He grinned, winking at Tish as he closed the umbrella. Pretending innocence, he said, "No idea."

"You guys!" I complained.

"What time is he getting back to town?" Case asked. It was Marshall's final year of school; he attended classes on Monday, Wednesday, and Friday.

I glanced at the wall clock. "In about two hours. The party starts at six. You can come help Tish and me decorate, if you want."

"I'd be happy to." Addressing Tish, he asked, "Baby, what time are you done here?"

"I'm heading out soon. I'll swing home to change and then we can meet Ruthie at The Spoke."

"Sounds good. Come here, I haven't kissed you in hours." He reached for her, adding apologetically, "I'm all wet…"

"I don't care," she said, roughing up his hair as he bent to kiss her.

Case, who'd parked in the lot at the law office, left a minute later and Tish and I returned to our desks. The rain began to slacken, the radio tuned to our preferred country station, a local one broadcast out of nearby Miles City. I was singing along under my breath when Tish suddenly muttered, "Uh-oh."

She was frowning at her phone. Her tone didn't convey extreme distress but I asked quickly, "What?"

"Robbie just texted there's trouble between Dad and Christina Turnbull."

"Trouble? What kind of trouble?"

"We use code names for Christina and Ron, which was Robbie's idea since most everything is a game to him. He gets off on thinking he's some kind of spy. She's 'Fancy Pants' and he's 'Hot Shot.' Apparently Fancy is angry at Dad."

"But why?" Even though both Tish and I had spoken to Dad in the past few weeks, neither of us had confronted him about Robbie's accusation; not the least of reasons being that our father was an adult and I felt no responsibility to or warmth for his current wife, Lanny, the woman who broke apart my parents' marriage once upon a time. Besides, we'd have to explain where we'd received the information in the first place. Dad had called me to ask about my decision to stay in Jalesville, of course, and wondered how I was adjusting, but nothing he said suggested he was anything other than his usual charming, busy self. I'd never fully recognized how expert my father was at concealing things.

Tish studied her phone's screen, chewing her lower lip. "Apparently Dad isn't returning Christina's calls anymore. Robbie thinks he's shutting her out but he doesn't know why."

"Is Fancy crazy?" The question sounded stupid but I was completely serious.

"No, I think she's actually quite intelligent, for all of the mean shit I say about her. Not that she couldn't be intelligent *and* crazy. She's clever enough to have multiple affairs behind Ron's back, which seems incredibly dangerous. I would bet she knows everything Ron's involved with, on and off the books."

"I meant will she resent what Dad's doing, not returning her calls?

I'm sure she's not used to hearing the word 'no.'"

Tish drummed her fingers on her desk. "That's a good point."

A beat of anger sounded inside my head. "I can't believe Dad. He calls me and acts like nothing's wrong, like I'm a little girl who needs to be pacified." Immediately the anger morphed to concern. "What if Dad's in trouble? What if he's involved in the Yancys' business here?"

Tish slowly removed her reading glasses. "I don't honestly believe that. I would tell you if I did, I promise. But I agree he's trying too hard to act natural whenever we talk. Something's off, I can tell, beyond cheating with Christina." She tapped her glasses on a stack of files, attention returning to her phone as it received another text. She read it and then murmured, "Shit."

"What?" I demanded, rising and heading across the room to perch on the edge of her desk.

Tish angled the phone so I could see Robbie's latest message.

Din-din tonight at the Lair. Looking into Number One = Top Priority. I'll let you know what I find. Over & out, Spice Lady.

"'The Lair?'"

Tish rolled her eyes. "I know, he's out of control with the code talk. He means he's attending a dinner party at Ron and Christina's townhouse."

"And looking into Franklin Yancy," I understood, rubbing my arms, which had broken out with sudden goosebumps. "I hate this, Tish. Something is so *wrong*."

Tish nodded, fingers flying as she composed a quick response. "I told him to lay low. I hate it, too, but maybe by some miracle he'll actually find something."

Recognizing that we would accomplish no more work this afternoon, Tish and I locked up the office; she headed home to change while I hurried across the street to my apartment for the same reason. I showered, leaving my hair to air-dry so it would be especially curly, and shimmied into my favorite cotton sundress, one the color of daisy petals and patterned in tiny orange flowers; it fit more snugly than it had a month ago, courtesy of the dessert Clark never failed to serve after his mouthwatering dinners.

I drove to The Spoke with warm afternoon sun streaming over my bare shoulders; I'd been correct in the assumption that the storm would blow over. The resultant light was nearly blinding in its intensity, striking the earth from beneath a lingering, steel-blue cloud ridge, spangling all objects with a glittery, otherworldly beauty. I absorbed the ocher heat of its glow, allowing it to settle the nervous tension hovering at the edges of my consciousness.

Wy met me in the parking lot at The Spoke, climbing from the high school bus just as I arrived; the driver had kindly dropped him off here instead of home. Grinning wide enough to showcase his molars, Wy called "Hey, Ruthie!" He was so effortlessly cheerful; I squeezed him close in an impromptu hug and he said in my ear, "You're gonna be so surprised!"

"*Marshall's* going to be surprised, you mean," I said.

"Yeah, that's what I meant! Come on, we gotta get decorating!"

I followed him to the front entrance, sidestepping puddles that reflected the lowering sun in dazzling copper flashes. Once inside we were embraced like old friends by music and scent – the jukebox was cranking tunes and the pork ribs smelled so good my mouth began watering. Clark, Garth and Becky, Julie and her husband, Aaron, and their three daughters, Netta, Pam, and Lee, were setting up long serving tables near the stage. They'd pulled the wagon-wheel tables to the edges of the room, allowing more space for what would become a buffet once the food was set out. Everyone we'd invited was supposed to arrive by five-thirty at the latest; Sean and Quinn had promised to stall Marshall until six.

Clark, wearing oven mitts, curled me close in a hug. "Hi, hon. Marsh will be so surprised!"

"I hope so!" I squeezed him tightly and it was right then, with my cheek resting on Marshall's father's steady shoulder that my unease returned, flickering like a distant beacon. My body went still as my mind screamed through an array of fearful thoughts – *what was it, what was wrong?*

I suddenly realized Marshall hadn't texted all afternoon; it hadn't occurred to me to worry because I'd been so preoccupied with the party and then Robbie's messages to Tish. A sick edge of fear sliced my heart – heavy rains had fallen most of the day.

Slippery two-lane roads.

Truck drivers who fell asleep at the wheel and crossed the yellow line…

"Lookit the banner Miss Hensley let us paint today," Wy was saying, brandishing a long, narrow roll of canvas paper, emblazoned with multi-colored birthday wishes. Behind him, Tish and Case entered the bar carrying wrapped presents and a small crockpot. I eased back from Clark's kind embrace, forcing a deep breath. Forcing myself to relax.

He's in class. He's all right. It's all right.

"Let's get it hung up," I told Wy.

By quarter to six The Spoke was bursting at its seams. Garth and Case were tuning their guitar and fiddle, respectively, sitting on barstools they'd dragged up on stage. The beer keg had been tapped; the food tables creaked under the weight of platters of pork ribs and grilled vegetables, bowls of baked beans and au gratin potatoes, fruit salad with whipped cream, spicy deviled eggs, chocolate cupcakes, and Julie's homemade bread pudding, drizzled with caramel-rum sauce. The painted birthday banner stretched over the tables, along with helium balloons; someone had brought along inflatable instruments that Wy and his friends were using to alternately rock out to the jukebox and bash one another over the head.

I'd managed to keep busy (and therefore shut out the worried thoughts that wanted to repeat like a broken turntable inside my head), but relief still almost brought me to my knees when Tish suddenly shrieked, "They're here!"

The room erupted with controlled chaos as everyone dropped what they were doing and crowded close, giggling and shushing each other, elbowing to claim a better view of the door. Tish motioned me up to the front and I clung to her waist, quivering with nervous excitement as we watched Marshall, Sean, and Quinn head for the main entrance, the sunset glinting on their dark hair. They were laughing about something – my pulse was absolutely galloping – Sean threw open the front door –

The roar of everyone yelling, "*Surprise!*" was deafening and Marshall's expression struck me straight through the heart. I knew he often down-played his emotions, underreacted to his own happiness, but such unin-hibited delight shone momentarily on his face that tears filled my eyes. He sought me in the crowd, throat bobbing; he reached and I flew. Safe in his arms, I cried, "Happy birthday!"

He crushed me close; I could feel his thundering heart. "Thank you, angel, I can't believe this is all for me!"

We were swarmed then, everyone wanting a hug or to offer him a drink, but Sean whistled shrilly, gaining attention. When he had the floor, Sean spoke with the air of a ringmaster. "Marsh has a birthday an-nouncement, y'all, *if* he could have your undivided attention!"

Marshall was all but hopping with barely-contained excitement and I crinkled my eyes at him, asking, *What's this?*

Garth and Case had positioned just to our left, instruments poised; everyone was murmuring anew in excited speculation. Tish was in on it, which I could have guessed from her behavior earlier today, beaming with her hands clasped beneath her chin. Clark was grinning, thumbing tears; Wy was practically turning cartwheels. Case and Garth began to play my favorite country song, "I Cross My Heart" by George Strait.

Marshall took my hands and dropped gracefully to one knee, amid a collective gasp from almost everyone observing; his gray eyes were lu-minous with emotion and unshed tears as he said, "I love you, Ruthann Marie Gordon. You mean more than the world to me. Will you give me the most beautiful birthday present I could ever dream of, could ever hope for…" His voice cracked and tears streaked past my eyelashes as he tenderly kissed the knuckles of my left hand and then slipped a ring onto my third finger. He steadied his voice. "Will you be mine, angel? For always?"

I nodded, laughing and crying and overcome, and the cheering around us threatened to raise the roof from its rafters. Marshall grinned so ra-diantly that back in Minnesota there was probably a burst of sunshine. He sprang to his feet and lifted me off of mine, whirling us in exuberant circles as everyone applauded and whistled.

"You knew about this, didn't you?" I asked Tish much later in the evening, the two of us sipping beers at our table and admiring my gorgeous engagement ring, a round solitaire diamond set on a delicate gold band and flanked by two garnets, my birthstone. It was an antique, having once belonged to Marshall's grandmother, and fit perfectly, courtesy of Tish's knowledge of my ring size.

She giggled, both of us giddy with happiness. My face felt hot from a pretty strong beer buzz; I'd been the recipient of more than a dozen toasts already this evening. Marshall was currently situated behind a drum set on stage, jamming with Case and Garth and a couple of other guys whose names I couldn't remember just now. He looked my way and winked, so damn sexy as he wielded his drumsticks I couldn't help but shiver; neither of us had stopped smiling.

"I did know," she admitted. "Case and I went with him to the jewelry store when they added the garnets. Those were Marsh's idea."

"Isn't it beautiful?" I enthused, turning my left hand one way and then the other. "It was Faye's mother's ring." My heart was warmed anew; I'd never been so stunned and delighted by a turn of events.

Tish clinked her beer bottle against mine. "You're engaged! I'm *so* happy, I can't even tell you."

"Marshall asked Mom for her permission, did he tell you? And he called Dad, too."

"Of course! Who do you think gave him Dad's number?"

"I wish Mom and everybody was here," I murmured, surveying the crowded dancefloor. The atmosphere in The Spoke always reminded me of Shore Leave – the same laughter and chatter, music and merriment. Of course Shore Leave didn't have a stage and The Spoke was without a set of porches and a lake view, but the level of comfort was equal. I watched waltzing couples through the tranquil, gold-tinted lens of one too many beers: Clark and Trudy (whose diner I lived above), Julie and her husband, Garth and Becky, Sean and Quinn and their girlfriends; even Wy was dancing with a giggly, redheaded girl about his age. I knew Marshall would sweep me into his arms the second he was done with this set; the Rawleys were all good dancers, having been taught by Clark.

"I know, I miss them, too," my sister said, downing the last of her beer. She replaced the bottle on the table and lightly drummed her fists. "Shoot, I told Becky I'd put that crockpot in their truck. I borrowed it from her a week ago, plus her tablecloth and that yellow serving tray. I'll be right back."

"I'll help," I said, deciding a dose of crisp night air would tamp down my buzz.

About three-quarters of the guests had headed home; the parking lot was no longer crowded. Carrying Becky's tablecloth, I slowly followed Tish to Garth's truck, parked near the wider back entrance where they'd carted the tables inside. I peered at the stars only to find them rotating on a slow axis; overwhelmed by dizziness I reeled straight into Tish, who laughed.

"You're drunk! Here, hold my elbow."

We reached Garth's truck, which was unlocked, and Tish pushed the passenger seat forward so we could load everything in the back. She bent inside and I clung to the edge of the open door with one hand. Neither of us heard approaching footsteps – at the last second a cold centipede of fear scurried up my neck, but he was already upon us.

"*I couldn't do it.*"

I startled so violently at the low, hissing words spoken just behind me that I bumped into Tish a second time, pitching us forward into the truck; drunk and frightened, I couldn't get my bearings and hampered Tish's efforts to stand upright. She untangled our limbs and sprang to her feet to confront the man looming near the open truck door and blocking all escape routes.

"Then who did?!" she cried.

I rolled to an elbow, peering up at the surreal scene – her back to me, Tish's hair created a nimbus around her head, curls highlighted in the bluish glow of the nearby streetlamp. Though the man was backlit by the same light source his sharp, wolflike features were visible; he and my sister stood not two feet apart. Tish's arms were tensed as though her next move included physical assault. My gut twisted. I had to help her and so I stood, steadying my legs with all the effort I possessed. The man, who could only be Derrick Yancy, did not spare me a glance, focusing solely on Tish; he spoke with quiet vehemence. "There are things you *don't know.*"

I sensed curiosity well within my sister, diluting her fury. She eased closer to him. We'd unwittingly stumbled upon the perfect opportunity for questions; this time her voice emerged softly. "What don't I know, Derrick? Tell me."

Instead of answering, his eyes detoured south on her body, coming to rest near her navel. He blinked in slow motion; he seemed confused, as though ensnared in a dream. I thought I heard wrong as he muttered, "I won't tell him about the child, I promise."

Tish froze. "What?" she gasped.

At the same instant the distant communication turned my bones to tuning forks – as though I knew what Derrick meant. He was responding to the same far-off message, I was certain, and a sudden connection was forged. I edged closer, driven by instinct. "Won't tell *who* about the child?"

Tish swallowed her shock and implored, "Who set fire to our barn? Who ordered it?"

Derrick's head wagged slowly side to side; I didn't think he was drunk but he was behaving similarly, unsure which question to answer first. At last his gaze sought and held Tish; he repeated, "I couldn't do it." And then, like the cherry atop this whole surreal exchange, he whispered, "I *love* you, for fuck's sake."

"Tish is your wife, isn't she?" I pressed; my beer buzz had vanished in the intensity of the moment. *Tell me the truth*, I thought, willing this plea into Derrick's mind. He was on the verge of revelation. "That's why you love her, isn't it?"

"I have always loved Patricia," he whispered haltingly, eyes fixed somewhere beyond our shoulders; I wasn't sure exactly what he was seeing, I only knew it was not the dark parking lot of The Spoke. "Even when she…did not return my affections. I purchased this land, just for her. But it wasn't enough."

Tish and I exchanged a horrified, two-second glance. Somewhere nearby, from within The Spoke, I heard the sound of Garth's laughing voice and Case's response, coming closer. Derrick blinked, seeming confused, and Tish clutched his forearm in a two-handed grip, refocusing his attention to her.

"I need to know the truth." She appeared as serious as I'd ever witnessed her. "Please, tell me the truth. What do you know?"

Derrick's mouth remained in a dire line as he studied Tish's face. When he spoke, hardly more than a breath emerged. "He's dangerous."

"Who?! Who do you mean?" I wished I was physically strong enough to shake answers from him.

"Is it Turnbull?" Tish was hoarse with fear.

At the name *Turnbull*, Derrick's eyes changed as swiftly as a switch being thrown. He blinked, staring wildly around, like he'd been dropped from the sky into this moment. His forehead wrinkled into deep lines of horrified disbelief; he jerked from Tish's grasp.

"Who's dangerous? What the fuck don't we know?!" Tish advanced on him but the connection was severed; Derrick made an abrupt about-face and stalked away, headed for the black SUV at the edge of the parking lot.

"Come on!" I cried breathlessly, and we chased after him.

Tish grabbed for his elbow but Derrick sidestepped. She reached again, this time succeeding, but Derrick stopped short and yanked roughly away, causing her to stumble; it wasn't his fault that Case exited the back door in time to see it happen.

Before my next breath, Case had a white-knuckled fist clamped around the front of Derrick's shirt, propelling him backward as he seethed, "I will break *every fucking bone in your body*."

"Get your hands off me!" Derrick threw his elbows outward, shrugging violently free; menace curled his mouth and eyebrows as his posture became more threatening.

Ten feet away and with a sinking heart, I thought, *Shit*.

Muscles bristling with rage, Case stood with shoulders squared, elbows bent, hands loosely curled. Low, almost singsong, he invited, "You want to hit me, Yancy? *Hit me*. Go for it."

Tish, out of breath at my side, cried, "No! Case…he didn't hurt me…"

I grabbed for her arm, scared she was about to spring between them. Tension surged, matching my heartrate.

Derrick's upper lip curled – he didn't want to back down but even an idiot could have predicted who would emerge victorious in the event of a physical confrontation. At last he muttered, "I'll remember you said that, Spicer."

My spine ached at the threat – what did I know that I could not explain? What did Derrick know?

Case jabbed a hard index finger into the air before Derrick's chest. "Get the *fuck* out of here."

Derrick resumed his stride toward his vehicle, not looking back. And this time, we let him go.

"You were surprised, weren't you?" Marshall asked for probably the tenth time.

We lay entwined in our bed, the sheet tangled around my thighs. My breasts rested flush on his sternum as Marshall played with a loose curl falling over my shoulder, winding and unwinding it. I made shallow trenches in his chest hair with widespread fingers, both of us too wound up after the evening's events to settle into sleep. We'd already exhausted the discussion of what had happened with Derrick in the parking lot.

"I had no idea. You are a master at keeping secrets, love."

His eyes crinkled at the corners as he grinned, lifting my left hand to gently kiss my new ring. "It looks perfect there, angel. This is the ring my grandpa gave my grandma when they were first engaged. I picked out the garnets for the jeweler to add so it would be unique to you. And because I cherish the month you were born."

"I love it so much," I whispered. He got me every time – he knew, *he saw*. I traced my fingertips across the bold lines of his dark eyebrows, following a familiar path over his eyes, which closed briefly as I marveled at the charcoal-black sweep of his lashes; my touch drifted along his sharply-angled cheekbones and long nose and then outlined his mouth, ending by pressing my thumbs to his chin. I leaned just close enough to lick his top lip, slow and deliberate, and his eyes kindled, from tender to scorching in less than a second. He grasped my hips, caressing the hollows there with both thumbs. My nipples were as hard as gems, teased by his chest hair. I took his lower lip between my teeth and fire sizzled between my spread legs.

Outside, fresh rain struck the ground and thunder growled in the distance, indicating an advancing storm which echoed the one in Marshall's eyes; I imbibed the sight of him as though I would not be allowed to look upon his face for ten lifetimes.

I whispered, "Happy birthday." Rain took up a steady clattering against the window glass. "The first of many to come."

His throat bobbed with emotion. He reached for my left hand, linking our fingers, pressing his thumb to my engagement ring. Quiet and intense, he murmured, "I can't do without you. I need you, Ruthie, more than I've ever needed anything in this life."

He brushed tears from my cheeks and I was swept away by the ardent joy his touch and his words unleashed. He cupped my shoulder blades and I kissed his forehead, smoothed hair from his temple and kissed him there, inhaling his scent; when I lifted my face to see his eyes, my heart jolted all over again.

I whispered, "I have another present for you."

"You are all the present I could ever need."

"It's right down here." My fingers trembled as I commandeered his hand.

Marshall exhaled in a passionate rush, caressing deeply. "Can I open it right now?" His voice was so husky my knees would have collapsed had I been standing. He rolled us to the side, drawing my thigh over his hip. "You don't know how beautiful you are." He studied me as though there might be a test later, one his life depended upon. "Ruthann. No one has ever looked at me the way you do."

"Marshall...*I need you*..."

He rolled me beneath him, fulfilling my breathless request, kissing me in a way that made all of space and time seem to twist inward on itself, as though something beyond us held its breath as our bodies joined. Later in life I was to wonder: had the bitter knowledge, sharper than any blade, already sliced through a part of my consciousness, making itself quietly known on the eve of Marshall's twenty-eighth birthday, the very night he proposed? Had the threat of our separation lurked at the back of my mind, in a way I could only understand looking back?

Had I known, then, what was to come?

Could I have prevented it?

It was a question that, now, I would die to answer.

Chapter Nineteen

October, 2013

AUTUMN IN MOUNTAIN COUNTRY ADVANCED, JALESVILLE and the surrounding foothills taking on a burnished appearance as leaves and brush blazed in hues of russet and ruby and bronze. Nightly frost began to frame the windows with lacy gilt by morning's light, while Marshall and I snuggled in those sweet, tender minutes before daylight tugged us from the luxury of our new queen-sized bed, which took up almost every available inch of floor space in our little bedroom.

"That twin mattress just *ain't* gonna cut it," Marshall had teased upon moving in, shortly after his birthday party at The Spoke.

Marshall was nearing midterms in his fall-semester classes while I continued my daily job at the law office, finding joy in the simple pleasure of seeing Tish every day, working alongside her like the old days back at Shore Leave; as always, there wasn't a subject we couldn't discuss. Despite all the issues demanding our attention, we spoke often of how much we anticipated the arrival of spring, with its promise of my wedding and a new cabin for Tish and Case; they pored over floorplans many a night when Marshall and I came to visit them, all of us making suggestions.

The cozy trailer with its chili-pepper lights had become as dear and familiar to me as Clark's house; many of those crisp autumn evenings were spent crowded around the little kitchen table, eating and talking, laughing and planning. Marshall and I acknowledged that we were spoiled; we rarely made dinner for ourselves. If we weren't with Case and Tish we were enjoying Clark's sumptuous cooking, or Julie's. More often than not when we ate at the trailer Case and Marshall would play for us after dinner. We'd relocate outside, sharing the front steps with the plump orange pumpkins Tish had set out as decorations, directing our singing voices at the rising moon; the music danced into the distance of the foothills.

Such moments with my sister and our men touched me as nothing had ever before; I sometimes found myself thinking, *What if the fire had never happened and I'd never traveled here to help Tish? What if I'd stayed in Minnesota and had never found Marshall?*

Such 'what-ifs' tortured me – and there were far too many of them in our lives.

"He must have been referring to Turnbull," Tish decided, not long after the confrontation in the parking lot at The Spoke. Since that night Derrick seemed nowhere to be found in the greater Jalesville area – we had not spied his SUV cruising slowly past the law office – nor had he reappeared in Chicago, to the best of Robbie's investigative knowledge. The hotel where Derrick stayed in Miles City told Tish when she called that a room under his name had been paid up through the end of November. But he was absent.

"Turnbull is undoubtedly dangerous. But exactly what threat do *we* pose to him?" Case asked during that conversation. "His property edges right up on ours but he must own over a hundred acres, straight out into the foothills. He built a mansion he stays in maybe two weeks of the year. What could he, or the goddamn Yancys for that matter, want so bad with the town? Why bother?"

"Yancy has repeatedly suggested an ancestor of his was cheated out of land around here," Marshall reminded us.

I added, not for the first time, "And if Derrick remembers a past life like we think he does, or if he actually *was* that ancestor in that life, it's possible those memories are clouding his mind in the here and now. He said he bought that land *for* you, Tish, but of course he never did that in this life."

"That makes sense," Tish said, and I saw her shoulders twitch with a shiver; Case put his arm over the back of her chair in a protective manner. "It's such a horrible thought, but it does make sense if you consider it from that angle. And now all our paths are colliding again."

Case said quietly, "But it's not just *us* on that path, much as I wish it. There's others we can't control."

"And some of them don't even live now," I whispered, edging closer to Marshall's warm strength, seeking reassurance. "It's like the past isn't just in the past. It's happening simultaneously. Somehow, that must be possible."

"Our understanding of time is too limited," Marshall said.

"Aunt Jilly said the same thing the last time I talked to her, about the nature of time being beyond comprehension. She's always been able to sense the future, though, not the past." Tish roughed up her curls, changing the subject. "Word around town is that Derrick is gone for good, pulled up stakes, all of that." She held Case's steady gaze as she recognized, "But it can't be that easy. And we still have no real answers."

Case was the one to suggest an alternative theory. "Forget for a minute why they want the town. Suppose what they're hiding isn't some illegal business dealing. What if they're covering up something even more sensational, like a family member with…bizarre abilities?"

"Such as disappearing into thin air," Tish supplied and I could see the effort it took for her to avoid looking my way; the very phrase froze my blood from the inside out.

The crease of worry between Marshall's eyebrows deepened, furrowing his brow; he instinctively tightened his grip on me. Before he'd known anything about my frightening encounters with the past, the topic of someone dissolving from sight had been one to spark his imagination and inspire discussions. Now armed with the sobering knowledge, he sat silent and watchful, troubled beyond words.

Not meeting Marshall's or my sister's eyes, keeping all thoughts of Una Spicer's letters from my mind, I added my own theory, through a raspy throat. "Maybe when Derrick disappears, he returns to a different time altogether."

Tish leaned forward, her expression gaining intensity. "Into the past, you mean?"

An awkward hush descended over the table.

"We have to consider the possibility," I insisted.

Case looked between Marshall and me, radiating concern. He asked quietly, "Do you suppose he has any control over it? Assuming he's able?"

"I don't think 'control' is a word you can apply to any part of it," I responded.

Later that same night, tucked in our bed, I whispered, "What if…"

Marshall heard the despairing notes in those two words and immediately rolled me to face him; we'd been snuggled with my shoulder blades against his chest. Our late-night bedroom was cloaked in tones of gauzy gray but I could still discern his eyes, and read the sincerity present there as he vowed, "I'm here, angel, and I'm not going anywhere. I will never let you disappear into thin air."

A trembling started in my thighs, moving outward, and Marshall issued a low sound of concern, hauling me closer. Hiding my face against his neck, my fear gushed forth. "It scares me so much, Marsh. I haven't wanted to talk about it because I'm so scared…"

Marshall buried a hand in my loose hair and cupped the back of my head, his strong arms and long legs anchored around my body – my body with its soft, ample curves and the few extra pounds that months of delectable dinners had added – which at times seemed so fragile and fleeting that a breath of wind could dissolve it. Twice now I'd experienced the loss of substance, of becoming…*nothing*.

"*Never*, do you hear me?" he whispered fiercely, his lips at my ear. "Never will I let you go, Ruthann. I would die first."

"But what if…" I couldn't stop shaking. I did my best, and was usually successful, not to think of those two times, first with Una's letter and then out near the old homestead. It was so much easier to pretend it had been something I'd seen on television or read in a novel…certainly not something from real life, let alone *my* real life.

"I'm here, love, right here." Marshall sheltered me against his naked body, his passion tempered to soothing reassurance in that moment. He did not release his hold and by morning's crystalline light my fears had been temporarily overridden.

Until the weather grew too cold Marshall and I rode the horses as often as we could, leaving from Clark's barn on Arrow and Banjo. I was proud of how well I'd taken to horseback, having learned primarily with Banjo; by now I loved the mare dearly. I loved her gentle strength and the way her ears pricked toward my voice. I loved her kind, intelligent eyes and velvet-plush nose. Her mane was coarse and black and sometimes I braided sections of it for her, much to Marshall's amusement. In the last few weeks I'd advanced to cantering, and loved watching Marshall canter Arrow; I could not describe what the sight of them at such speeds did to my heart.

Marshall rode as though born to a saddle, his every movement effortless; he reminded me of a dancer flowing in perfect harmony with a partner, Arrow responding to the slightest shift of Marshall's position. When saddled up, he was never without his black hat, sometimes donning a pair of worn leather riding chaps over his jeans. He knew damn well how incredible he looked in these, though he pretended innocence when I first saw him and almost fell from Banjo's saddle. He and I spent many a beautiful evening riding the horses through the wild foothill plains – avoiding, by tacit agreement, the site of the old Rawley homestead and instead angling the horses east.

Time seemed suspended in a glass jar during those gorgeous dusks, when the setting sun gilded our bodies and sparked from the horses' manes, and I was so happy my soul was like a singing bird – deliriously joyful. I should have realized such happiness always comes with a price; the universe rebalancing itself, maybe. Surely it was selfish, indulging so freely in this joy, wrapping within it. We'd ride far from sight before tethering the horses and spreading out the camp blanket Marshall always tied neatly behind his saddle. Scarcely would we strip free of our jeans before need overpowered all else. The sweet passion of kisses, wordless sounds of love, my thighs curving around his hips atop that faded old blanket spread over hard ground.

These things remain etched in my memory, the sharp blade of remembrance scouring the softer, more vulnerable surface of my mind – the last of the sun dancing over our bare skin before we turned gray with the gloaming light, Marshall at times pinning our linked hands above my head as we sated ourselves on each other, our eyes holding just as tightly as our bodies. Arrow and Banjo grazing nearby, tails swishing, unconcerned.

I love you, Marshall Augustus Rawley, I think now, when the unbearable pain of being without him hammers anew at my senses. I whisper these words aloud, with all of my willpower, praying for him to somehow hear me. *I never stopped loving you, no matter what you may have thought. I still long to be your wife. You have to know this.*

I didn't die. I know that was the only likely conclusion you could have reached, but I didn't die.

Please know this, sweetheart…

"Ten minutes or so," Sean announced from his lawn chair, cracking the top of another beer. His girlfriend was snuggled on his lap, a blanket over them, while Quinn and Wy lay on a quilt to their right, taking turns pointing out constellations, Wy making lazy pinwheels with a sparkler he'd just lit with Sean's lighter.

Quinn said, for the second time, "Watch it with that thing, buddy, I don't want to lose an eyebrow."

Becky and Garth sat close on the dropped tailgate of their pickup, while Clark cuddled the baby in a nearby sling chair. Marshall and I shared the bed of his truck with Case and Tish; the guys sat with their spines braced against the cab, knees widespread, so Tish and I could lean back against them. I was bundled in a scarf and mittens, furry boots, a green wool sweater of Marshall's, and a puffy, down-filled vest. Clark had lit three candle lanterns and there were orange and purple lights strung all along the front of the RV set up by The Spoke, so the buoyant delight on everyone's faces was plainly visible.

It was Halloween, a holiday that Jalesville celebrated with gusto; earlier in the week we'd visited the pumpkin patch and carved what the Rawleys called 'pumpkin moonshines,' two of which now graced the counter in our apartment. I'd given mine a cheerful lopsided smile while Marshall's leered wickedly; he'd gone so far as to add pumpkin-seed teeth, anchoring them with toothpicks. Halloween was serious business around here. The entire town had been festively adorned since the first week of October, complete with bats and spiders and ghosts; hay bales piled with gourds and pumpkins were stationed on every corner. Al let Tish and I have free reign decorating the law office's front walk and we'd decked it out.

We had all spent the evening on a haunted hayride through the foothills. Never mind the vampires and ghouls; everyone's resultant shrieks and screams had bounced across the rocky spires and echoed in the distant formations, as frightening as any carnival funhouse. To top off the overall merry mood, Camille and Mathias had welcomed their fifth baby early this morning, naming him James Boyd Carter after two of Mathias's ancestors. Now, as it approached ten, we were gathered to watch the annual Halloween fireworks display just south of town – or, as Marshall explained, annual as long as it hadn't yet snowed.

It appeared most of the mobile population of Jalesville had turned out for the show; the Hellers set up a makeshift bar in the back of their RV, complete with a cardboard, hand-lettered sign reading *Have Bar, Will Travel*. Instead of peddling icy beers, this evening they offered hot chocolate or apple cider, liberally spiked with rum, and Irish coffee. I'd finished my second cider-n-rum and nestled contentedly in the security of Marshall's arms. Leaning back against his chest, drowsy with warmth and a long day spent outside, I studied the black crystal of the nighttime sky as he, Tish, and Case talked about past Halloweens; I let their words and laughter flow around me like pleasant eddies in a slow-moving stream, absently rubbing the band of my engagement ring with my thumb.

"We'd go door-to-door down the hall in our townhouse in Chicago, but that was pretty lame," Tish was saying. "It was always way more fun after we'd moved to Landon and took Millie Jo and Rae around town. Then you could really get into the whole Halloween mood."

"I remember carrying a pillowcase to hold candy. Talk about lame," Case said, laughing. "Marsh, remember that year an ice storm blew in while we were still running around?"

"Yeah, we were half-frozen by the time Mom found us. Mom always drove us all into town to trick-or-treat," Marshall explained to Tish and me. His left hand had found its way just beneath the hem of my sweater and he traced gentle patterns on my belly as he spoke.

"That was a hell of a storm. We were stranded in town that night, at your aunt's," Case added. "But at least we had our entire haul of treats…"

Lulled by their conversation and the rum flowing in my veins, my eyelids sank and I drifted away in the leisurely current, half-asleep.

Mom always drove us…

A strange feeling I didn't want to answer…

After the sheriff questioned him that terrible day, the driver seemed to disappear…

There's been an accident…

I sank deeper into sleep, my temple resting against the inside curve of Marshall's outstretched left arm.

Ruthann…

The soft, whispered request for my attention made my legs twitch.

I'm here, I murmured in response.

The forest path beckoned, littered with natural debris; I smelled the rot of dead leaves. My feet were bare, the contours of the surrounding trees blurred and shadowy with advancing dusk. Slowly I lifted my hands, palms up, a gesture of surrender, but to whom or what I was surrendering, I did not know. The air was too quiet, the kind of tense, fragile stillness about to be fractured by unimaginable violence –

The voice came again, but this time shrieking.

He's coming! Run!!

But I was helpless to move, solid as a block of ice cut from the surface of a wintertime lake, eyes wide and fixed on the sight of a man stepping from the trees not a dozen feet away; his appearance was so sudden it seemed as though patches of darkness had simply melded to form the outline of a human. I became glass – fragile and see-through and immobile. He approached, gaze locked on mine. He halted within three steps of my transparent body.

I figured it would be one of your sisters. Funny that it's you. His voice was low and deceptively soft, almost caressing. *I didn't think you had it in you.*

Fair hair, dark clothing; hollow cheeks and eyes like narrow holes, the sort made by plunging the tip of a ski pole into fresh snow. I stared dumbly at his face, trying with all my strength to place him in context – he was familiar. Somehow I knew his face, though I was sure I'd never seen him in this life. He spoke again.

I killed her. And I will kill you, Ruthann, mark my words.

His lips widened, exposing the top row of his teeth. I realized he was smiling and tasted vomit. He shifted just slightly and I threw my arms forward in a gesture of primal fear – a wordless plea for him to halt.

You can't stop me, he whispered. *No one can.*

A tremendous explosion shattered the forest, flooding the darkness with bursts of red-orange light. I fell to a crouch, protecting my head, and when I looked up again, seconds later, he was gone –

At the same instant I gasped awake, both legs jerking as another firework lit the night sky over Jalesville, detonating in a shower of indigo sparkles. My heart was going like a jackhammer and I clung to Marshall's arms, wrapped around me from behind.

"You were sleeping," he murmured in my ear. "The fireworks are starting, love, that's all."

It's not all! I wanted to scream. *It's not all by a long shot.*

Rendered wordless, I scoured my memory for a picture of the man from the forest – it was real, wherever I'd been just now. It was not a simple nightmare, I was certain. My body craved the only security it recognized and I clung tightly to Marshall, hardly registering the Halloween fireworks display, trying my best to recall the man's exact words…*his face…*

But all that remained was dread.

Chapter Twenty

HEAVY SNOW AND AN EARLY TWILIGHT CAST MUTED GRAY light through the windows at Clark's that chilly Thursday evening, our first Thanksgiving as an engaged couple. Inside it was cozy and warm, the fireplace roaring and candles lit all along the mantle; the big blue spruce, unimaginably fragrant, that Marshall and his brothers had chopped down just this afternoon glowed with lights shaped and tinted like old-fashioned gumdrops. The entire household was scented by more than a dozen delicious aromas; cooking was a family affair that had begun at dawn.

Everyone was gathered for turkey dinner, crowded in either the kitchen where appetizers and wine were plentiful, or the living room, where I lounged on one of the leather sofas along with Tish, Jessie, and Becky, the four of us offering suggestions as the guys decorated the tree; baby Tommy lay dozing in my arms and as a result I was about two hundred degrees. Becky, clad in a festive maternity sweater patterned in maple leaves, was pregnant enough that moving from place to place required real effort; we'd already gifted her with an enormous piece of pumpkin pie and she balanced the plate on her bulging belly. The local radio station played Christmas songs and Marshall sent me a grin as he knelt to hang an angel ornament made from a painted gingerbread cookie.

"I made this in sixth grade," he explained. "I knew even back then that someday I'd find my real angel."

We were so in love I could not fully express it in words. The joy of it pierced my heart in a hundred thousand places.

"It reminds me of the decorations at Shore Leave," I said. "Remember, Tish, Aunt Ellen always used to say that some drunk fisherman was going to eat our ornaments one day?"

Tish sat to my right, legs tucked beneath her, repeatedly feathering Tommy's soft hair with the tips of her fingers; it was why he'd dozed off in the first place. The baby was so chubby he appeared to have no neck; a soft but poignant pang resounded inside me as I studied his sweet sleeping face.

"Of course! No one ever did, though. Remember how Grandma always hung about a thousand yards of tinsel?"

Another pang struck at me, a small rush of homesickness; Case, Tish, Marshall and I had made plans to visit Landon this upcoming spring, but that suddenly seemed very far away. I nodded. "Aunt Jilly said they're putting up the trees in the cafe this weekend."

"Mom said it's been snowing there since early this morning." And in Tish's voice I heard an acknowledgment of how much we both missed Shore Leave, especially at this time of year.

Wy was busy adding finishing touches to the adjacent dining table, which was set with burnt-orange linens and Faye's good white china, which only ever made an appearance during the holiday season. I'd arranged small, autumn-hued gourds and bright orange jack-be-little pumpkins as a centerpiece but it was Wy's idea to place pinecones tied with silver ribbon at the top edge of each plate.

"I'm impressed," I told him again, watching as he tied neat bows.

He flushed with half-bashful pride.

"If I find pinecone bits in my food, I'm blaming you, little bro!" Sean said, ruffling Wy's hair as he walked past en route to the kitchen for another beer.

We were nearly a full house this evening; only Gus and his girlfriend were absent, having attended dinner with Lacy's family in town. Wy had even invited a guest, a girl from his class named Hannah Jasper, whom he was "kind-of" dating, as he'd explained to Marshall and me not long ago. With her wavy, golden-red hair, Hannah could have been Case's little sister. She proved sweet and shy, and blushed easily – much to her detriment in a family of men who loved to tease their youngest brother. Apparently once upon a time Wy had tried to kiss her and aimed wrong, getting a mouthful of her earring instead. Hannah was currently in the kitchen with Clark; if there was anyone to put a person at ease, it was him. They were whipping the cream for the pumpkin pies.

"Here it is!" Quinn suddenly yelped, on his knees on the rug, rooting through an ornament box.

There was a minor scuffle among the brothers.

"The Conestoga?" Becky questioned, her mouth full of pie.

"It's my turn this year!" Sean yelled from the kitchen.

"No way, it was yours last time," Garth said.

"Dad, whose turn is it this year?" Marshall called, and Clark leaned around the doorframe, adjusting his glasses with one hand.

"I believe it's Case's turn this year," Clark said, with a half-teasing air of exaggerated patience.

Case apprehended the ornament from Quinn with a smug smile.

"Bring it over here!" Tish insisted, leaning forward to look.

"It's a little wagon," I marveled as Case bent to showcase the favorite ornament, holding it cupped in his broad palms like a magician. It was a beautiful, detailed carving, complete with all the parts I assumed a real covered wagon possessed, down to toothpick-slim wheel spokes. A tiny wooden man, woman, and baby bundled in a scrap of red cloth were seated at the front, the man holding leather reins that were connected to two wooden horses. Just like a wagon in a movie, the top was covered with a perfect arch of ivory canvas. The entire piece spoke of loving craftsmanship.

"See right here, where the covering makes a little oval, you attach it to one of the tree lights so the whole thing glows like there's a lantern inside," Case explained.

Marshall squatted beside me, resting his forearms on the sofa cushion near my feet. He leaned to kiss my knee before saying, "Grandpa Clem carved that for Mom and Dad for their first Christmas together."

I reached to touch his face and he cupped a hand over mine and kissed my palm. "Your mom's dad?" I clarified.

Marshall nodded.

"Clem was so talented," Becky said. "Garth and I have a few things he made over the years." Smiling up at her husband, she held out her empty plate. "The baby wants more pie."

"Your wish is my command, sweet darlin'," Garth said, with a bow.

Case twined one of Tish's curls around his index finger as he said softly, "Baby, why don't you hang it this year? It's our first Thanksgiving together."

Wy, finished with his ribbon-tying, hopped over the back of the sofa, plunking down between Becky and Jessie. Tommy was jostled and blinked open his eyes; I kissed his forehead, smiling at the startled expression on his round, dimpled face.

Wy agreed, "Yeah, your turn this year, Tish!"

"And yours next year, angel," Marshall told me, rubbing a gentle thumb over Tommy's downy hair. A sweet smile lit his gray eyes. "It'll be our first year married."

If only it would have been.

"I'd be honored," Tish said emotionally, kissing her man before Wy, Sean, and Quinn crowded around to show her how to properly hang the wagon.

"Is anyone hungry?" Clark called. "Because I think this turkey is done!"

We all helped haul food from the kitchen, with the exception of Becky. Clark went around the table pouring wine while Wy followed with ginger ale for everyone not drinking alcohol. The table creaked under the weight of roasted turkey, creamy mashed potatoes, delectable gravy, and every other side dish imaginable.

Once everyone was seated, Clark folded his hands and led a simple grace. "Dear Lord, we are so thankful to be here together at this Thanksgiving feast. Please bless each of my sons, all seven of them, and the dear, lovely women they have chosen as partners in life." Marshall squeezed our linked fingers as Clark continued. "We look forward to the upcoming year, when Marshall and Ruthann will be married and little Tommy will be blessed with a new brother or sister. Lord, please continue to look after my sweet Faye. I know she would be so happy to see how her family has grown in the past ten years." Clark paused briefly before concluding, "Amen," echoed quietly by all of us.

We all fell to loading our plates but I noticed Garth and Becky exchange a look; Garth grinned as she offered him an almost imperceptible nod.

"Brother," he announced quietly.

Becky's smile widened as she looked around the table, smoothing one hand over her belly. "We didn't plan to find out but at this last appointment we just couldn't resist."

The table erupted with congratulations.

"Another boy! I knew it!"

"Your beard is going to be ankle-length before long!"

Garth had joked he didn't plan to shave until he and Becky had a daughter.

"That's so exciting, you two!"

"Have you picked any new names now?"

"We'll try for a little girl next time around." Garth winked at his wife.

"But Rawleys make boys," Wy contradicted, as though everyone should simply know this fact; he spoke around a mouthful of stuffing, seeming to have forgotten there was a female guest at his elbow. Poor Hannah turned the shade of a sliced watermelon, falling into an immediate giggling fit.

It was too much for Sean, who cried wickedly, "No baby-making for a few years yet, you two! *Damn.* Wyatt, you listen to me, buddy."

Wy hung his head in mock shame, shaking it side to side while everyone laughed uproariously. Since Wy told me almost everything, I happened to know that he and Hannah had only recently kissed – this time on the mouth, with no earring interference.

"We've been so excited to tell you guys," Becky said. "This time they were sure it was a boy. At my first ultrasound, last summer, they *thought* they saw a tiny little penis but it's so hard to tell. To me those pictures just look like gray static…"

"Hold up now!" Sean choked out around a mouthful of ham, lifting both hands in the air; Quinn pounded helpfully on his brother's back. Sean wheezed, "Becky, don't let me *ever* catch you using those words to describe a Rawley's penis…"

I couldn't stop laughing, along with the entire table; Hannah covered her face, shoulders shaking. I hoped she was a good sport.

"Hey, that *is* a good point," Marshall agreed, and I flicked his knee under the table.

"Honeybunch, we've been over this," Garth teased his wife.

"Well it is teeny-tiny, at first," Becky insisted. "Not like *yours*, honey…"

A sudden sharp knocking on the front door startled all of us, cutting short the good-natured banter; the dogs, lounging near the warmth of the fire like furry throw rugs, leaped to attention, barking furiously. It was dark as charcoal outside, no telling who was suddenly here at dinnertime on Thanksgiving evening, with no warning. It couldn't have been Julie and her family, since they wouldn't have knocked. I hadn't even noticed headlights on the driveway. Quinn reached the entryway first, as he happened to be closest; there was only a limited view from the dining room table, but we all shifted and leaned to catch a better glimpse of the visitor. Clark rose from his chair at the head of the table and I felt the first rush of fear.

Quinn shooed the dogs away as he opened the door and we all stared in wordless shock as we beheld none other than Derrick Yancy, tall and imposing, clad in a black wool greatcoat and tweed scarf. He'd grown a goatee since we'd seen him last and if he seemed surprised to observe so many people staring blankly at him, he gave no outward sign. I saw his dark eyes fixate upon Tish before darting with instant apprehension to Case, who'd almost knocked over his chair as he stood up.

"You'd show your *goddamn face* here?" Case's control hung by the thinnest of threads; though he didn't lift his hands, his knuckles stood out like ridges on his bunched fists.

Tish's wide, anxious gaze flashed between her husband and Derrick. I knew she, like me, was envisioning a violent physical confrontation, right here in front of everyone.

Clark was already standing and all of the men, including Wy, simultaneously rose, their sheer physical presence as potently threatening as loaded guns. I looked up at Marshall, whose eyes had narrowed, his shoulders taut, and then back at Derrick, whose chin had lifted. I had to give Derrick credit, at least fractionally, as he didn't immediately retreat; he refused to respond to Case and instead cleared his throat. He spoke with stiff formality, no trace of mockery. "I didn't realize the entire family would be here."

"It's Thanksgiving." Clark retained a reasonable tone but there was a subtle undercurrent of tension, and perhaps even menace, also present.

Derrick did not reply and in the resultant thick silence I could hear the fire crackling. Marshall curved a protective hand over my right shoulder. Tish looked ready to attack, her blazing eyes locked on Derrick. A log snapped in the hearth, sending a shower of red sparks outward.

As though this was his cue to speak, Clark inquired, "What is your business here this evening, Mr. Yancy?"

Derrick blinked slowly and then shifted, reaching into the breast pocket of his greatcoat. My heart seized; for a horrible instant I imagined him extracting a handgun. Instead he produced something that proved almost worse, though for that moment it was simply pieces of paper, folded as though to slide into a business-sized envelope.

"My business is brief and I will be on my way." Though I assumed Derrick meant to keep his eyes on Clark they strayed again to my sister. As though speaking just to Tish, he added, "It's actually quite fortunate that all of you are here."

"Spit it out, Yancy," Case ordered, low and dangerous, and Derrick's composure flickered, the loathing between the two men almost visible in the air – their two lives, long connected in ways I could only imagine, with Tish unwittingly in the middle.

"I have here a copy of the deed to my family's former acreage, which I have been searching for without rest since I first arrived in this godforsaken place." Derrick squared his shoulders. As he spoke, he approached Clark at the head of the table, seeming to draw all of the air in the room with him. He placed said document in Clark's hands; Clark unfolded the paper while the rest of us observed woodenly, audience members watching a drama play out on a theater stage.

"Thomas Yancy lawfully obtained and homesteaded this very land," Derrick said. "And he never sold, rented, or bestowed any portion of it, not in his lifetime. In the event of his death, the land passed to his two sons. As this deed unequivocally demonstrates, the land upon which we are currently standing belongs to *my* family, as it has for well over a century."

Clark remained unruffled. "This land was purchased by Grantley Rawley in the nineteenth century and I have proof of this bill of sale."

"False, as are those purchase claims of one Henry Spicer, on the adjacent property. That land was unlawfully seized from Thomas Yancy after his murder. Stolen," Derrick clarified, growing more heated with every word.

"That is *bullshit*," Case said, with absolute certainty.

"Explain your justification for these claims," Tish demanded of Derrick; though her demeanor was confrontational, even haughty, I heard the fear in her voice. "Statute of limitation, for one thing. Where is your evidence?"

"Oh, it's my honor to provide justification, *counselor*." Derrick bared his teeth in a smile. "As I will, in the court proceedings," and he indicated another document, "that will follow if you do not comply with our stipulations to vacate the allotted land within sixty days. Consider this your service of process notification."

An eruption of angry words followed this statement. Derrick would be lucky to make it out retaining all of his limbs.

"Who's representing you?" Tish demanded. She flew around the table to study the claim over Clark's shoulder. And then I saw her face drain of all color.

"Turnbull and Hinckley, of course," Derrick said. He allowed this to sink in before adding, "I'll let you finish your dinner," and though he didn't quite run, he certainly didn't linger. The headlights I hadn't noticed earlier blinked to existence outside, the eyes of a hungry predator gazing at the Rawleys' house, intent on claiming the home for itself.

It was well after midnight before Marshall and I got home; he'd driven us through the snowy darkness. Jalesville was peaceful beneath a heavy, starless sky and a quilt-layer of fresh, powdery snow. Inside our little apartment the fragrant balsam fir we'd hauled home from Clark's only yesterday lit the space with warm white twinkle-lights. Upon our tree hung a variety of ornaments, some gifted by my family back in Landon, some from Clark, and a handful Marshall and I had chosen on our own; Nelson's Hardware was the place in Jalesville for such things. We'd found a family of painted wooden cardinals we especially loved. Marshall had taken great care to hang the little nest with its two baby cardinals between the mama and daddy, and then he'd cradled me close, resting a palm upon my belly as he whispered, "Maybe by this time next year."

In the glow of our Christmas tree we settled our coats on the wall-mounted hooks that Marshall had hung back in September; among other ways in which the apartment was lacking, it had no closet space. We vowed that as soon as Marshall graduated and we were married, we would build a beautiful, well-organized, and efficient cabin. We'd spent many a cozy autumn evening evaluating sample blueprints and had even chosen the building site, a quarter-mile from Clark's house.

On land that the Rawleys were now ordered to vacate by the end of January.

I slipped my arms around Marshall's waist and pressed my face to his back; he was wearing his dark green flannel shirt, the material soft against my cheek, and he covered my arms with his and held. I loved how I knew his every last piece of clothing, down to his socks and underwear. I wore his sweaters all the time and kept them out of the washer (we took our laundry to Clark's on Friday nights) so that they would retain the scent of him; throughout any given day, I would periodically tug the collars of those sweaters over my nose so I could smell him. I knew it touched him deeply that I did this, and he loved to tease me that he kept a pair of my panties in his coat pocket, for a similar reason.

Before we left Clark's, it seemed there was nothing that hadn't already been said, the festive mood having vanished into a black hole of disbelief and fury. Only Garth, who'd built his and Becky's house on their own land, gifted to them by Becky's family, was not in danger of imminent potential eviction.

"It will be all right," Marshall murmured, turning to encase me in his arms. "I don't know how exactly, but it will. We have to believe that."

"But how?" I whispered, hiding my face against his warm chest, too overcome and exhausted to be rational.

"Hey," he murmured, stroking my hair with both hands. "It's our first Thanksgiving together. No matter what, I consider that special. More beautiful than anything I've ever known."

One of my Christmas presents for Marshall was a little red bulb decorated with the words *Our First Christmas, 2013*. It was also painted with two Canadian geese whose beaks were touching, and I knew he would love it. At last I whispered, "I do too, sweetheart. I know we'll do everything we can."

After perusing the documents Derrick had left behind, Tish called both our father and Al, demanding to know what could be done. Dad didn't answer and Al was on vacation in Colorado for the week, visiting his children. Tish left each of them two messages and would have kept going strong except for the fact that Case insisted, with gentle firmness, that she needed to rest. I knew Tish would do anything for her husband and though she was reluctant to let up, Case had successfully gotten her calmed and headed for home an hour or so before Marshall and I left.

What frightened me most was the evidence of Clark's worry; despite his flurry of frenetic activity, unearthing legal documents from cabinets, spreading them chronologically on the floor before the fireplace and assuring us we were in the right, he was truly concerned. Fear that perhaps the Yancys, especially the Yancys backed by a powerful Chicago law firm like Turnbull and Hinckley, had concocted enough evidence to somehow prove ownership of the land pierced all of us. Marshall said the same thing as we lay snuggled in bed minutes after arriving home, naked beneath flannel sheets and Faye's patchwork quilt, snow falling like feathers at the window. Neither of us could sleep.

"Dad was trying to hide it, for our sakes. But I can tell. This is such a nightmare. Ruthie, that's been our land for generations. Mom is buried there, for Christ's sake." Marshall and I had visited her grave on the anniversary of her death, just two days after Marshall's birthday, to leave flowers and "show" her my engagement ring, which had once, after all, belonged to Faye's mother. "All of us would die before anyone takes our land. And there is no doubt in my mind that it is legally *our* land, no matter what that son of a bitch Yancy says otherwise. But it may be that there's no way to avoid going to court."

"Tish said there will be a hearing, there's no avoiding that." It seemed unimaginable, almost surreal. "Derrick has enough of a claim to justify it. From there it's in a judge's hands."

"We'll just have to prove him wrong. Show that there's no reason to move forward with a trial."

"But what if…"

"What if Case's ancestor really murdered Derrick's?" Marshall whispered, tucking his chin over my shoulder, from behind; he knew what I meant. I clung to the security of him, squeezing shut my eyes. But the images appeared anyway, on the shifting blackness of my eyelids. I saw the Rawley family at the creek, playing in the sunset glow.

"That night…out at the old homestead…" I clenched my muscles to keep from shivering, picturing that magenta light – a sunset from the distant past – cutting through the darkness and contradicting what I understood as reality. The memory of it hollowed out my gut. "That night, your family was right there, Marsh, right *there*…"

"I felt them, too, Ruthie, I swear to you." He had mentioned this the very night it had happened, months ago now; neither of us had since returned to the site of the old homestead. I traced the bones of his forearms, enclosing his wrists in my fingers and entwining our legs; the ferocity of my fear at the idea of him disappearing from me was almost too much to bear.

"But it never happened to you before?" I demanded.

"No, never. We used to play out there all the time, all those summers, but I never remember being afraid. Or sensing people from the past. It was always a peaceful place."

"*Marshall*," I whispered, wilting against him. There were too many puzzles, too many unanswered questions…

He snuggled me closer, settling my shoulder blades more firmly against his chest hair, nuzzling my neck. He spoke with gentle reassurance, setting aside his own fears and worries to comfort me, as he so often did. "I'm going to think about spring and our wedding. If it's all right with you, let's have the whole thing in Dad's backyard. Because it will still be ours, I swear. We'll have a hell of a party right after our vows, how's that sound, my sweet darlin' angel-woman?"

"Perfect," I whispered, my hot tears dripping to the sheets. "Just perfect, sweetheart."

Just before dawn I had a dream.

I stood in a clearing, certain I'd been here before even though I had no actual memory of the place – only the echo of a powerful feeling. My eyes darted like moths, seeking a safe place to land. Tension and desperation hammered my breastbone, in equal parts.

He was close.

An agony of need engulfed me and I ran, toward the edge of the clearing, toward *him*.

Dear God, let me get there. He's in danger!

My bare feet were bloody; each new breath scraped my lungs.

They're going to hang him…

Hurry!

But I was already out of time.

Chapter Twenty-One

January, 2014

MY TWENTY-THIRD BIRTHDAY WAS A DAY AWAY BUT I'D hardly thought about it, far too preoccupied, spending every free moment working with Tish as we helped Al gather evidence for the hearing that had been scheduled next month, on our behalf. Three days after Valentine's, on February seventeenth, Clark and Case, as the primary landowners in this dispute, were scheduled to appear for a hearing at Rosebud's county seat in Forsyth, an hour's drive from Jalesville. There at the courthouse, a judge would determine whether the Yancys possessed enough evidence to go forward in court.

And, since they were working with Turnbull and Hinckley associates, we would be fools to assume they did not possess ample evidence.

Tish and I were alone in the law office, Al in court across the town square. Outside, snow fell from the cold, bright gloss of a January sky. I was used to hip-high drifts, as I'd spent my teenage years in northern Minnesota, though here in Jalesville the snow was often what locals called 'dry,' consisting of small, pellet-like flakes. I hated letting Marshall out of my arms in the mornings but most especially when he had to drive through the snow and ice, over to Billings as he did three days a week.

It was his final semester; he would receive his bachelor's degree on May third. He'd already put in an application with the local Fish, Wildlife, and Parks department. Both he and I were quietly excited about this, though it wasn't easy to concentrate on anything past the date of the February hearing, including our wedding. Looking out the window at the snow-globe world encased in midwinter I felt the way I used to at Shore Leave, studying the frozen surface of Flickertail Lake and longing for the sunny yellows and minty greens of early spring, the renewal that it always promised. I prayed this spring would be no different.

"Ruthie, you and Marsh head over around six," Tish said, drawing me back to the present. She had planned dinner for the four of us, to celebrate my birthday. "Case is going home early to make that spinach lasagna you like."

I sent her a smile but Tish knew me too well.

"You look tired, Ruthie. Are you sleeping enough? I know everyone's so worried, it sucks…"

"I'm fine," I whispered. I didn't always get enough sleep but it was because Marshall and I stayed up late, making love and talking, then usually making love again, hoarding our precious night hours, when we were alone together. "It's hard to feel too much like celebrating, when we're all so worried."

"I know," she acknowledged. "But it's your birthday. That's special no matter what."

"Thanks, Tish."

Her phone made a noise, distracting her attention. She muttered, "It's Robbie. I'll let it go to voicemail. I'm just not in the mood to hear about what he *hasn't* found out."

That evening there was a blizzard watch posted but just like back in Minnesota it didn't deter most people's plans. Marshall had put snow tires on both of our vehicles back in October; fortunately, I didn't have far to travel on any given day. Marshall drove us through the snow to Case and Tish's place; there, the new barn glowed with warm light.

"Hi, guys, we're out here!" Tish called as we climbed from the truck, sticking her head out the wide double doors, which were propped open a couple of feet.

Both Marshall and I were clad in our puffy winter outer gear, and we held mittens as we navigated the snowplowed path to the barn, built last summer for Case and Tish with such great care; I knew Marshall was also thinking of those weeks, working so damn hard on something that now might be lost to Derrick Yancy in the end anyway.

Tish explained, "Carrot just had a litter out here, so we're making sure they're all warm."

Carrot was one of their cats. Case was kneeling beside a wooden crate, bundled in a plaid wool coat and a brown hat with fur earflaps. Case had grown a full beard, complete with mustache, to combat the cold of the winter months. Tish liked to tease him about the variety of colors, from russet to scarlet to gold, that were blended in his facial hair; he really did have about the prettiest shade of hair I'd ever seen. Case turned to greet us, inviting, "Come see, you guys. They're so little their eyes aren't even open yet."

Marshall and I dropped to our knees while Case reached for Tish, angling his right thigh for her to sit upon. Tish wrapped her arms around his neck and snuggled close, kissing his forehead. She nodded at the litter of tiny kittens, with a grin. "We're still trying to determine paternity."

"Definitely a local cat," Marshall joked. He was wearing his black cowboy hat, which he favored even in the cold, the black wool scarf he'd had since he was a teenager (knitted by Faye), and his black goose-down jacket. His nose and cheeks were red from the brisk air, his jaws and chin a little raw from a fresh shave, his wavy hair wild along the back of his neck. He looked so handsome and he was so dear to me; I felt a smile overtake my face.

"And I'm guessing he had black fur," I added, getting into the spirit.

"We only know for sure that it wasn't Peaches," Case said, naming their other cat, a fluffy white female.

Inside the trailer it was warm and cozy, combating the frozen night, and smelled like a fancy Italian restaurant. Tish had decorated with silver and pink streamers and there was a cake from Trudy's Diner on the counter, a big, gooey, chocolate one. Tish had written *Happy Birthday Ruthann* across the top with pink gel frosting. I giggled at her efforts; she wasn't incredibly gifted in this regard.

"It's beautiful," I pronounced, with a smile. At Shore Leave, Grandma and Aunt Ellen were the cake experts; it was tough to live up to their example.

Tish rolled her eyes, arranging sliced garlic bread in a basket lined with a red-checkered napkin. "Hey, it's chocolate fudge cake with three layers, so I don't want to hear any shit."

"You throw back a couple of shots first?" Marshall asked, coming behind me to examine the wobbly writing.

"Speaking of that, grab us some drinks, Marsh," Tish ordered, nodding at the fridge.

Dinner was delicious (Case was a great cook and his spinach lasagna was to die for) and the mood remained festive. Maybe it was the weeks of increasing tension that simply needed release, but we all laughed and joked as though we hadn't a care in the world, sipping wine or beer and talking about springtime and planning a visit to Landon.

"Do you think we'll ever convince Carter and Camille to move out here?" Case asked. "Goddamn, I miss those two."

Tish shook her head. "That would be wonderful, but they love Minnesota too much."

"We'll keep working on them," Marshall said. "But I understand it. Shore Leave being right on the lake like that is hard to resist."

The mention of Flickertail sparked a new round of stories about waterskiing and fishing and swimming – specifically skinny-dipping – learning to drive the motor boat and sneaking out on hot, humid summer nights to meet our friends from Landon.

"You swam naked at night?" Case asked for the second time. "But what about the fish?"

We could hardly catch our breath from laughter.

"Like, they get scarier at night?" Marshall demanded.

"The *night* fish?" I managed to gasp.

"But didn't they try to bite…"

"Our nipples, is that what you mean?" Tish interrupted her husband, inspiring another round of near-hysteria.

"I'm not gonna lie, I kept my trunks on when we swam those nights in Landon," Marshall said, once we'd regained control. "I wouldn't chance a fish mistaking parts of me for food."

"Who was your first kiss, Ruthanna-banana?" Tish asked, changing topics. I loved that the four of us moved so easily through many levels of conversation, at times serious and intent but always relaxed enough to discuss anything one of us suggested. She marveled, "I can't believe I don't remember."

"Hal Worden, summer after ninth grade. Remember, we dated for a little while?" I shook my head at the memory. I explained to the guys, "His sisters were my good friends. It was at a sleepover at their house and Fern dared us. I didn't really want to kiss him, but it was a dare." I giggled, remembering. "I didn't even spit out my gum first. And then he stuck his tongue in my mouth and I almost bit it. Isn't that awful, that was my first reaction…"

Marshall said, "That's not as bad as your braces clinking and grinding together."

"So that wasn't just Wy making things up?" I asked, thinking of hearing that story the first time I'd ridden in Marshall's truck, last August.

"No, it was true, but we didn't *actually* get stuck together. The fire department never showed up. Let's just say it was still really awkward. Katie Nelson could hardly look at me for the next year."

Tish said, "That reminds me what I found last night!"

Since dinner was winding down, the lasagna pan nearly empty, Tish dug out a couple of yearbooks from Jalesville High, one each from Case's last two years in high school, and I dove into the one she handed me. It was dark green, gilded with silver letters that read *Go, Raptors!*

Marshall protested, "Oh God, not those…"

"No way, I want to see you," I insisted, flipping at once to the index while Tish did the same with the other book. "Were you one or two years behind Garth and Case?"

"Two," Marshall said, with a grin, peering over my shoulder at the yearbook.

"Jesus, I think I was drunk by noon just about every day of that year," Case said, shuddering a little as Tish found his senior picture. As though in reaction, he set aside his beer.

"Look at you, honey, you're adorable," Tish said in response, tracing her fingertip over the image of his face. "And also drunk."

"Ha!" I proclaimed, locating Marshall's freshman picture in the other book. He was grinning for the camera with his usual good humor, string-bean slim and with his dark hair buzzed close to his head. At this age he still wore braces and his eyes were as full of mischief as ever. "Here you are! You're so cute. And you look so naughty. Did you get in trouble all the time?"

Marshall rested his arm over the back of my chair as he shook his head, with a rueful snort. "After Garth, all the teachers were just plain ruined. Then they heard there were three *more* Rawleys coming through after me, and most of them either quit or retired."

I giggled, flipping to the sports section, where he, Garth, and Case had all played football and run track. I recognized on Marshall several of the M. RAWLEY t-shirts that were now mine.

"Aren't these great?" Tish enthused. "Oh look, here's Becky…"

"She looks just the same," I observed, glancing at the pages open over Tish's lap.

"Shit, there's Garth with the flame guitar," Case said, laughing and indicating another image, clearly Garth's senior picture, in which he posed clutching the neck of a black guitar painted with brilliant red flames. Instead of smiling Garth was giving the camera his best mugshot. To make matters worse, the background was a swirl of green neon.

"Fuck, that was *so* cheesy, but he still loves that picture," Marshall said.

"Ruthie, I have a present for you but I didn't wrap it," Tish said, handing the yearbook to Case. "You know I'm not the best wrapper. Let me grab it before we have cake…"

I was about to tell her we could have cake first when something fell out of the back pages of the yearbook I was holding. It fluttered to my feet and I bent to retrieve it from the floor. Everyone else was still laughing about Garth's picture as I sat up and smoothed my fingers over a sheet of paper, figuring it was an old school assignment. It took a second for me to understand that I was holding a letter. It wasn't Una Spicer's handwriting on the old paper; these words were hastily scrawled in faded ink, the message brief.

May 28, 1882

Dearest Una,

At this moment I am riding hard to Iowa and have posted this letter at an office near the Minnesota border. Please know I will do my best to locate Cole. I have written Grant of my intentions in a separate letter and will look in on his parents as I pass through their territory. I know they are yet unhealed at Miles's passing. God willing, we will all be reunited before the end of summer.

Regards,

Malcolm A. Carter

The letter drifted from my numb fingertips but it was already too late. *Marshall.*

I called for him with no sound; my lips were too wooden. But Marshall looked my way at once and I felt it more strongly than ever – the force of the past, attempting to drag me from them. Marshall's eyes flashed with horrified understanding and he dove for me, his chair crashing over behind him. The force of his movement took us to the floor. Reality flickered like fireflies at dusk. I was instantaneously alone in a small, confined space – damp rock walls and the smell of wet earth, my back upon rough, uneven ground.

I could hear Marshall shouting my name but he was far away, and drifting farther. A smothering force assaulted my body and I tried to breathe, tried to claw my way back to him.

RUTHANN!

Marshall's voice was more frantic than I'd ever heard a person sound. Tish was screaming.

Please, I begged with every ounce of my strength. *Not yet. Please not yet…*

Pressure built to bursting in my skull as I was returned.

"We have to burn them," Marshall was saying again, venom harsh in his voice. "Case, burn those *goddamn fucking things*. I never want to see them again."

He meant the letters.

I was crammed securely between my sister and Marshall, the three of us situated on the couch, Tish's hands bracketing my head. The familiar scent of Marshall's neck was the only thing keeping me sane right now. I clung to his sweatshirt with both fists. I didn't have the strength to open my eyes.

"What in the hell just happened?" Case asked for the third or fourth time. He was agitated, pacing the living room, stopping only to place his hands on Tish time and again, certainly fearful that she too might disappear before his eyes, completely out of his control.

The helplessness was the worst part.

"It was too close." Marshall's heartbeat had not yet slowed, his blood still flowing hard. A tremor passed through him and he crushed me closer.

"Ruthie, you *weren't here*," Tish whispered. "Where did you go?"

I could not answer.

"Now isn't the time! She doesn't know!" Marshall snapped.

"I'm scared, too!" Tish threw right back; fear shortened her temper. She pressed, "Ruthie, do you remember?"

I didn't answer even though the earthy scent of the cave remained strong in my nostrils.

"It's the letters that trigger it," Tish said, and I knew she was simply trying to make sense of something that defied all logic.

"That's why I want them destroyed!" Marshall yelled, and the edge of his fury was growing stronger.

"Don't fight," I whispered. I couldn't open my eyes. I promised, "I won't touch them ever again."

"We're not fighting," Tish assured me.

"I want to go home. Tish, I'm sorry…"

"Don't be sorry," my sister insisted. "Ruthie, you're so pale…"

"C'mon, angel, I'll bring you home," Marshall murmured and I opened my eyes to his, which were red-rimmed, wet with unshed tears. I knew, without a doubt, that his presence was what had allowed me to return to this winter's night in 2014, to return from wherever it was I had gone. I knew I could never touch those letters again.

But Malcolm Carter's words were burned into my brain.

They are yet unhealed at Miles's passing…

I will do my best to locate Cole…

God willing we will all be reunited by the end of summer…

Marshall retained calm as he helped me into my coat and hugged Case and Tish good-bye. Outside, the sky was dense with a thick layer of clouds, dark as the inside of a coat pocket. Marshall lifted me into the truck.

"You rest, I'll get us home," he said as he started the engine. As though against his will, but needing to tell me, he acknowledged, "It was somewhere outside, wasn't it? I could smell wet rocks…"

I didn't question how he knew this, only reached and gripped his hand.

Chapter Twenty-Two

February, 2014

THE MONDAY FOLLOWING VALENTINE'S DAY DAWNED leaden and overcast, not exactly a cheerful prediction of how the day would play out; Clark and Case were scheduled to appear before a judge in roughly five minutes, at the courthouse over in Forsyth. Though all of us wanted to be in attendance, Al explained that it would be in our best interest to remain in Jalesville.

"What we don't want is a maelstrom of emotion," Al said before they left this morning. "Judge Hall is unmoved by displays of feeling. If anything moves him, it's empirical evidence."

Al had accompanied them, of course, as their counsel. Clark and Case were both armed with as much hard evidence as possible, proving the land in question was indeed lawfully theirs, and with something perhaps even more important in the long run – their conviction. Unfortunately, we were certain that Derrick's own conviction was as strong. The only hope we retained was that his proof of claim was lacking. Marshall had left for Billings hours ago to attend his Monday classes, all of us attempting to keep the day as otherwise normal as possible; outside, the atmosphere was eerie, too still – as though holding an angry breath. A snow cloud was massing on the western horizon. I felt restive, unable to sit quietly, fighting the urge to text him; besides, I knew his phone would be turned off while he was in class.

Being left behind to wait for news was unimaginably difficult. I wandered to the radio propped on the window ledge near my desk and cranked the volume, earning an irritated look from Tish, who was wearing her glasses, poring over a stack of papers. She was more on edge than ever; on top of the worry over today's hearing, Robbie had sent her a strange text on Friday afternoon, written in his coded language: *Big news. Think I found something on Number One. P.S. Fancy is smarter than I thought.*

Tish had called Robbie immediately after receiving this message. He'd still been at work and promised to call her back. It was Monday now and she hadn't heard from him yet, but that wasn't unusual; they rarely communicated on the weekends anyway. I sat in front of my computer to avoid annoying Tish any further. There were numerous little things with which I could have occupied myself but I remained idle, staring at the screensaver. When my phone flashed with an incoming call I jumped, almost knocking it to the floor. I saw that Mom was calling, surely wondering if we'd had any news from Clark and Case.

"Hi, Mom. Nothing yet," I said upon answering. "They're probably just getting in front of the judge right now."

"Ruthie." Mom's voice was low and quiet; I knew instantly that she wasn't calling about the hearing.

"What's wrong?" I sat straight. Tish's eyes flashed my way.

Mom, I mouthed at her.

"I wasn't sure if I should call you at first," Mom said, stalling. And then she spoke in a rush. "Ruthie, Liam admitted to Clint last night that he's been considering suicide. He requested a leave of absence from work. He's in a bad place, honey."

"What?" I whispered, stomach shriveling into a tight little ball. It was very nearly the last thing I had expected her to say. "Oh, Mom…"

"This is not your fault," she said at once.

"But he's all right? He didn't actually do anything?" I pressed.

"He's all right," Mom said. She paused and I could almost hear her thoughts. "Ruthann, I am not saying I think you should have stayed with him, not at all. I know you're happy, my little one, but I think it might be a good idea for you to make a quick trip home, to come and see Liam, and at least have a face-to-face conversation with him. You never did that. I think it might help him."

"Stop," I pleaded softly. I could not hear another word. I knew she was right.

Hovering over my desk like a drill sergeant, Tish demanded, "What?!"

"I'll call you back," I told Mom. "I promise."

I hung up before she could answer and lowered my head onto my forearms. Behind my closed eyes I saw a fast-flowing parade of images from all the years I had known Liam, his perpetual smile and good-natured attitude. I could not reconcile these memories with the idea of him confessing to my cousin that he wanted to take his own life.

Valentine's Day, I realized. That had always been Liam's favorite holiday. He'd always made a big deal for us.

"Ruthie!" Tish ordered.

I lifted my face. "Liam told Clint that he's suicidal."

"Oh. *My God.*" Tish sank to an adjacent chair and covered my hands with hers.

"Mom thinks I should come to Minnesota and talk with him." I was hardly able to swallow past the expanding guilt.

"This is *just* what you need, on top of everything else. Oh, Ruthie…"

Tish and I had avoided talking about what had happened at my birthday dinner, as if pretending it hadn't occurred somehow negated the horror of it, but I knew it was what she meant right now. She held fast to my hands, eyes full of agony as she whispered, "Do you feel like you should drive to Landon?"

My voice full of gravel dust, I admitted, "Mom's right. I should have broken up with him in person last summer. This is my fault, in its own way. I'm just so shocked, Tish…"

She regrouped then, insisting, "First of all, it's *not* your fault. Ruthann, Jesus Crimeny. It's not as though you have control over Liam's words or actions. He's a grown man, for fuck's sake." She sighed and added, more softly, "But I think maybe you should go see him. Maybe it would be better closure for him. Clint told me a while back that Liam bought you a ring last summer, that week you guys drove out here because of the fire. He never returned it."

I flinched as hard as if she'd slapped my face. I looked at the ceiling of the law office and felt a horrible shifting in my gut, a sense of something terrible approaching that I could not control. It was powerful enough I couldn't catch my breath. I suddenly heard that old wives' tale in my mind, as clearly as though whispered in my ear – *bad things come in threes.*

I leaped to my feet, rife with desperate urgency. "I have to call Marshall…"

I tried and got his voicemail, but didn't leave a message. I needed to see him so badly that I felt ill with longing, tempted to call the college in Billings. Instead I texted, *Please call me right away.*

Not an hour later Tish's phone buzzed with a call from Case. I think we already knew it was not good news but Tish answered with forced cheer in her tone. Even as one-sided as it was, I heard clearly through her conversation with Case that what we feared was indeed happening: Derrick had obtained ample enough documentation to allege that Thomas Yancy was cheated out of his land in the nineteenth century. Once a court date was settled upon by all parties, Case explained, the legal proceedings would begin in earnest.

The snowstorm had not yet broken over Jalesville by the time Marshall and I got home late that afternoon. This may have contributed to the tension that was palpitating between us; we were both ready to crack apart from the strain this day had wrought upon not only us, but our families. A small part of me believed that if the sky would just split open and release its burden of snow, I might be able to draw a full breath. The back of my neck ached. Inside our apartment I shed my outer clothes and moved through the dimness, clicking on lights. Finally I stopped my frenetic movement and simply leaned against the counter, lowering my head. I sensed Marshall come into the kitchen behind me; I could feel his eyes, intent as he studied me without a word.

"Just say what you're thinking," I said at last.

"You don't want to hear it," he figured, just as low-voiced. In addition to the devastating news that his family may very well lose their land, the land upon which his beloved mother had been laid to rest and where we planned to build our future home, I'd been forced to tell him about Liam and how I had decided I would drive to Minnesota for a few nights' stay. I told Marshall I wouldn't leave until tomorrow, Tuesday the eighteenth, that I would call him every night I was away, and that I would be back before the end of this week.

He hadn't spoken a word to me since I'd made these pronouncements, until just now.

"Well, I better hear it whether I want to or not." My voice was acidic, though Marshall was the last person in the world I wanted to fight with. I hated this barbed tension. I wanted him to understand I had a responsibility I'd never carried out; I wanted him to accept that I had made a necessary decision and needed his support. Instead, here I stood facing his anger.

"You aren't going," he announced, and his tone was final, further spiking my ire. "It's winter and it's dangerous, for Christ's sake. Roads are shit. I won't have it."

"I've driven in winter plenty of times." I sounded petulant and immediately changed tone. "I'll drive straight through. It's nothing but interstate the entire way there."

"It's *dangerous*," he repeated, controlling his voice with tremendous effort.

"That's not why you're mad," I challenged, turning around. My heart hammered at the sight of the man I loved, who was so jealous that it manifested as anger, I clearly understood.

Didn't he trust me?

Marshall's eyes flashed like iron-colored clouds about to unleash hail. I straightened my spine. He said quietly, "You realize Liam is saying these things to *hurt* you, don't you? It's attention-seeking. It's also spineless and fucking cowardly and here you are, going to him even so."

I couldn't breathe past the anger in my chest; a small part of me reflected that Marshall did have a point, but I couldn't see beyond the fact that Liam had sunk low enough to consider taking his own life. I owed it to my former boyfriend to talk to him and explain in no uncertain terms he must move on – that killing himself was the wrong decision no matter what, that he had a future ahead of him – and he must accept that this future did not include me.

And Marshall owed it to me to trust my decision.

When I didn't immediately answer, Marshall insisted, "I won't have you going to him, not in winter, not in summer. Call him if you have to, but that's where it ends."

"Marshall!" I implored. "You're spinning my words! You're being mean. It's not that way at all! I'm not *going* to him like you make it sound. I'm driving to my former hometown to talk to him, which I should have had the courage to do from the start. I should have broken up with him in person. It was cowardly that I called back *then*. I have to make this right, don't you understand?"

"'Being mean?'" he repeated. The heat of his anger rippled like a living thing between us. "I'm so worried about you, about everything that's been happening, that *I can hardly think straight*, and you think I'm being *mean*?"

"Then try to understand what I'm saying!" I wanted so badly to touch him, just angry enough that pride prevented me from closing the distance between us. "I won't be gone even three days. I'll call you every night. I'm not going to stay there…how could you even think such a thing?"

"You won't stay there, because you're not leaving *here*," he ordered, his throat tight with emotion. Our eyes clashed.

"Don't tell me what to do!" I would not cry right now, I would *not*.

Marshall drove both hands through his hair. His voice was agonized. "*You* should have enough common sense to realize that it's *dangerous* to drive that far this time of year."

I softened a little, knowing he was thinking of Faye. "I'll be all right, sweetheart. You don't have class tomorrow and we can talk on the phone the entire way there. I have to do this. Please understand."

"I can't understand," he said, his chest nearly heaving. Though I'd witnessed him every bit as passionate many times, I had never seen it manifest as anger this extreme.

"You have to trust me," I persisted. "I trust *you*."

"I do trust you!"

"Then show me!"

"This is not how I prove that I trust you!" he said heatedly, eyes blazing. "I will not have you throw that in my face this way! It's not fair!"

"Just admit that you *don't* trust me!" I fired right back, even though I didn't truly believe this; my voice was uncomfortably close to a shriek. "I'm going and I will be back and you have to *deal with that!*"

I knew he had a hair-trigger temper but I still jumped a little when he absolutely raged, "You're doing this despite what I think?! Despite me *fucking begging* you not to go?!"

"Don't swear at me," I cried, throat clogged with tears. I tried to grasp his forearms, to force him to calm down, but the extremes of his emotions possessed him and he jerked away from my hands, instead leaning to direct his fierce words into my face.

"Oh, so I can't say it to you, only do it?! *Is that it?!* Since your *fucking boyfriend* could never give it to you that way, *couldn't fuck you like I can?!*"

"*Stop it,*" I sobbed, shocked at the force of his anger, hurting so much he might as well have been striking me with closed fists. Then I realized he was striking me, just as brutally, with his words.

"I won't!" he yelled, and I could hear the husk in his voice. He turned away from me altogether and then directed his fury at the table, sweeping everything atop it to the floor, loose papers, the fruit bowl, our coffee cups.

"*Marshall,*" I cried, reaching to stop him, but he moved immediately away, putting the now-empty table between us. There were tears in his eyes; I felt as though a knife was carving out the inside of my heart. Fruit seemed to be rolling all across the floor.

"Go then." All the fight had left his voice. His throat was choked and his words low-pitched, rough and terrible, as he looked directly into my eyes and said, "Just go."

I reeled backward, those words as deadly as a firmly-applied razor. Numb, more stunned than ever before in my life, I grabbed my coat and purse, my scarf and keys. My fingers were so stiff that I could hardly grasp these things.

And I left without looking back, leaking the contents of my heart all over the place.

Chapter Twenty-Three

In our trailer that night, after the hearing, Case and I lay awake.

"Sweetheart, we'll get through this," he whispered again, our fingers linked over my belly.

"It's just been one thing after another," I whispered. "I'm exhausted."

"You work too hard," Case said. "You always do. I'm putting my foot down. I want you to tell Al that you need a few days off from work."

"You're putting your foot down?" I repeated, teasing him a little.

"Yes," he said, with certainty, kissing my collarbones. His familiar touch was so wonderful, so welcome, and I tilted my head to give him better access to my bare skin. Case rubbed his chin against my neck, which he knew I loved, especially now that he had a soft beard. He murmured, his voice vibrating against me, "And that's final."

"I know you worry about me," I acknowledged. "And I know we'll get through this. I just hate feeling so helpless. I feel like everything we hold secure is in jeopardy."

"No matter what, we have each other. We have our family. If we have to start over somewhere else, we will. I hate that thought, I hate the thought of not living here in Jalesville, of losing to Yancy, but in the end he's the one who's lost. Truly lost, I mean. He has no one who gives a shit about him in the world, I really believe that, Tish. You should have heard him at the courthouse. I almost felt sorry for him. Almost…but not quite."

"You're right," I whispered, though I was in no way sympathetic to

Derrick Yancy's plight in this life. I kissed my husband's lips and told him for the countless time, "I love you so much."

Case rested his forehead gently to mine. "I count my blessings every day, sweetheart. Every minute. When I think of all those lonely years I spent without you, longing for you. I used to lie right here and study your beautiful blue eyes in that old picture of you. Baby, do you know how many blue things I bought with your eyes in mind? Everything – clothes, towels, even my electric guitar…"

My heart melted away at this confession; I reflected that we did own a great many dark blue possessions. "I'm the one who should be counting my blessings. That you still loved me after all those years, and how I acted at Camille's wedding…oh, *Case*…"

"I knew if I couldn't be with you then there was no one for me, not in this lifetime. I love you more than I even realized I was capable of loving. And now you're my wife and I could never be thankful enough."

I held him with all my strength, wrapping arms and legs around him. I thought back to the days he lay immobile in the hospital bed in Bozeman, the agony of being without him. Never again. I would never let that happen again. I kissed his mouth as he caressed my hair, stroking along the length of my curls, which fell past my shoulders now. Against his lips I whispered, "I can never get enough of you touching me."

Case smoothed his warm touch down my spine, teasing the interior of my mouth with his tongue, gliding his hands to cup my breasts. "Just so happens that touching you is my very favorite thing in the world." He grinned speculatively. "Remember what we were talking about the other night?"

I grew increasingly breathless as he played with my nipples, gently stroking them as if attempting to pick up stacked coins. I nodded, whispering, "Yes, I think you could bring me to orgasm just doing that."

"There's no greater pleasure than bringing you to orgasm, love," he whispered, and in response I reached down to take him in hand, nipping his lower lip; his grin widened and he kissed me in earnest.

I bowed to Case's concern and called Al in the morning, explaining that I was not coming downtown to the office today.

Al said, "I was going to suggest that yesterday. To Ruthie as well, but she must have subconsciously taken my advice, since she didn't show up for work this morning."

"She didn't call?" I was surprised. Now that I considered it, I hadn't heard from my sister since she left work yesterday, even though I knew she meant to leave for Landon today, much to Marshall's obvious distress. Ruthie had intended to call me last night to let me know what time she was leaving this morning.

"No, but I didn't pester her," Al was saying. "I'm sure she's sleeping in and I hope she gets some good rest. Besides, it snowed so much last night I almost threw in the towel this morning, too."

"I'll try her a little later," I said. Before I made coffee I also shot Robbie a text —*taking a couple days off. Talk to you later this week.* Even though I hadn't heard from him in three days and he hadn't explained his 'Number One' text from Friday, I didn't want to think about anything work-related, Yancy-related, or Dad-and-Christina-related, for at least twenty-four hours. But then I sent a final text to Robbie.

Unless of course you actually found something!

Maybe by some miracle he had discovered something concrete, but Robbie was prone to the dramatic and I didn't want to get my hopes up just yet.

Case plowed out our driveway and drove to town for groceries around noon; it was snowy enough that he didn't bother to open our music shop downtown. School was canceled for the day and Wy called to see if he and Hannah Jasper could come grab the snowshoes he'd forgotten over here last month.

"Of course," I said, and then trudged out to the barn in my winter clothes and enormous furry boots, flanked by Mutt and Tiny, intending to check on Cider and Buck, and our rabbit and chickens. I also found five eggs, feeling like a real farm wife, and then peeked at Carrot and her growing kittens, snuggled in their box in the warm, pleasant, hay-scented barn. Carrot preferred to avoid the trailer, while Peaches, our other cat, rarely ventured outside.

Wy and Hannah arrived in Clark's big diesel truck an hour later, and Wy surprised me by tattling, "Marsh slept at our house last night because they had a fight. He looks like crap today, Tish, I'm worried. He wouldn't tell me or Dad anything."

"*Shit*," I muttered. I decided I better call Ruthie right away. I knew Marshall didn't like the idea of her driving to Minnesota, nor what she intended to do there. Surely Ruthann was still in Jalesville, hiding out in their apartment; I hoped she had decided against making the drive altogether, especially considering the weather.

After Wy and Hannah left I tried Ruthie's cell phone, which went straight to voicemail. I felt a small wrenching in my gut, thinking of things I tried very hard to mentally avoid, such as the picture of my sister disappearing before my eyes less than a month ago, right here in my kitchen. The letters that seemed to spark this horror were hidden away; we hadn't burned them, despite Marshall's orders, instead tucking them into a trunk, deeply buried. Ruthann would never have to see them again. I listened to the recording of her sweet voice asking me to leave a message after the beep, and my heart bumped in unmistakable fear.

There's nothing to be afraid of. For one thing, people fight all the time.

I debated calling Mom, but refrained. I didn't want to hear more about Liam right now.

Dammit, Marshall, I thought next, certain he had been a jerk about his opinions yesterday; as much as I loved Marsh and considered him a brother, I knew he wasn't the world's most tactful man and he had a shit temper. I tried his phone next but he didn't answer either; I left a brief, irritated message to call me as soon as humanly possible. I knew he didn't have college classes today; where the hell was he? No one answered at Clark's, further inciting my aggravation. By the time Case got home a few hours later it was late afternoon. He'd stopped at the law office to chat with Al for a spell; as he parked the truck the heavy, overcast sky was already darkening, courtesy of winter's short days. I met my husband at the door and he saw my concern.

"What's wrong, baby?" he asked immediately, jogging up the steps.

"I'm not sure." I shook my head. "I just have a bad feeling..."

I explained what I thought must have happened, about Marshall and Ruthie fighting and Marshall sleeping at Clark's. I'd tried both Marshall and Ruthie yet again in the last five minutes, growing seriously annoyed that no one would answer their phone today.

"Dammit!" I said, tossing mine with a little more force than necessary onto the kitchen table.

Case put his hands on my shoulder blades. "I'll make some supper, baby, it's all right."

"I'm going to go see Cider for a minute," I muttered. The horses always made me feel better and I hadn't lingered in the barn after feeding them, as I usually did on mornings I wasn't headed to work. I assured him, "I'll be right back."

The air was crisp after last night's snow, stark and chilly, the sky the shade of tarnished silver. As I walked between the trailer and the barn, praying that it would still be ours at this time next year, a rogue beam of sun shot from beneath the edge of the low-slung cloud ridge on the western horizon, sudden and dazzlingly bright in my eyes, momentarily blinding me. Its scarlet-red light glinted magnificently upon everything in sight, dancing over the snow with a million rubies, gilding the yard with a radiance we hadn't seen in days.

It was a breathtakingly gorgeous sight.

Why, then, did my stomach seem to bottom out? Why did this lovely red sunburst strike me as deeply ominous?

I heard the growl of a truck engine, coming closer. I looked down the road, already realizing the driver was going far too fast on the snow hard-packed over the loose gravel.

"Case!" I yelled, and even though the windows were closed he heard my voice and appeared in the door. I pointed wordlessly.

"It's Marshall," Case recognized, deep voice rife with sudden concern, and I watched in silence as the familiar rusted-out black truck skidded to a stop across the road from the trailer, back tires fishtailing on the slippery snow.

"What..." I faltered, my heart struck by a hard mallet of fear.

"Wait here, love," Case ordered, and then jogged toward the truck.

I clasped my mittened hands and watched, uncharacteristically speechless, only able to observe as Marshall stormed out the driver's side door, slamming it like an enemy against the truck. I heard him demand, "Where is Ruthann?"

Sickness penetrated my gut, the inevitable knowledge of something monstrous I was about to have to face. My fingernails dug into my palms inside my mittens, throat already closing with dread, even as Case caught Marshall by both shoulders, halting his progress.

Marshall threw off Case's light grip and directed his words at me. Only then did I realize he wasn't furious as much as terrified. He begged, "Tish, where is she? Is she here? Jesus, tell me, *please tell me.*"

I hurried to him, seeking answers in his gray eyes. What I saw was raw desperation, deep shadows of strain. "Marsh, what are you talking about?".

My lips began to tremble even before Marshall spoke. Case saw the white sheen to my face, as he gathered me close and ordered, "Answer her, little bro."

Marshall gripped my upper arms with fingers that seemed talon-like even through the layers of my down coat. He wasn't wearing gloves, a scarf or a hat, not so much as a jacket, his jaws with a good two days' growth of dark scruff. In a hollow voice that begged me to understand, he said, "She left yesterday, Tish, to go to Minnesota. She was going to drive straight through."

"Yesterday?" I interrupted, furious now, as fury was a thousand times preferable to fear. My words became a lava flow, pouring hotly forth. "I thought she was going to leave today! Why didn't she call me first? Why did you sleep at Clark's? What did you *say to her?*"

Tears streaked Marshall's face and he choked out, "We had a fight, a horrible fight, just before she left. Oh God, and now...just now..." His frantic words fell atop one another. "I've tried her phone at least fifty times since then. But just now I called Shore Leave, and she never got there, Tish. Oh Jesus Christ, *she never got there.* She should *be there by now...*"

I shoved at his chest, blindly wanting to hurt him for what he'd just forced me to hear, and Case moved swiftly, catching me close and turning us away, as Marshall's harsh sobs scratched like ripsaws along my flesh. In my ear, my husband spoke quietly and firmly. "Tish, calm down, baby. We'll figure this out."

I could sense his agony over what to do next but he remained calm, leading me inside and seating me at the table before doing anything else. He bent close so that he could look into my eyes and said, "Stay right here. Wait for me, all right, sweetheart?"

I managed to nod because it was Case, because I would do anything for him. He was so worried, and controlling it, and so I nodded a second time, a terrible, jerking bob of my head. Case jogged back outside. I spied my phone on the tabletop and when I picked it up in fingers gone nearly bloodless, I saw that I had two missed calls in the past five minutes, both from the phone at Shore Leave. As though sunk in tar, ridiculously sluggish, I tried to call the cafe. The phone fell to the kitchen floor with a dull thud. Case hadn't closed the outer door and through the screen I heard him order in no uncertain terms, "Marsh, tell me everything from the start."

It was clear to me that Marshall was in absolute torture. I fumbled to my knees, trying to get the phone back in my grasp, but I was gripped by a dizzy rush of nausea and sank to sit cross-legged on the floor. The air flowing inside was icy.

I heard Marshall gasping out his words. "She left…and she should have been there by now. Oh God, Ruthann should *be there by now…*"

"Why did she leave yesterday instead of today?" Case asked, and I could hear how he was trying to stay calm, to get the answers before Marshall went completely ballistic. Case urged, "What happened?"

"Did she come here? Did she call Tish?" Marshall demanded.

"No," Case said quietly and Marshall's cry of anguish ripped through my heart.

"I called the cafe, I talked to Joelle." Marshall heaved, gasping between every few words. "What if…what if Ruthie was in…*a car accident*…" And then I could hear him vomiting.

"Marsh, come inside," Case pleaded; I could hear the way he was controlling his terror. "Come inside, little bro, please."

"*No*," Marshall groaned.

Case pounded back up the steps and into the trailer, where I reached my arms to him.

"Help me up," I whispered and he did, cradling me to his chest, pressing his face to my hair.

"I felt dizzy," I explained, but I was unwilling to waste time on myself right now and so I said, "I have to call Mom, she's at Shore Leave…"

"I'll do it," Case said.

"I'm so scared…"

"Me too," he admitted in a whisper.

My mother answered the cafe phone immediately. I imagined her at the familiar counter at Shore Leave, with the old-fashioned till and the toothpick dispenser-wheel.

"Joelle, this is Case, I'm here with Tish," my husband said, his voice calm and steady. "Is Ruthann there? Is she in Landon?"

"No," Mom wept; I could hear her through the phone. "She's not here and she never called…"

A roaring in my ears, a buzzing in my skull. I gripped Case as though he was the only thing keeping me from going under forever.

Case was saying, "Marshall is here and he said that she left for Minnesota yesterday afternoon. She was going to drive straight there. She never called to tell you she was coming?"

"No." Mom was crying hard and then I heard Blythe; he'd obviously taken the phone from her.

"Case, it's Bly. I'm calling the state patrol," my stepdad said. "Then I will call you right back."

"We'll do the same here," Case said, and hung up. Before he could stop me, I stormed back outside to confront Marshall.

"What did you *say to her*?" I screamed for the second time.

Marshall was on his knees, hunched over his stomach and dry-heaving now, his dark hair falling across his face and bare hands sunk into the snow to his wrists as he braced himself. He must have been freezing.

He said brokenly, "I told her to go. I told her to leave. I was so mad…so goddamn jealous…oh *Jesus*…"

"This is *your fault!*" I shrieked, grabbing his shoulder, wanting to hit him, even knowing that it was utterly unfair for me to pin blame this way.

"I know," he rasped painfully. "I know. I didn't mean it, I was just so angry…oh God, *Ruthann*…"

"Your fault!" I couldn't quit screaming this at Marshall.

Case was on me again, carrying me back inside. A detached part of me felt terrible for what I was putting my husband through by acting this way; his cinnamon-brown eyes were wet with unshed tears as he set me gently onto the couch and whispered, "Please sit here, love." He implored me with both eyes and voice. "Please, sweetheart, for me."

I nodded weak agreement.

"I'll be right back," Case promised, and went outside again.

Ruthann, I begged, gripping my forehead and reaching out with my mind, trying to sense her. Maybe she had stayed at a motel, maybe she was somewhere in North Dakota right now. But I knew she wouldn't let us worry this way. Even if she was furious at Marshall, surely hurt by his angry words, she was softhearted enough that she would never make us worry. Even if we deserved it.

My phone rang. I was sure it was Mom or Aunt Jilly; when I saw Dad's work number, his office at Rockford, Gordon and Bunnickle in downtown Chicago, I immediately assumed that Mom had called him. And then, my mind ignoring rationale and clinging to a spark of hope, I thought, *Maybe Ruthie went there. Maybe she bought a plane ticket!*

"Dad, is she there?" I asked upon answering.

A brief, surprised silence before my father said gravely, "Tish, I'm so upset…"

"Did Mom call you?" I interrupted. Dad's voice was so familiar and there was a tiny, undying part of me that still longed to believe in him, to hero-worship, despite everything.

"No," he said, and his voice was gruff with both puzzlement and concern.

Then how had he heard about —

"Tish, honey, I hate to tell you this, I hate it deeply," Dad began.

"I know," I said, interrupting him.

"You know?" Dad asked incredulously, this time interrupting me. "How did…they only just found him…"

I was so confused. Dumbly, I echoed this phrase. "Found him?"

"Rob," Dad said, and roughly cleared his throat.

"What?" I could hardly force the sound of this single word from my mouth.

Dad said somberly, "He overdosed, Tish. Probably three days ago now. They found him in his apartment just this afternoon…"

Once, as a kid, I'd begged Camille to spin me on one of those rare tiny merry-go-rounds, the ones with a base no more than two feet in diameter, basically the equivalent of a single-seater. It was in a park somewhere on the way to Landon from Chicago, in a summer years past. Camille warned me that I would be sick but I'd insisted and she finally relented. The way I felt right now could only be compared to that long-ago afternoon, when I'd staggered to the reeling ground and threw up all my lunch.

Whirling and revolving, the merry-go-round completely out of control.

Like a mechanical toy I lurched to my feet and walked with jerky steps across the kitchen to the bathroom. Later, Case would find my phone in the garbage, where I unconsciously chucked it right then. I fell to my knees beside the toilet and heaved into the bowl.

Ruthann.

Robbie.

Oh God…

This can't be happening…

But the world would not stop spinning.

"They're searching for her car," Case told me, coming into the darkened bedroom. I lay curled on our bed, despising my own weakness, my inability to face everyone gathered in our tiny living room. At Case's words I pressed both hands to my face. Case closed the bedroom door and joined me, his big, strong body so warm as he gathered me close and held securely. I could feel his heartbeat and I twined my fingers through his. He kissed the top of my head; his concern was palpable.

"My heart is breaking to see you this way," he whispered, nose against my hair. "I'm so sorry. I hate this so much."

In the past few hours I'd told Case about Robbie's death, our local sheriff Jerry Woodrow had come and gone, and all the Rawleys flooded to our side; in times of need, they gathered, without question. Marshall was more of a wreck than me, if that was even possible. He refused to be comforted and had instead driven back to his and Ruthann's little apartment, in the hope that she might show up there before morning. I felt, childishly, that all hope had been extinguished, at least momentarily. At least until tomorrow. Tomorrow I would have to get up and face this, find a grain of hope, but for tonight I could not muster the strength to climb from the trench and instead clung to my husband.

"Can't they trace her phone?" I asked again.

"The battery must be dead, because they couldn't," Case whispered. "Baby, you need to eat something. Will you eat something, please, sweetheart? I'm so worried."

I whispered, "I can't right now. I will tomorrow..."

Tomorrow, which would not restore Robbie to life; somehow I knew that neither would it restore Ruthann to us.

Oh God, oh please no...

I wept, unable to stop. "Don't let go..."

"I'm here," Case said, with quiet passion. "I love you and I'm right here, sweetheart. I will never let you go."

Midnight came and went. The state patrol put out an APB on Ruthie's car, as it had been over twenty-four hours now. No word. Minutes ticked by as though counting down to a detonator. Clark brought Wy home; Garth, Sean, and Quinn went to the apartment, desperate to talk to

Marshall, but Sean called to tell us that Marshall wouldn't let them inside.

"We'll try again tomorrow," he concluded.

I dozed for no more than fifteen minutes once our house was empty, my head aching and congested with tears, and yet it was enough time for a dream to spring to life on the screen of my closed eyelids. In the dream I was following Ruthie. My heart beat joyously to see her. I tried to call to her but no sound emerged from my dry throat. She was moving swiftly away from me, her long curls swinging down her slender spine, barefoot along a path that led into a forest. Setting sunlight created an auburn halo around her entire body. The sight both transfixed and horrified me; the light was not angelic, as it should have been, but instead deeply ominous.

Ruthann! I tried to scream.

But then, before my eyes, she vanished.

I woke sweating and disoriented, my heart cramping with fear.

Sharp knocking on the outer door.

For a moment, still enmeshed in the dream, I couldn't make sense of the sound. Mutt and Tiny weren't barking. Case wasn't beside me – but then I could hear him, out in the living room.

Marshall's voice then, heated and frantic, yet there was a note of something in it that had not been present earlier, a note of resolve. I sat up, still seeing the image of Ruthann moving away from me and then disappearing…

Disappearing right before my eyes.

I suddenly knew, deep in my innermost heart, where all the things I could not explain were stored, what she had done. I also knew that she was in unimaginable danger.

Through the bedroom door, Case asked, "Tish, are you awake? Marshall wants to talk to you."

I clicked on the lamp and immediately squinted at the brightness. "I'm awake!"

Marshall all but burst into the small bedroom and sank to his knees beside the bed. I had never seen such blatant desperation on anyone's face, such agonized urgency. His gray eyes were wrecked, tangled with torture. "Where are those letters, Tish? Did you burn them? Oh Jesus, tell me you still have them."

He knew. He had realized the same thing.

"I can't go there. I can't go with you, Marshall. It has to be you alone." I was shaking so hard that my teeth rattled; Case moved immediately to the bed and curled me close to his warm chest.

"I know," Marshall said, having regained tentative control, a fraction of his fear replaced by determination. "I need those letters."

It would be dawn in just a few hours. I looked hard into Marshall's eyes and begged, "Find her. Oh God, what if..."

"No," Marshall said intently. "Don't say it. Don't even think it. I will find her. I will find her or I will die trying. *I love her.* Oh God, I love her and I hurt her so much. I will bring her back. I swear on my life, I will bring Ruthann back."

Excerpt from The Way Back

Smothering.

Unable to breathe, I floundered, ripping at my face to tear away the blanket covering it, only to encounter nothing but emptiness. I screamed so hard my throat was shredded, I tasted blood, but no sound met my ears. There was only a pulsing pressure that threatened to shatter the curved boundaries of my skull, the sound of an unforgiving January wind streaking across the frozen surface of a shrouded lake.

Though the words were incomplete in my mind, the sense of them hovered somewhere near –

Help me!

I was insubstantial, not so much a physical body as a rush of air. I hurtled motionlessly through open space, the way you would feel as a stationary passenger in a fast-moving airplane, a soap bubble, a husk, as fragile as an eggshell emptied of its liquid contents.

Dear God, help me!

I clung to the one name that had brought me back twice before, had pulled me from the brink of this empty, echoing terror. Need for him was stronger than my fear; need inundated my hollow body.

Marshall! Please hear me, Marshall!

But this time, I was not returned.

I became conscious in splintered fragments. Sharp points of light darted into my mind and then away, carrying bits of awareness. For a time I fought full consciousness. At last I could no longer resist and squinted at the blinding brilliance. Sunlight stuck fingers down my eye sockets.

Pain.

I attempted to sit; it didn't take long to understand I was incapable.

"Help…please, help me…"

The words rasped against my paper-dry throat. My tongue felt three times its usual size, a flopping cartoon tongue. Instinct led me to curl around the pain in an attempt to center it; this motion sent agony exploding like small, powerful firecrackers attached to my nerves. Tears stung the rims of my eyes. My shaking hands encountered the source before my brain stumbled to the same conclusion – broken ribs. I whimpered, unable to help it.

I let my eyelids sink, not caring in that moment if I died.

Night was a cloak anchoring my body to the earth. I lay with shoulder blades flat against the ground, unable to shift to another position. For an unknown reason – or maybe many unknown reasons, I couldn't begin to guess, not just now – I was outside and all sensory evidence suggested it was not in fact wintertime, even though the last memory I was able to conjure through the vice grip of physical pain involved heaping snow, and ice, and sadness –

"No," I begged, shying away from whatever the memory contained.

I was an unchained prisoner, trapped on the ground, surrounded by empty land and chilly night air, hearing what seemed like every cricket on earth sawing a tuneless, repetitive chorus. My skin rippled with goosebumps and was blistered by mosquito bites, my limbs jittering with cold. I had no idea where I was. My body hurt so much I was certain I would be dead before morning and still it didn't come close to rivaling the gouging ache in my heart.

Just go, I begged the memory. *Please, just go…*

A deep, gruff voice demanded, "What in God's name?"

Heavy rumbling and the clinking of metal links invaded my ears, sounds I could not place into context. But then there was the unmistakable whoosh of a horse exhaling through its nostrils. Seconds after that I heard stomping hooves.

It was daylight once again.

A second voice, younger than the first, exclaimed, "Why, it's a woman!"

"Jump down, boy, quick!"

"A woman, lying right here in the grass!"

"Quit flapping your jaws and get to her. Is the poor thing dead?"

Running footsteps approached and I sensed someone kneeling near my head. I heard the dry crackle of grass stalks and a shadow fell over my face, at once blocking the hammer of midday sun. The smell of an unwashed body hit my nose with enough force that I cringed away, groaning. The man connected to the voice and the smell placed his fingertips on my neck, gently probing for a pulse. He called, "She's alive!"

His voice was immediately closer to my face. "Miss? Can you hear me?" When I couldn't manage to respond or open my eyes, he persisted, "Miss! You're hurt. Can you hear me?"